"Stayed in from recess to read it . . . **CAN'T WAIT FOR NEXT ONE!**"
—Zac A., age 9, Hood River, Ore.

"**GINA WAS MY FAVORITE** character because she's into science and soccer like me! I also liked D.J.'s family because it looks like mine!"
—Kiran M., age 7, Carlsbad, Calif.

"*Hilo* is **REALLY, REALLY FUNNY.** It has a **LOT OF LAUGHS.** The raccoon is the funniest."
—Theo M., age 7, Miami, Fla.

"**HIGH ENERGY** and **HILARIOUS!**"
—Gene Luen Yang, National Ambassador for Young People's Literature

"**FANTASTIC. EVERY SINGLE THING ABOUT THIS . . . IS TERRIFIC.**"
—Boingboing.net

"My students are obsessed with this series. **OBSESSED!**"
—Colby Sharp, teacher, blogger, and co-founder of the Nerdy Book Club

"More **GIANT ROBOTIC ANTS . . .** than in the complete works of Jane Austen."
—Neil Gaiman, author of *Coraline*

"My big brother and I **FIGHT OVER THIS BOOK.**"
—Nory V., age 8, Montclair, N.J.

"*Hilo* is loads of **SLAPSTICK FUN!**"
—Dan Santat, winner of the Caldecott Medal

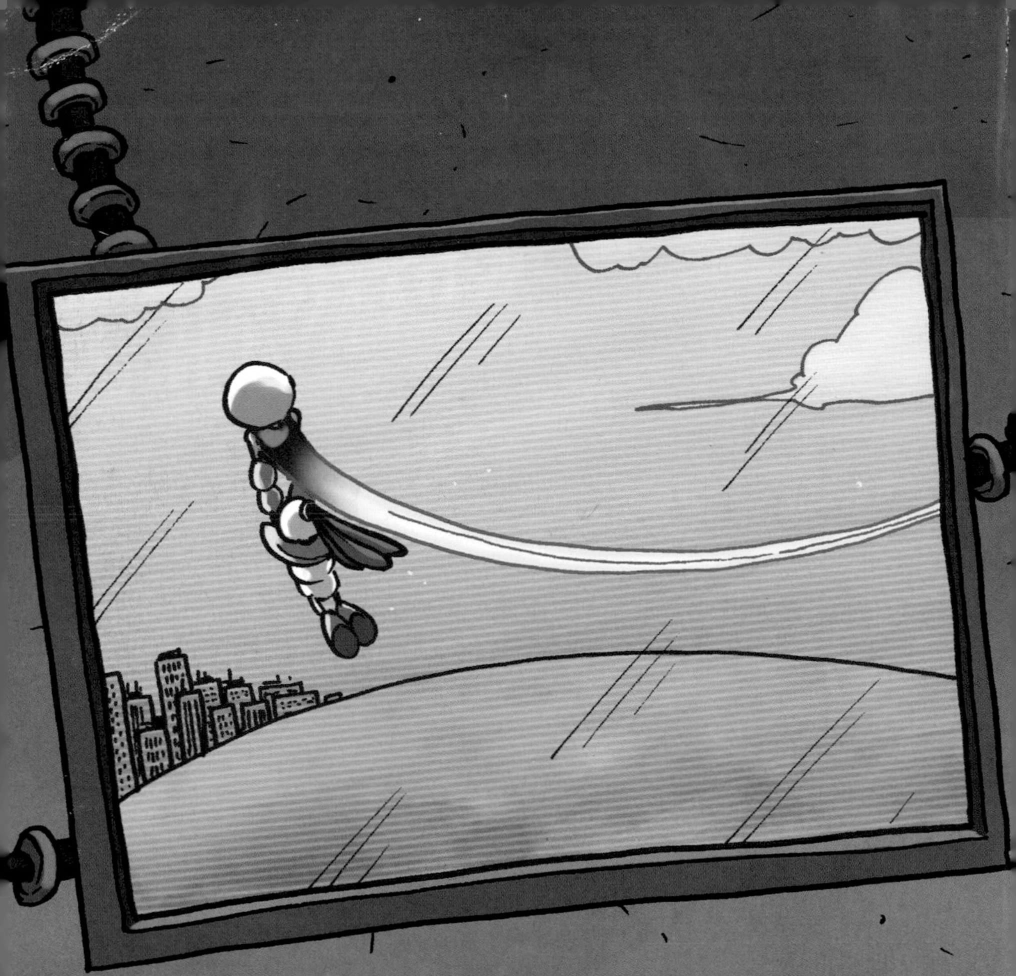

READ ALL THE HILO BOOKS!

HILO #1 THE BOY WHO CRASHED TO EARTH

HILO #2 SAVING THE WHOLE WIDE WORLD

HILO #3 THE GREAT BIG BOOM

HILO #4 WAKING THE MONSTERS

BOOK 4

HiLO

WAKING THE MONSTERS

BY JUDD WINICK

COLOR BY
STEVE HAMAKER

RANDOM HOUSE 🏠 NEW YORK

Copyright © 2018 by Judd Winick

All rights reserved. Published in the United States by Random House Children's Books, a division of Penguin Random House LLC, New York.

Random House and the colophon are registered trademarks of Penguin Random House LLC.

Visit us on the Web! rhcbooks.com

Educators and librarians, for a variety of teaching tools, visit us at RHTeachersLibrarians.com

Library of Congress Cataloging-in-Publication Data

Names: Winick, Judd, author.

Title: Hilo. Book 4, waking the monsters / by Judd Winick.

Description: First edition. | New York : Random House, [2018] | Summary: Hilo and his friends learn more about Hilo's past while they battle robots that were buried underground on Earth a thousand years ago.

Identifiers: LCCN 2016052236 | ISBN 978-1-5247-1493-2 (hardcover) | ISBN 978-1-5247-1494-9 (hardcover library binding) | ISBN 978-1-5247-1495-6 (ebook)

Subjects: LCSH: Graphic novels. | CYAC: Graphic novels. | Robots—Fiction. | Extraterrestrial beings—Fiction. | Friendship—Fiction. | Identity—Fiction. | Science fiction.

Classification: LCC PZ7.7.W57 Wl 2018 | DDC 741.5/973—dc23

MANUFACTURED IN CHINA

10 9 8 7 6 5 4 3

Book design by Bob Bianchini

First Edition

FOR MY BIG
BROTHER,

ORIN

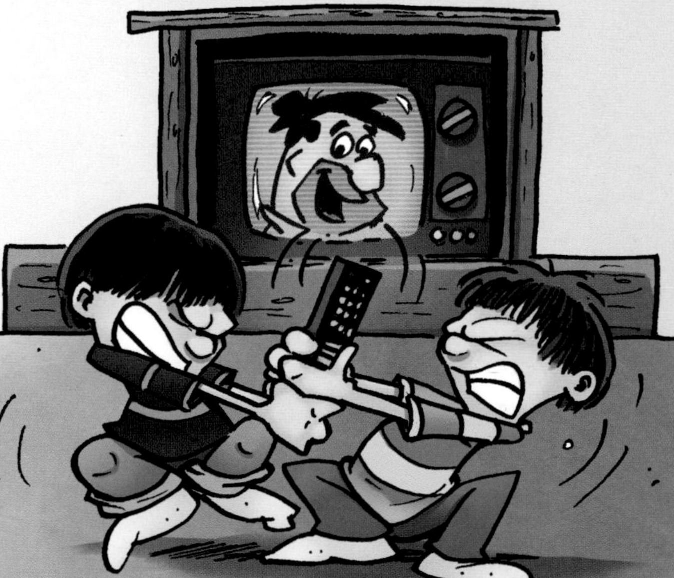

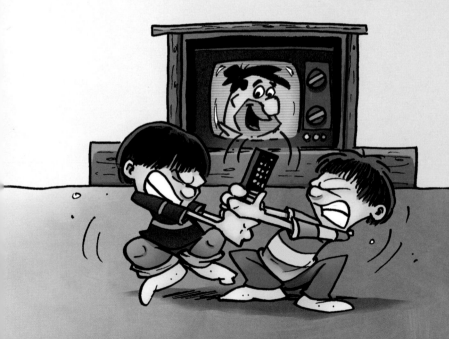

CHAPTER 1

WHOA

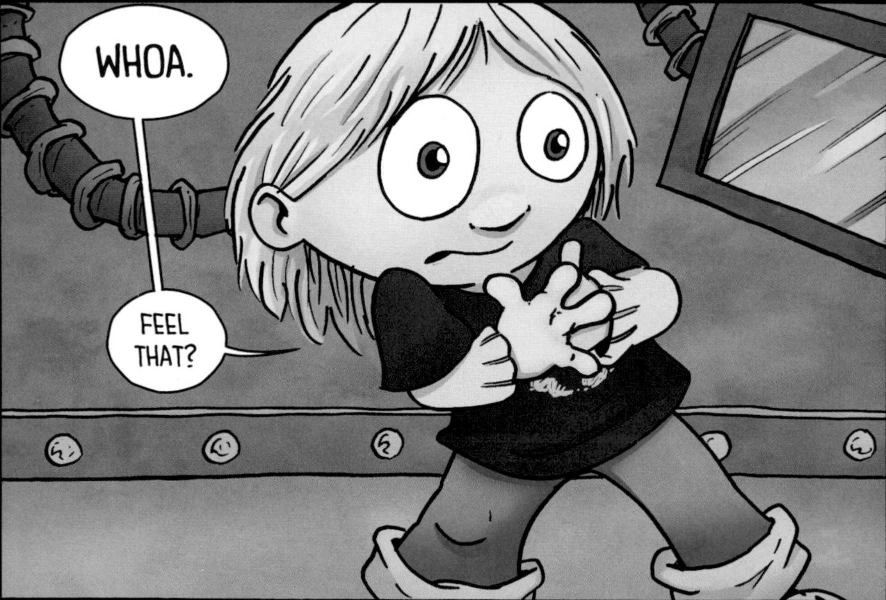
WHOA.
FEEL THAT?

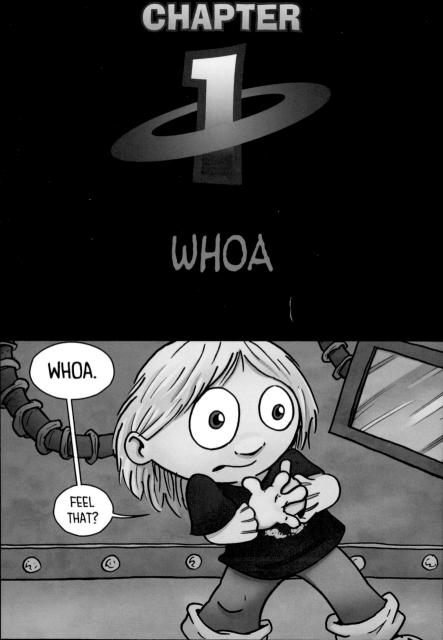

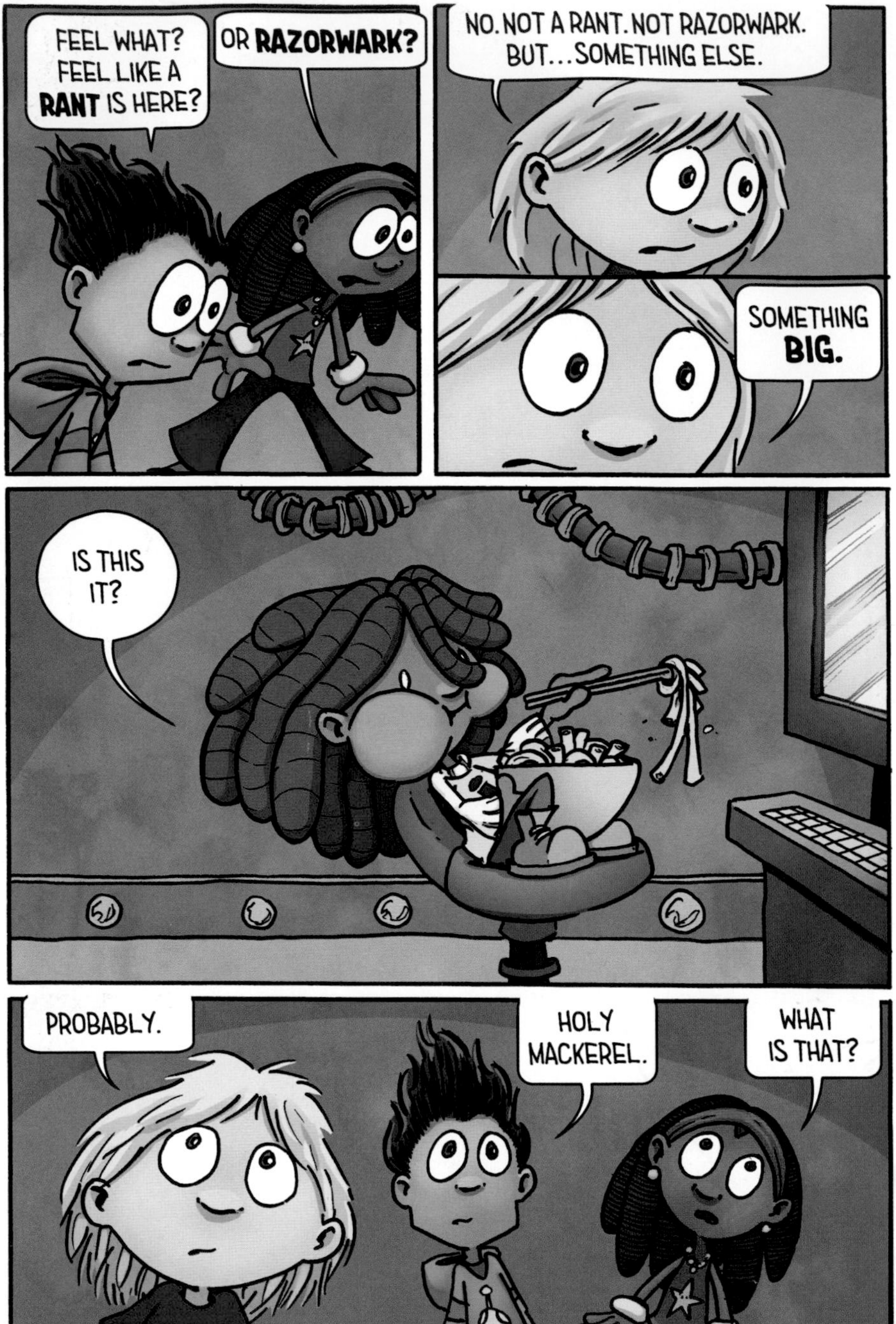
FEEL WHAT? FEEL LIKE A **RANT** IS HERE?
OR **RAZORWARK?**
NO. NOT A RANT. NOT RAZORWARK. BUT... SOMETHING ELSE.
SOMETHING **BIG.**
IS THIS IT?
PROBABLY.
HOLY MACKEREL.
WHAT IS THAT?
NOT SURE, BUT IT LOOKS LIKE ...

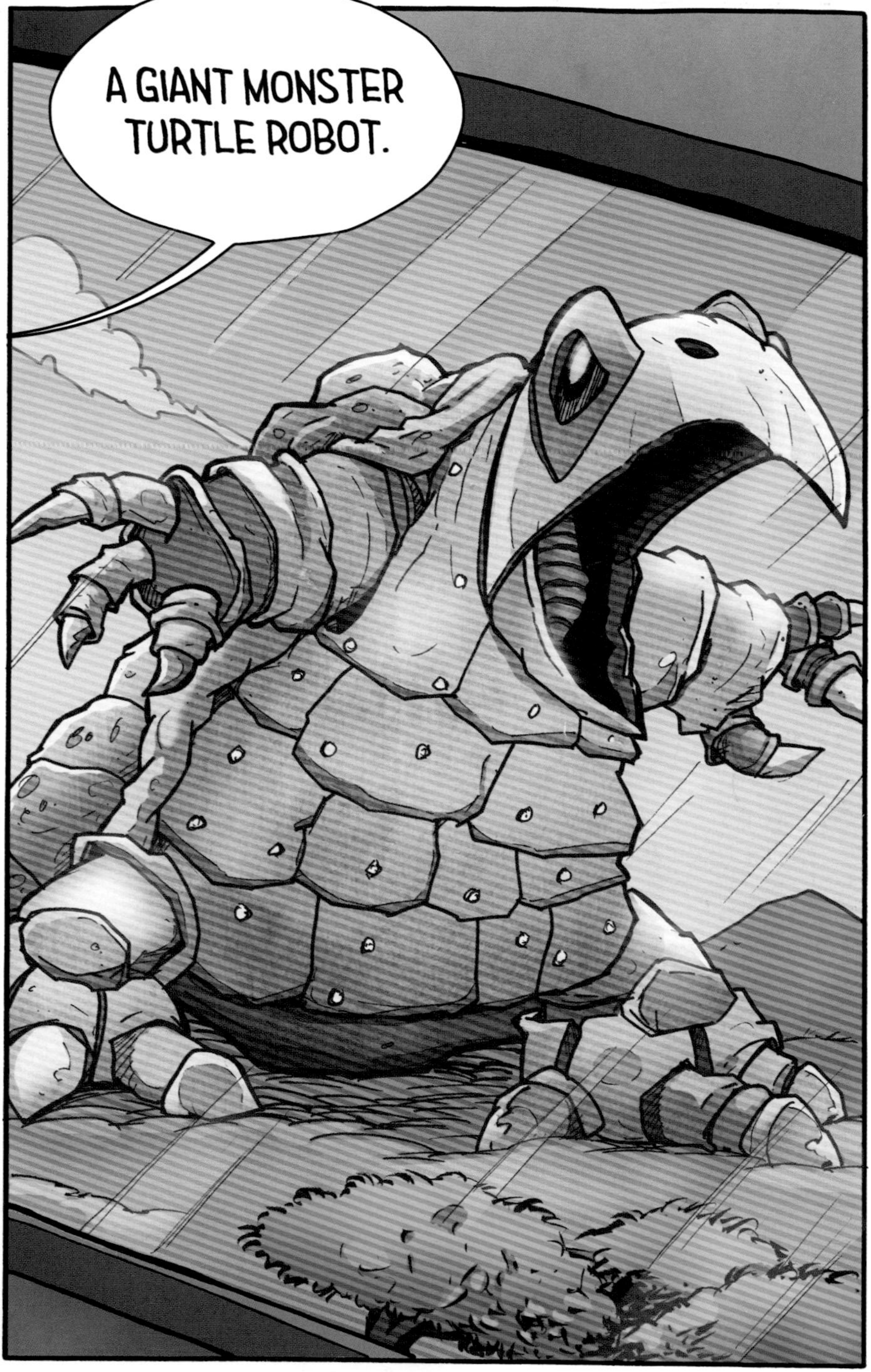
A GIANT MONSTER TURTLE ROBOT.

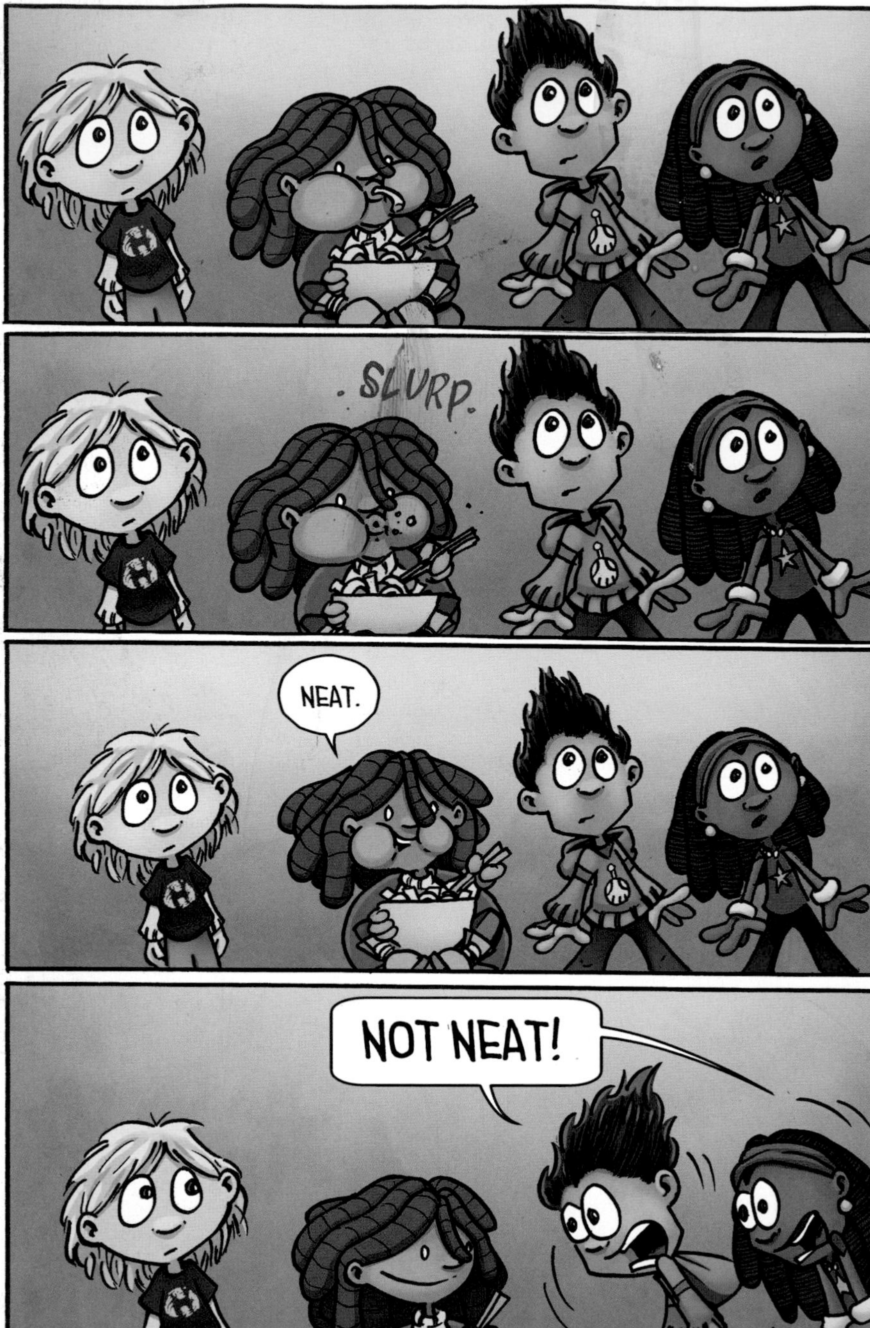
SLURP
NEAT.
NOT NEAT!

CHAPTER 2

HERE TO HELP

TWO MONTHS EARLIER.

MY NAME IS **DANIEL JACKSON LIM.** BUT EVERYONE CALLS ME **D.J.**

THIS IS MY BEST FRIEND, **HILO.**

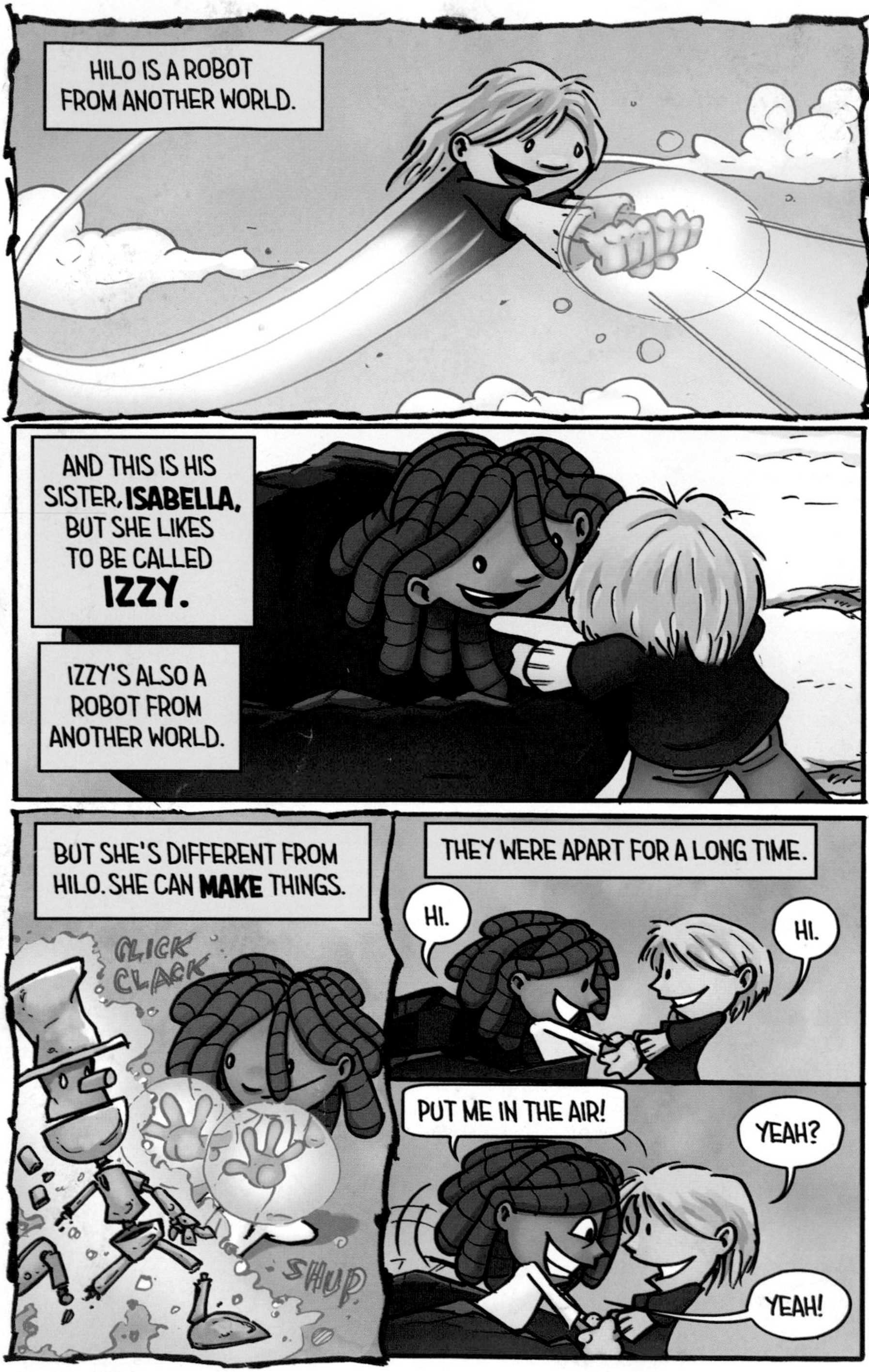
HILO IS A ROBOT FROM ANOTHER WORLD.
AND THIS IS HIS SISTER, ISABELLA, BUT SHE LIKES TO BE CALLED IZZY.
IZZY'S ALSO A ROBOT FROM ANOTHER WORLD.
BUT SHE'S DIFFERENT FROM HILO. SHE CAN MAKE THINGS.
CLICK CLACK
SHUP
THEY WERE APART FOR A LONG TIME.
HI.
HI.
PUT ME IN THE AIR!
YEAH?
YEAH!

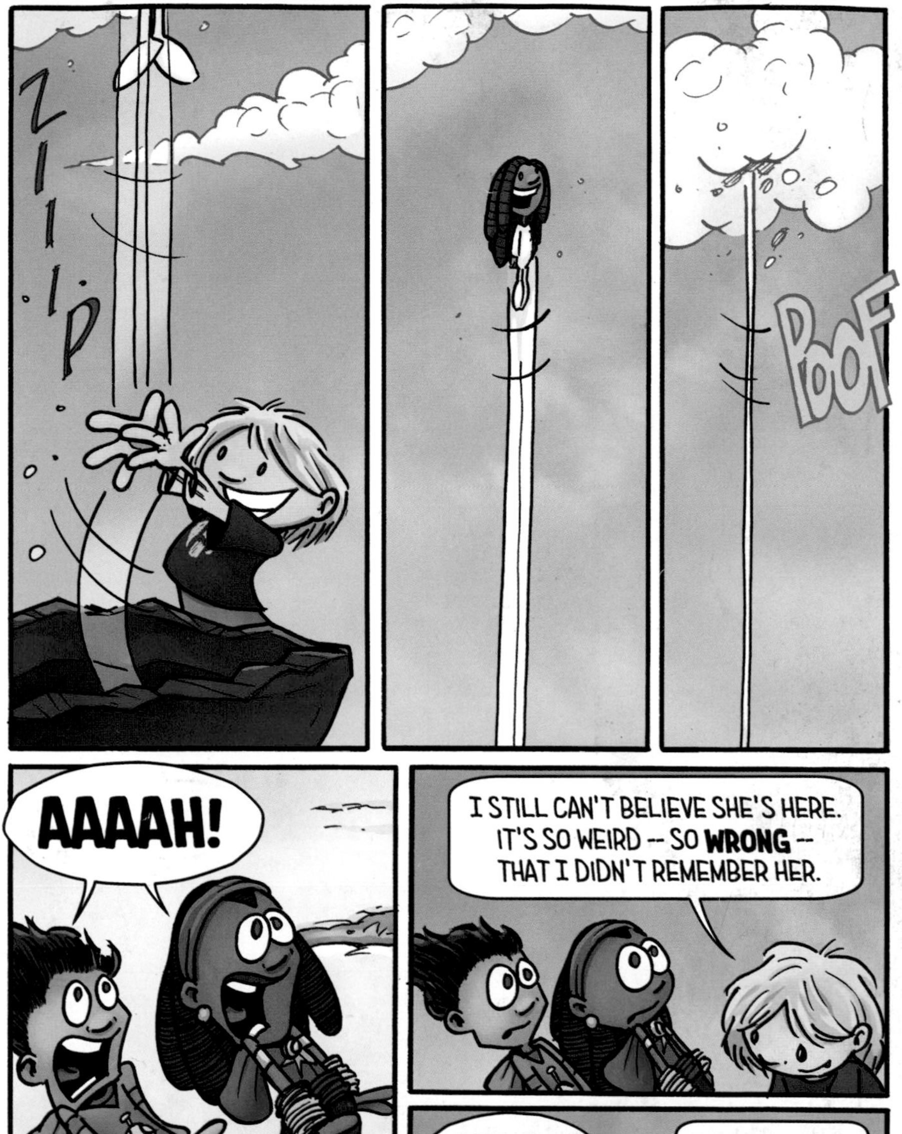
ZIIIP
POOF
AAAAH!
I STILL CAN'T BELIEVE SHE'S HERE. IT'S SO WEIRD -- SO **WRONG** -- THAT I DIDN'T REMEMBER HER.
HILO!
THERE'S JUST NOTHING . . .

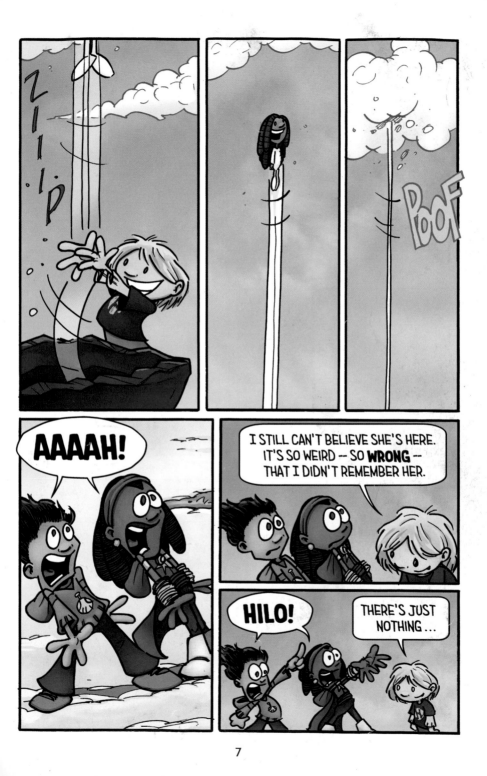

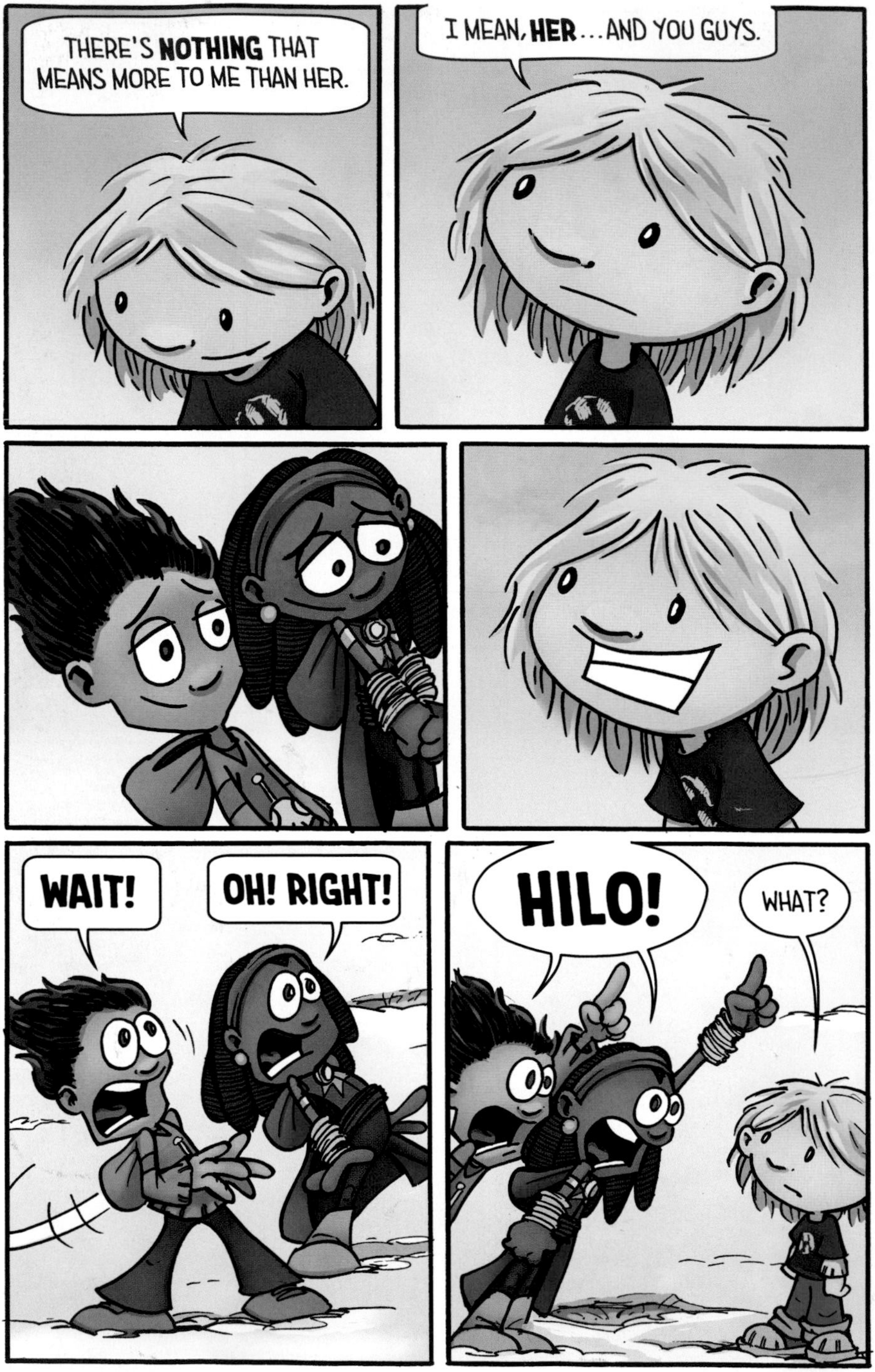
THERE'S **NOTHING** THAT MEANS MORE TO ME THAN HER.
I MEAN, **HER**... AND YOU GUYS.
WAIT!
OH! RIGHT!
HILO!
WHAT?

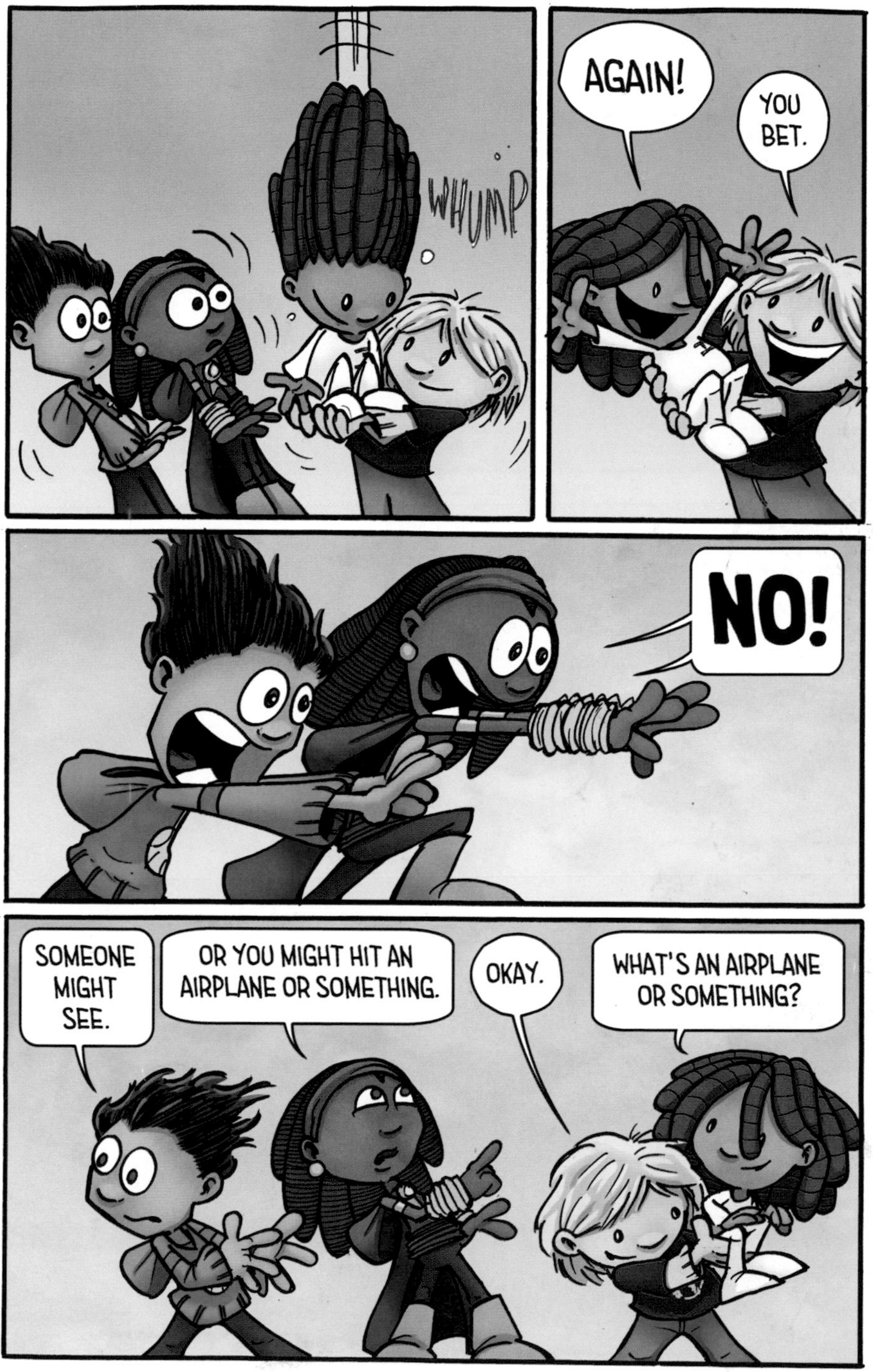
WHUMP
AGAIN!
YOU BET.
NO!
SOMEONE MIGHT SEE.
OR YOU MIGHT HIT AN AIRPLANE OR SOMETHING.
OKAY.
WHAT'S AN AIRPLANE OR SOMETHING?

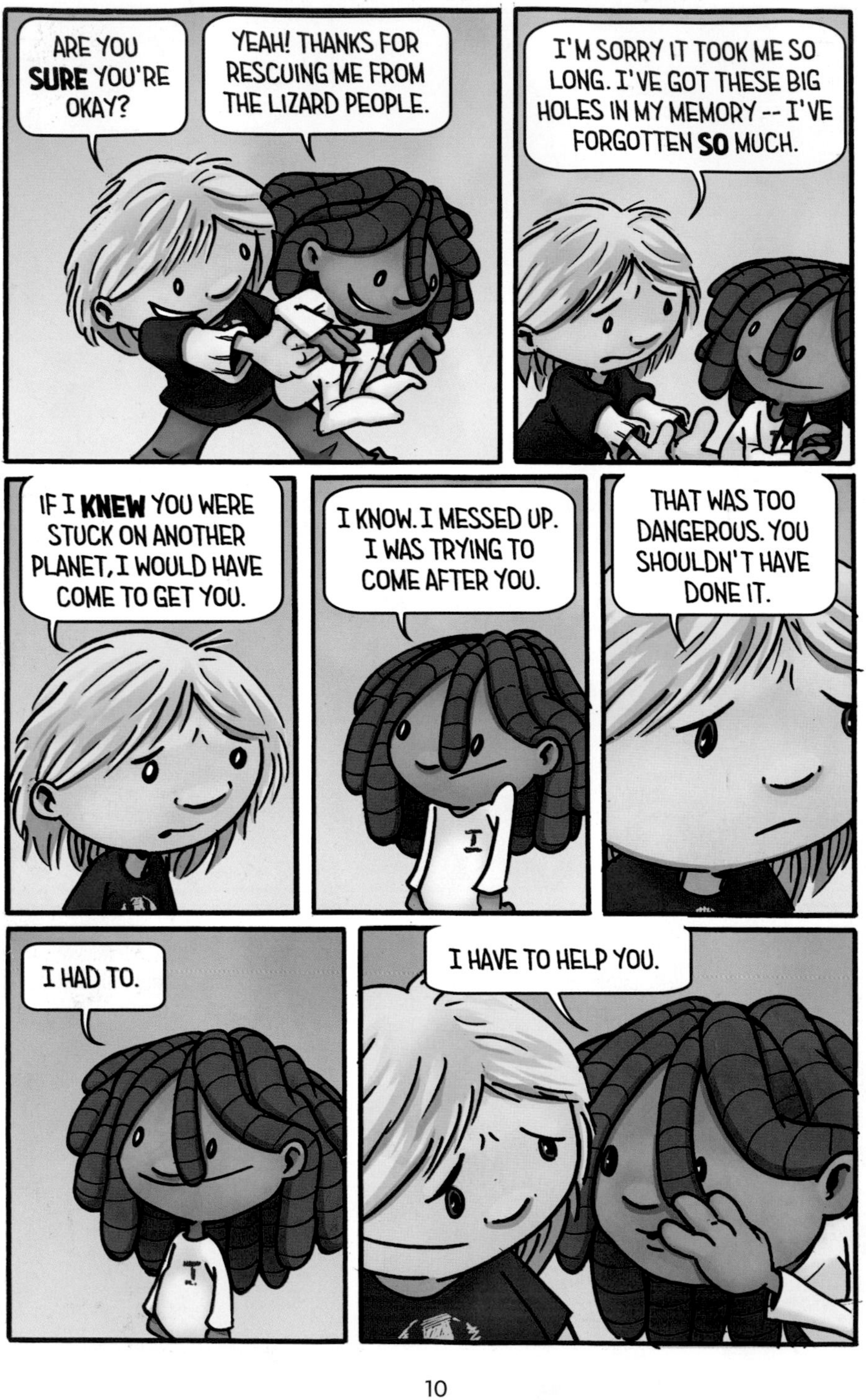
ARE YOU **SURE** YOU'RE OKAY?
YEAH! THANKS FOR RESCUING ME FROM THE LIZARD PEOPLE.
I'M SORRY IT TOOK ME SO LONG. I'VE GOT THESE BIG HOLES IN MY MEMORY -- I'VE FORGOTTEN **SO** MUCH.
IF I **KNEW** YOU WERE STUCK ON ANOTHER PLANET, I WOULD HAVE COME TO GET YOU.
I KNOW. I MESSED UP. I WAS TRYING TO COME AFTER YOU.
THAT WAS TOO DANGEROUS. YOU SHOULDN'T HAVE DONE IT.
I HAD TO.
I HAVE TO HELP YOU.

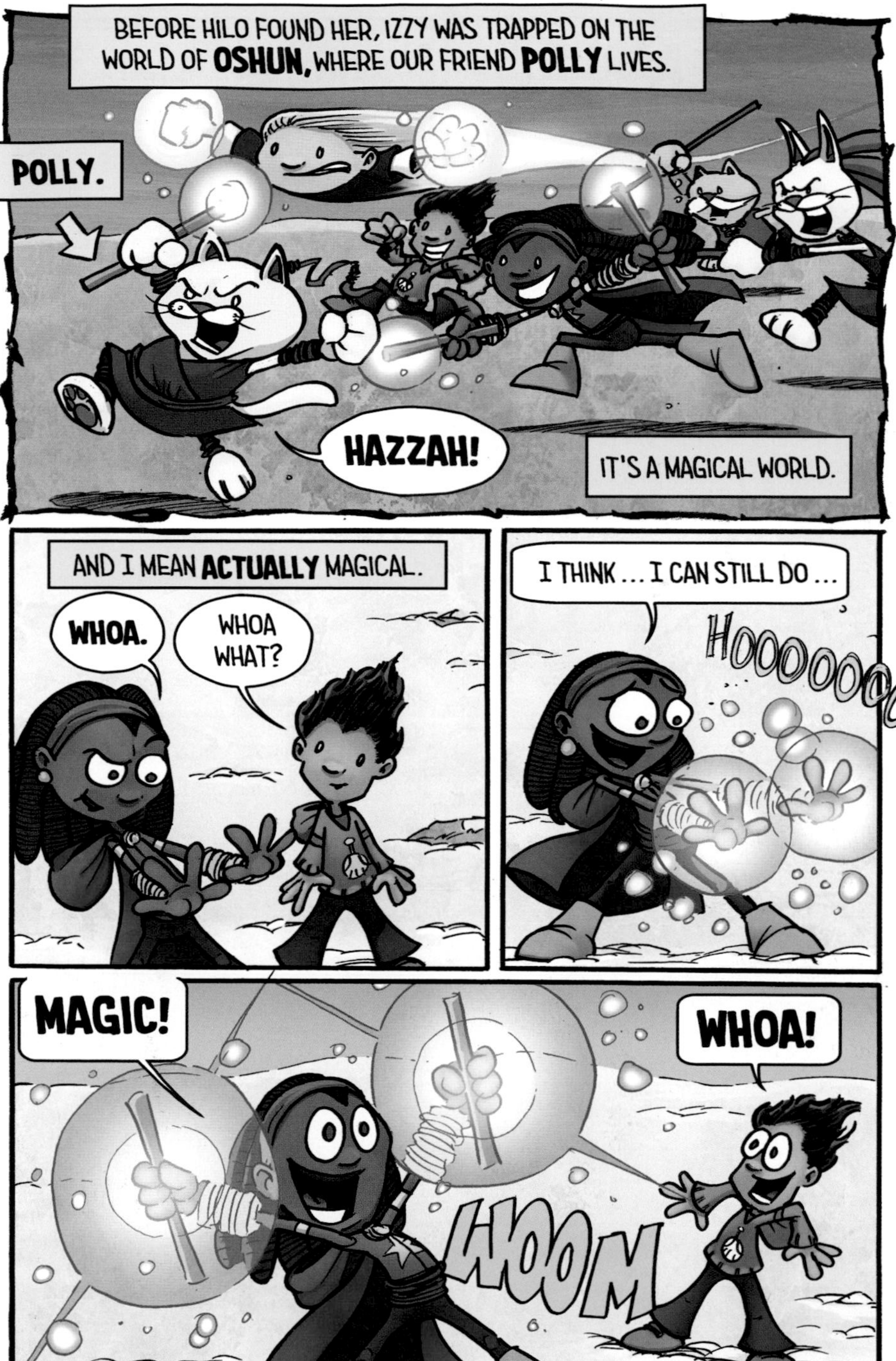
BEFORE HILO FOUND HER, IZZY WAS TRAPPED ON THE WORLD OF OSHUN, WHERE OUR FRIEND POLLY LIVES.
POLLY.
HAZZAH!
IT'S A MAGICAL WORLD.
AND I MEAN ACTUALLY MAGICAL.
WHOA.
WHOA WHAT?
I THINK . . . I CAN STILL DO . . .
HOOOOOOOO
MAGIC!
WHOA!
WOOM

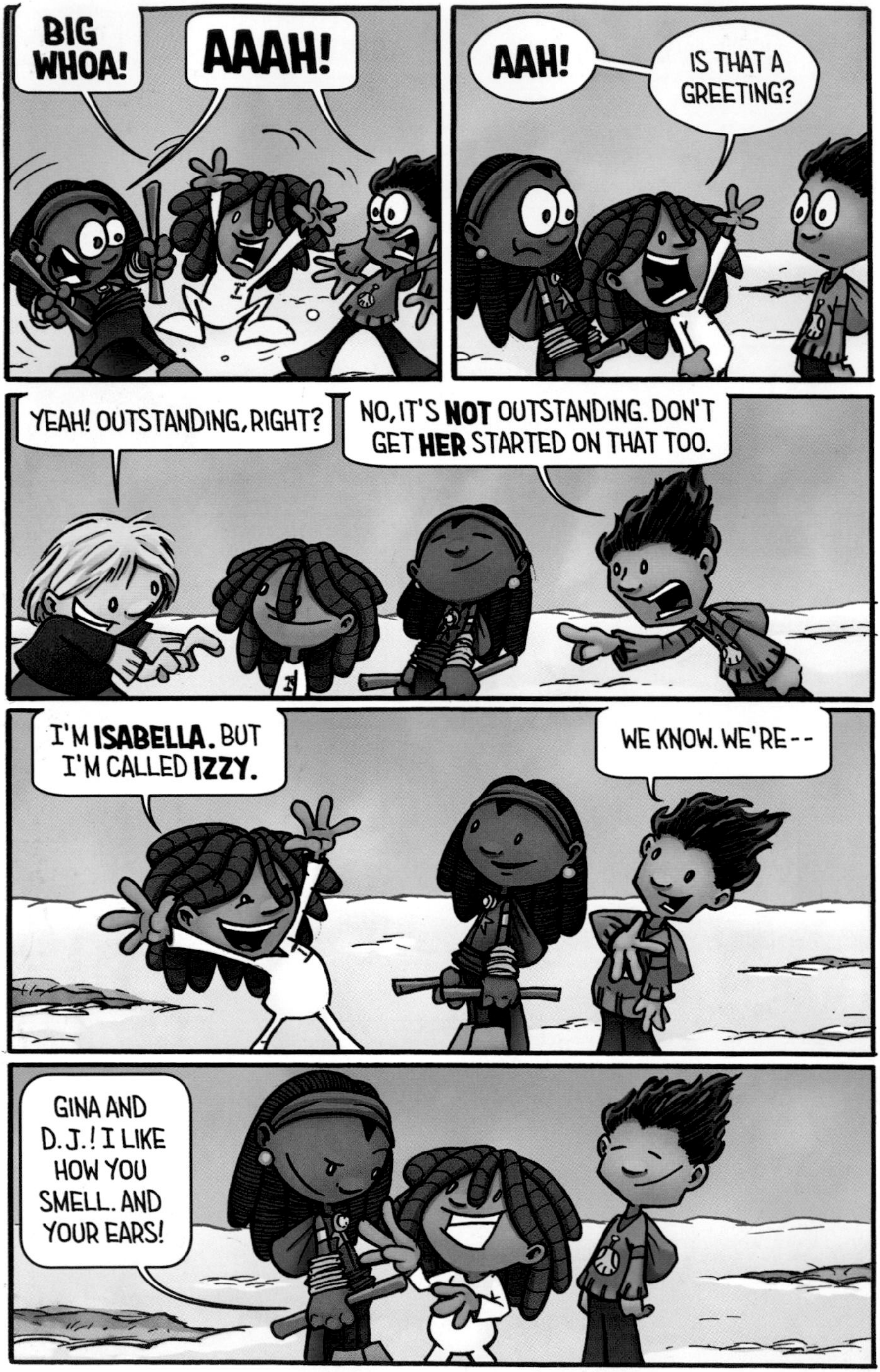
BIG WHOA!
AAAH!
AAH!
IS THAT A GREETING?
YEAH! OUTSTANDING, RIGHT?
NO, IT'S NOT OUTSTANDING. DON'T GET HER STARTED ON THAT TOO.
I'M ISABELLA. BUT I'M CALLED IZZY.
WE KNOW. WE'RE--
GINA AND D.J.! I LIKE HOW YOU SMELL. AND YOUR EARS!

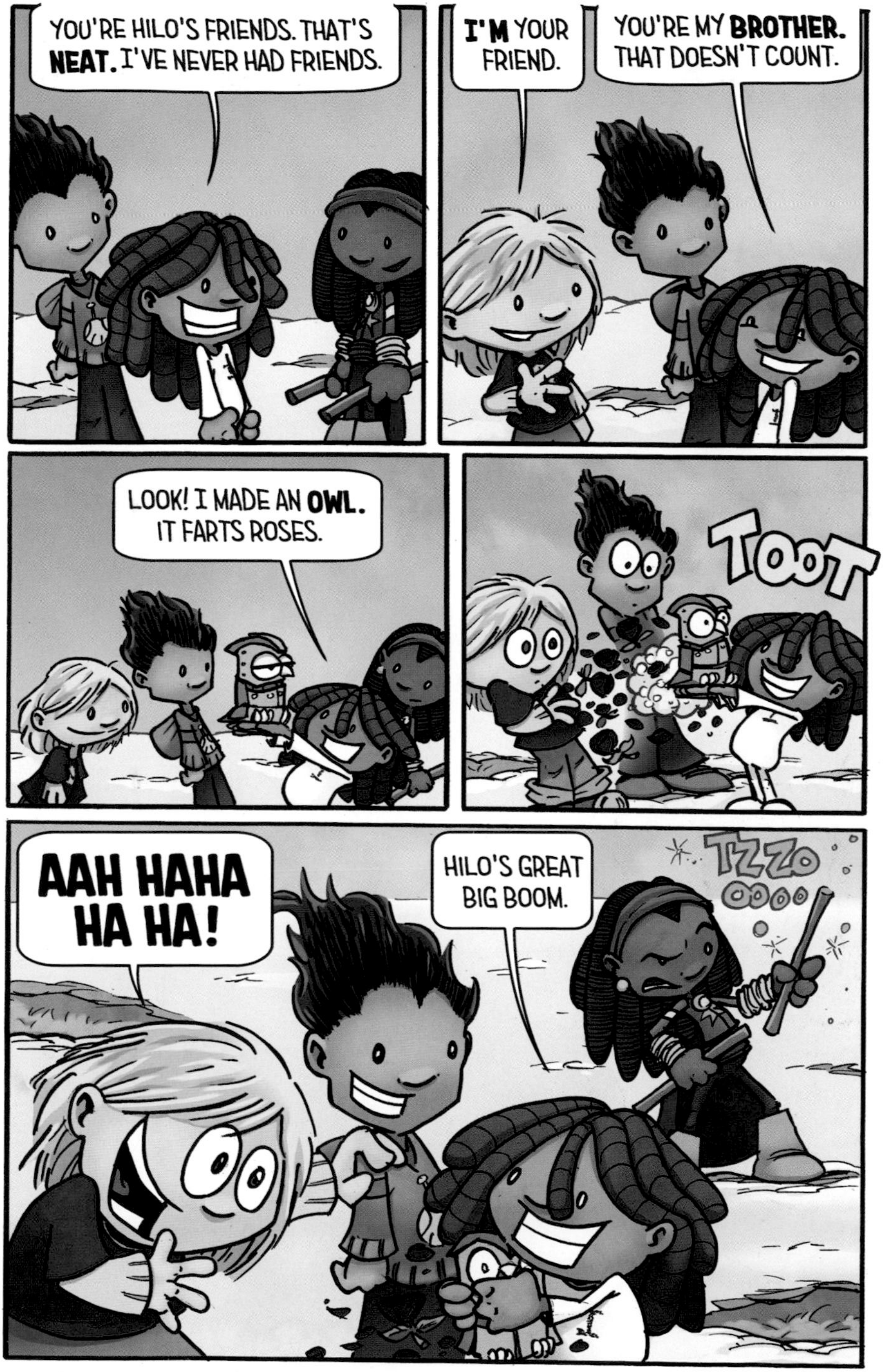
YOU'RE HILO'S FRIENDS. THAT'S NEAT. I'VE NEVER HAD FRIENDS.
I'M YOUR FRIEND.
YOU'RE MY BROTHER. THAT DOESN'T COUNT.
LOOK! I MADE AN OWL. IT FARTS ROSES.
TOOT
AAH HAHA HA HA!
HILO'S GREAT BIG BOOM.
TZZO

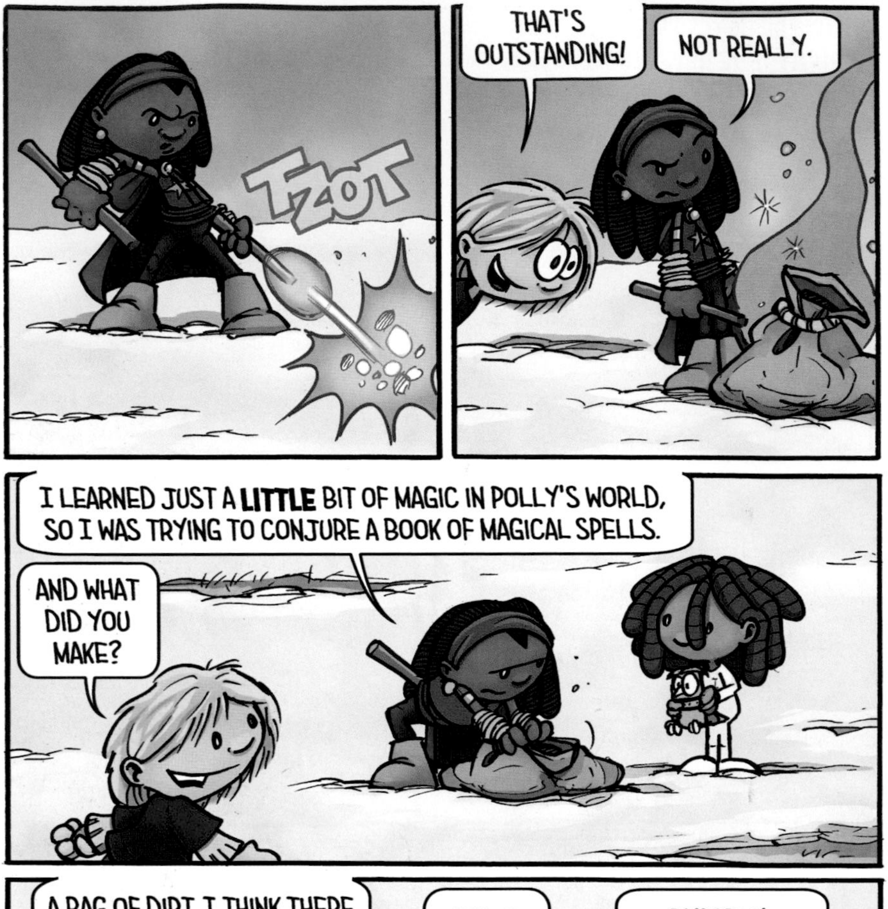
TZOT
THAT'S OUTSTANDING!
NOT REALLY.
I LEARNED JUST A **LITTLE** BIT OF MAGIC IN POLLY'S WORLD, SO I WAS TRYING TO CONJURE A BOOK OF MAGICAL SPELLS.
AND WHAT DID YOU MAKE?
A BAG OF DIRT. I THINK THERE MIGHT BE AN ONION OR SOMETHING IN THERE TOO.
AND IT SMELLS REALLY BAD.
EXACTLY. OUTSTANDING.

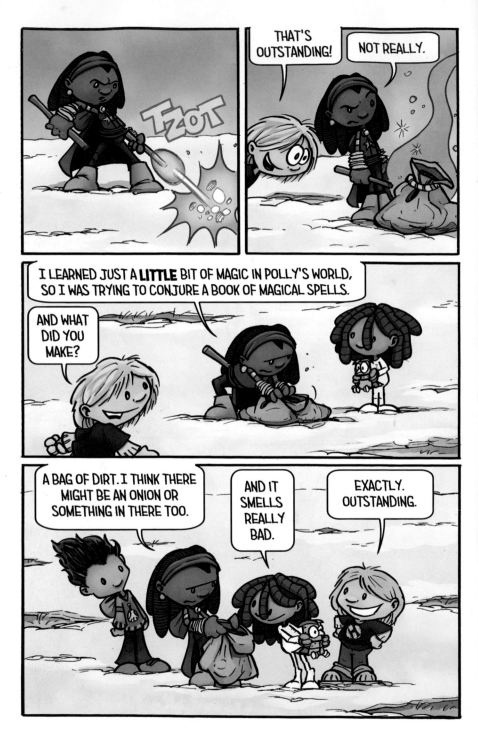

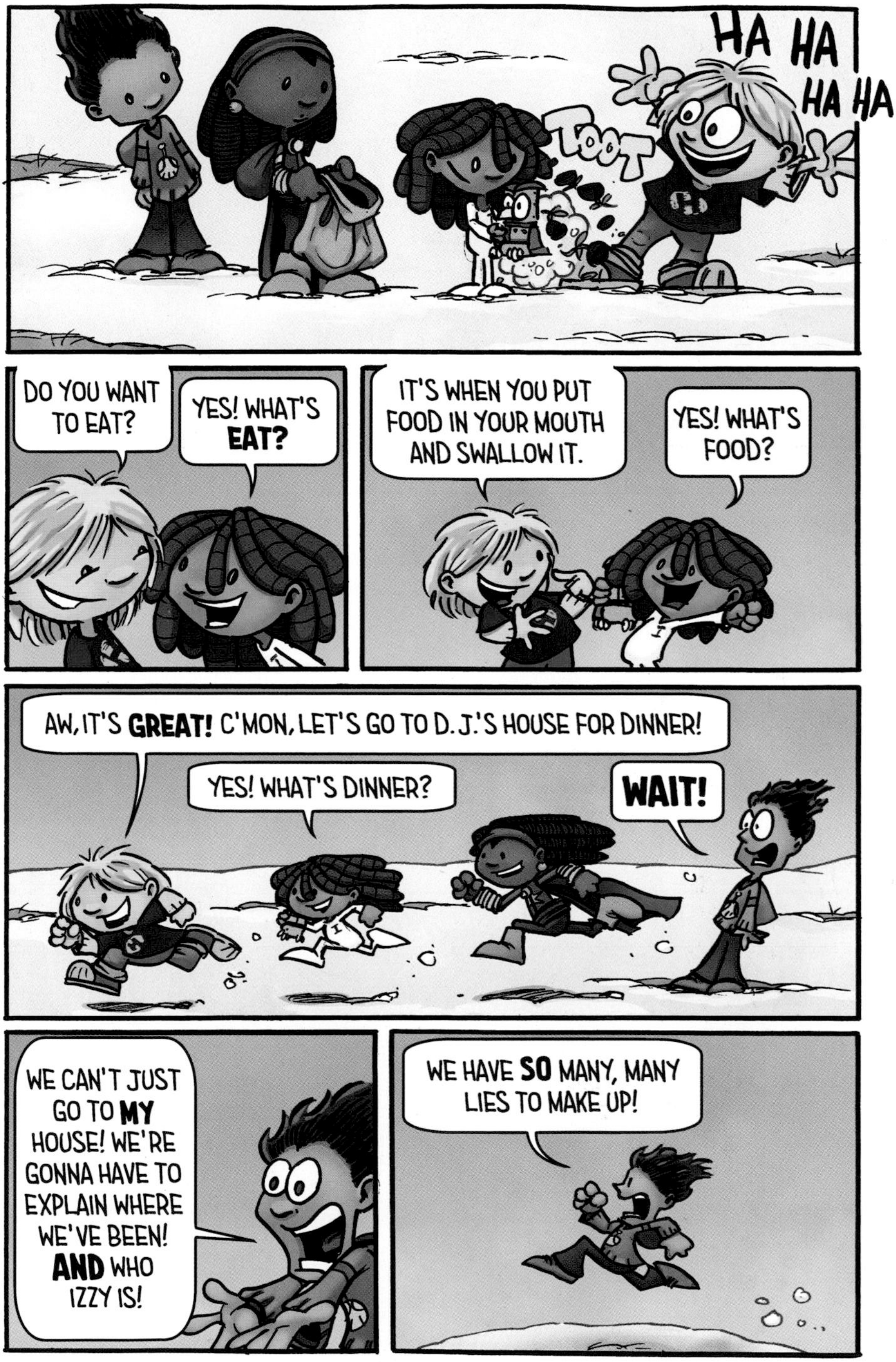
HA HA HA HA
TOOT
DO YOU WANT TO EAT?
YES! WHAT'S EAT?
IT'S WHEN YOU PUT FOOD IN YOUR MOUTH AND SWALLOW IT.
YES! WHAT'S FOOD?
AW, IT'S GREAT! C'MON, LET'S GO TO D.J.'S HOUSE FOR DINNER!
YES! WHAT'S DINNER?
WAIT!
WE CAN'T JUST GO TO MY HOUSE! WE'RE GONNA HAVE TO EXPLAIN WHERE WE'VE BEEN! AND WHO IZZY IS!
WE HAVE SO MANY, MANY LIES TO MAKE UP!

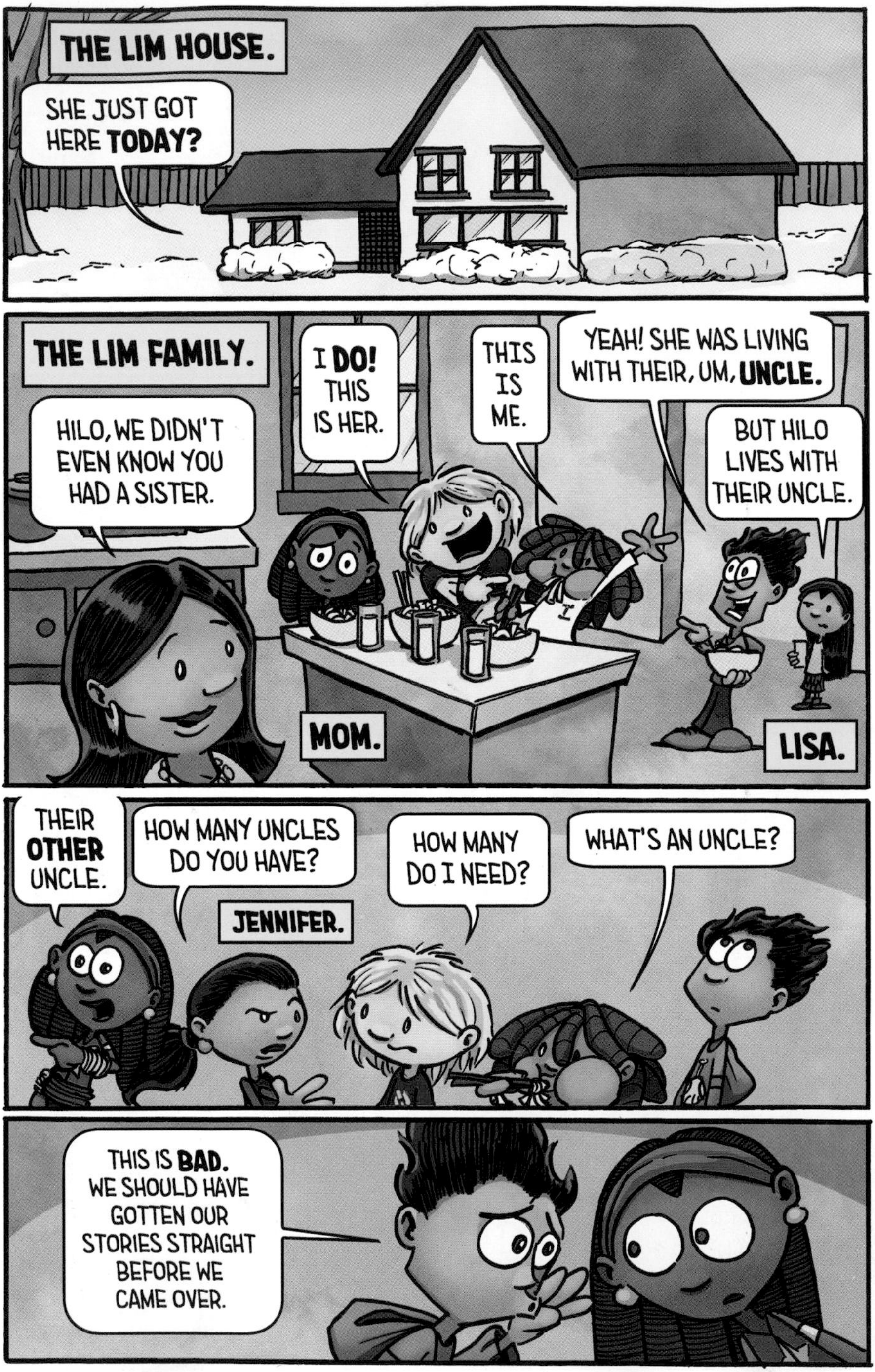
THE LIM HOUSE.
SHE JUST GOT HERE TODAY?
THE LIM FAMILY.
HILO, WE DIDN'T EVEN KNOW YOU HAD A SISTER.
I DO! THIS IS HER.
THIS IS ME.
YEAH! SHE WAS LIVING WITH THEIR, UM, UNCLE.
BUT HILO LIVES WITH THEIR UNCLE.
MOM.
LISA.
THEIR OTHER UNCLE.
HOW MANY UNCLES DO YOU HAVE?
JENNIFER.
HOW MANY DO I NEED?
WHAT'S AN UNCLE?
THIS IS BAD. WE SHOULD HAVE GOTTEN OUR STORIES STRAIGHT BEFORE WE CAME OVER.

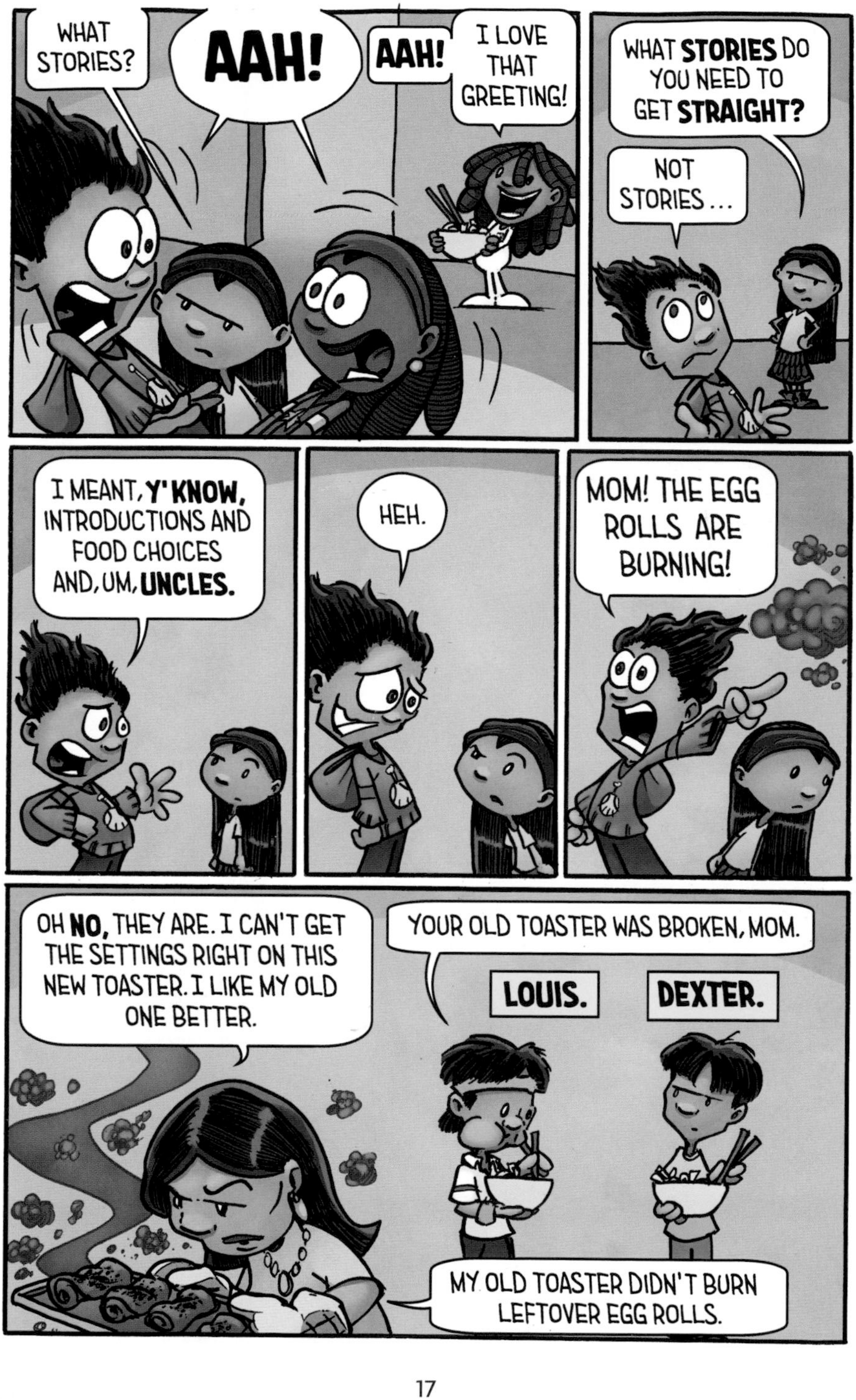
WHAT STORIES?
AAH!
AAH!
I LOVE THAT GREETING!
WHAT STORIES DO YOU NEED TO GET STRAIGHT?
NOT STORIES . . .
I MEANT, Y' KNOW, INTRODUCTIONS AND FOOD CHOICES AND, UM, UNCLES.
HEH.
MOM! THE EGG ROLLS ARE BURNING!
OH NO, THEY ARE. I CAN'T GET THE SETTINGS RIGHT ON THIS NEW TOASTER. I LIKE MY OLD ONE BETTER.
YOUR OLD TOASTER WAS BROKEN, MOM.
LOUIS.
DEXTER.
MY OLD TOASTER DIDN'T BURN LEFTOVER EGG ROLLS.

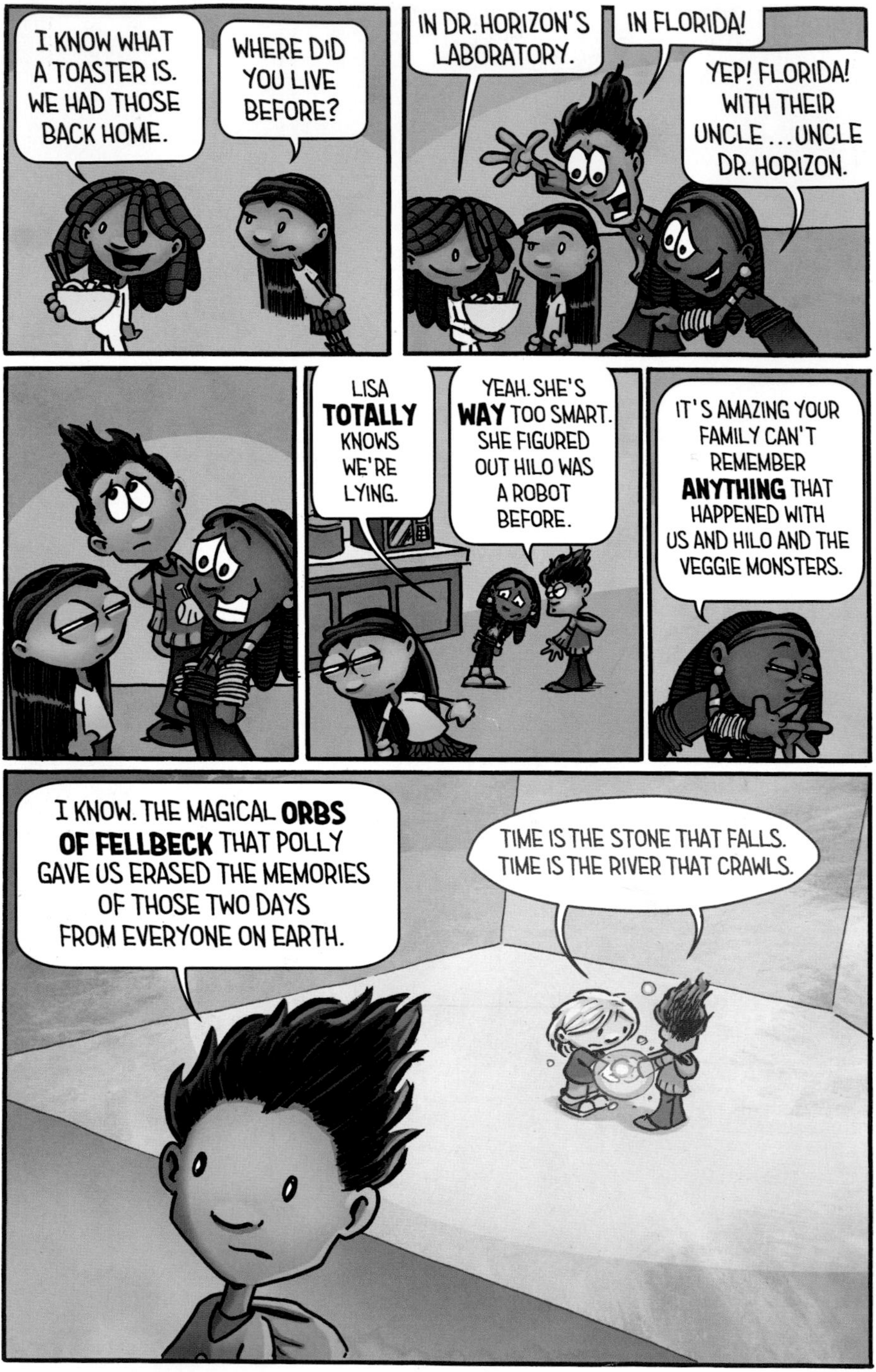
I KNOW WHAT A TOASTER IS. WE HAD THOSE BACK HOME.
WHERE DID YOU LIVE BEFORE?
IN DR. HORIZON'S LABORATORY.
IN FLORIDA!
YEP! FLORIDA! WITH THEIR UNCLE . . . UNCLE DR. HORIZON.
LISA **TOTALLY** KNOWS WE'RE LYING.
YEAH. SHE'S **WAY** TOO SMART. SHE FIGURED OUT HILO WAS A ROBOT BEFORE.
IT'S AMAZING YOUR FAMILY CAN'T REMEMBER **ANYTHING** THAT HAPPENED WITH US AND HILO AND THE VEGGIE MONSTERS.
I KNOW. THE MAGICAL **ORBS OF FELLBECK** THAT POLLY GAVE US ERASED THE MEMORIES OF THOSE TWO DAYS FROM EVERYONE ON EARTH.
TIME IS THE STONE THAT FALLS. TIME IS THE RIVER THAT CRAWLS.

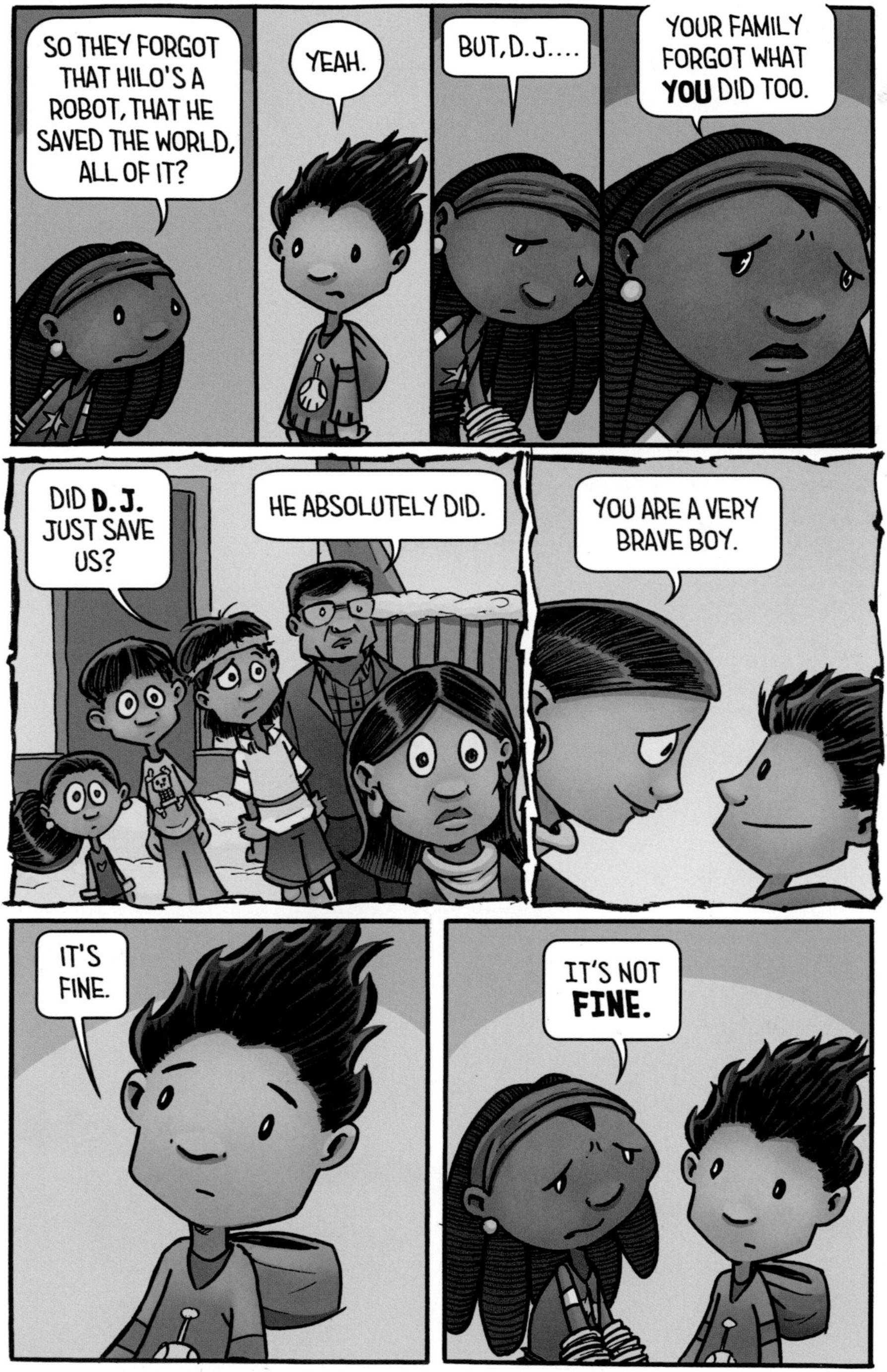
SO THEY FORGOT THAT HILO'S A ROBOT, THAT HE SAVED THE WORLD, ALL OF IT?
YEAH.
BUT, D. J....
YOUR FAMILY FORGOT WHAT **YOU** DID TOO.
DID **D. J.** JUST SAVE US?
HE ABSOLUTELY DID.
YOU ARE A VERY BRAVE BOY.
IT'S FINE.
IT'S NOT **FINE.**

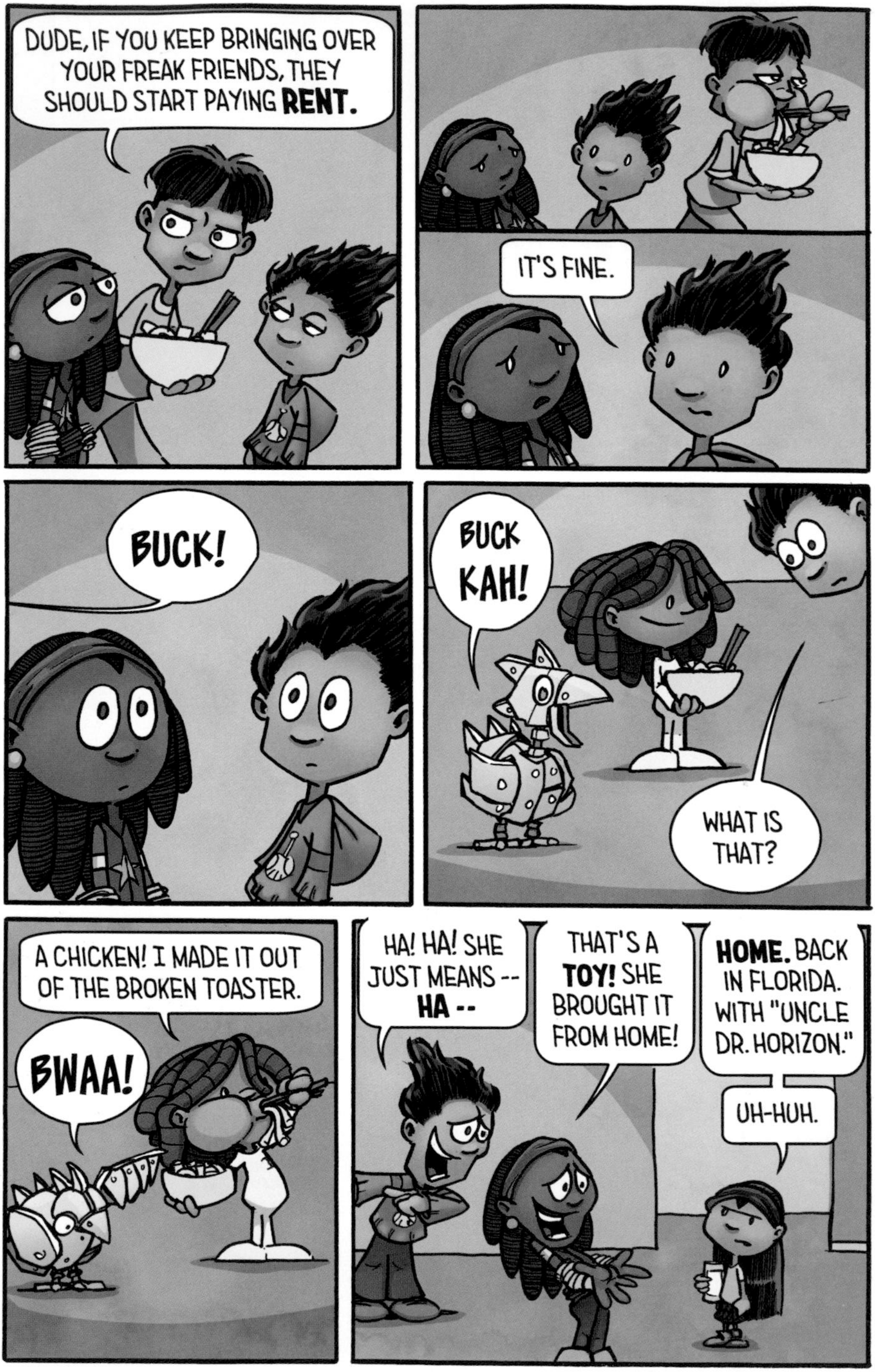
DUDE, IF YOU KEEP BRINGING OVER YOUR FREAK FRIENDS, THEY SHOULD START PAYING **RENT.**
IT'S FINE.
BUCK!
BUCK KAH!
WHAT IS THAT?
A CHICKEN! I MADE IT OUT OF THE BROKEN TOASTER.
BWAA!
HA! HA! SHE JUST MEANS -- **HA** --
THAT'S A **TOY!** SHE BROUGHT IT FROM HOME!
HOME. BACK IN FLORIDA. WITH "UNCLE DR. HORIZON."
UH-HUH.

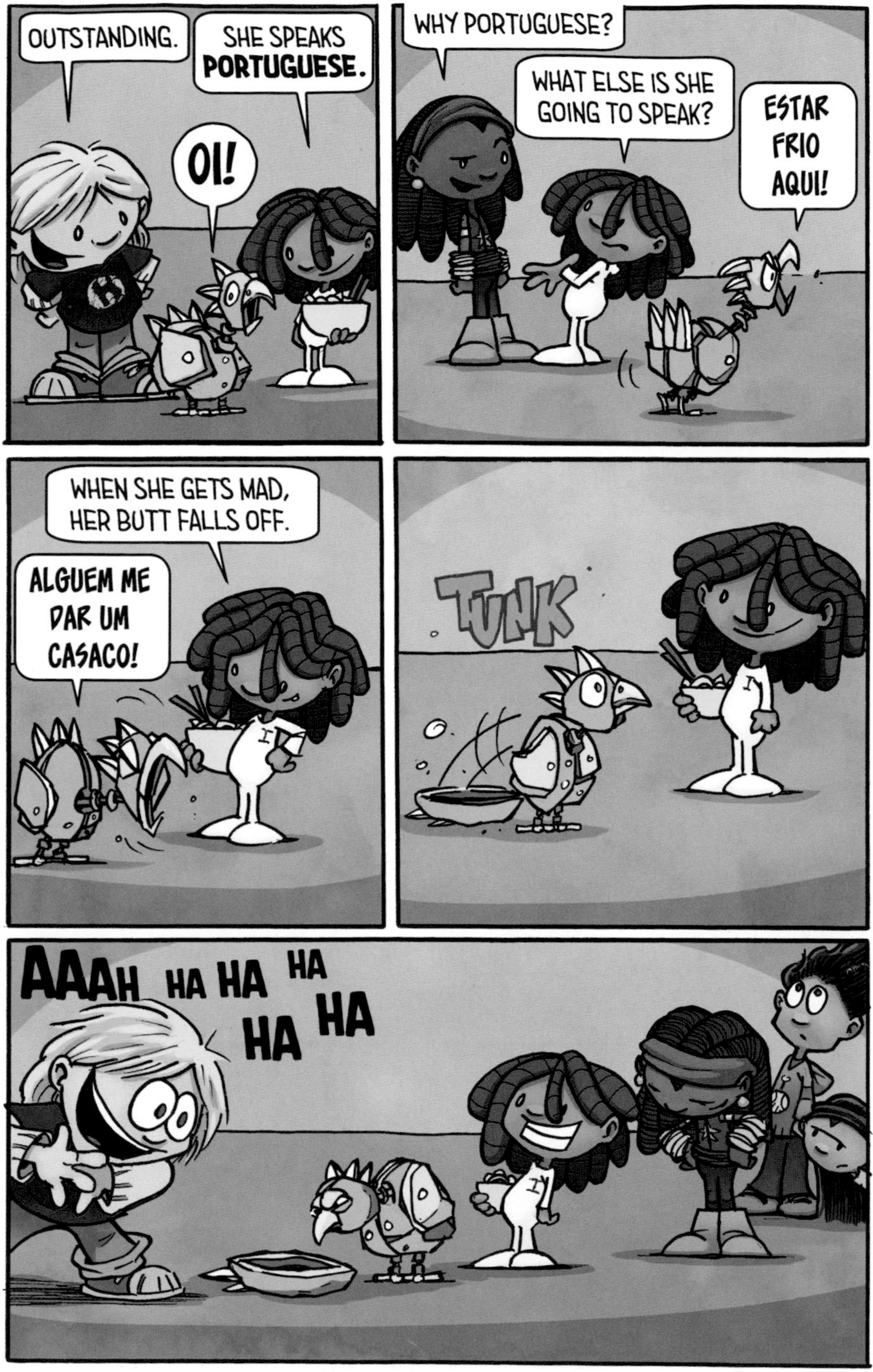
OUTSTANDING.
SHE SPEAKS **PORTUGUESE.**
OI!
WHY PORTUGUESE?
WHAT ELSE IS SHE GOING TO SPEAK?
ESTAR FRIO AQUI!
WHEN SHE GETS MAD, HER BUTT FALLS OFF.
ALGUEM ME DAR UM CASACO!
TUNK
AAAH HA HA HA HA HA

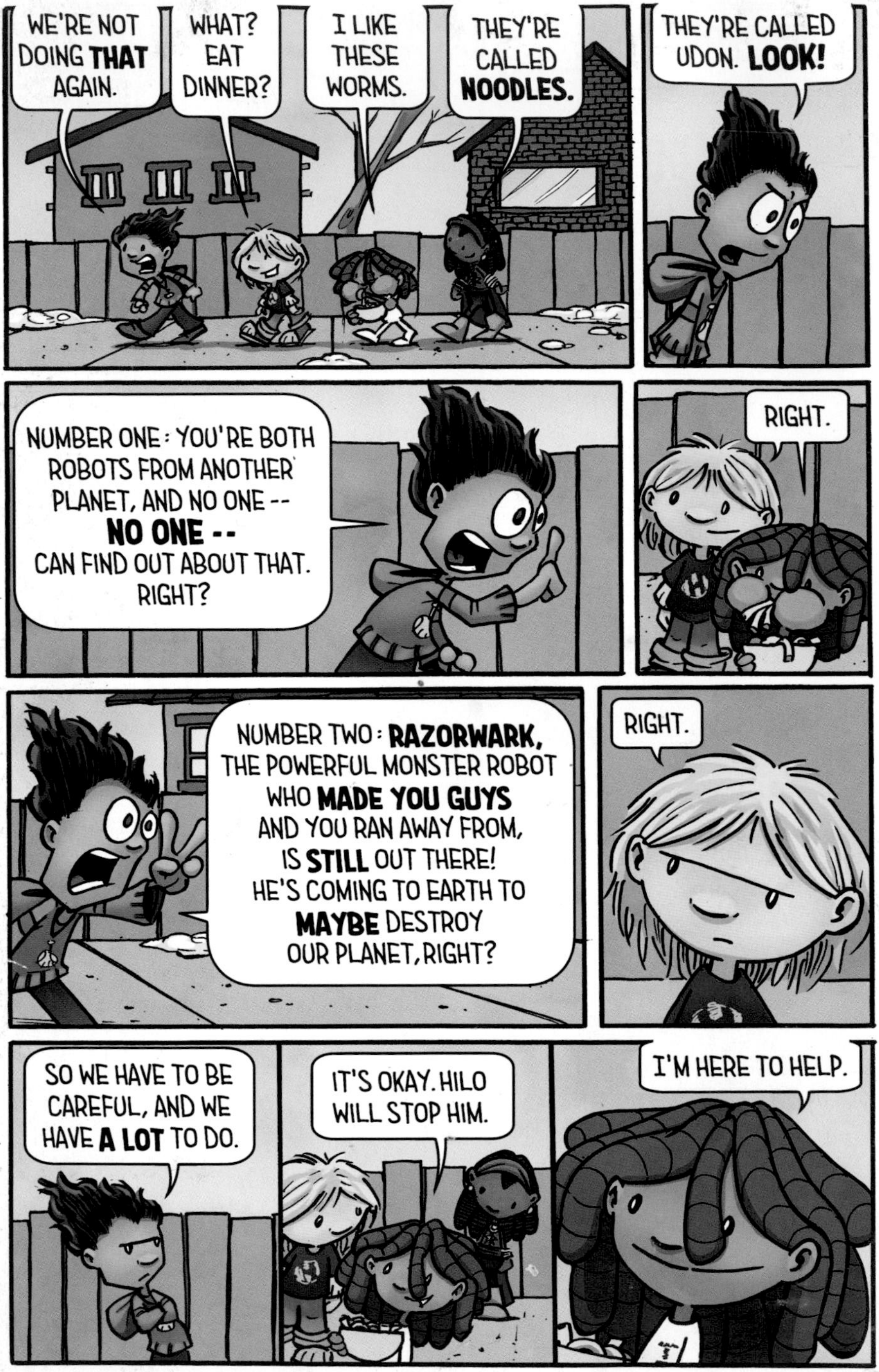
WE'RE NOT DOING THAT AGAIN.
WHAT? EAT DINNER?
I LIKE THESE WORMS.
THEY'RE CALLED NOODLES.
THEY'RE CALLED UDON. LOOK!
NUMBER ONE: YOU'RE BOTH ROBOTS FROM ANOTHER PLANET, AND NO ONE -- NO ONE -- CAN FIND OUT ABOUT THAT. RIGHT?
RIGHT.
NUMBER TWO: RAZORWARK, THE POWERFUL MONSTER ROBOT WHO MADE YOU GUYS AND YOU RAN AWAY FROM, IS STILL OUT THERE! HE'S COMING TO EARTH TO MAYBE DESTROY OUR PLANET, RIGHT?
RIGHT.
SO WE HAVE TO BE CAREFUL, AND WE HAVE A LOT TO DO.
IT'S OKAY. HILO WILL STOP HIM.
I'M HERE TO HELP.

CHAPTER 3

A LOT TO DO

JUST LIKE HILO, NOBODY CAN KNOW IZZY'S A ROBOT. SO WE HAD A LOT TO DO. LIKE, HER **CLOTHES.**
WHAT WAS WRONG WITH MY OLD CLOTHES?
THEY LOOKED LIKE PAJAMAS.
GOTCHA. WHAT'S PAJAMAS?
SHE LOOKS SO CUTE, I'M GONNA EXPLODE!
I KNOW, RIGHT?
TYSON

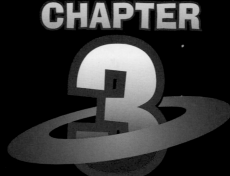

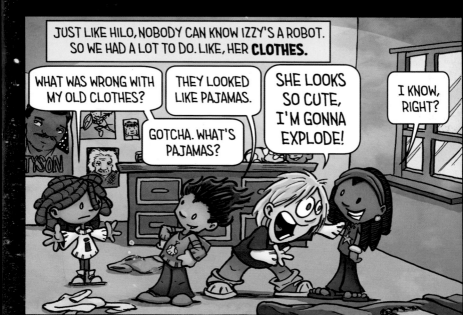

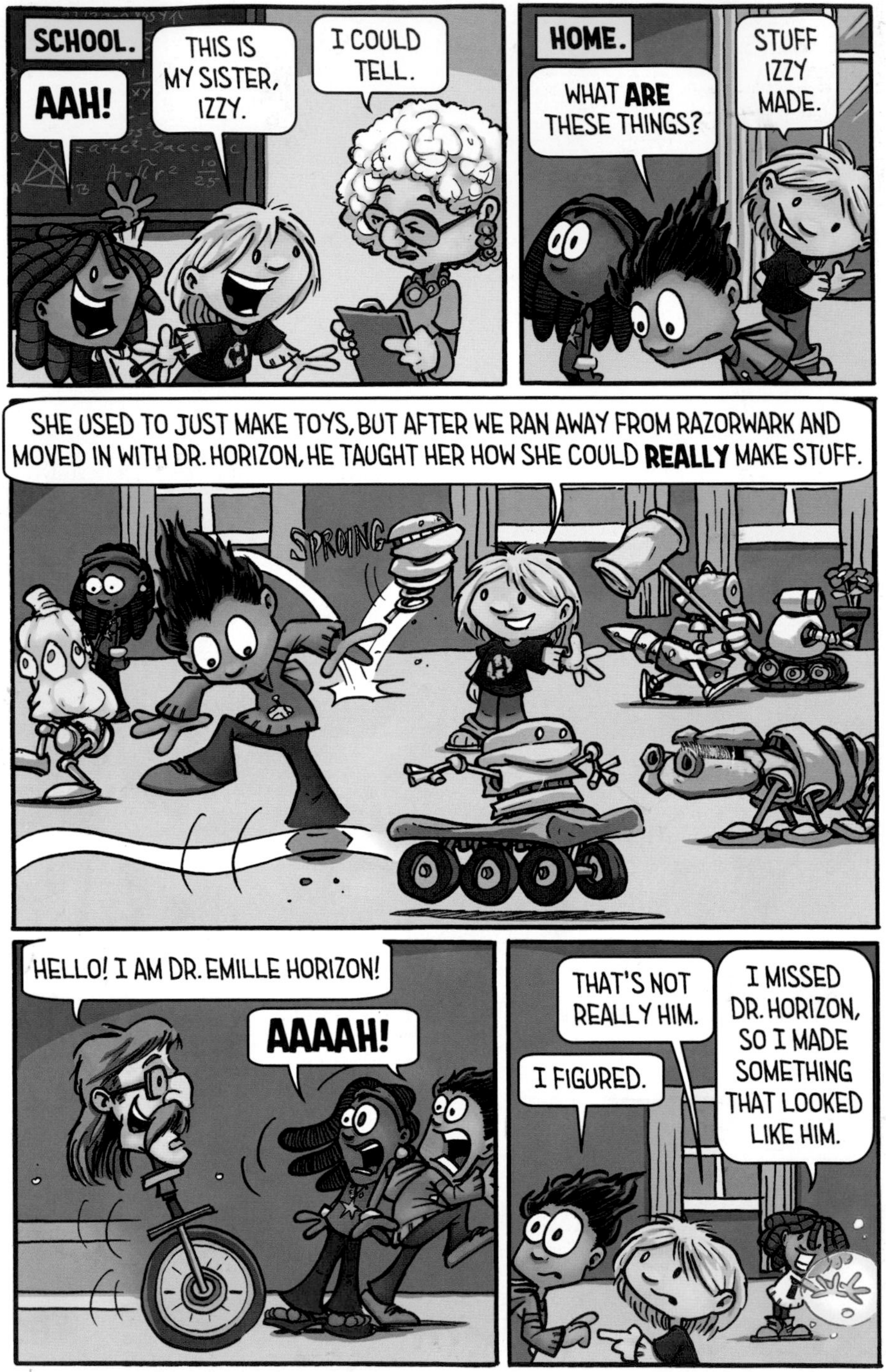
SCHOOL.
AAH!
THIS IS MY SISTER, IZZY.
I COULD TELL.
HOME.
WHAT **ARE** THESE THINGS?
STUFF IZZY MADE.
SHE USED TO JUST MAKE TOYS, BUT AFTER WE RAN AWAY FROM RAZORWARK AND MOVED IN WITH DR. HORIZON, HE TAUGHT HER HOW SHE COULD **REALLY** MAKE STUFF.
SPROING
HELLO! I AM DR. EMILLE HORIZON!
AAAAH!
THAT'S NOT REALLY HIM.
I MISSED DR. HORIZON, SO I MADE SOMETHING THAT LOOKED LIKE HIM.
I FIGURED.

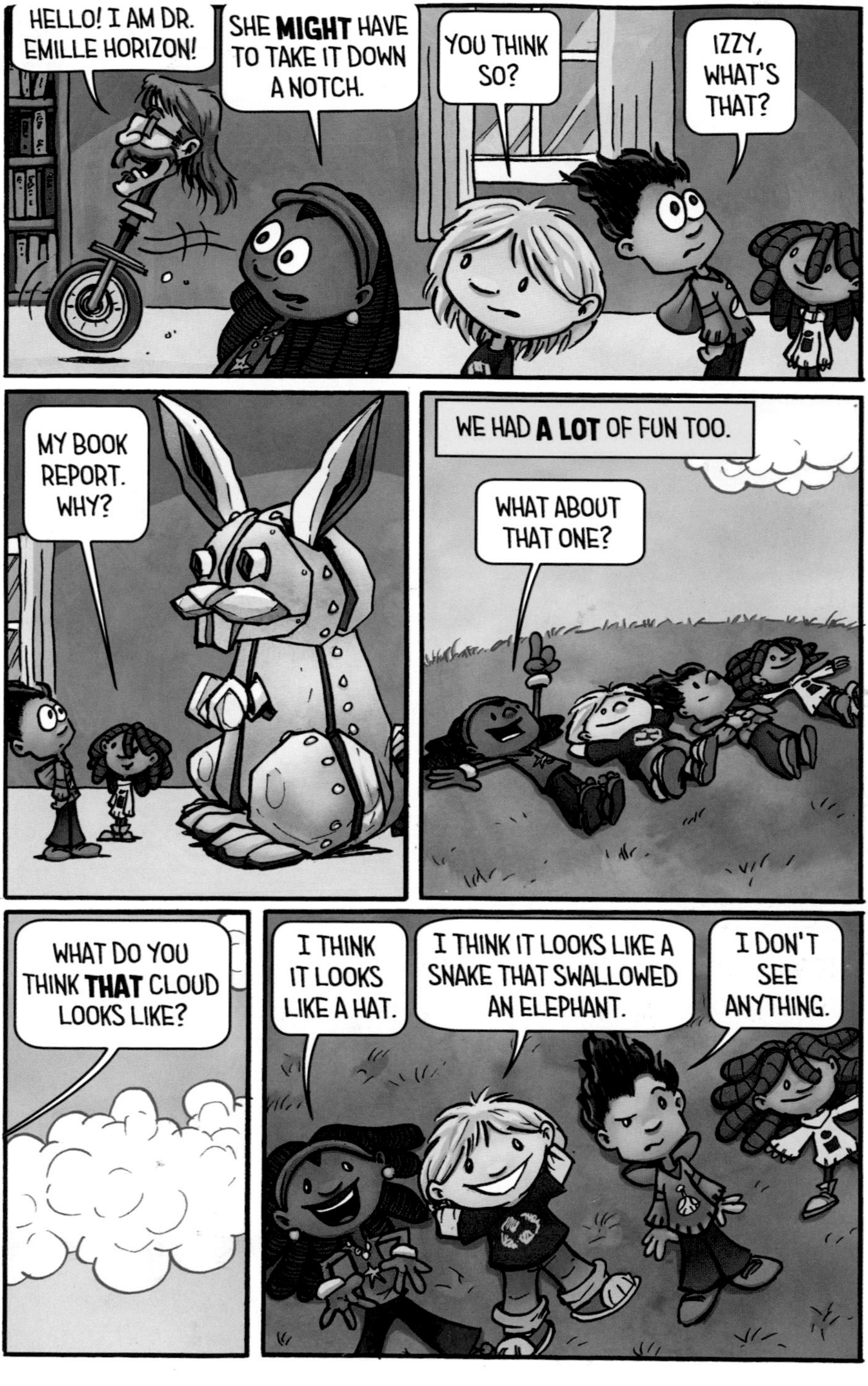
HELLO! I AM DR. EMILLE HORIZON!
SHE **MIGHT** HAVE TO TAKE IT DOWN A NOTCH.
YOU THINK SO?
IZZY, WHAT'S THAT?
MY BOOK REPORT. WHY?
WE HAD **A LOT** OF FUN TOO.
WHAT ABOUT THAT ONE?
WHAT DO YOU THINK **THAT** CLOUD LOOKS LIKE?
I THINK IT LOOKS LIKE A HAT.
I THINK IT LOOKS LIKE A SNAKE THAT SWALLOWED AN ELEPHANT.
I DON'T SEE ANYTHING.

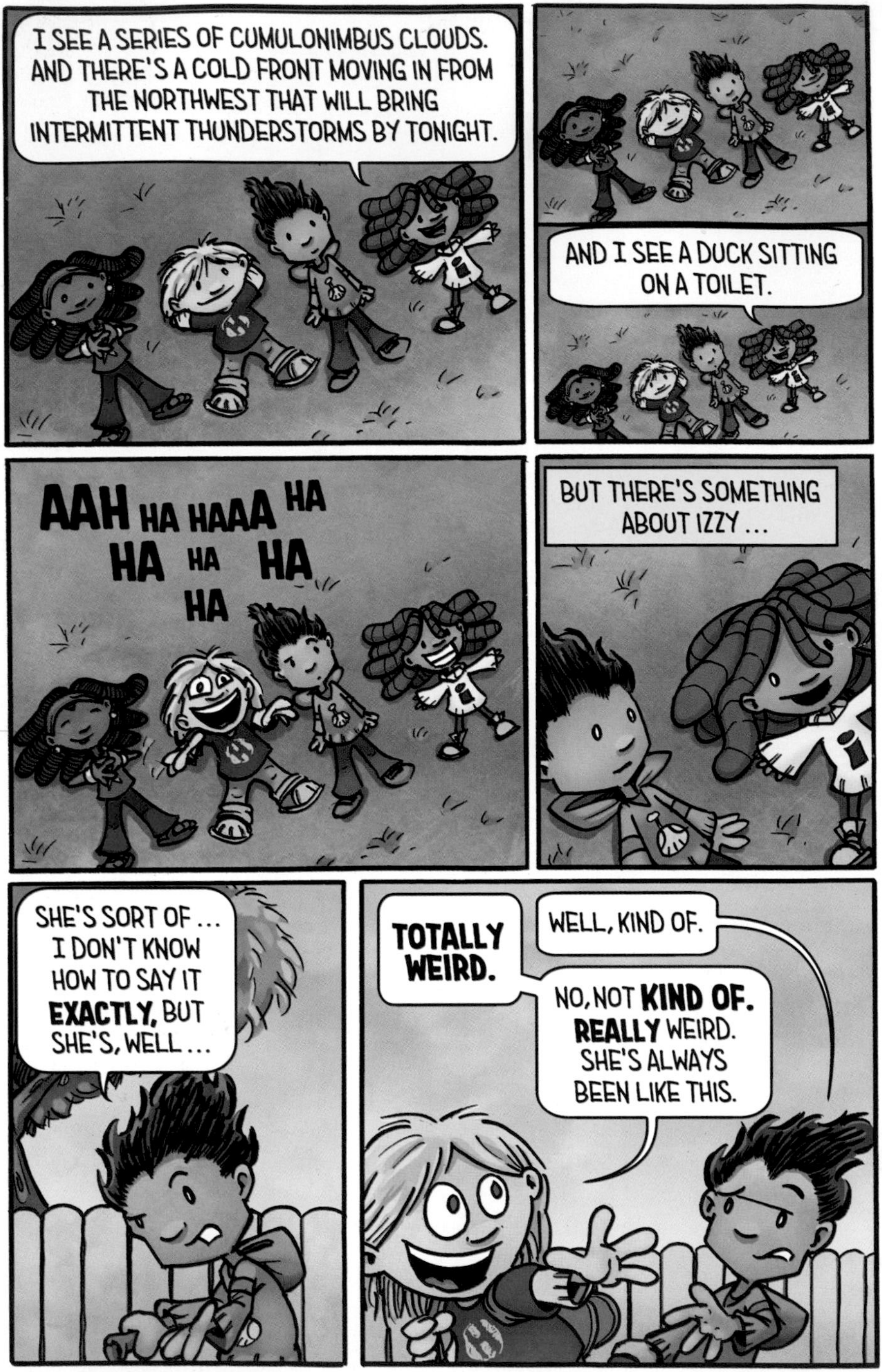

I SEE A SERIES OF CUMULONIMBUS CLOUDS. AND THERE'S A COLD FRONT MOVING IN FROM THE NORTHWEST THAT WILL BRING INTERMITTENT THUNDERSTORMS BY TONIGHT.
AND I SEE A DUCK SITTING ON A TOILET.
AAH HA HAAA HA HA HA HA HA
BUT THERE'S SOMETHING ABOUT IZZY . . .
SHE'S SORT OF . . . I DON'T KNOW HOW TO SAY IT **EXACTLY,** BUT SHE'S, WELL . . .
TOTALLY WEIRD.
WELL, KIND OF.
NO, NOT **KIND OF. REALLY** WEIRD. SHE'S ALWAYS BEEN LIKE THIS.

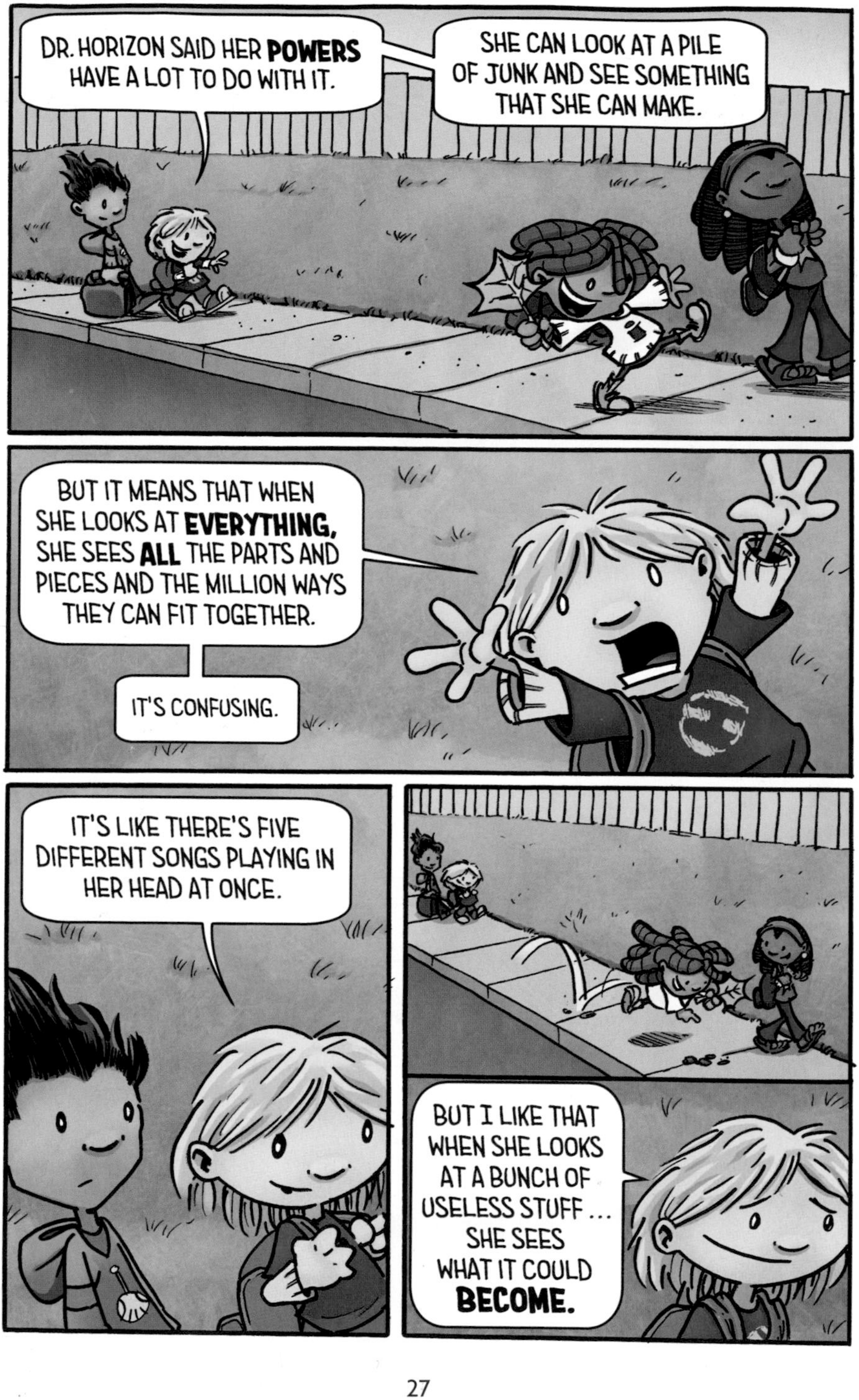
DR. HORIZON SAID HER **POWERS** HAVE A LOT TO DO WITH IT.
SHE CAN LOOK AT A PILE OF JUNK AND SEE SOMETHING THAT SHE CAN MAKE.
BUT IT MEANS THAT WHEN SHE LOOKS AT **EVERYTHING,** SHE SEES **ALL** THE PARTS AND PIECES AND THE MILLION WAYS THEY CAN FIT TOGETHER.
IT'S CONFUSING.
IT'S LIKE THERE'S FIVE DIFFERENT SONGS PLAYING IN HER HEAD AT ONCE.
BUT I LIKE THAT WHEN SHE LOOKS AT A BUNCH OF USELESS STUFF ... SHE SEES WHAT IT COULD **BECOME.**

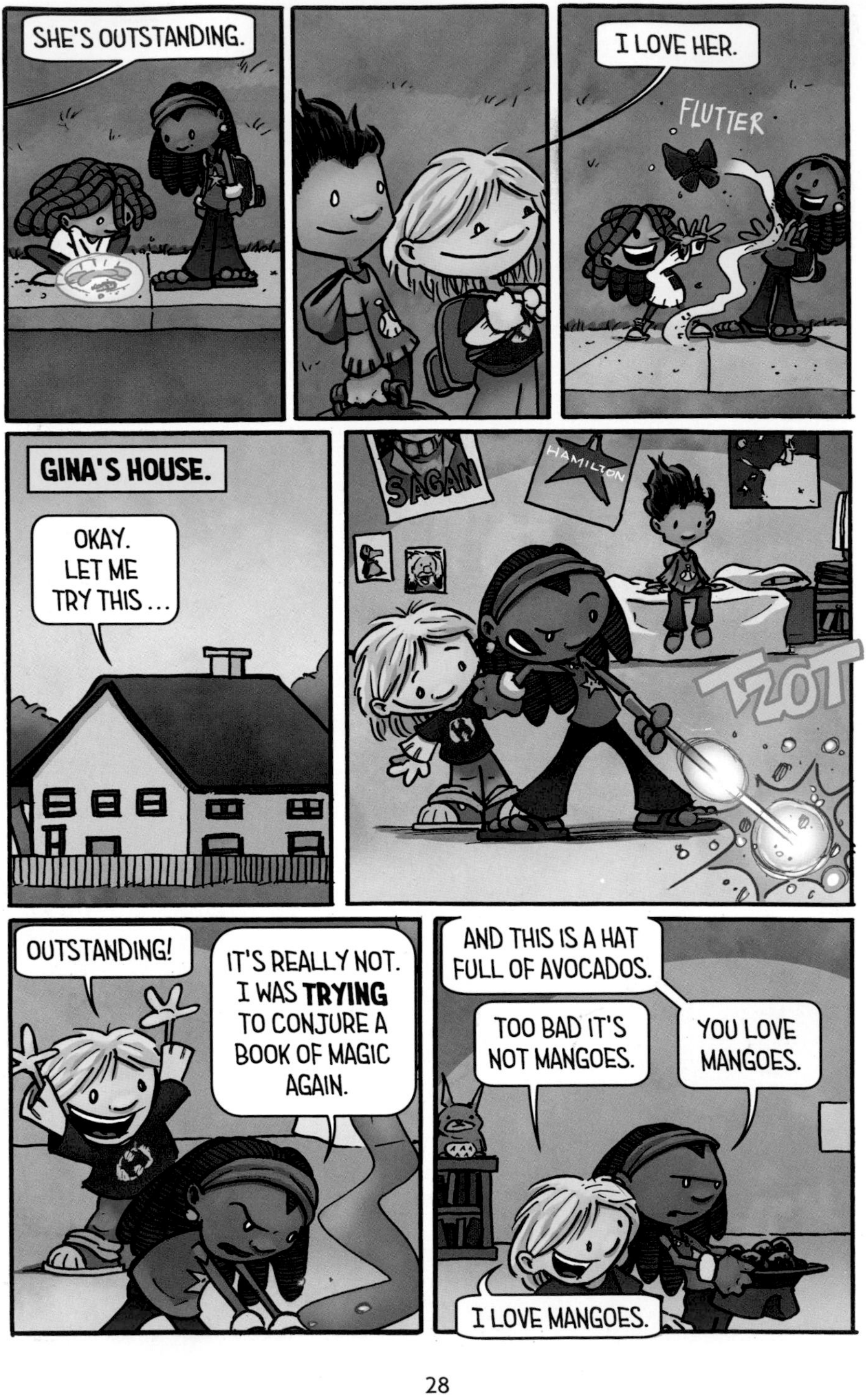
SHE'S OUTSTANDING.
I LOVE HER.
FLUTTER
GINA'S HOUSE.
OKAY. LET ME TRY THIS . . .
SAGAN
HAMILTON
TZOT
OUTSTANDING!
IT'S REALLY NOT. I WAS **TRYING** TO CONJURE A BOOK OF MAGIC AGAIN.
AND THIS IS A HAT FULL OF AVOCADOS.
TOO BAD IT'S NOT MANGOES.
YOU LOVE MANGOES.
I LOVE MANGOES.

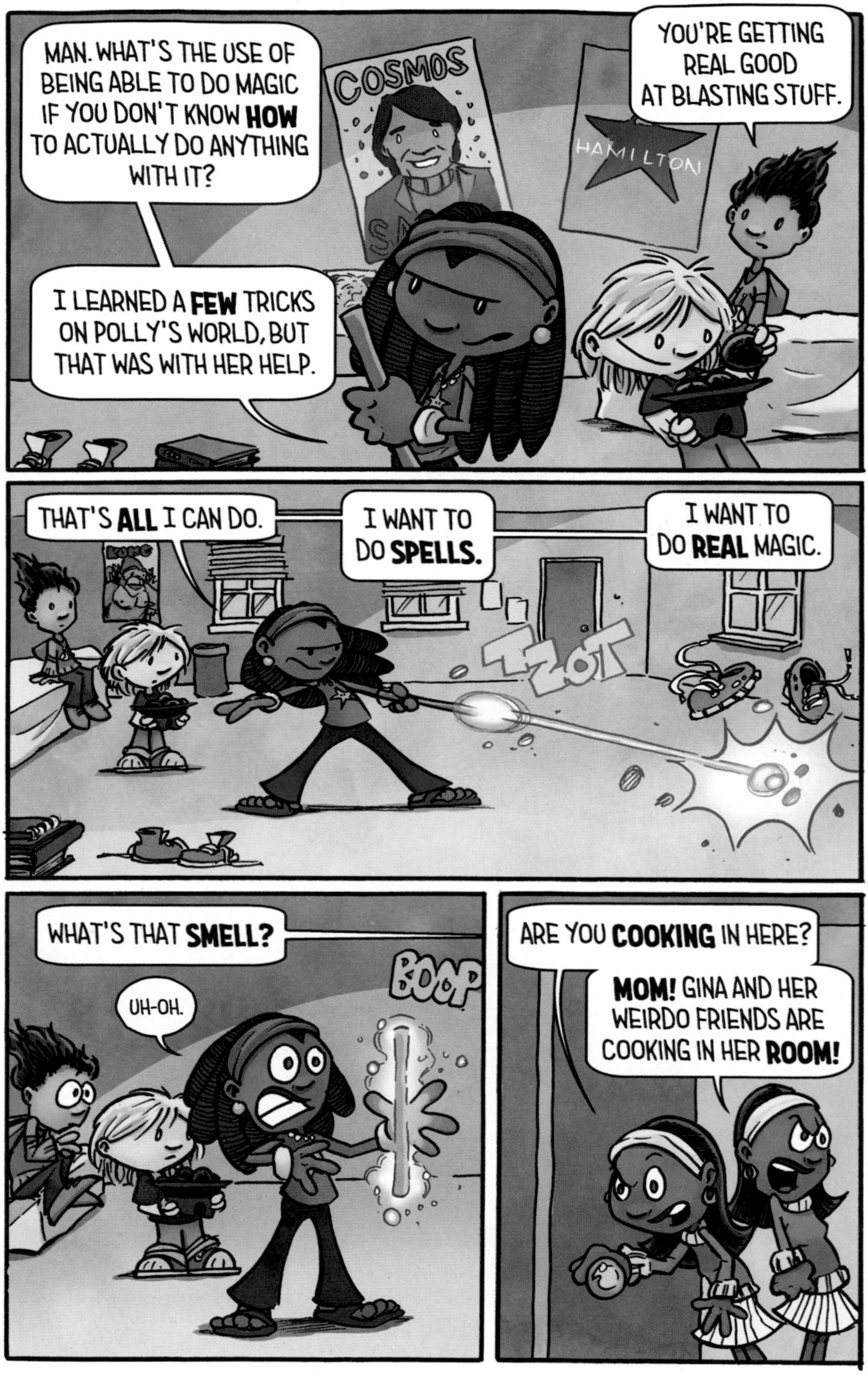
MAN. WHAT'S THE USE OF BEING ABLE TO DO MAGIC IF YOU DON'T KNOW **HOW** TO ACTUALLY DO ANYTHING WITH IT?
COSMOS
HAMILTON
YOU'RE GETTING REAL GOOD AT BLASTING STUFF.
I LEARNED A **FEW** TRICKS ON POLLY'S WORLD, BUT THAT WAS WITH HER HELP.
THAT'S **ALL** I CAN DO.
I WANT TO DO **SPELLS.**
I WANT TO DO **REAL** MAGIC.
KONG
TZOT
WHAT'S THAT **SMELL?**
BOOP
UH-OH.
ARE YOU **COOKING** IN HERE?
MOM! GINA AND HER WEIRDO FRIENDS ARE COOKING IN HER **ROOM!**

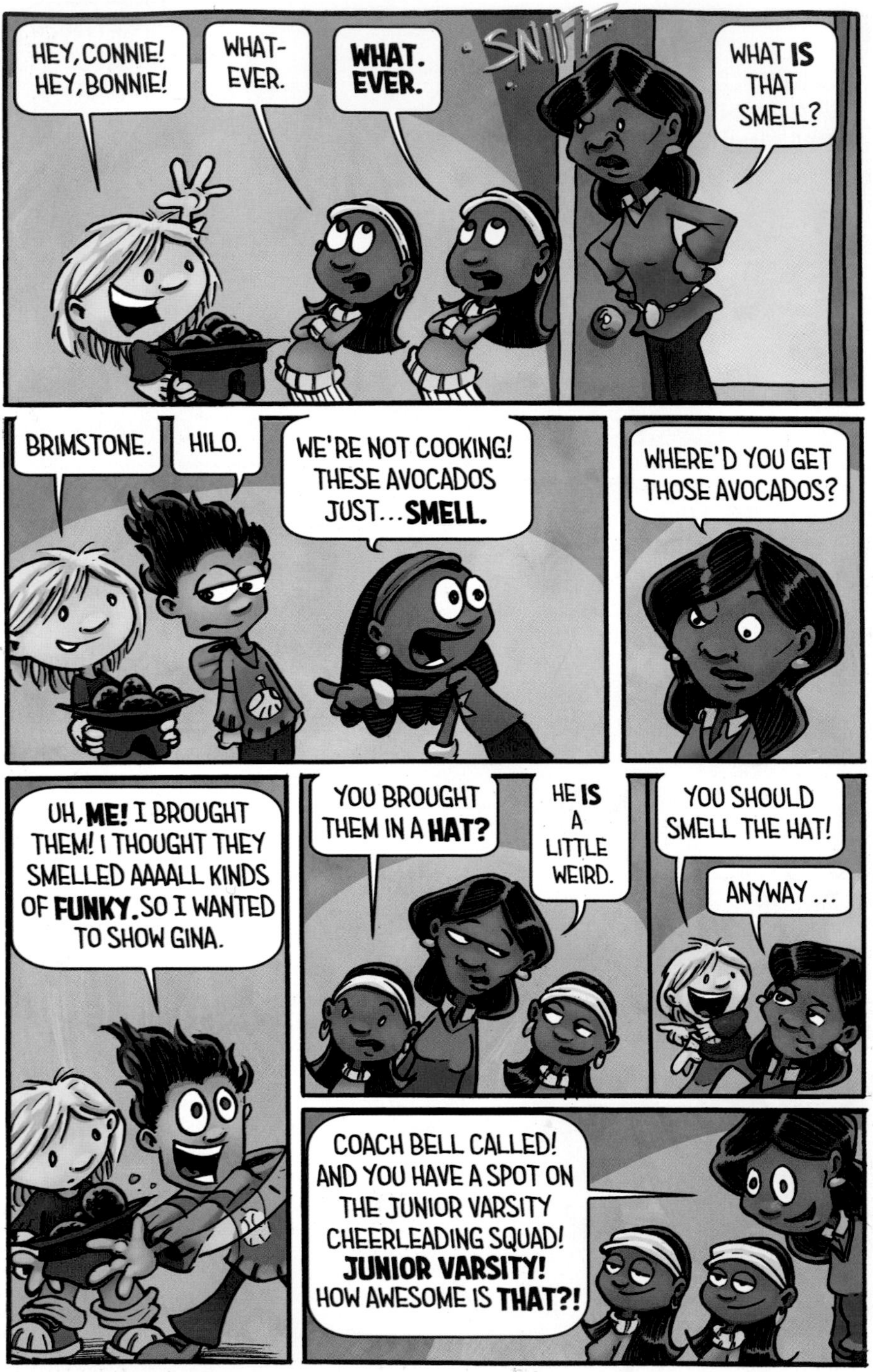
HEY, CONNIE! HEY, BONNIE!
WHAT-EVER.
WHAT. EVER.
SNIFF
WHAT **IS** THAT SMELL?
BRIMSTONE.
HILO.
WE'RE NOT COOKING! THESE AVOCADOS JUST... **SMELL.**
WHERE'D YOU GET THOSE AVOCADOS?
UH, **ME!** I BROUGHT THEM! I THOUGHT THEY SMELLED AAAALL KINDS OF **FUNKY.** SO I WANTED TO SHOW GINA.
YOU BROUGHT THEM IN A **HAT?**
HE **IS** A LITTLE WEIRD.
YOU SHOULD SMELL THE HAT!
ANYWAY ...
COACH BELL CALLED! AND YOU HAVE A SPOT ON THE JUNIOR VARSITY CHEERLEADING SQUAD! **JUNIOR VARSITY!** HOW AWESOME IS **THAT?!**

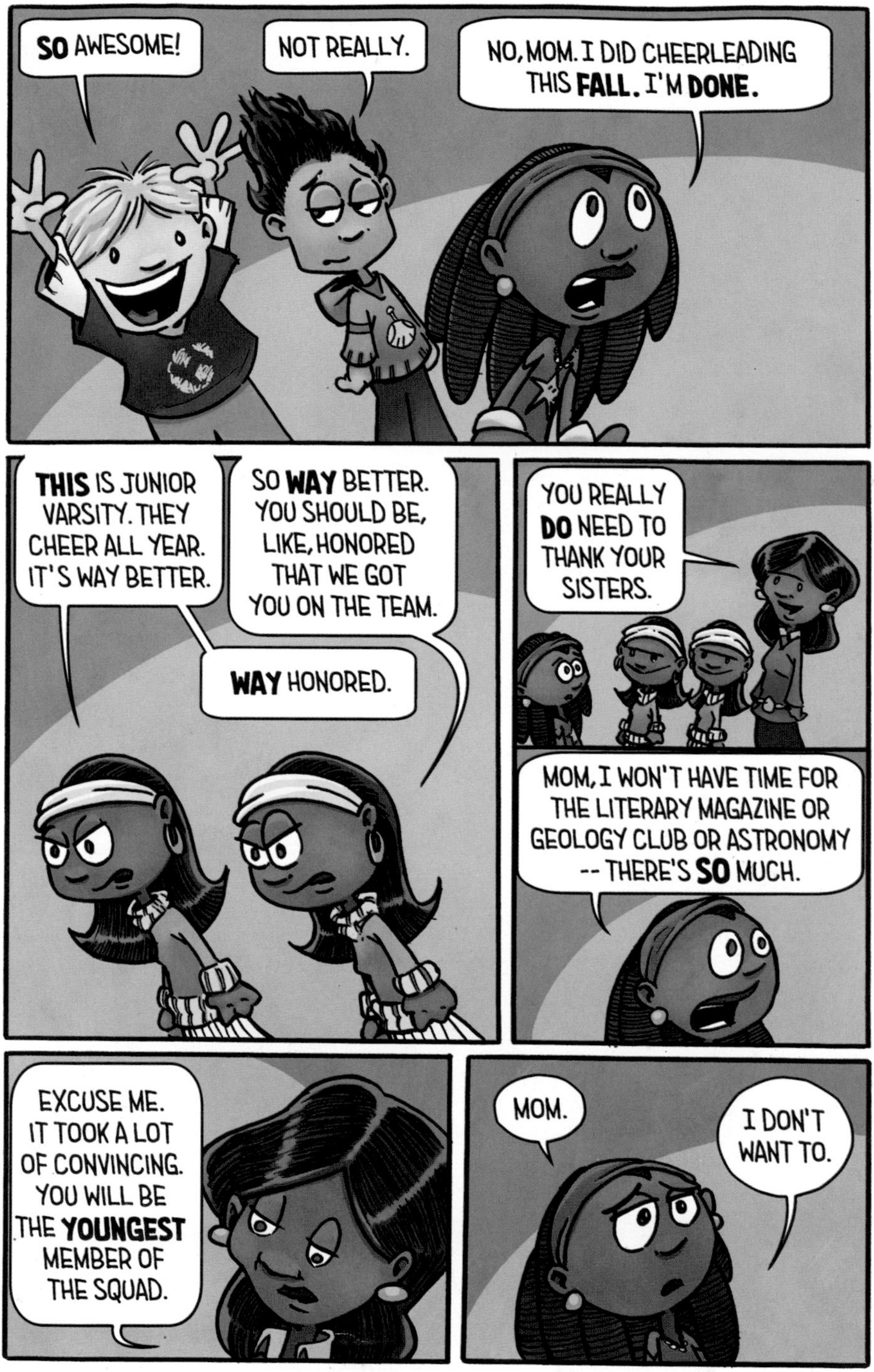
SO AWESOME!
NOT REALLY.
NO, MOM. I DID CHEERLEADING THIS FALL. I'M DONE.
THIS IS JUNIOR VARSITY. THEY CHEER ALL YEAR. IT'S WAY BETTER.
SO WAY BETTER. YOU SHOULD BE, LIKE, HONORED THAT WE GOT YOU ON THE TEAM.
WAY HONORED.
YOU REALLY DO NEED TO THANK YOUR SISTERS.
MOM, I WON'T HAVE TIME FOR THE LITERARY MAGAZINE OR GEOLOGY CLUB OR ASTRONOMY -- THERE'S SO MUCH.
EXCUSE ME. IT TOOK A LOT OF CONVINCING. YOU WILL BE THE YOUNGEST MEMBER OF THE SQUAD.
MOM.
I DON'T WANT TO.

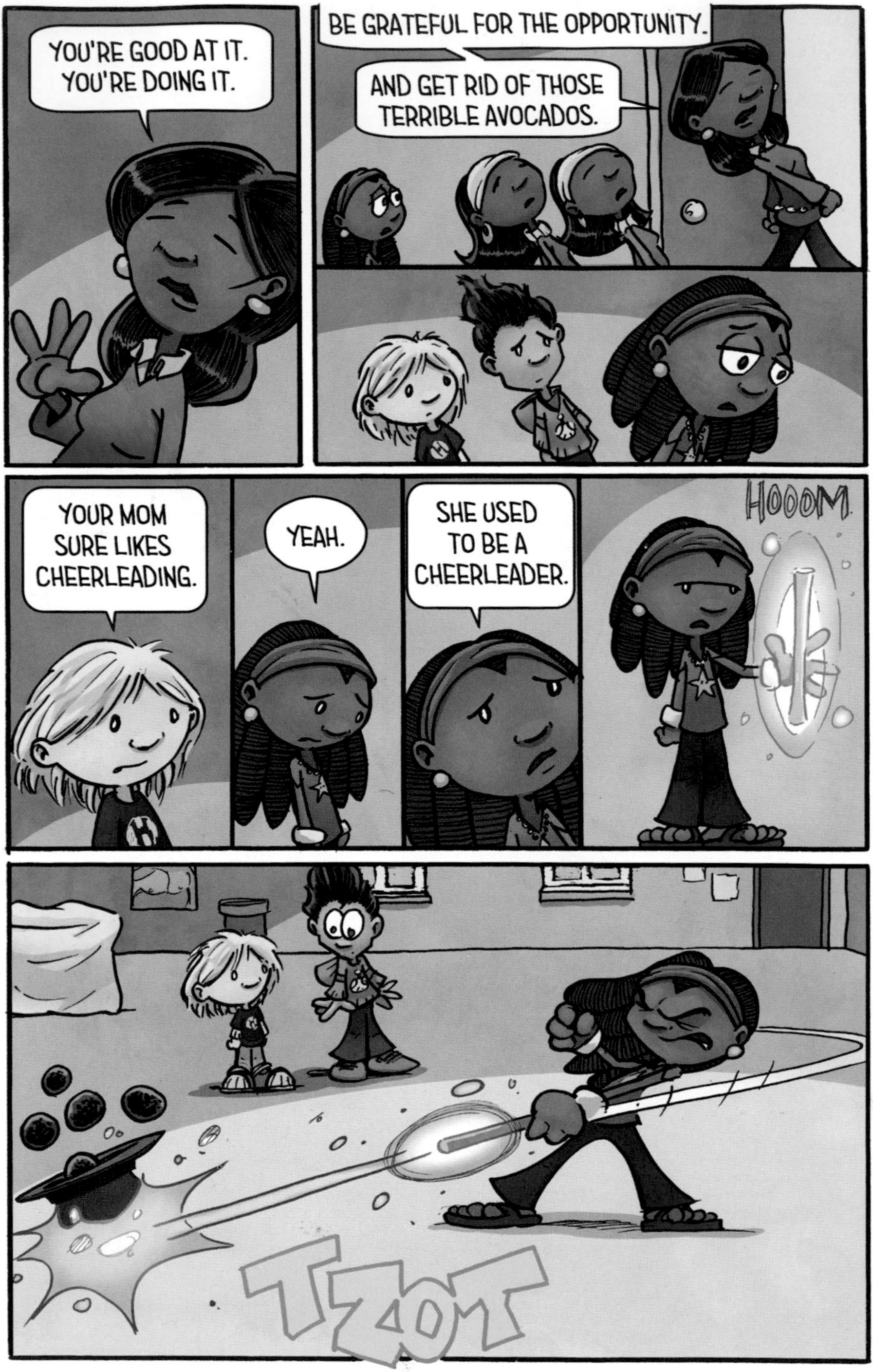
YOU'RE GOOD AT IT. YOU'RE DOING IT.
BE GRATEFUL FOR THE OPPORTUNITY.
AND GET RID OF THOSE TERRIBLE AVOCADOS.
YOUR MOM SURE LIKES CHEERLEADING.
YEAH.
SHE USED TO BE A CHEERLEADER.
HOOOM
TZOT

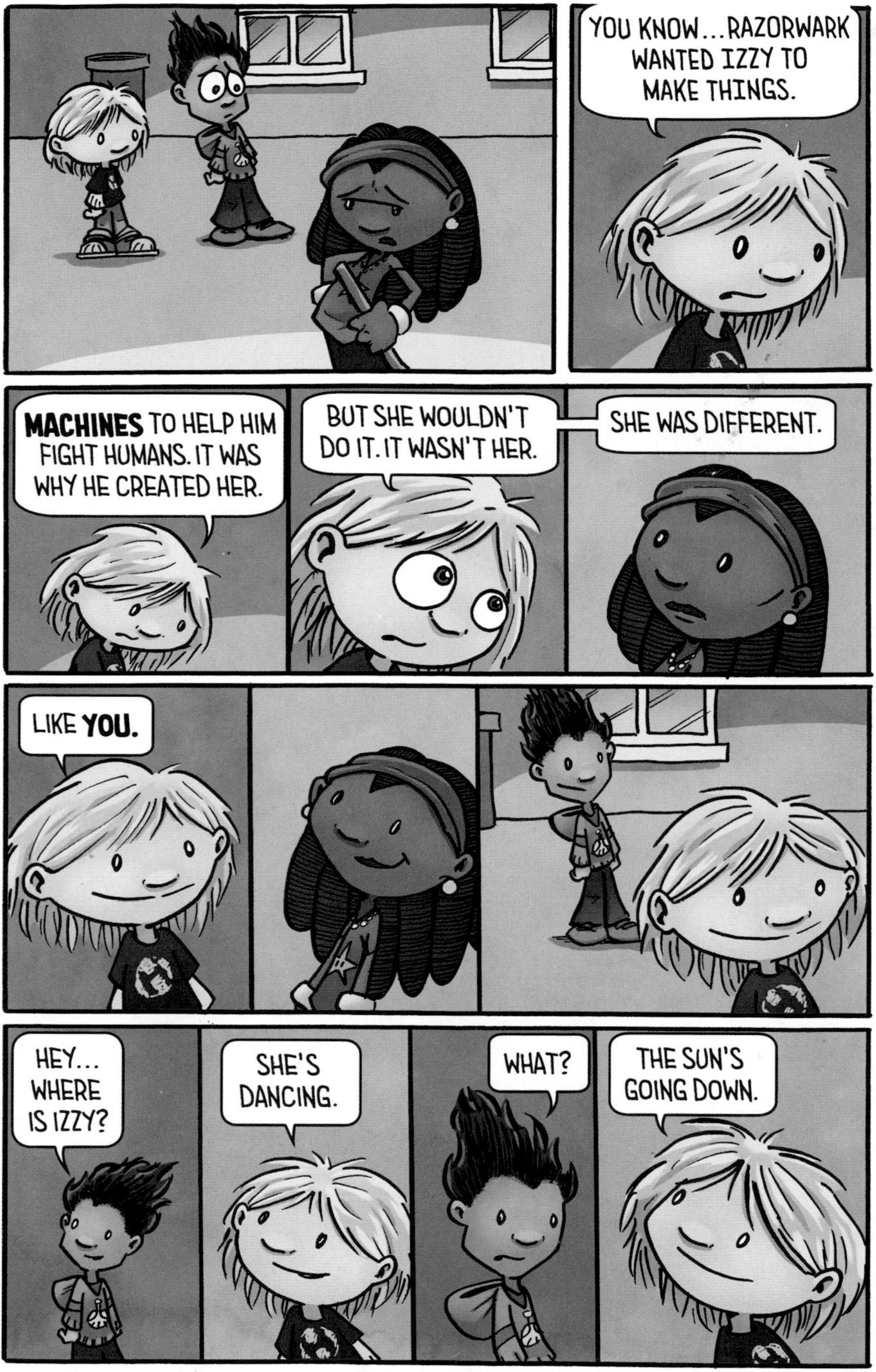
YOU KNOW... RAZORWARK WANTED IZZY TO MAKE THINGS.
MACHINES TO HELP HIM FIGHT HUMANS. IT WAS WHY HE CREATED HER.
BUT SHE WOULDN'T DO IT. IT WASN'T HER.
SHE WAS DIFFERENT.
LIKE **YOU.**
HEY... WHERE IS IZZY?
SHE'S DANCING.
WHAT?
THE SUN'S GOING DOWN.

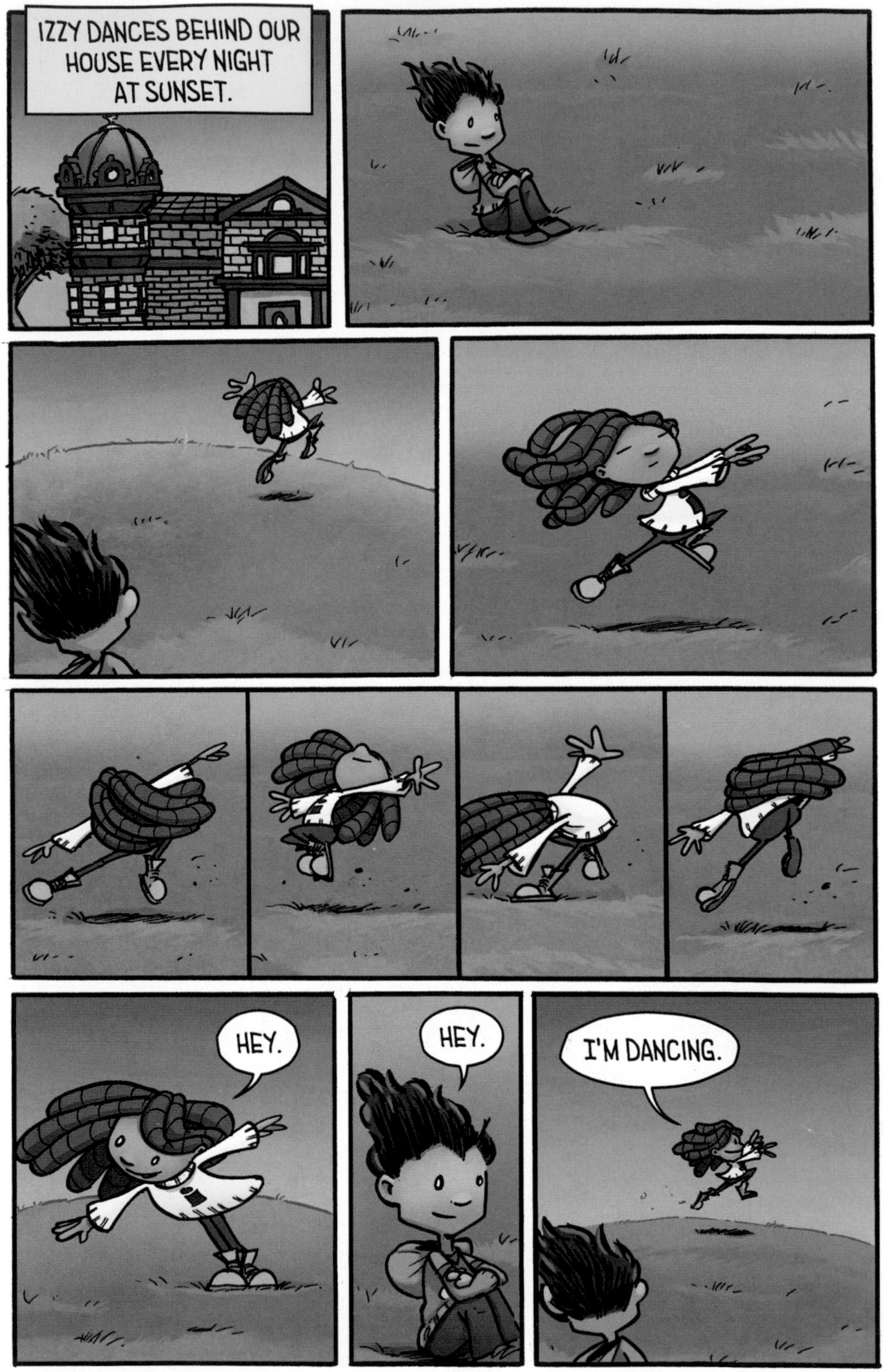
IZZY DANCES BEHIND OUR HOUSE EVERY NIGHT AT SUNSET.
HEY.
HEY.
I'M DANCING.

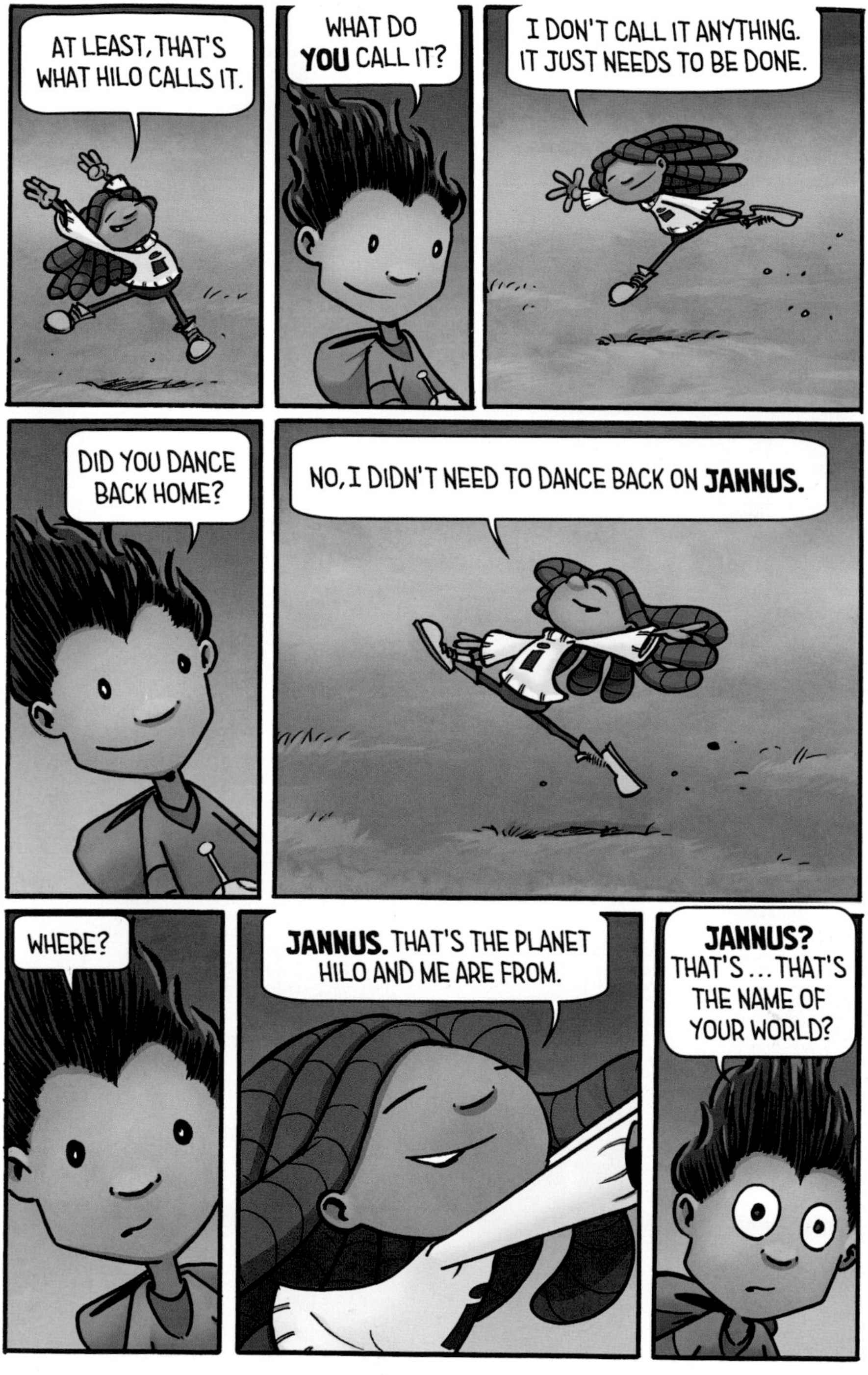
AT LEAST, THAT'S WHAT HILO CALLS IT.
WHAT DO **YOU** CALL IT?
I DON'T CALL IT ANYTHING. IT JUST NEEDS TO BE DONE.
DID YOU DANCE BACK HOME?
NO, I DIDN'T NEED TO DANCE BACK ON **JANNUS.**
WHERE?
JANNUS. THAT'S THE PLANET HILO AND ME ARE FROM.
JANNUS? THAT'S ... THAT'S THE NAME OF YOUR WORLD?

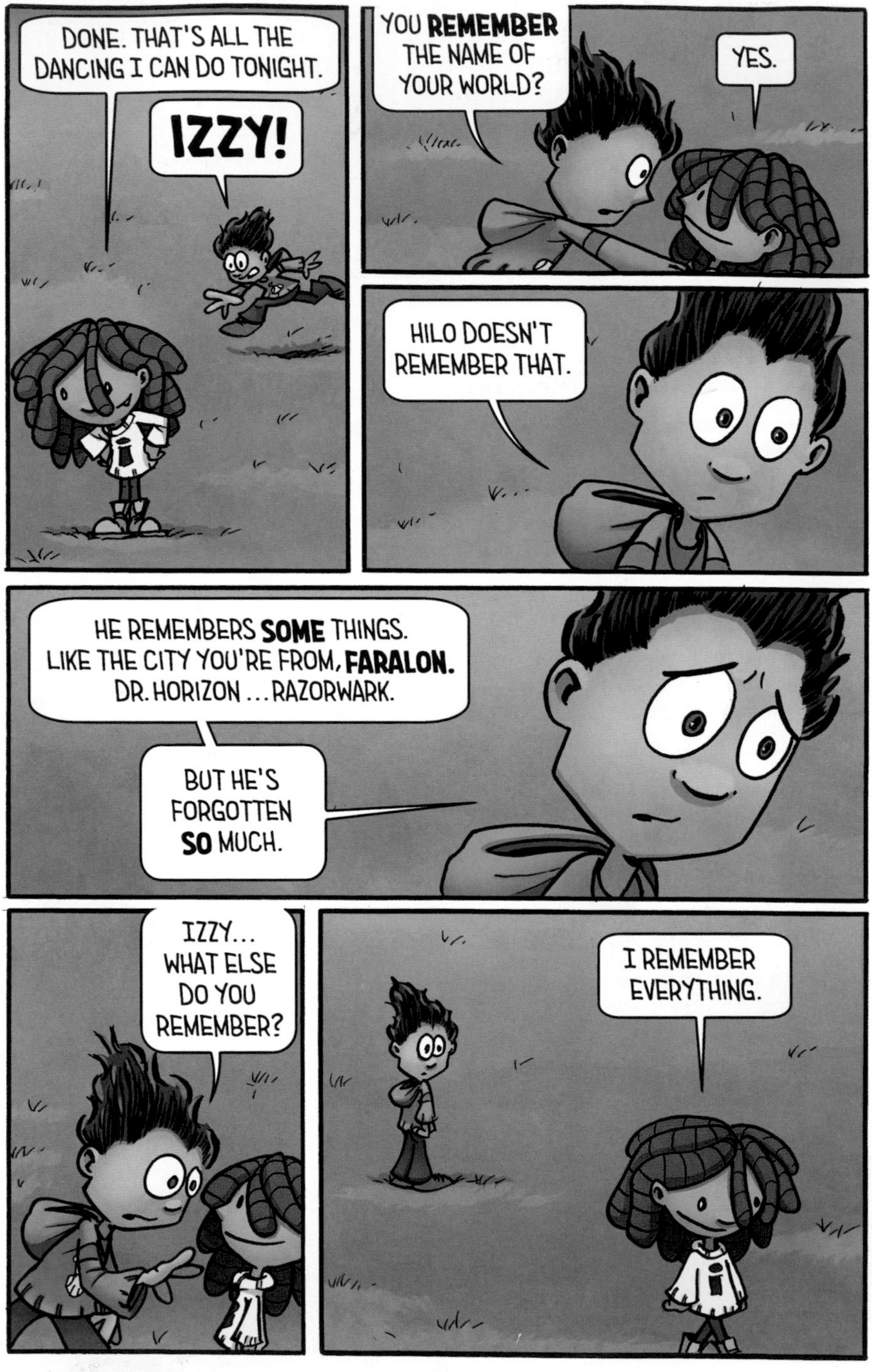
DONE. THAT'S ALL THE DANCING I CAN DO TONIGHT.
IZZY!
YOU REMEMBER THE NAME OF YOUR WORLD?
YES.
HILO DOESN'T REMEMBER THAT.
HE REMEMBERS SOME THINGS. LIKE THE CITY YOU'RE FROM, FARALON. DR. HORIZON ... RAZORWARK.
BUT HE'S FORGOTTEN SO MUCH.
IZZY... WHAT ELSE DO YOU REMEMBER?
I REMEMBER EVERYTHING.

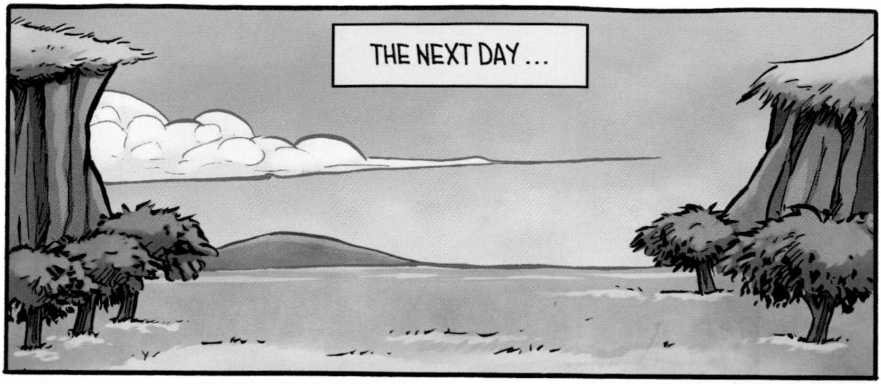
THE NEXT DAY . . .

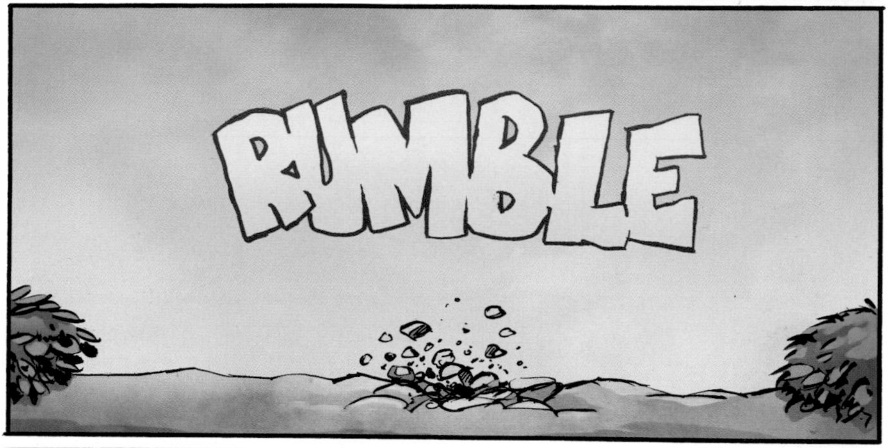
RUMBLE

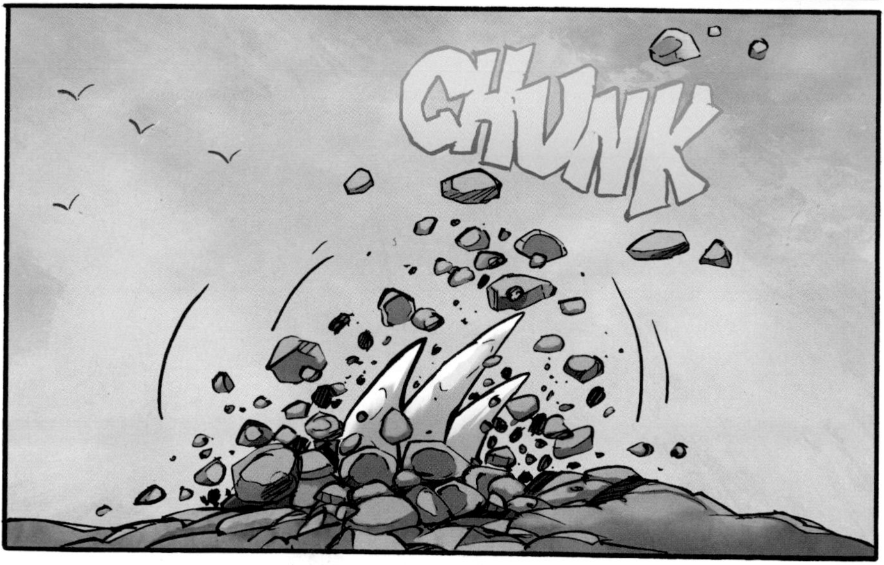
CHUNK

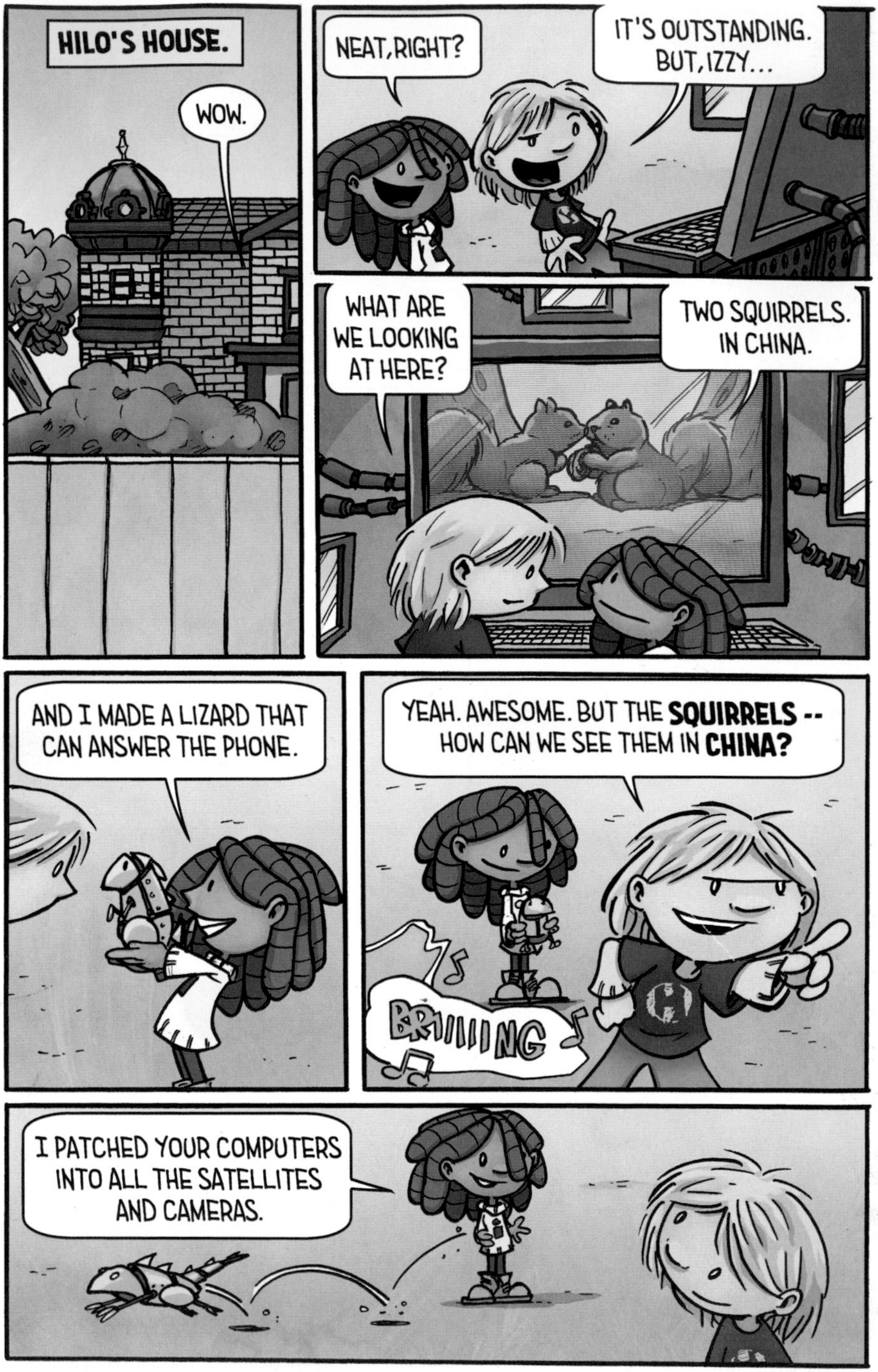
HILO'S HOUSE.
WOW.
NEAT, RIGHT?
IT'S OUTSTANDING. BUT, IZZY...
WHAT ARE WE LOOKING AT HERE?
TWO SQUIRRELS. IN CHINA.
AND I MADE A LIZARD THAT CAN ANSWER THE PHONE.
YEAH. AWESOME. BUT THE SQUIRRELS -- HOW CAN WE SEE THEM IN CHINA?
BRIIIIING
I PATCHED YOUR COMPUTERS INTO ALL THE SATELLITES AND CAMERAS.

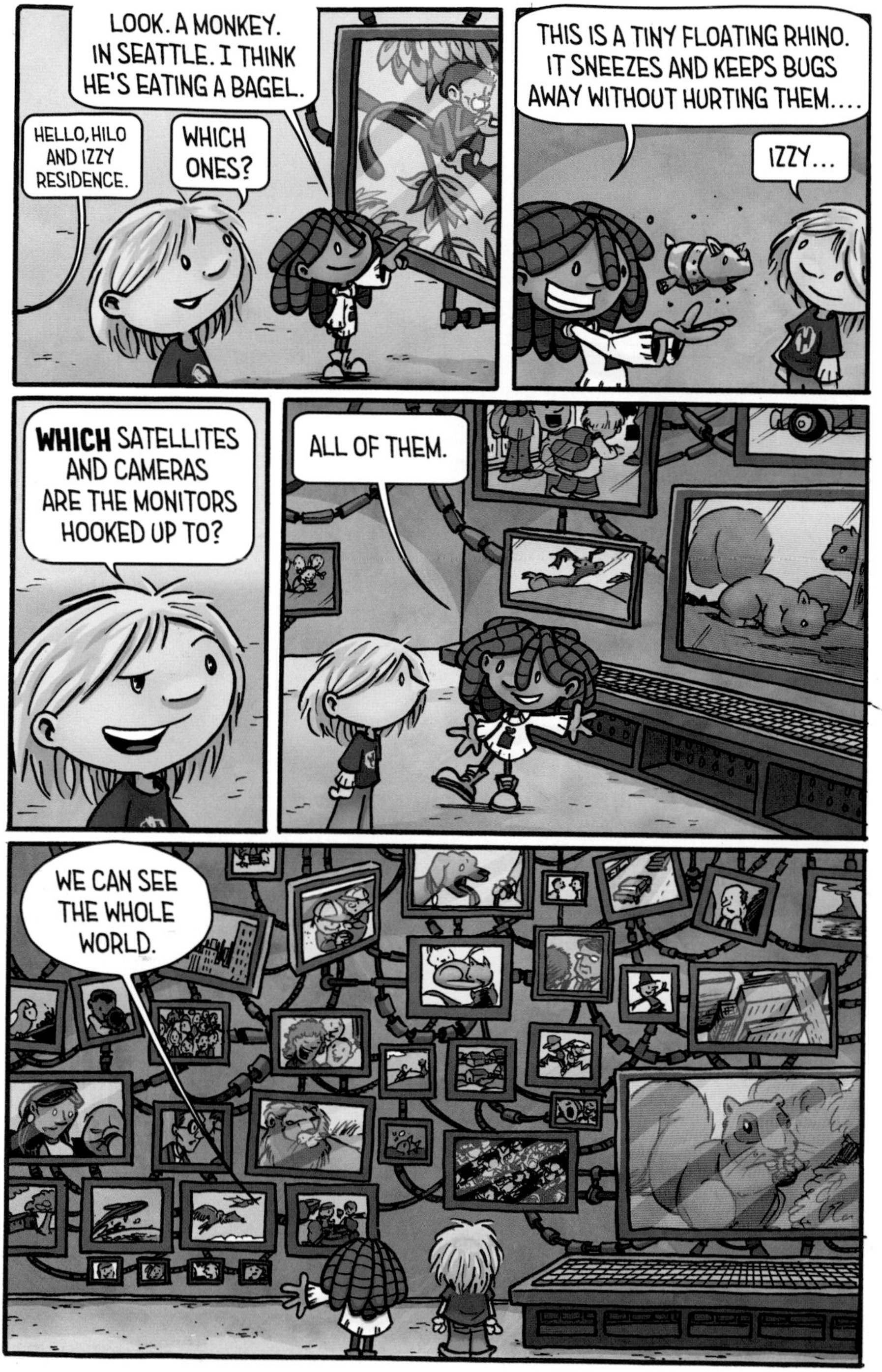
HELLO, HILO AND IZZY RESIDENCE.
WHICH ONES?
LOOK. A MONKEY. IN SEATTLE. I THINK HE'S EATING A BAGEL.
THIS IS A TINY FLOATING RHINO. IT SNEEZES AND KEEPS BUGS AWAY WITHOUT HURTING THEM....
IZZY...
WHICH SATELLITES AND CAMERAS ARE THE MONITORS HOOKED UP TO?
ALL OF THEM.
WE CAN SEE THE WHOLE WORLD.

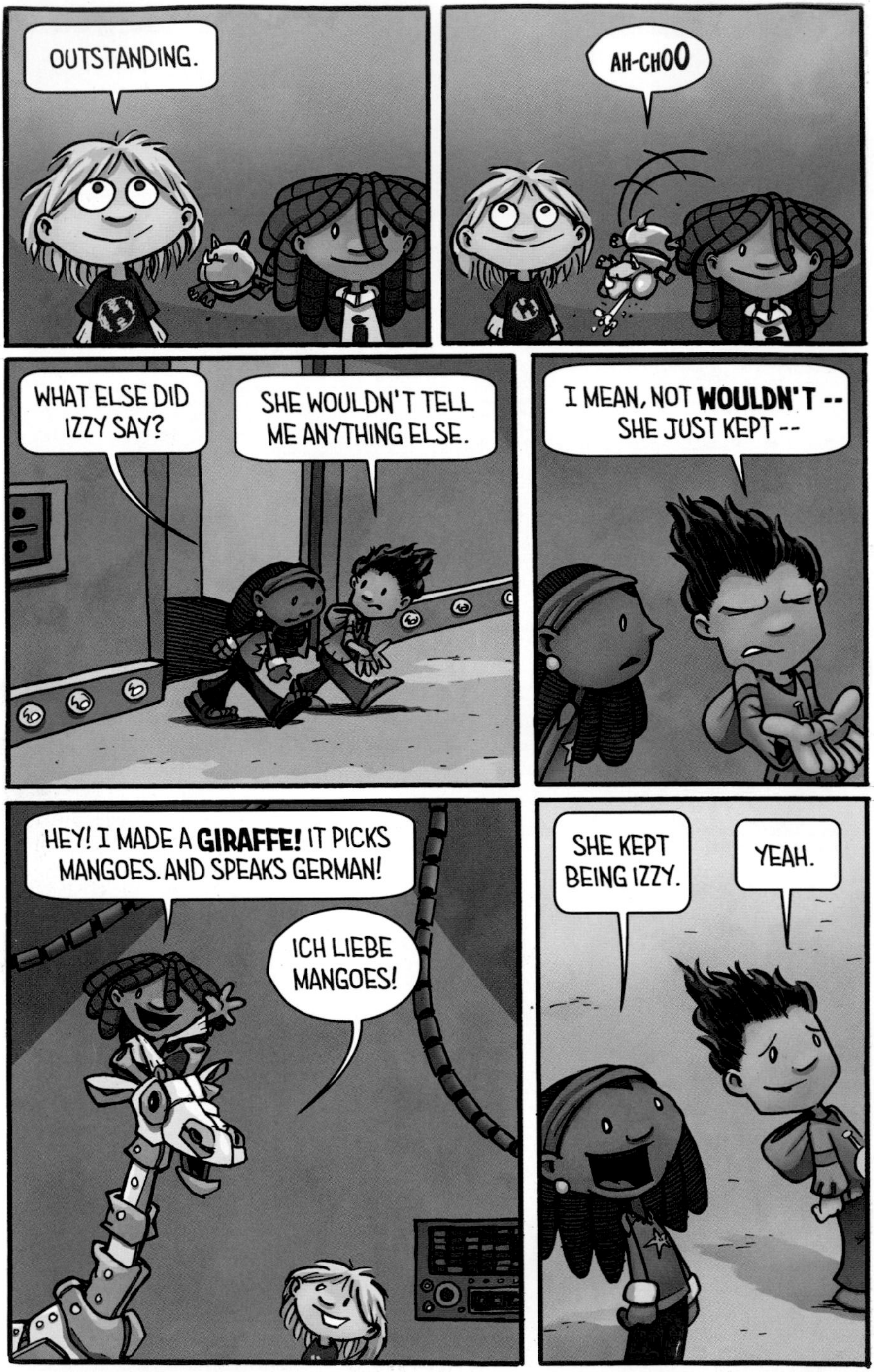
OUTSTANDING.
AH-CHOO
WHAT ELSE DID IZZY SAY?
SHE WOULDN'T TELL ME ANYTHING ELSE.
I MEAN, NOT **WOULDN'T --** SHE JUST KEPT --
HEY! I MADE A **GIRAFFE!** IT PICKS MANGOES. AND SPEAKS GERMAN!
ICH LIEBE MANGOES!
SHE KEPT BEING IZZY.
YEAH.

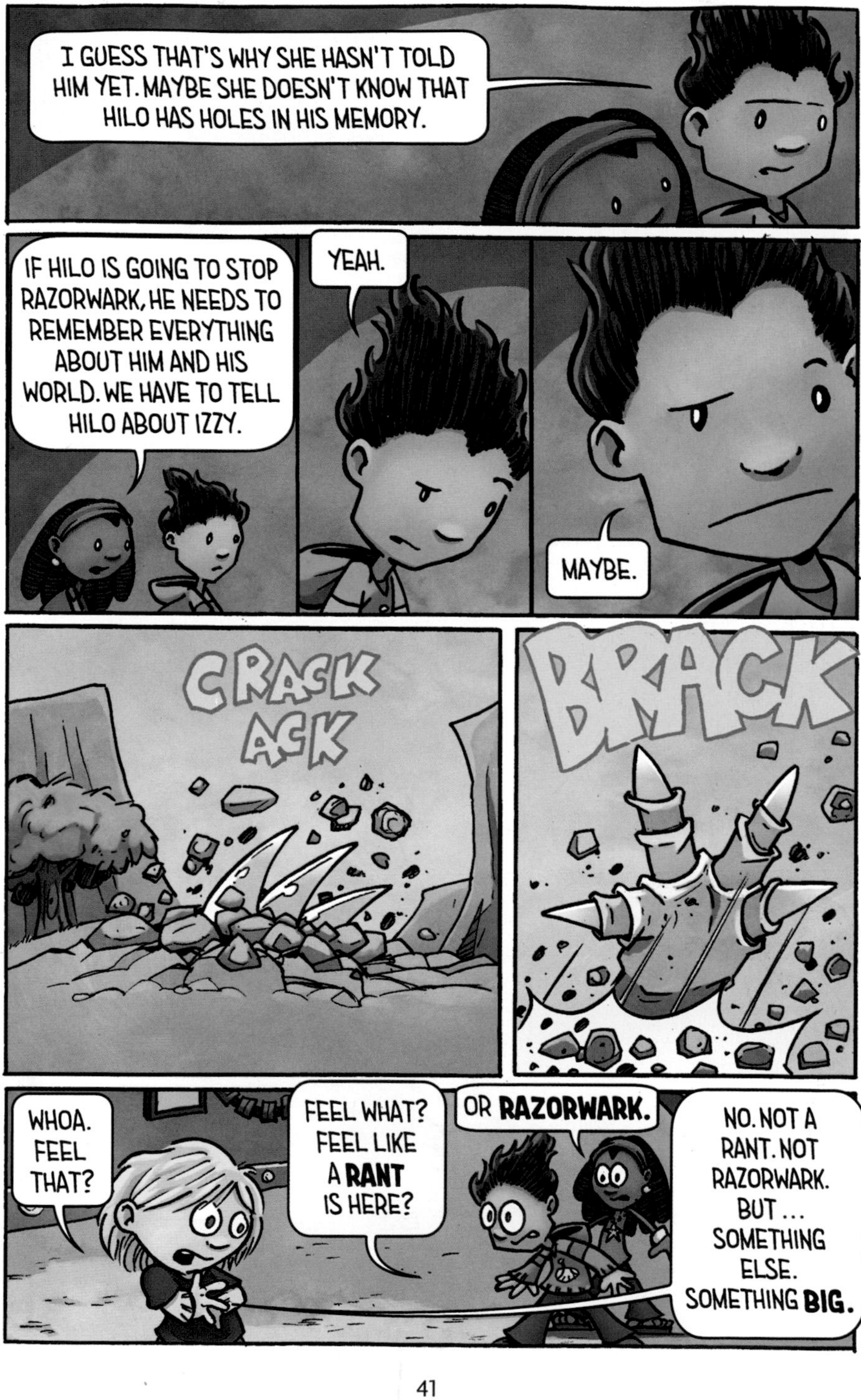
I GUESS THAT'S WHY SHE HASN'T TOLD HIM YET. MAYBE SHE DOESN'T KNOW THAT HILO HAS HOLES IN HIS MEMORY.
IF HILO IS GOING TO STOP RAZORWARK, HE NEEDS TO REMEMBER EVERYTHING ABOUT HIM AND HIS WORLD. WE HAVE TO TELL HILO ABOUT IZZY.
YEAH.
MAYBE.
CRACK
ACK
BRACK
WHOA. FEEL THAT?
FEEL WHAT? FEEL LIKE A **RANT** IS HERE?
OR **RAZORWARK.**
NO. NOT A RANT. NOT RAZORWARK. BUT . . . SOMETHING ELSE. SOMETHING **BIG.**

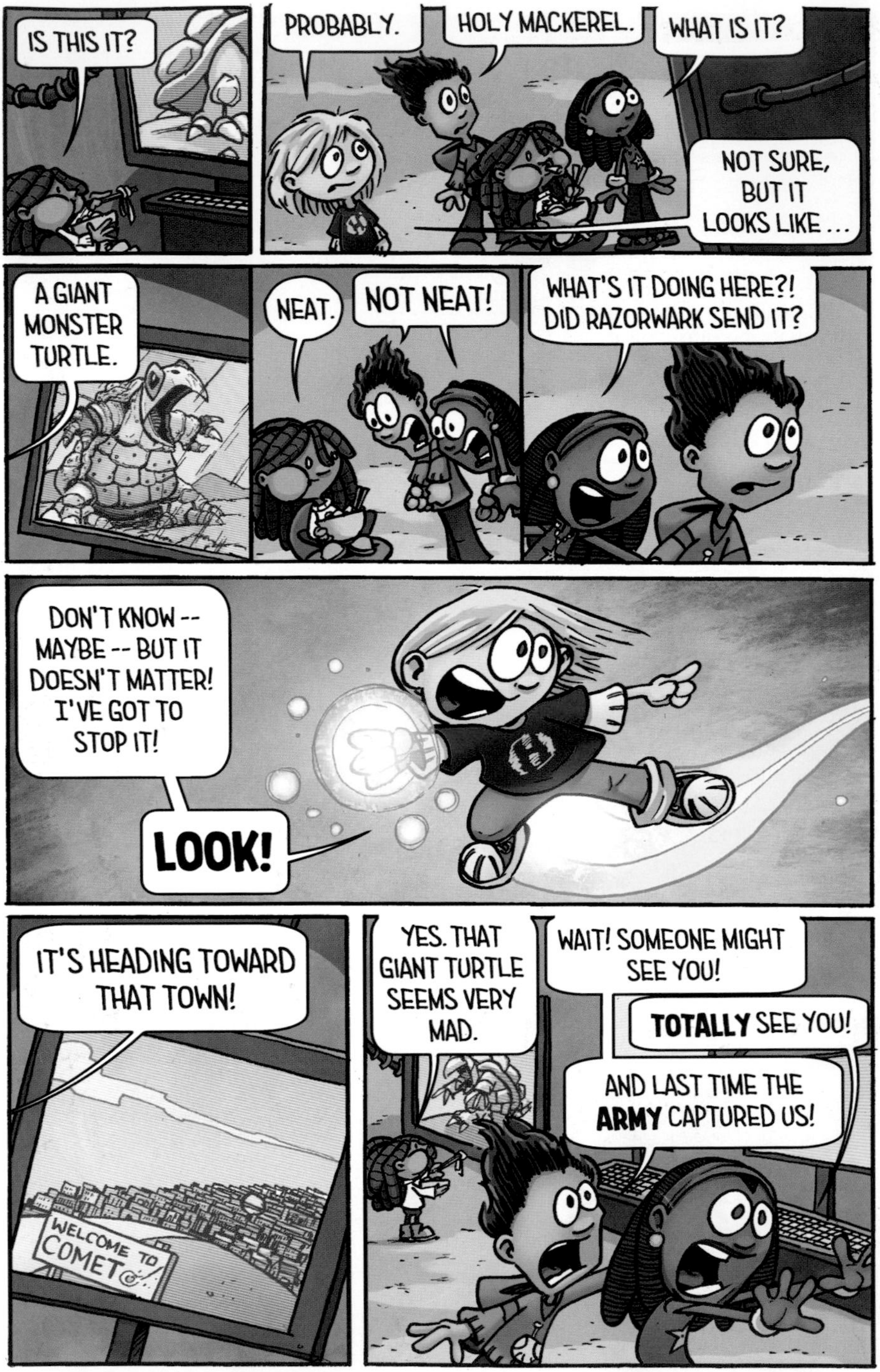

IS THIS IT?
PROBABLY.
HOLY MACKEREL.
WHAT IS IT?
NOT SURE, BUT IT LOOKS LIKE . . .
A GIANT MONSTER TURTLE.
NEAT.
NOT NEAT!
WHAT'S IT DOING HERE?! DID RAZORWARK SEND IT?
DON'T KNOW -- MAYBE -- BUT IT DOESN'T MATTER! I'VE GOT TO STOP IT!
LOOK!
IT'S HEADING TOWARD THAT TOWN!
WELCOME TO COMET
YES. THAT GIANT TURTLE SEEMS VERY MAD.
WAIT! SOMEONE MIGHT SEE YOU!
TOTALLY SEE YOU!
AND LAST TIME THE ARMY CAPTURED US!

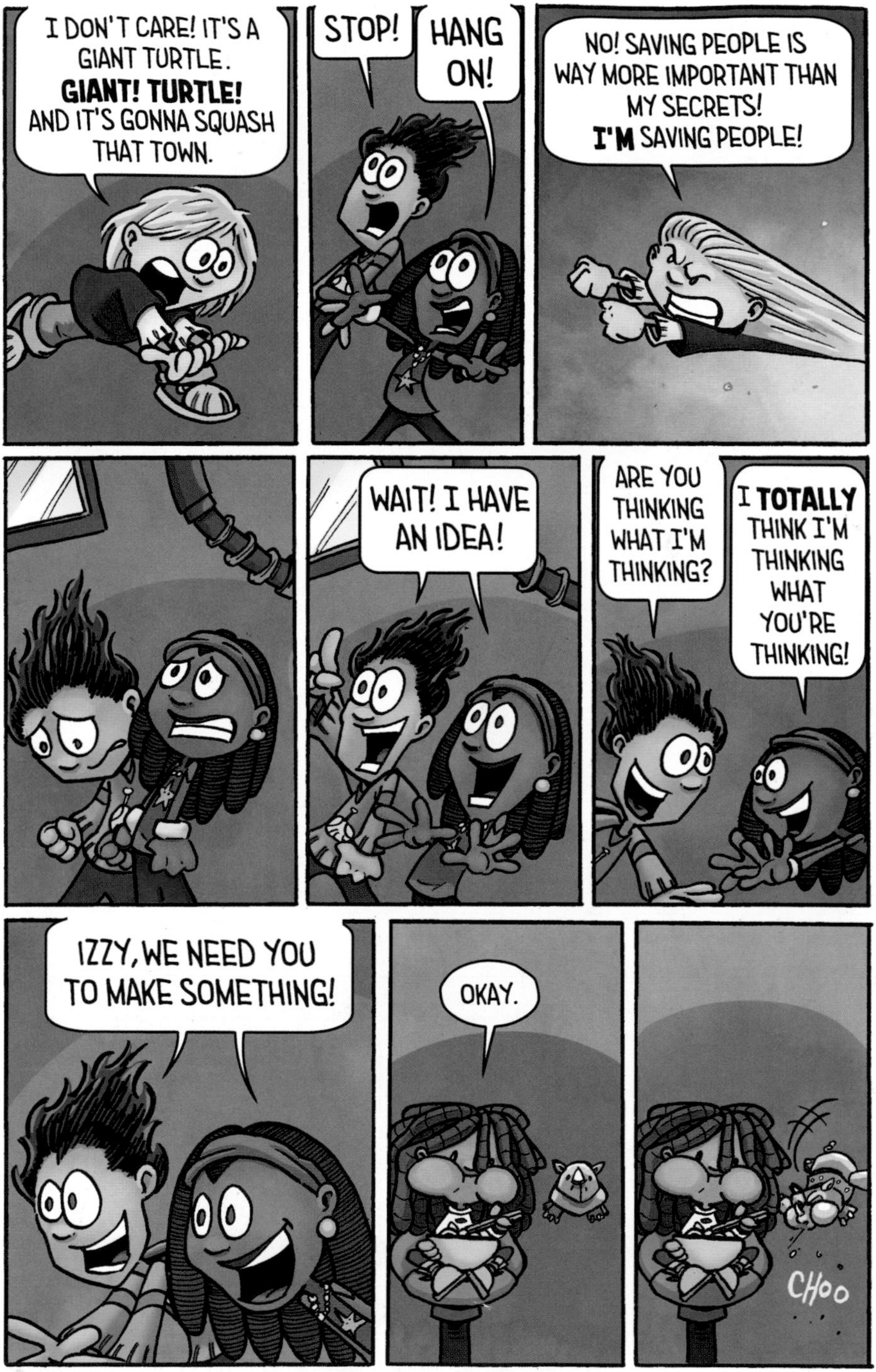
I DON'T CARE! IT'S A GIANT TURTLE. **GIANT! TURTLE!** AND IT'S GONNA SQUASH THAT TOWN.
STOP!
HANG ON!
NO! SAVING PEOPLE IS WAY MORE IMPORTANT THAN MY SECRETS! **I'M** SAVING PEOPLE!
WAIT! I HAVE AN IDEA!
ARE YOU THINKING WHAT I'M THINKING?
I **TOTALLY** THINK I'M THINKING WHAT YOU'RE THINKING!
IZZY, WE NEED YOU TO MAKE SOMETHING!
OKAY.
CHOO

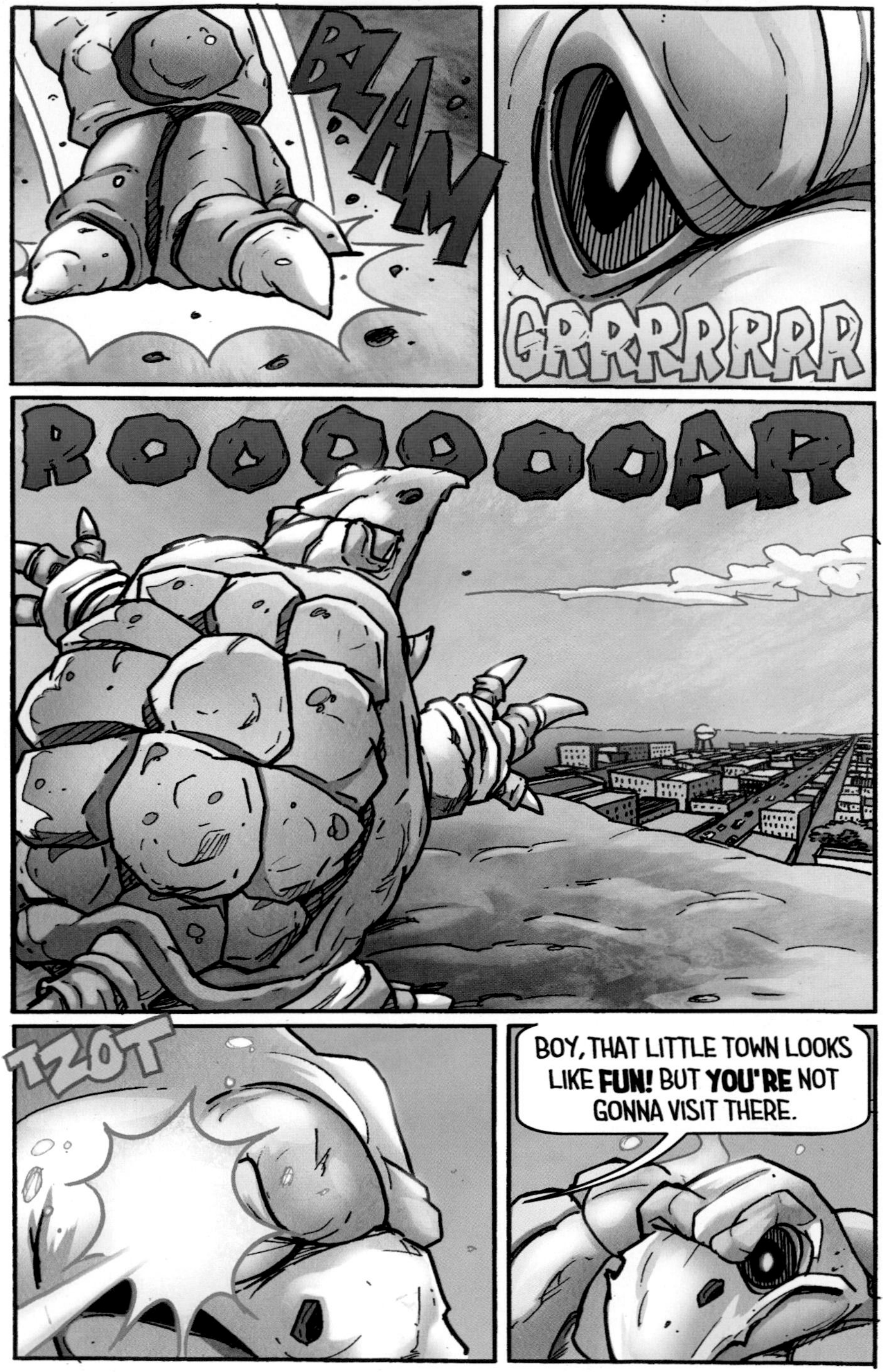
BLAM
GRRRRRRR
ROOOOOOAR
TZOT
BOY, THAT LITTLE TOWN LOOKS LIKE **FUN!** BUT **YOU'RE** NOT GONNA VISIT THERE.

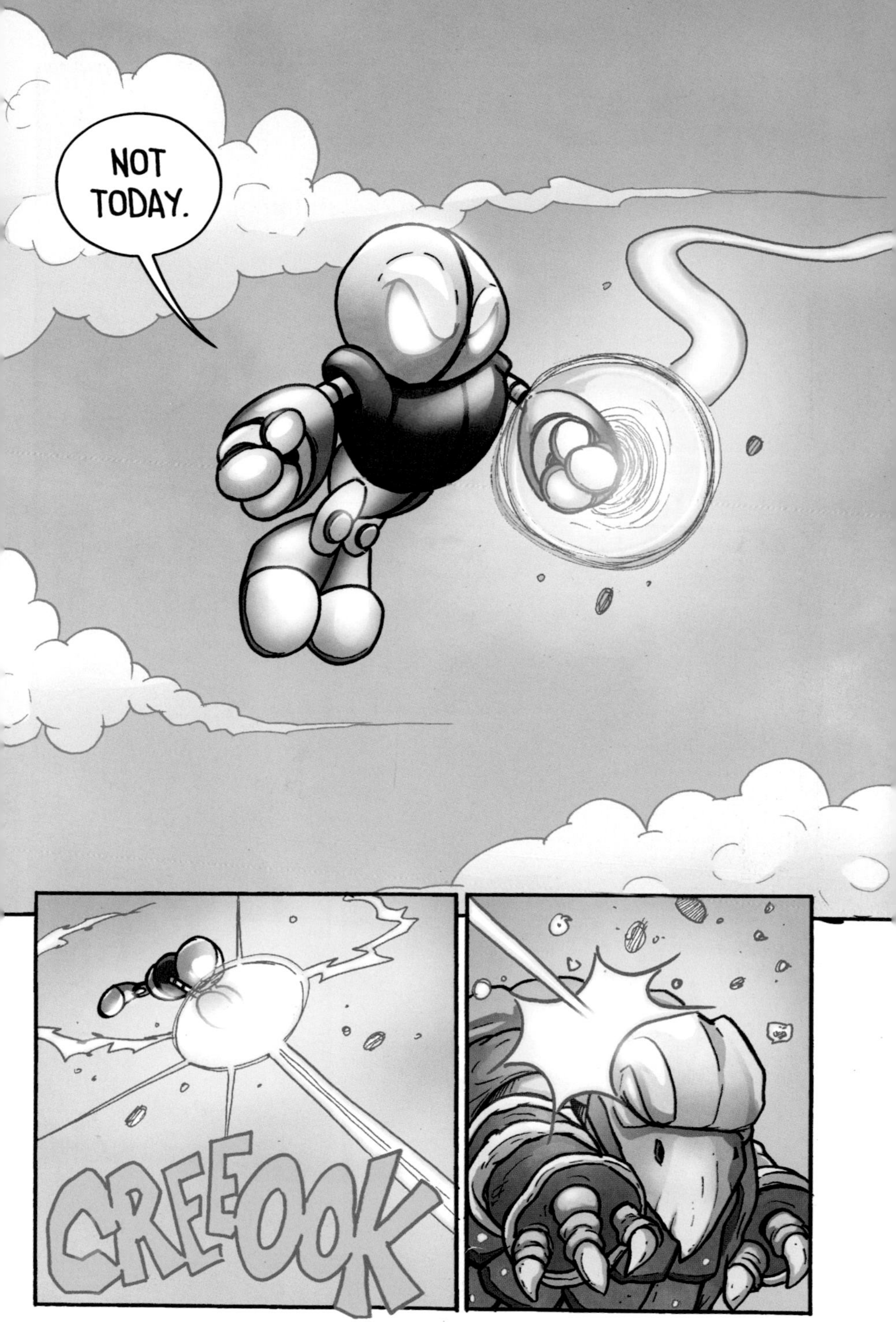
NOT TODAY.
CREEOOK

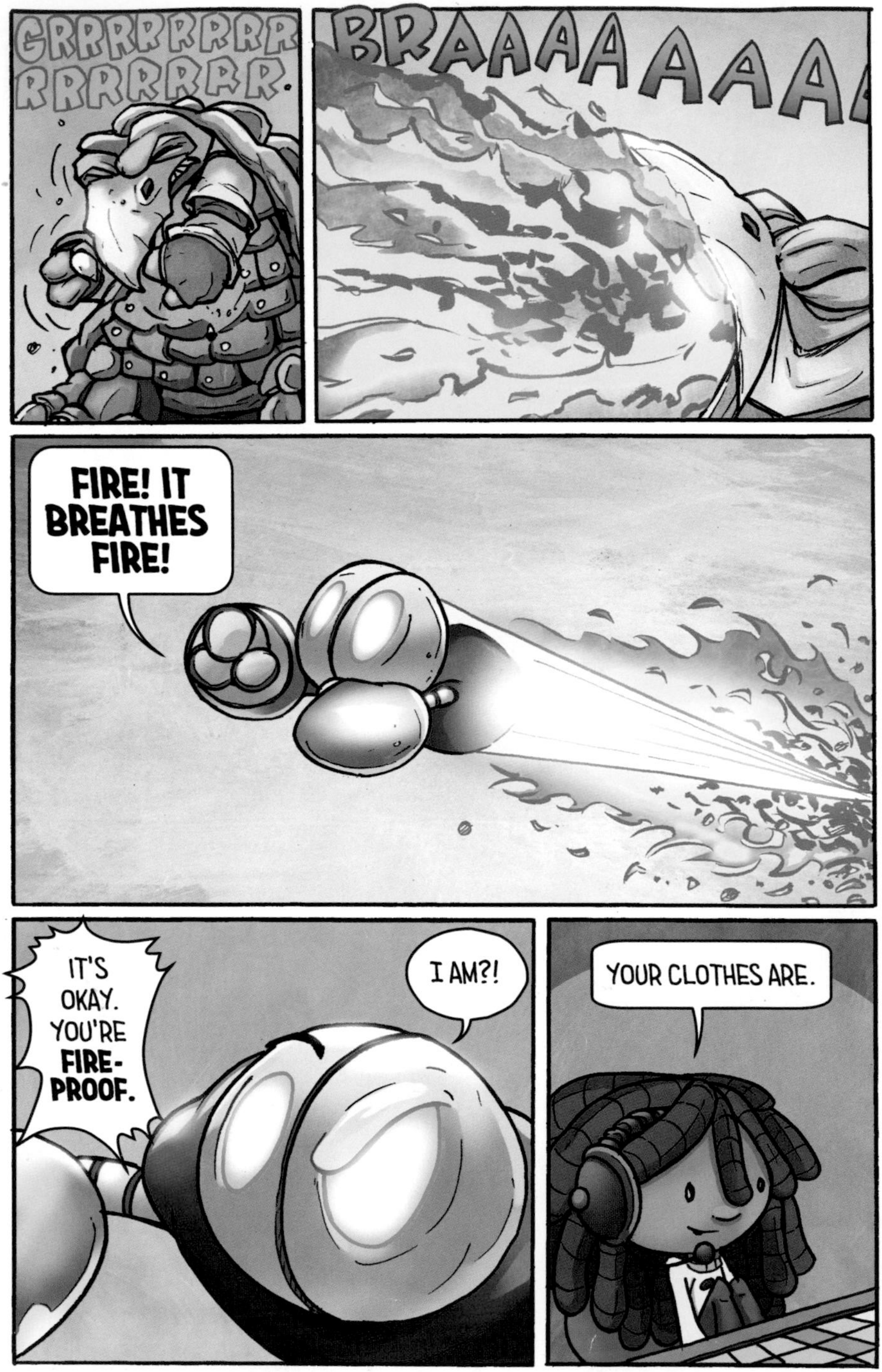
GRRRRRRRR RRRRRRR.
BRAAAAAAAA
FIRE! IT BREATHES FIRE!
IT'S OKAY. YOU'RE FIRE-PROOF.
I AM?!
YOUR CLOTHES ARE.

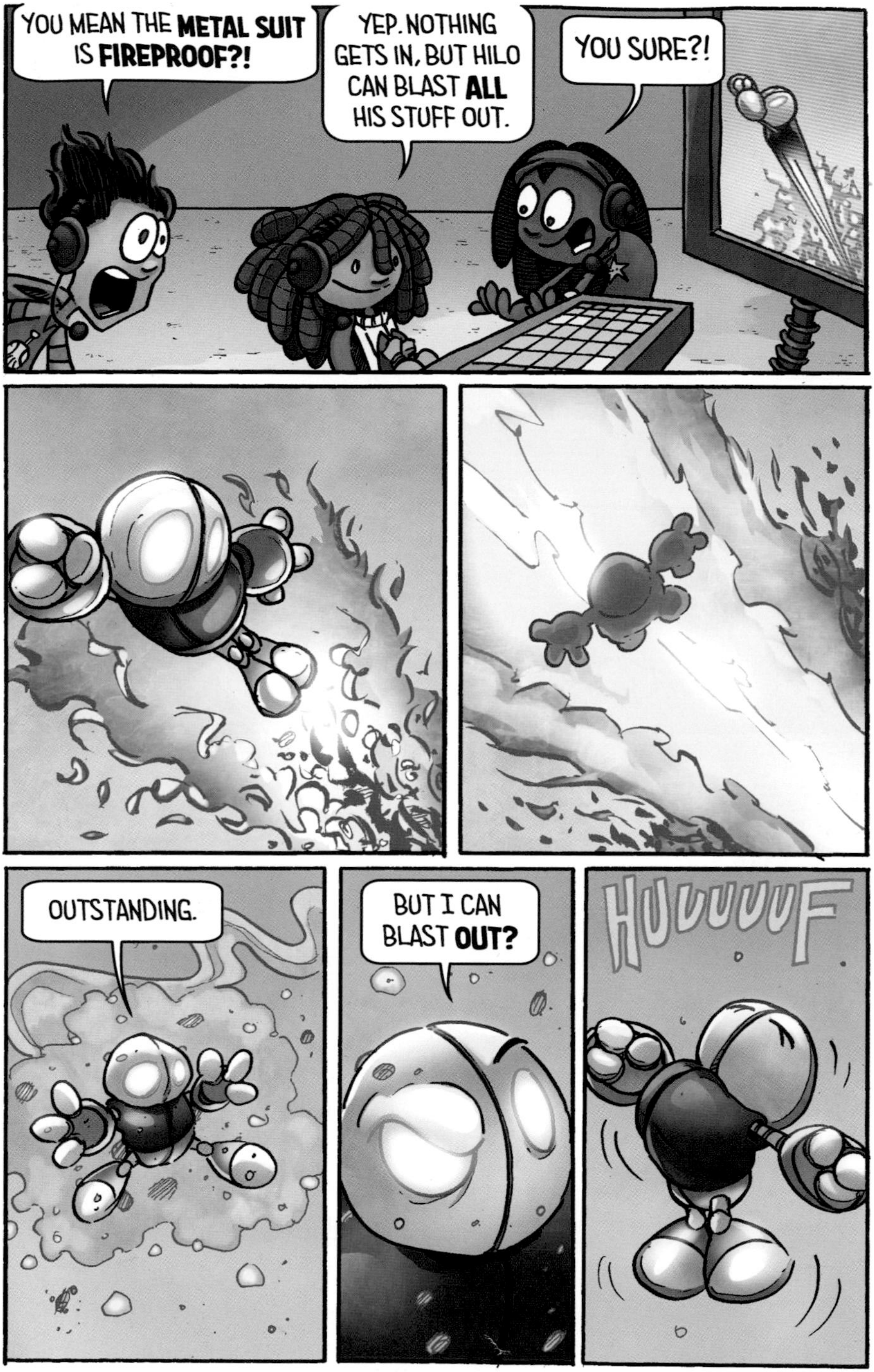
YOU MEAN THE METAL SUIT IS FIREPROOF?!
YEP. NOTHING GETS IN, BUT HILO CAN BLAST ALL HIS STUFF OUT.
YOU SURE?!
OUTSTANDING.
BUT I CAN BLAST OUT?
HUUUUUF

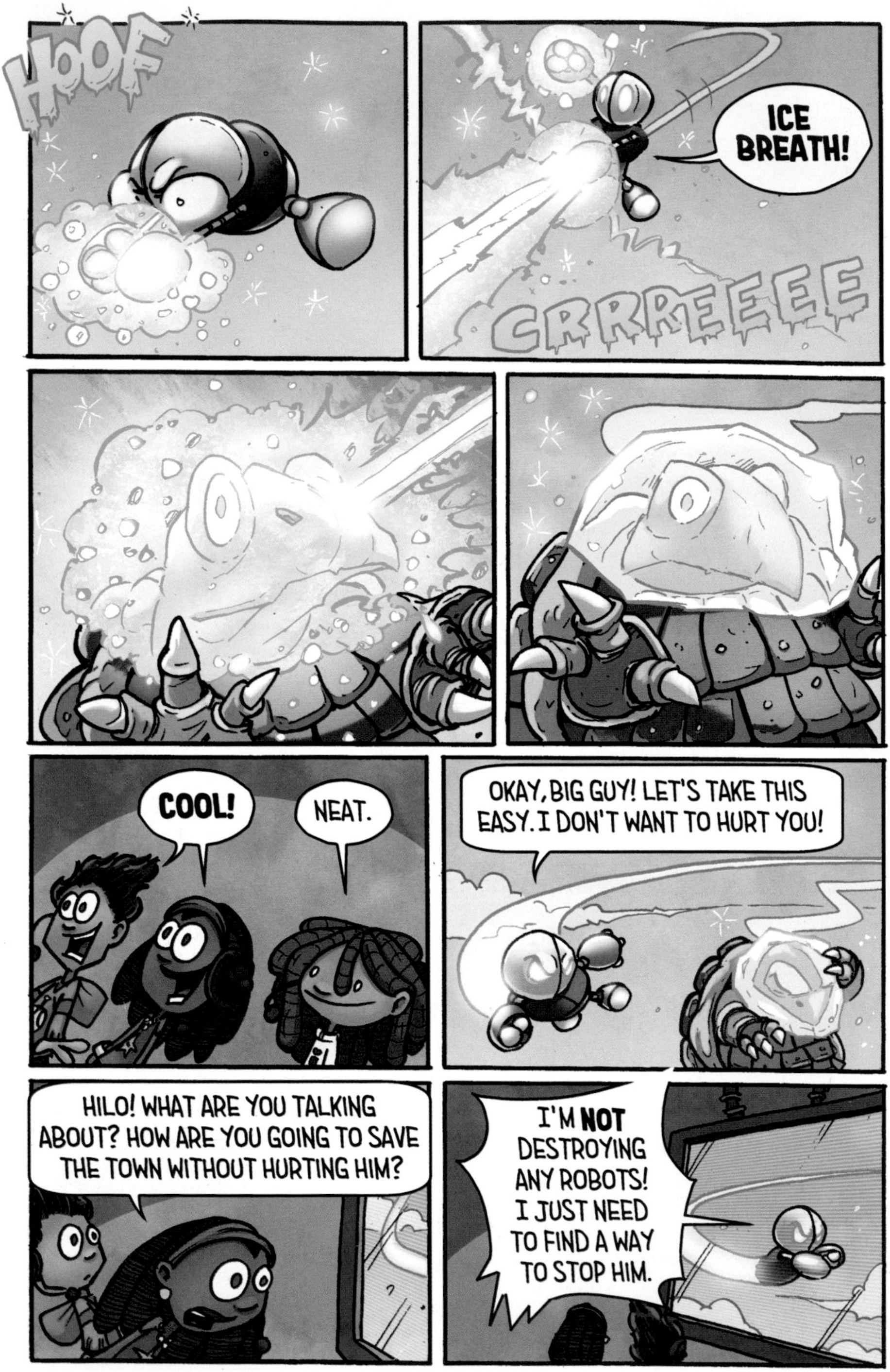
HOOF
ICE BREATH!
CRRREEEE
COOL!
NEAT.
OKAY, BIG GUY! LET'S TAKE THIS EASY. I DON'T WANT TO HURT YOU!
HILO! WHAT ARE YOU TALKING ABOUT? HOW ARE YOU GOING TO SAVE THE TOWN WITHOUT HURTING HIM?
I'M **NOT** DESTROYING ANY ROBOTS! I JUST NEED TO FIND A WAY TO STOP HIM.

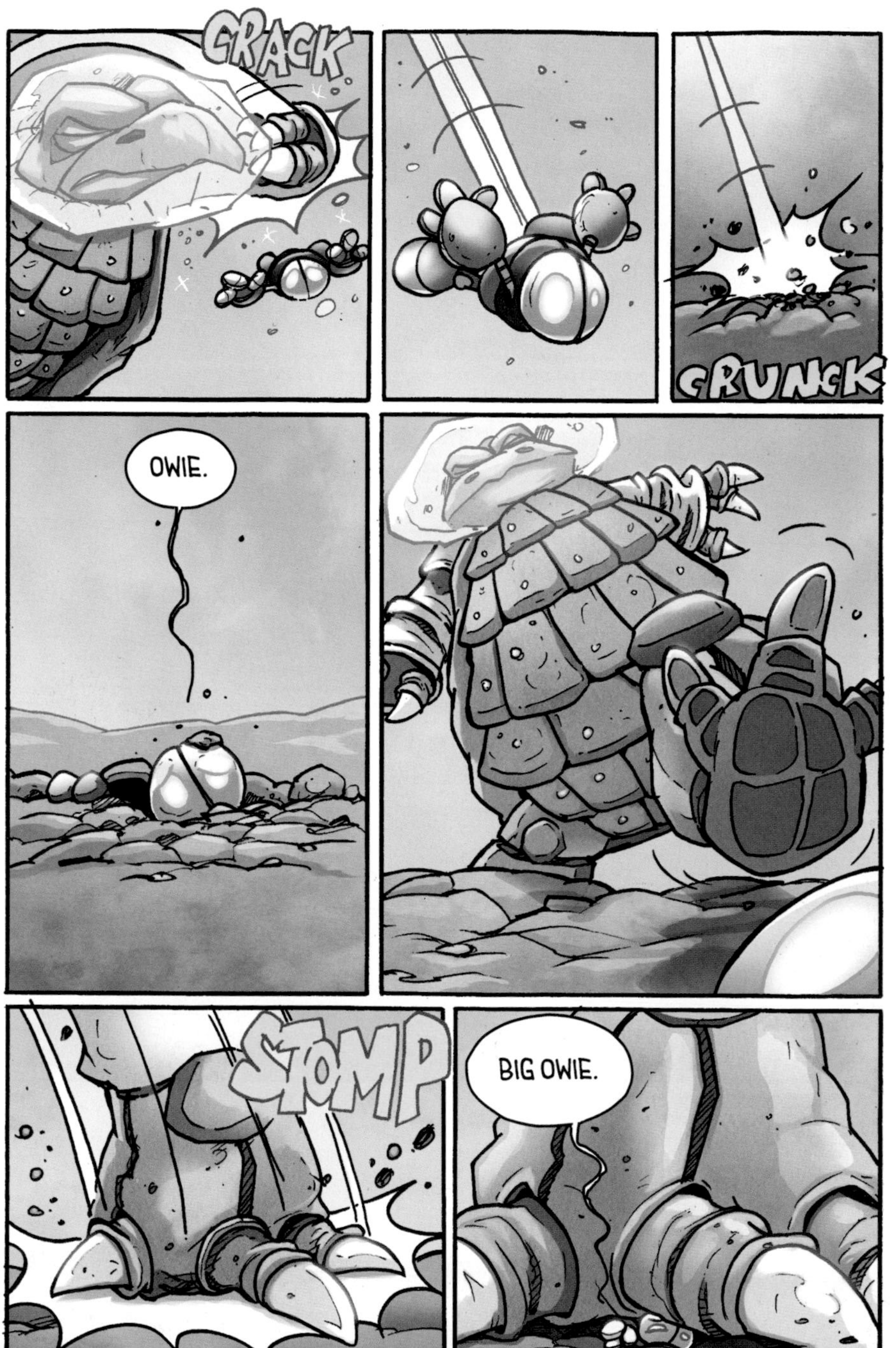
CRACK
CRUNCK
OWIE.
STOMP
BIG OWIE.

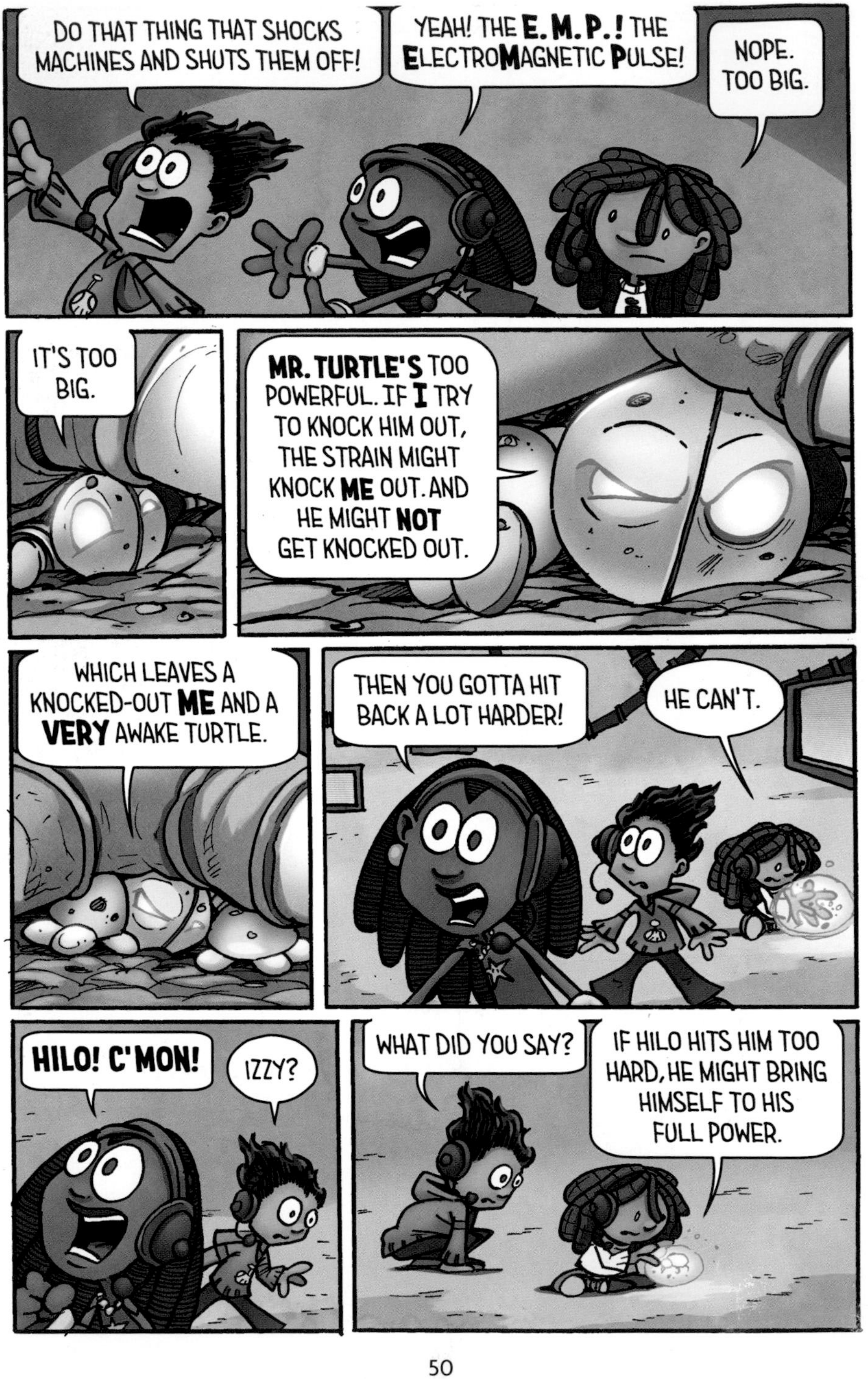

DO THAT THING THAT SHOCKS MACHINES AND SHUTS THEM OFF!
YEAH! THE **E.M.P.!** THE **E**LECTRO**M**AGNETIC **P**ULSE!
NOPE. TOO BIG.
IT'S TOO BIG.
MR. TURTLE'S TOO POWERFUL. IF **I** TRY TO KNOCK HIM OUT, THE STRAIN MIGHT KNOCK **ME** OUT. AND HE MIGHT **NOT** GET KNOCKED OUT.
WHICH LEAVES A KNOCKED-OUT **ME** AND A **VERY** AWAKE TURTLE.
THEN YOU GOTTA HIT BACK A LOT HARDER!
HE CAN'T.
HILO! C'MON!
IZZY?
WHAT DID YOU SAY?
IF HILO HITS HIM TOO HARD, HE MIGHT BRING HIMSELF TO HIS FULL POWER.

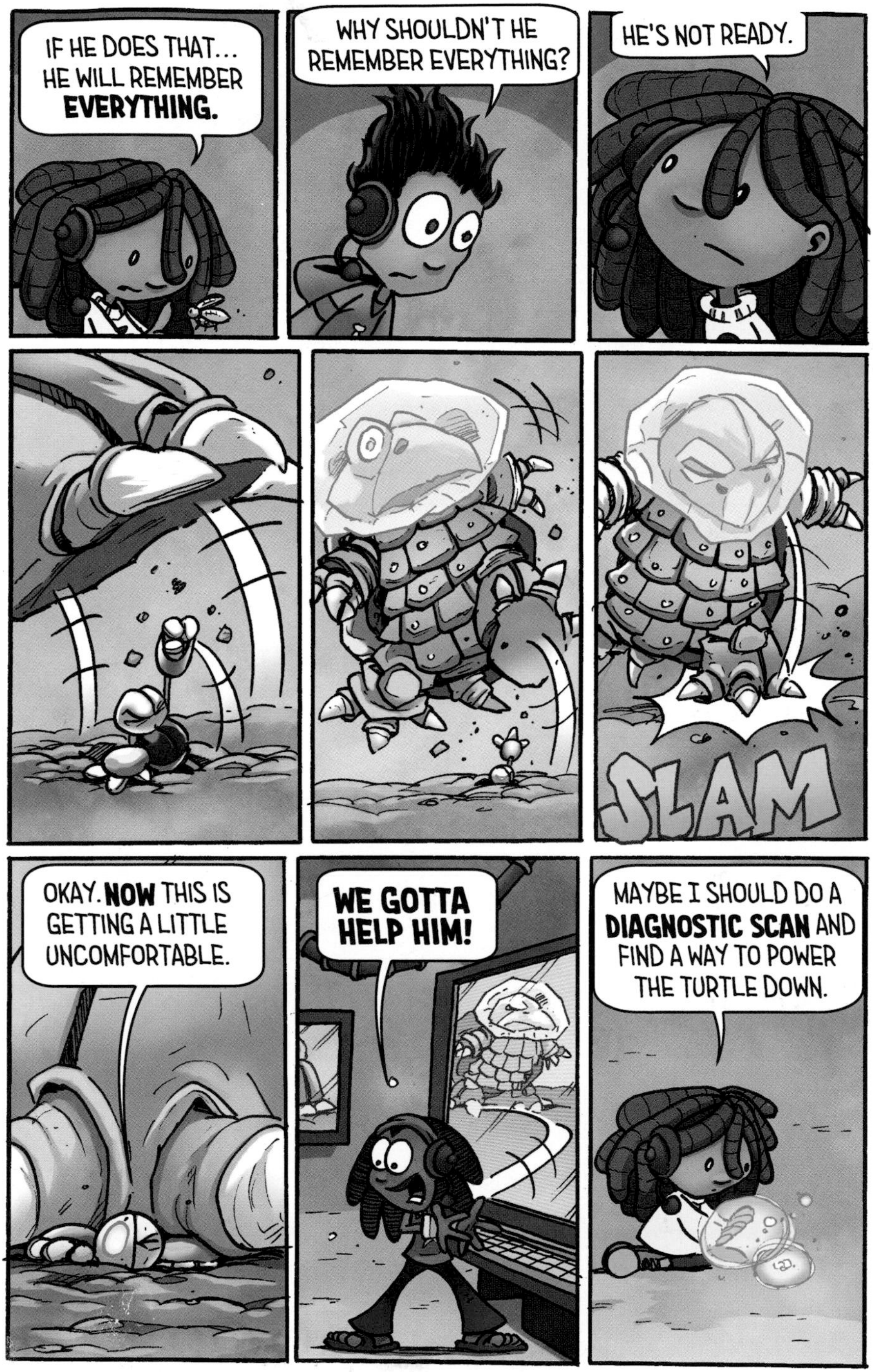
IF HE DOES THAT... HE WILL REMEMBER **EVERYTHING.**
WHY SHOULDN'T HE REMEMBER EVERYTHING?
HE'S NOT READY.
SLAM
OKAY. **NOW** THIS IS GETTING A LITTLE UNCOMFORTABLE.
WE GOTTA HELP HIM!
MAYBE I SHOULD DO A **DIAGNOSTIC SCAN** AND FIND A WAY TO POWER THE TURTLE DOWN.

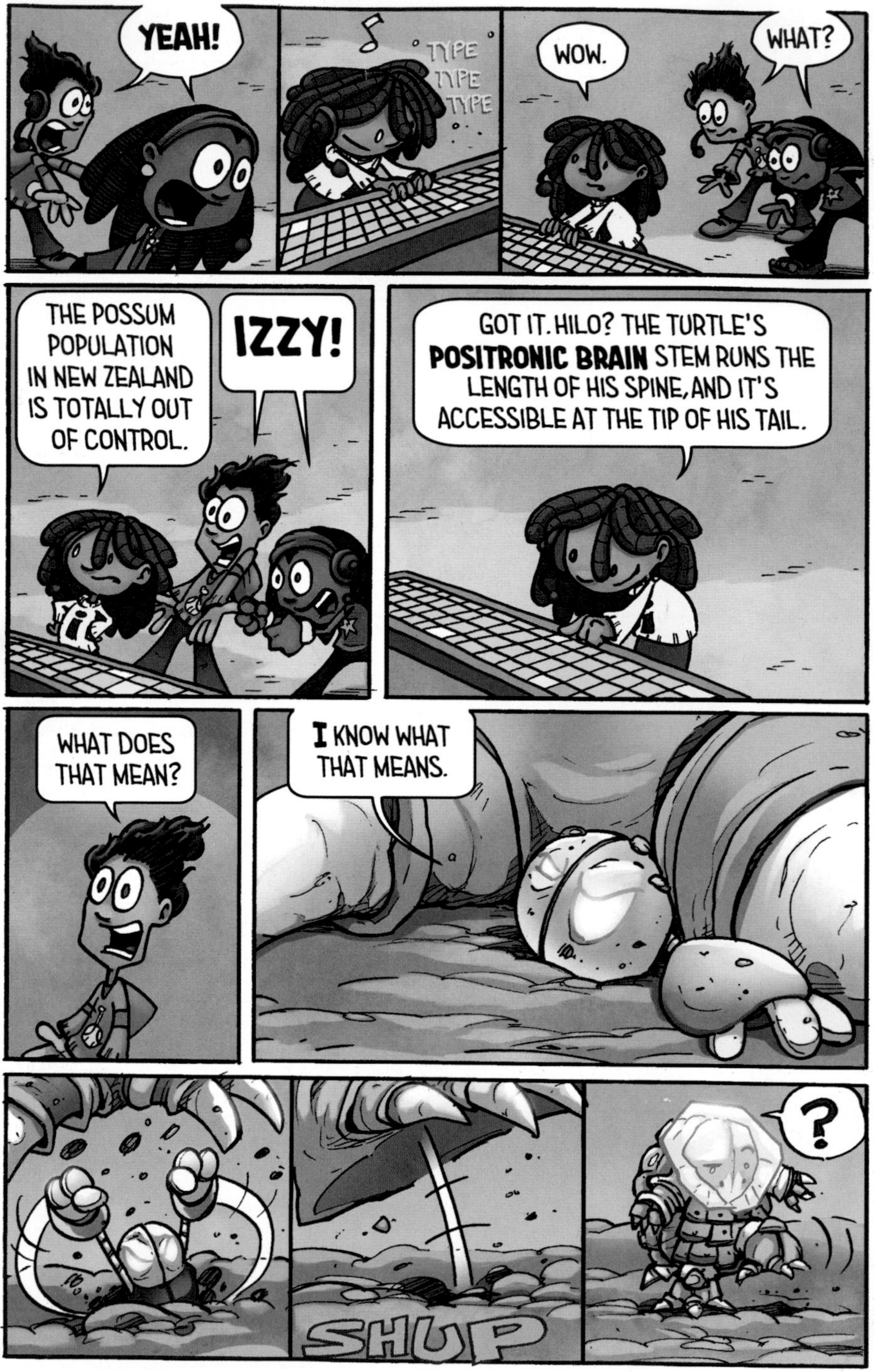
YEAH!
TYPE
TYPE
TYPE
WOW.
WHAT?
THE POSSUM POPULATION IN NEW ZEALAND IS TOTALLY OUT OF CONTROL.
IZZY!
GOT IT. HILO? THE TURTLE'S POSITRONIC BRAIN STEM RUNS THE LENGTH OF HIS SPINE, AND IT'S ACCESSIBLE AT THE TIP OF HIS TAIL.
WHAT DOES THAT MEAN?
I KNOW WHAT THAT MEANS.
SHUP
?

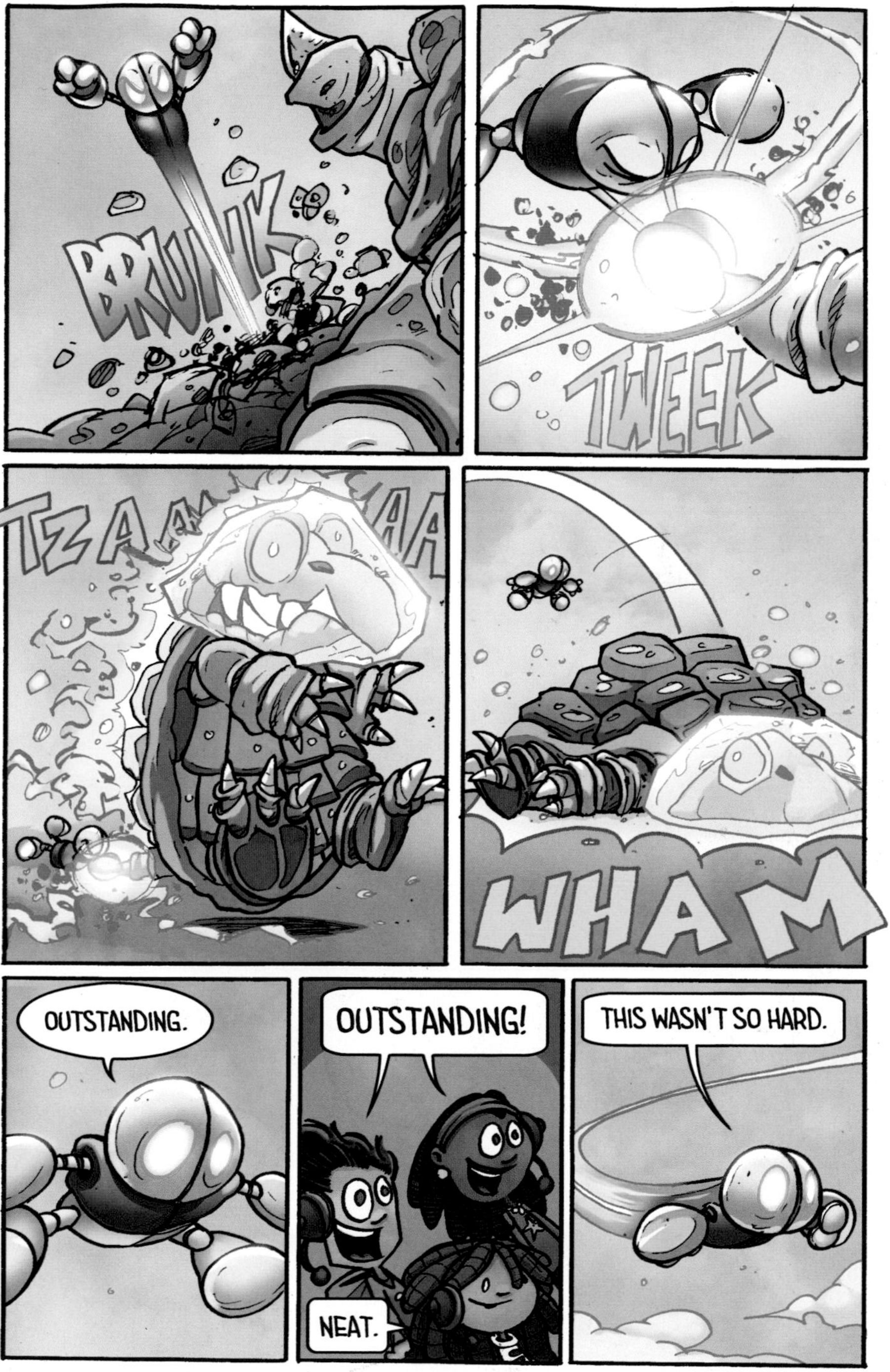
BRUNK
TWEEK
TZAAAAA
WHAM
OUTSTANDING.
OUTSTANDING!
NEAT.
THIS WASN'T SO HARD.

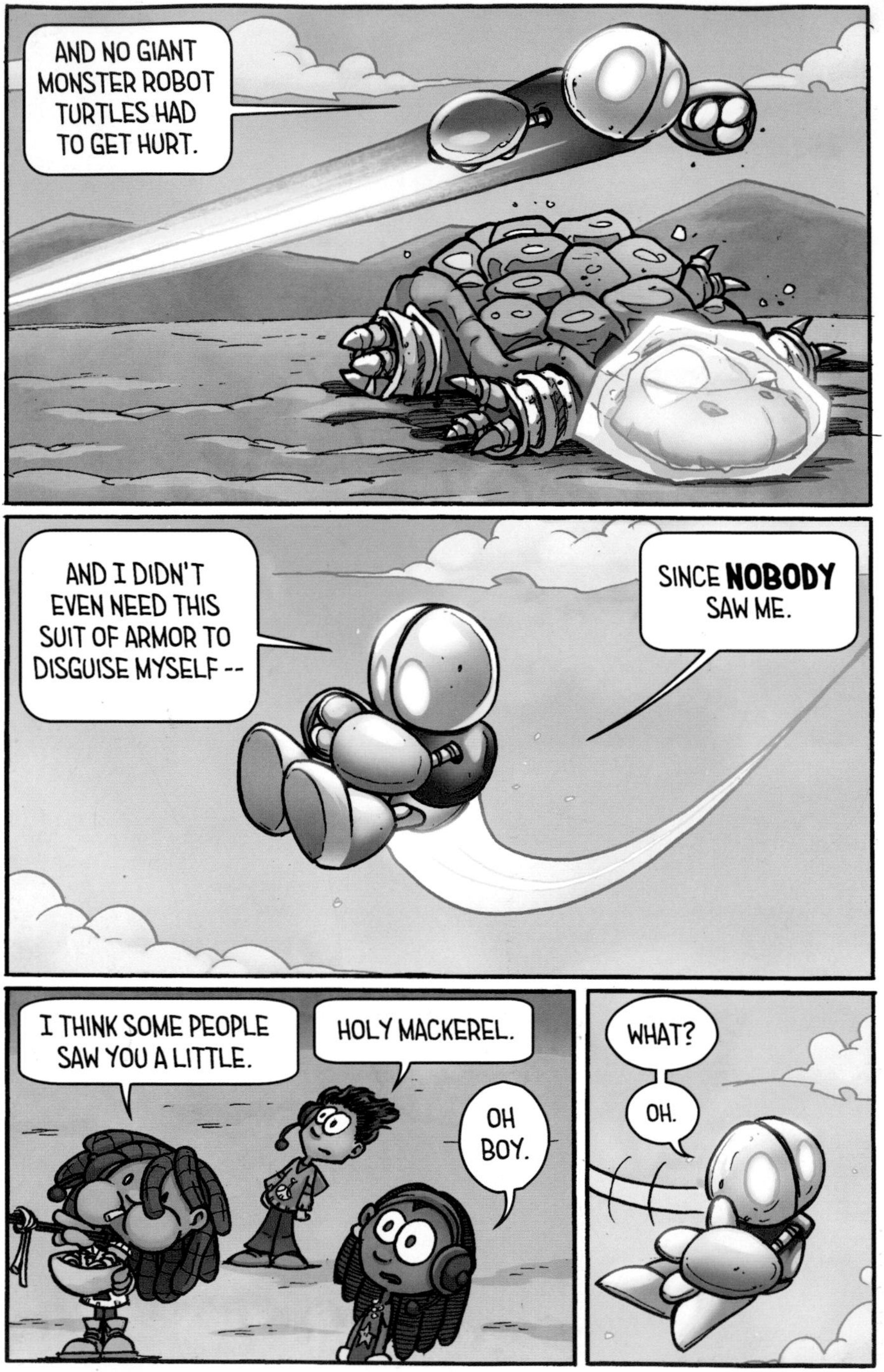
AND NO GIANT MONSTER ROBOT TURTLES HAD TO GET HURT.
AND I DIDN'T EVEN NEED THIS SUIT OF ARMOR TO DISGUISE MYSELF --
SINCE **NOBODY** SAW ME.
I THINK SOME PEOPLE SAW YOU A LITTLE.
HOLY MACKEREL.
OH BOY.
WHAT?
OH.

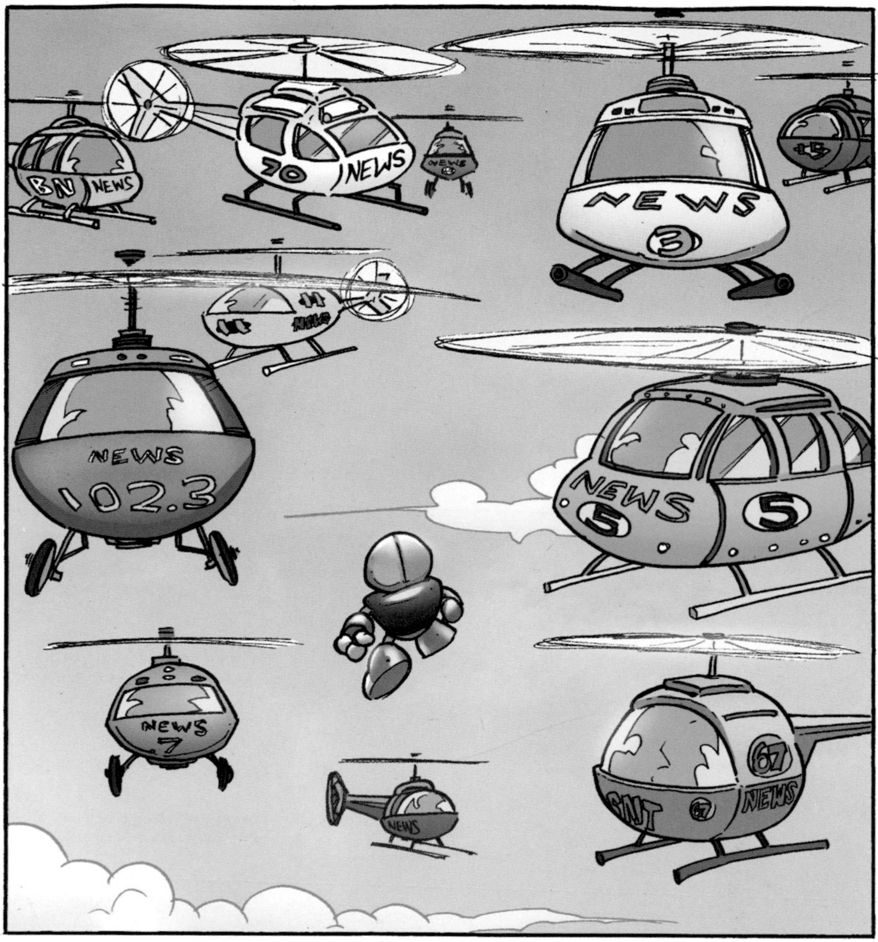
BN NEWS
70 NEWS
NEWS 3
NEWS 102.3
NEWS 5 5
NEWS 7
NEWS
GNJ 67 67 NEWS

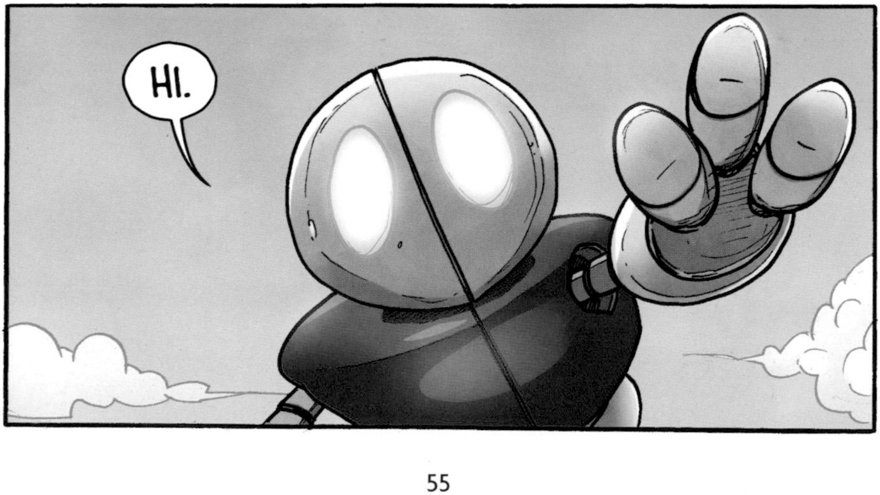
HI.

CHAPTER 4

NEWS

INCREDIBLE!
ASTONISHING!
UNBELIEVABLE!

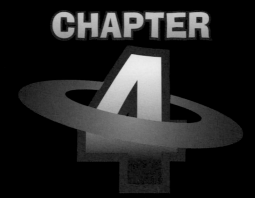

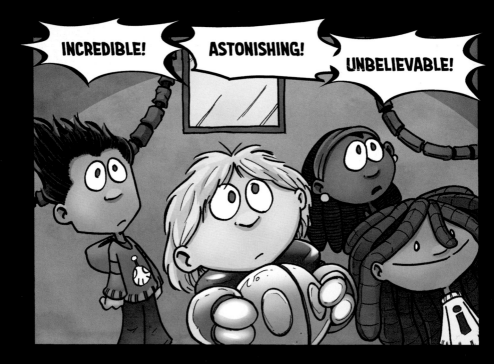

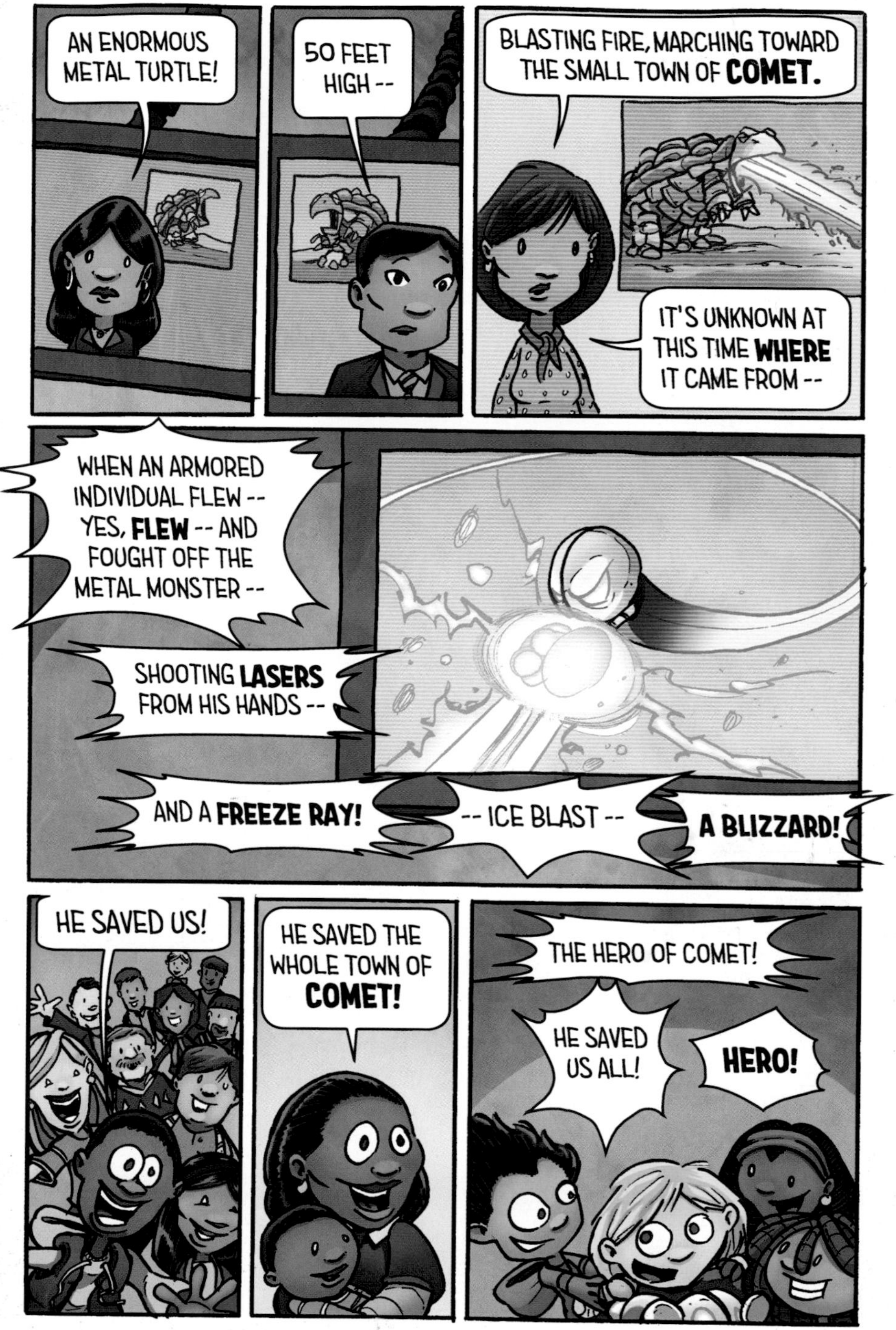
AN ENORMOUS METAL TURTLE!
50 FEET HIGH --
BLASTING FIRE, MARCHING TOWARD THE SMALL TOWN OF COMET.
IT'S UNKNOWN AT THIS TIME WHERE IT CAME FROM --
WHEN AN ARMORED INDIVIDUAL FLEW -- YES, FLEW -- AND FOUGHT OFF THE METAL MONSTER --
SHOOTING LASERS FROM HIS HANDS --
AND A FREEZE RAY!
-- ICE BLAST --
A BLIZZARD!
HE SAVED US!
HE SAVED THE WHOLE TOWN OF COMET!
THE HERO OF COMET!
HE SAVED US ALL!
HERO!

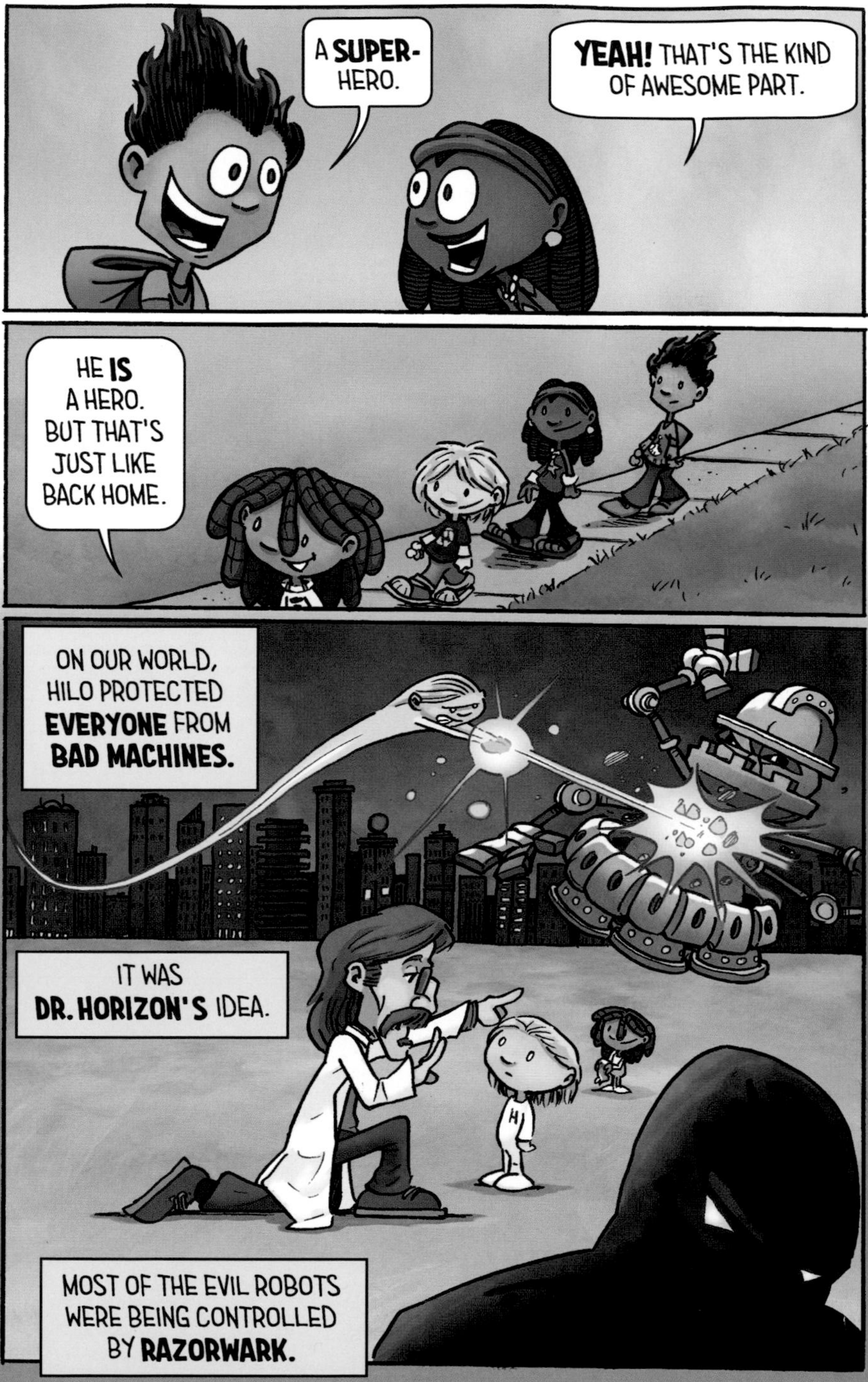
A SUPER-HERO.
YEAH! THAT'S THE KIND OF AWESOME PART.
HE IS A HERO. BUT THAT'S JUST LIKE BACK HOME.
ON OUR WORLD, HILO PROTECTED EVERYONE FROM BAD MACHINES.
IT WAS DR. HORIZON'S IDEA.
MOST OF THE EVIL ROBOTS WERE BEING CONTROLLED BY RAZORWARK.

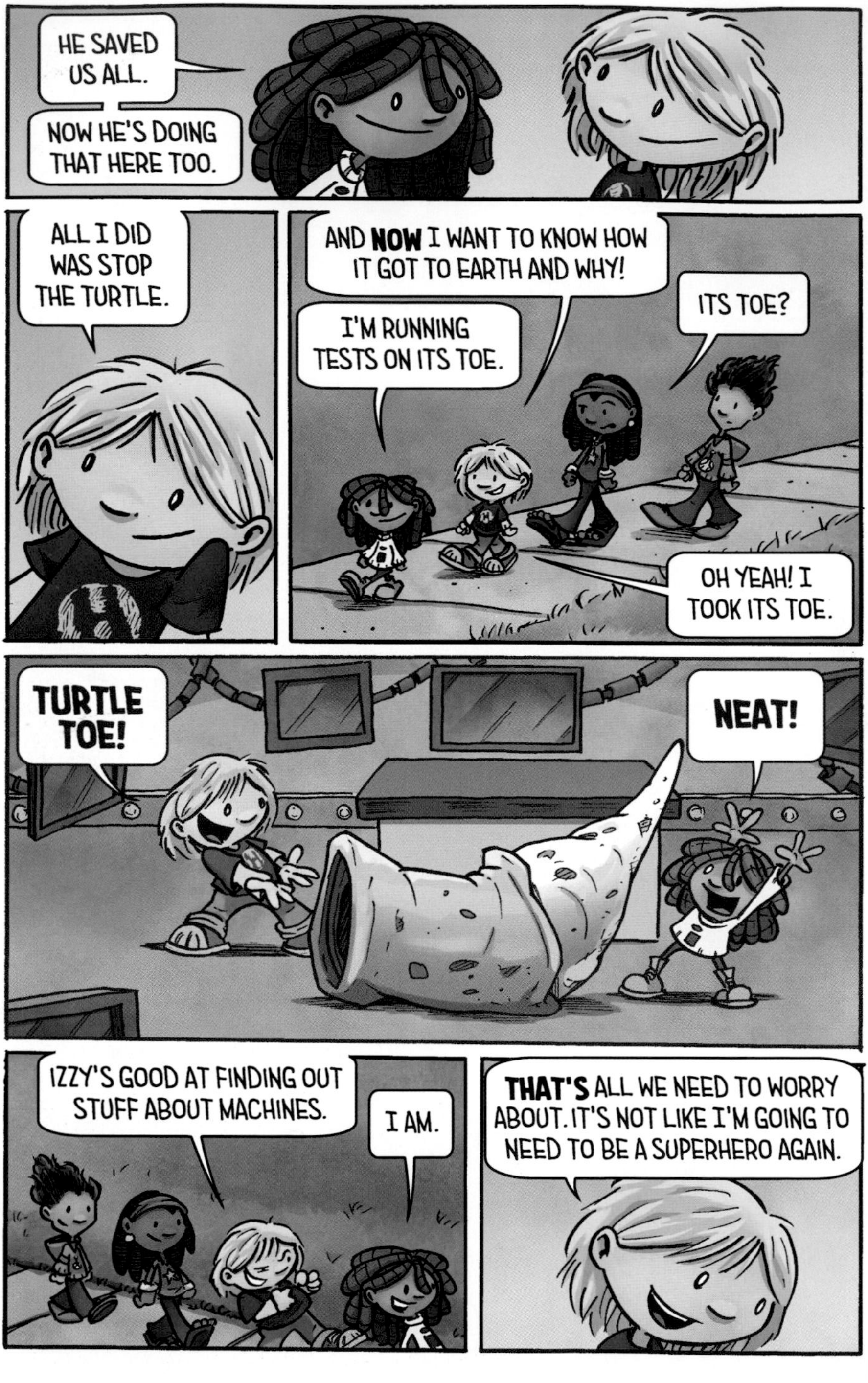
HE SAVED US ALL.
NOW HE'S DOING THAT HERE TOO.
ALL I DID WAS STOP THE TURTLE.
AND **NOW** I WANT TO KNOW HOW IT GOT TO EARTH AND WHY!
I'M RUNNING TESTS ON ITS TOE.
ITS TOE?
OH YEAH! I TOOK ITS TOE.
TURTLE TOE!
NEAT!
IZZY'S GOOD AT FINDING OUT STUFF ABOUT MACHINES.
I AM.
THAT'S ALL WE NEED TO WORRY ABOUT. IT'S NOT LIKE I'M GOING TO NEED TO BE A SUPERHERO AGAIN.

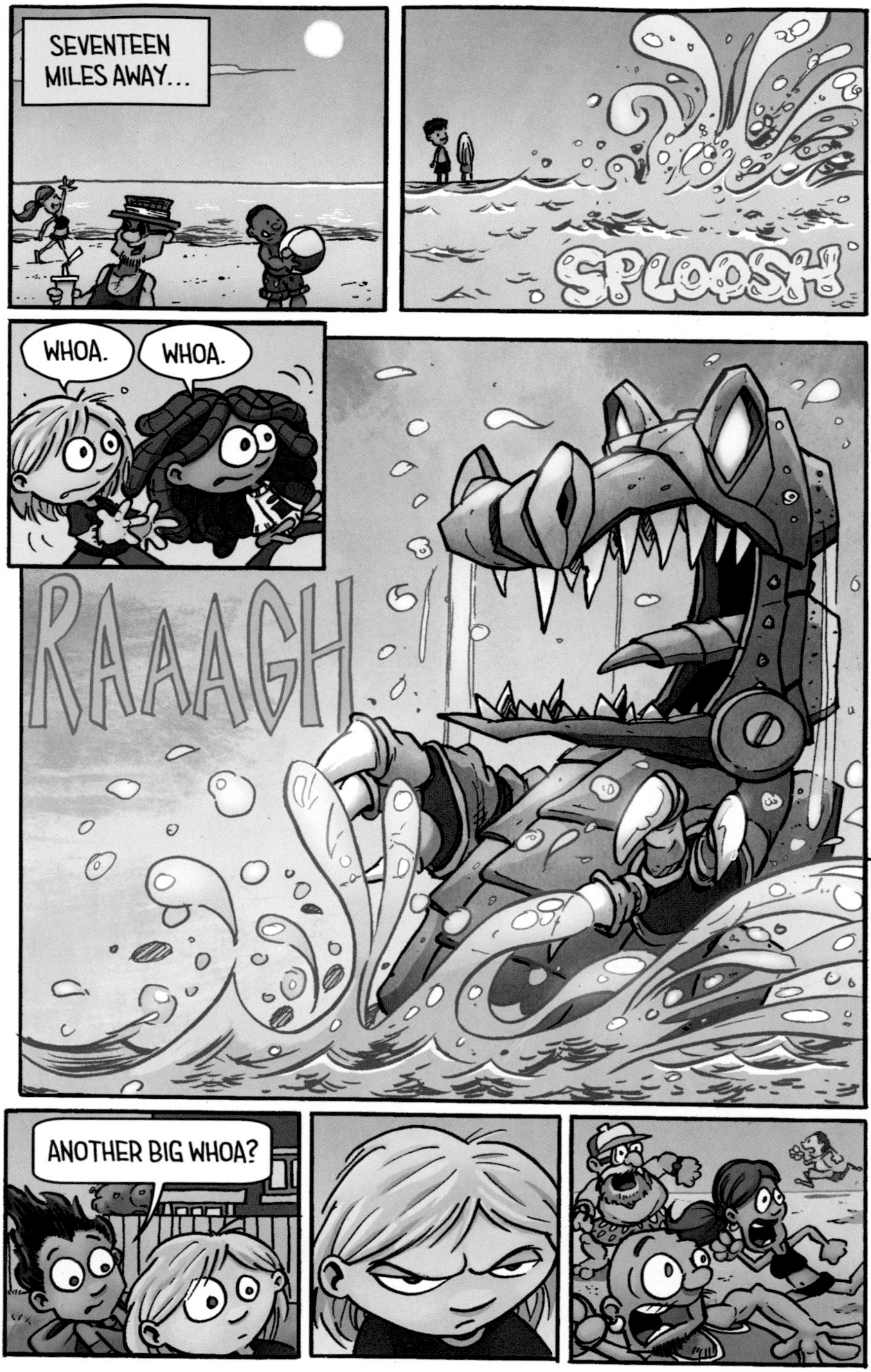
SEVENTEEN MILES AWAY...
SPLOOSH
WHOA.
WHOA.
RAAAGH
ANOTHER BIG WHOA?

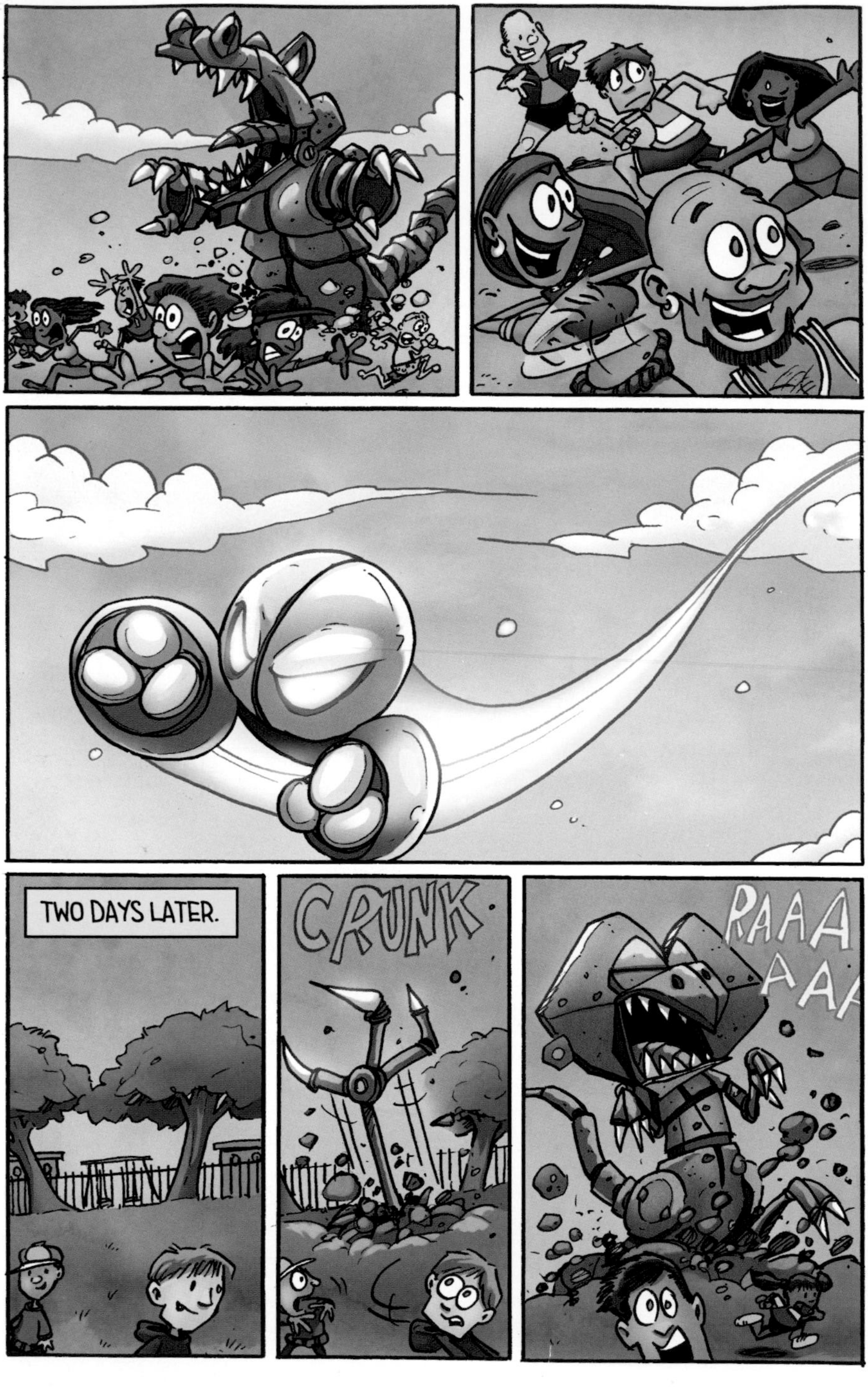

TWO DAYS LATER.
CRUNK
RAAA AAA

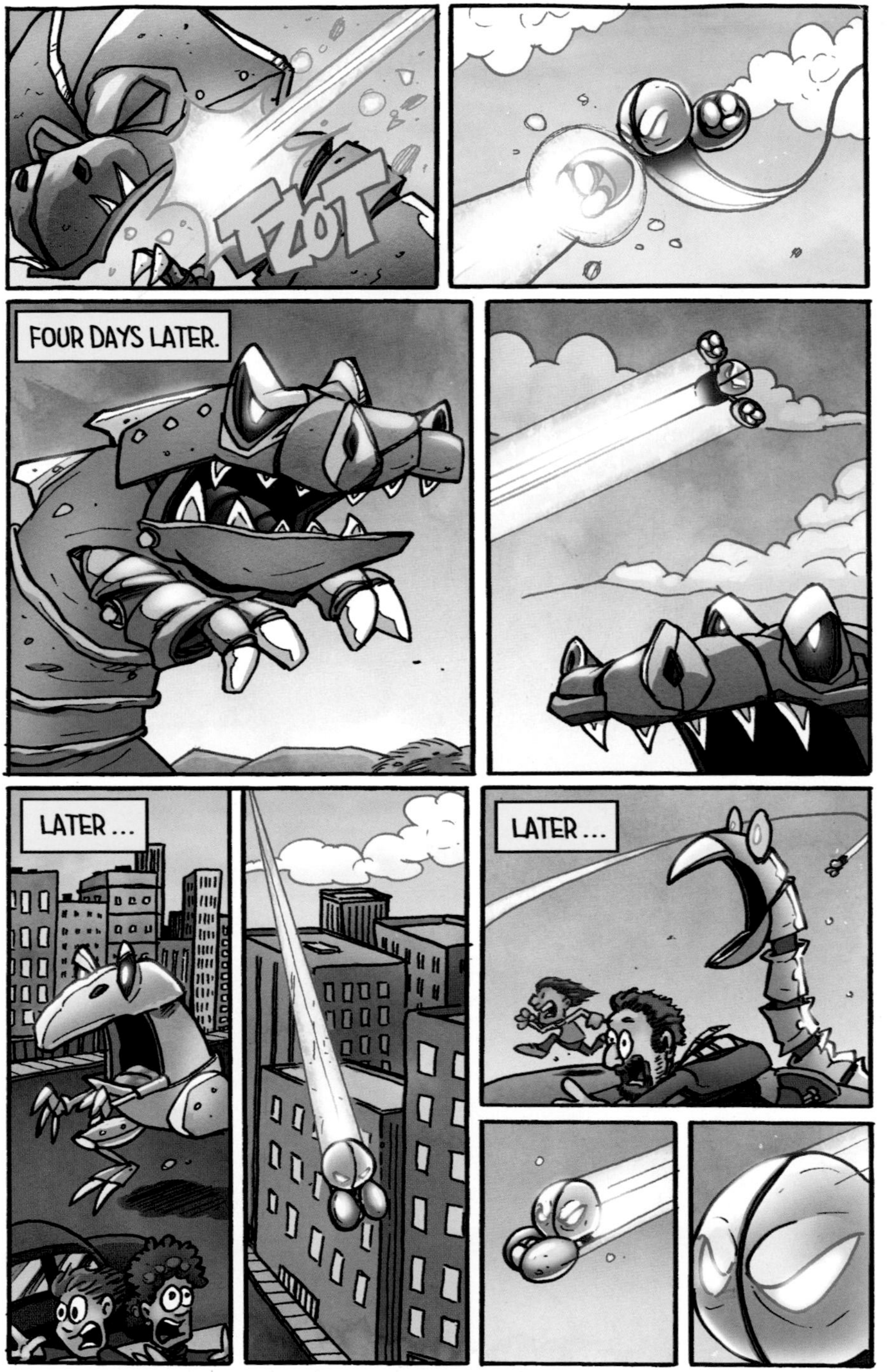
TZOT
FOUR DAYS LATER.
LATER ...
LATER ...

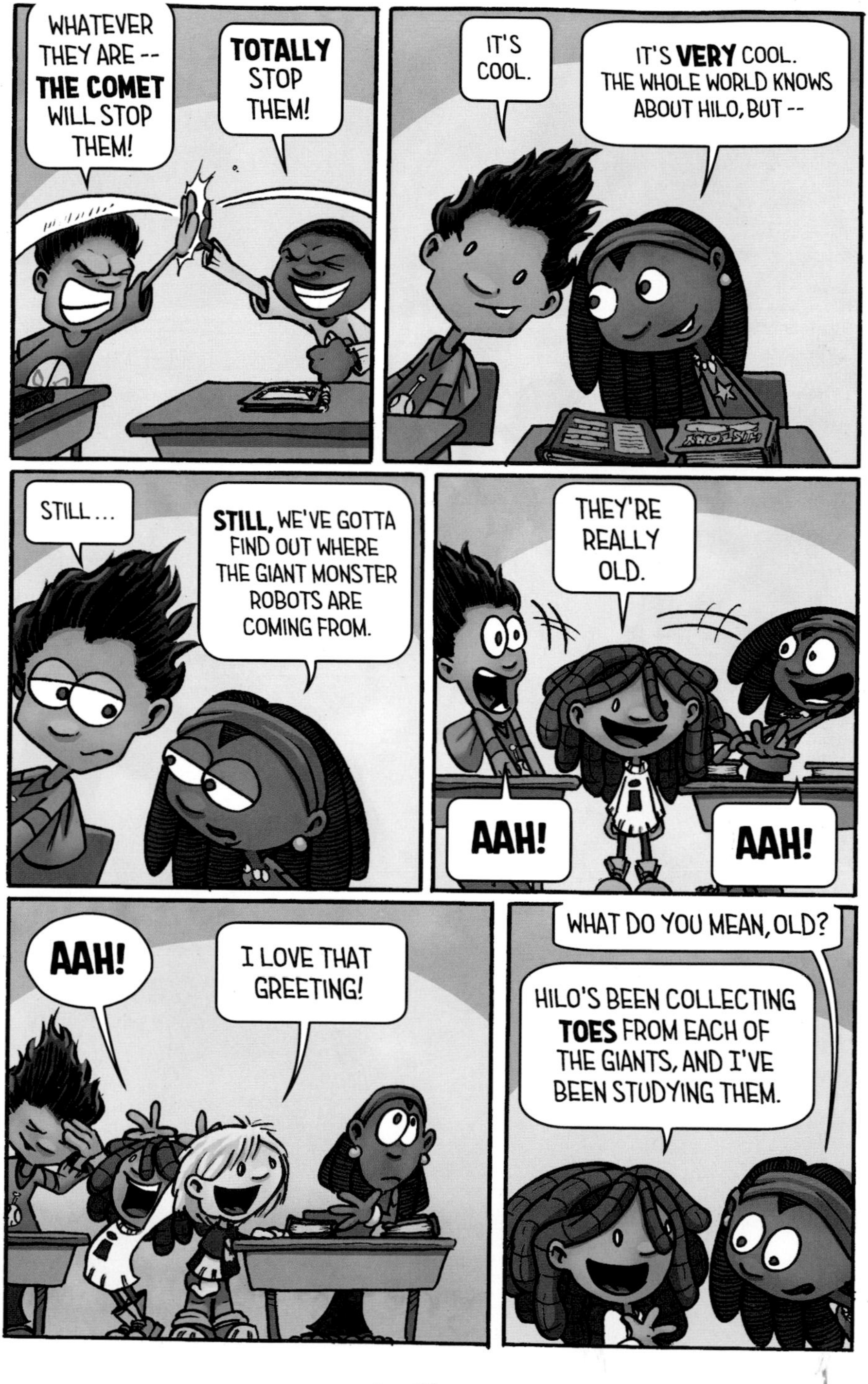
WHATEVER THEY ARE -- THE COMET WILL STOP THEM!
TOTALLY STOP THEM!
IT'S COOL.
IT'S VERY COOL. THE WHOLE WORLD KNOWS ABOUT HILO, BUT --
STILL...
STILL, WE'VE GOTTA FIND OUT WHERE THE GIANT MONSTER ROBOTS ARE COMING FROM.
THEY'RE REALLY OLD.
AAH!
AAH!
AAH!
I LOVE THAT GREETING!
WHAT DO YOU MEAN, OLD?
HILO'S BEEN COLLECTING TOES FROM EACH OF THE GIANTS, AND I'VE BEEN STUDYING THEM.

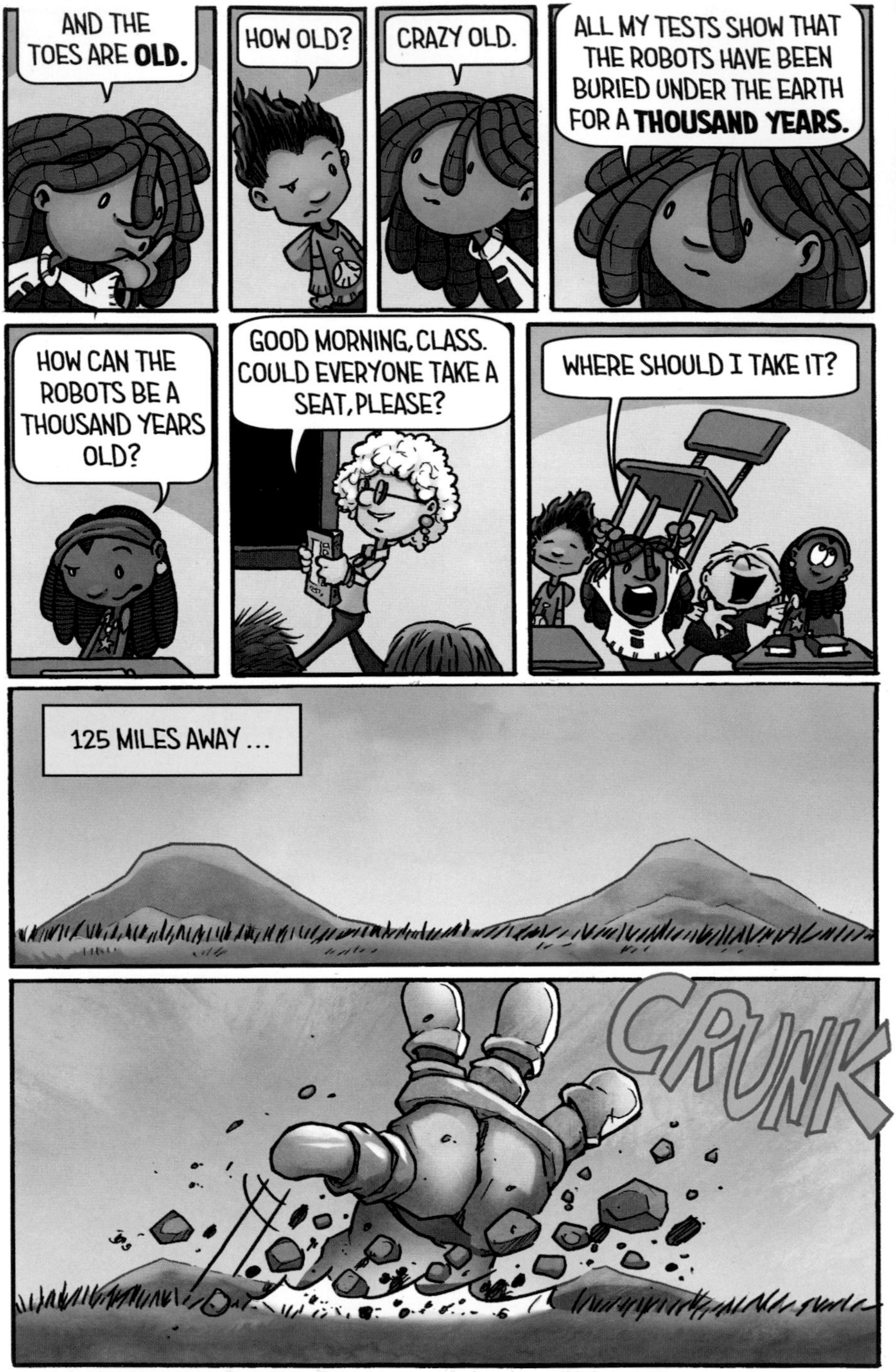
AND THE TOES ARE **OLD.**
HOW OLD?
CRAZY OLD.
ALL MY TESTS SHOW THAT THE ROBOTS HAVE BEEN BURIED UNDER THE EARTH FOR A **THOUSAND YEARS.**
HOW CAN THE ROBOTS BE A THOUSAND YEARS OLD?
GOOD MORNING, CLASS. COULD EVERYONE TAKE A SEAT, PLEASE?
WHERE SHOULD I TAKE IT?
125 MILES AWAY ...
CRUNK

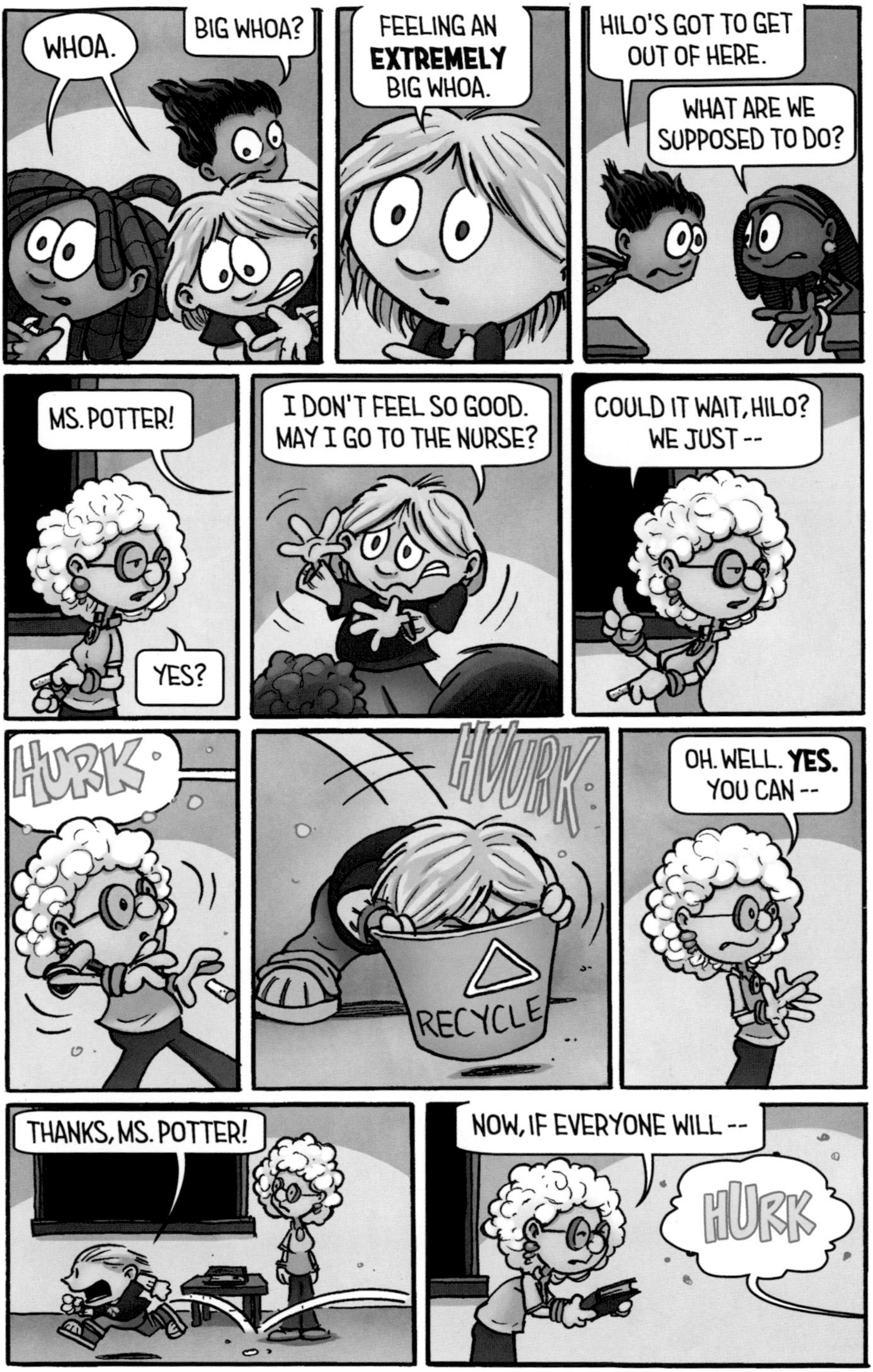
WHOA.
BIG WHOA?
FEELING AN **EXTREMELY** BIG WHOA.
HILO'S GOT TO GET OUT OF HERE.
WHAT ARE WE SUPPOSED TO DO?
MS. POTTER!
YES?
I DON'T FEEL SO GOOD. MAY I GO TO THE NURSE?
COULD IT WAIT, HILO? WE JUST --
HURK
HUURK
RECYCLE
OH. WELL. **YES.** YOU CAN --
THANKS, MS. POTTER!
NOW, IF EVERYONE WILL --
HURK

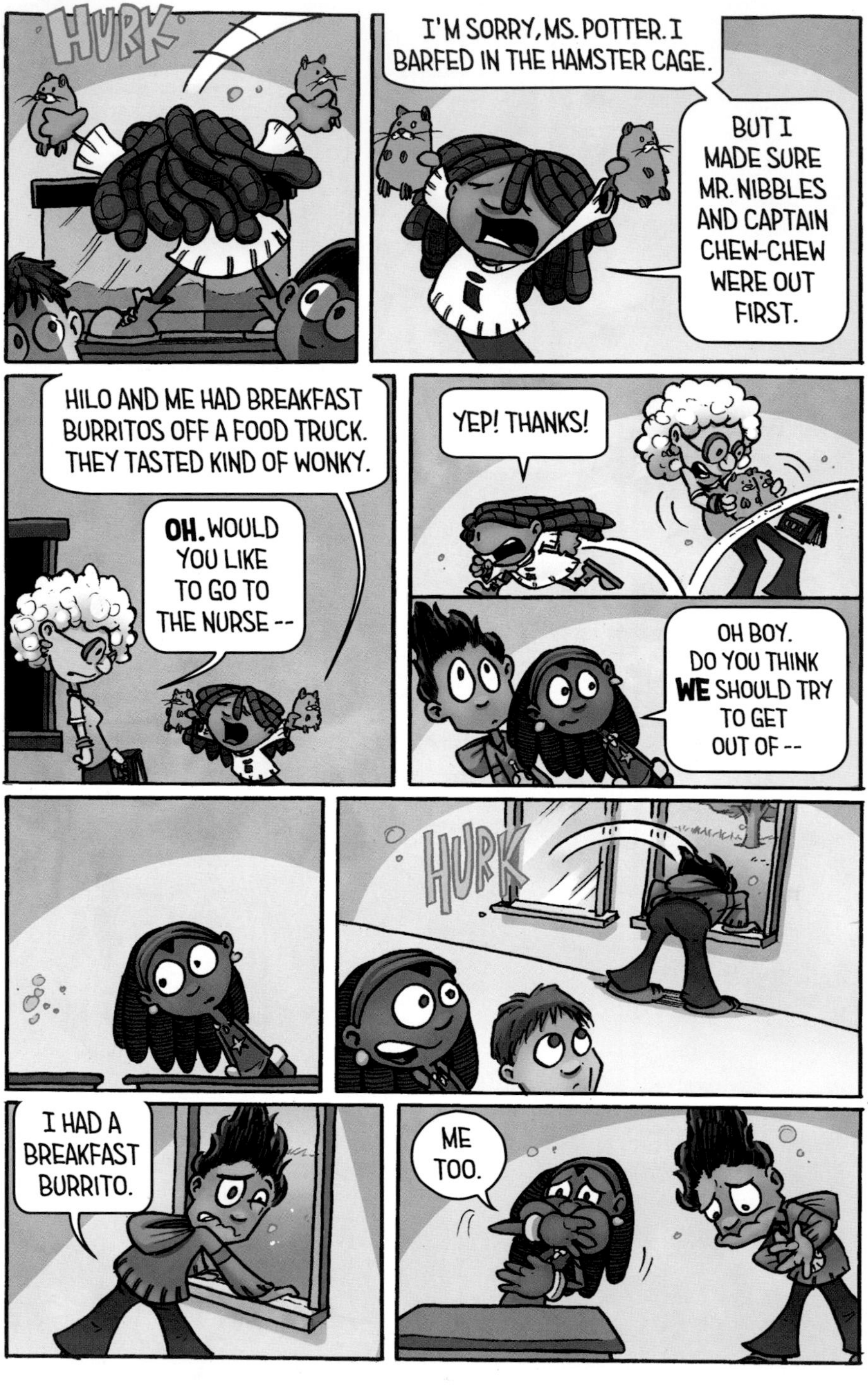
HURK
I'M SORRY, MS. POTTER. I BARFED IN THE HAMSTER CAGE.
BUT I MADE SURE MR. NIBBLES AND CAPTAIN CHEW-CHEW WERE OUT FIRST.
HILO AND ME HAD BREAKFAST BURRITOS OFF A FOOD TRUCK. THEY TASTED KIND OF WONKY.
OH. WOULD YOU LIKE TO GO TO THE NURSE --
YEP! THANKS!
OH BOY. DO YOU THINK WE SHOULD TRY TO GET OUT OF --
HURK
I HAD A BREAKFAST BURRITO.
ME TOO.

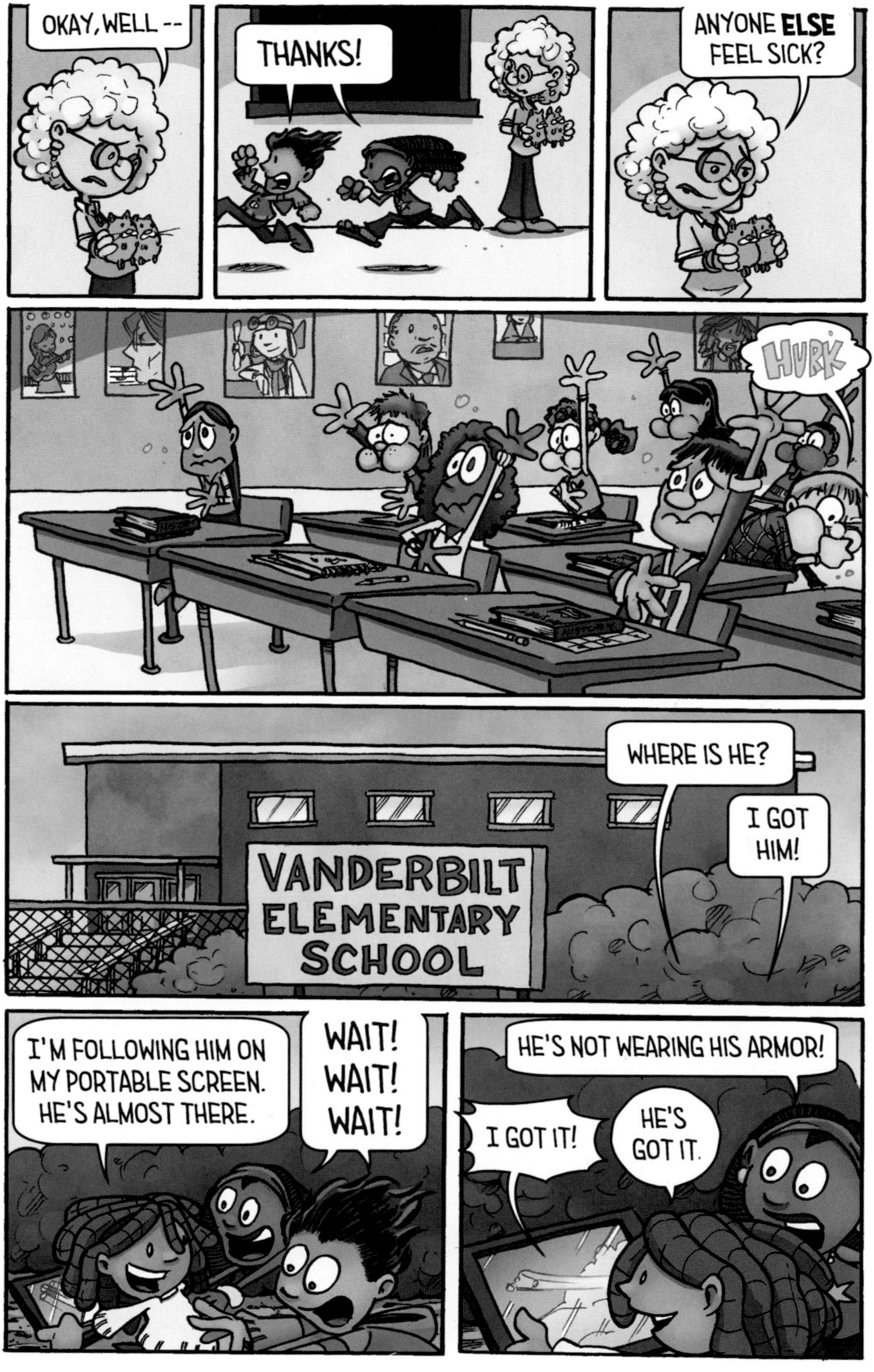

OKAY, WELL --
THANKS!
ANYONE ELSE FEEL SICK?
HURK
VANDERBILT ELEMENTARY SCHOOL
WHERE IS HE?
I GOT HIM!
I'M FOLLOWING HIM ON MY PORTABLE SCREEN. HE'S ALMOST THERE.
WAIT! WAIT! WAIT!
HE'S NOT WEARING HIS ARMOR!
I GOT IT!
HE'S GOT IT.

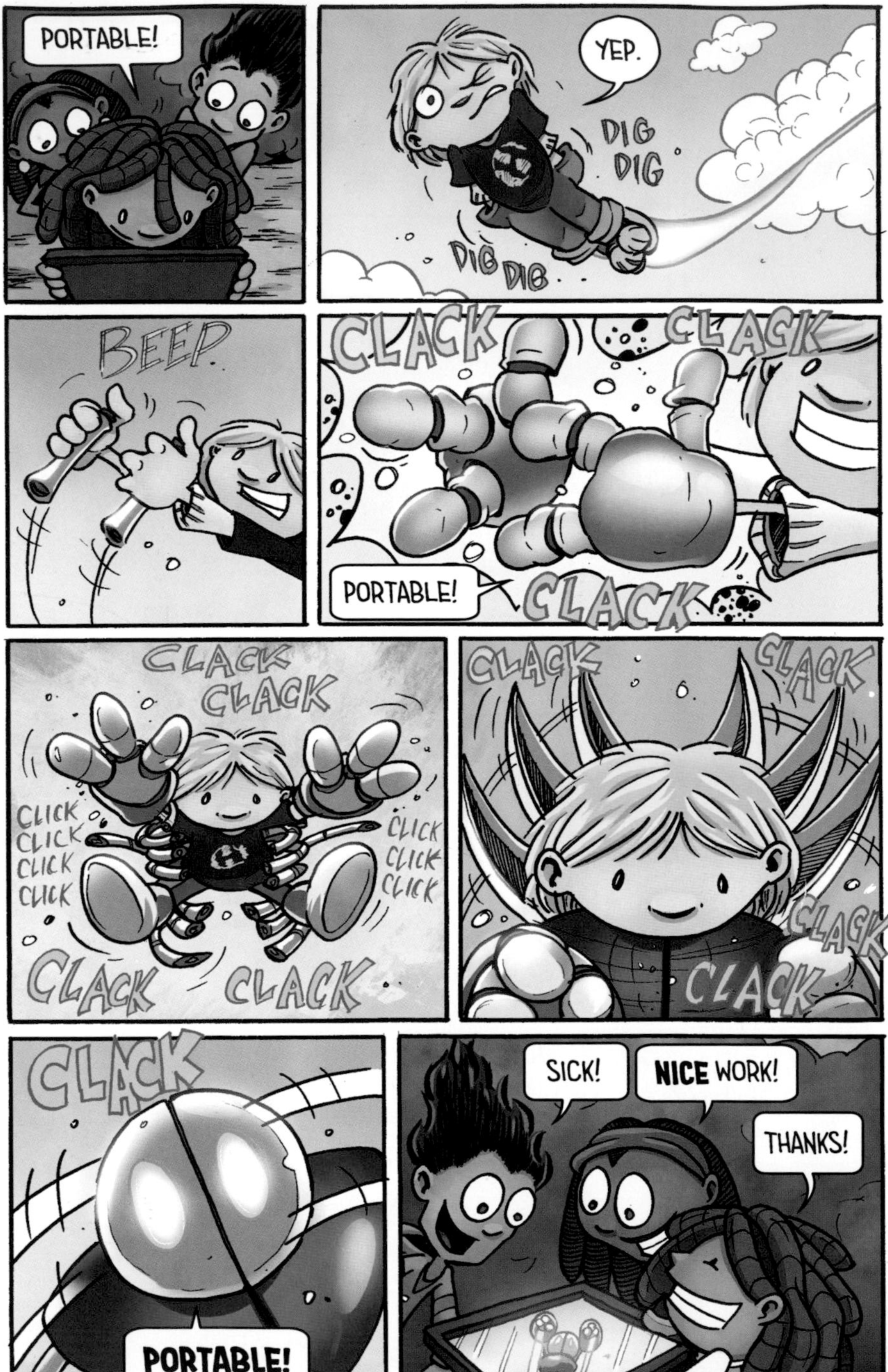
PORTABLE!
YEP.
DIG
DIG
DIG DIG
BEEP
CLACK
CLACK
PORTABLE!
CLACK
CLACK
CLACK
CLICK
CLICK
CLICK
CLICK
CLICK
CLICK
CLICK
CLACK
CLACK
CLACK
CLACK
CLACK
CLACK
CLACK
PORTABLE!
SICK!
NICE WORK!
THANKS!

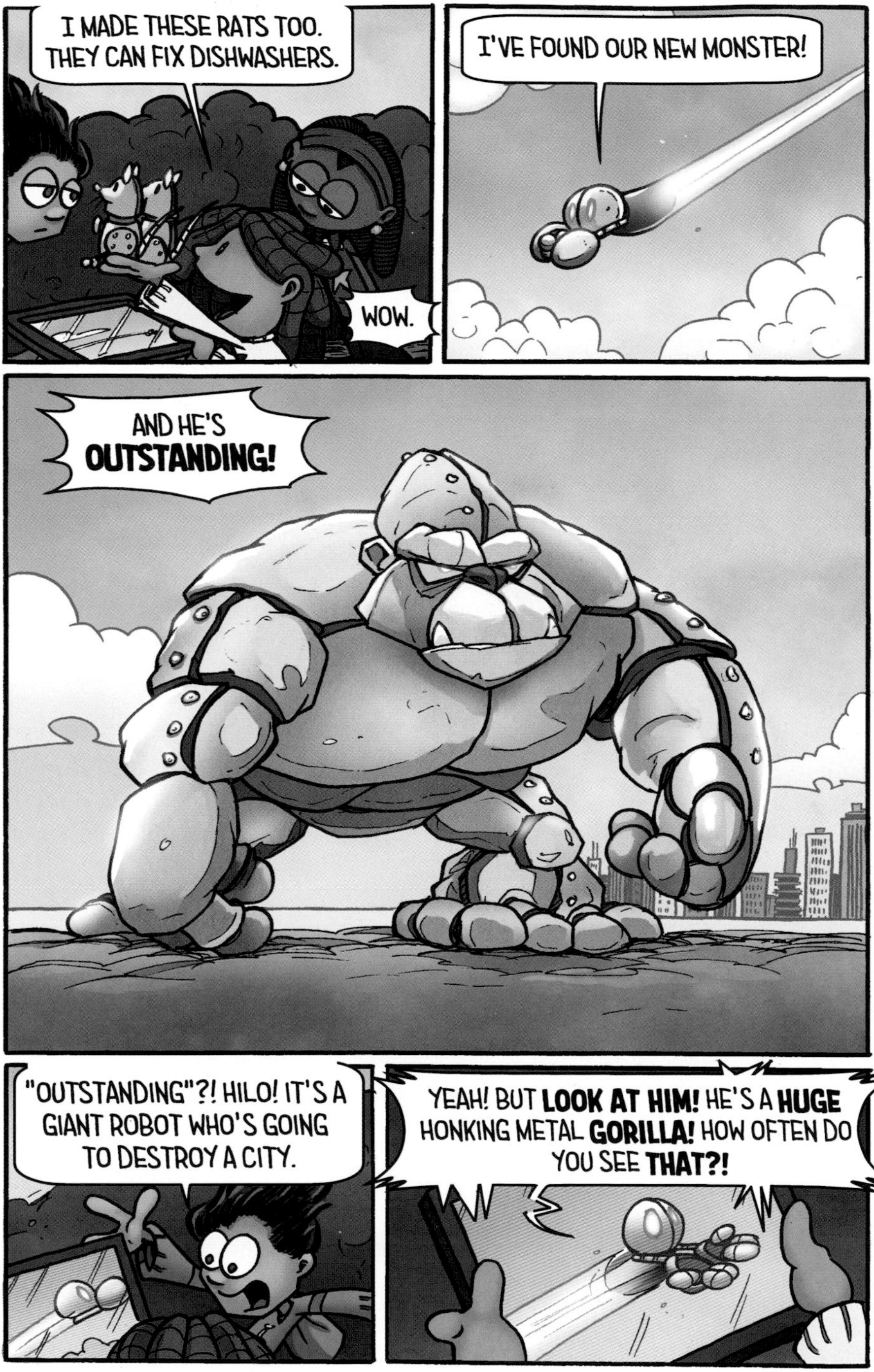
I MADE THESE RATS TOO. THEY CAN FIX DISHWASHERS.
WOW.
I'VE FOUND OUR NEW MONSTER!
AND HE'S **OUTSTANDING!**
"OUTSTANDING"?! HILO! IT'S A GIANT ROBOT WHO'S GOING TO DESTROY A CITY.
YEAH! BUT **LOOK AT HIM!** HE'S A **HUGE** HONKING METAL **GORILLA!** HOW OFTEN DO YOU SEE **THAT?!**

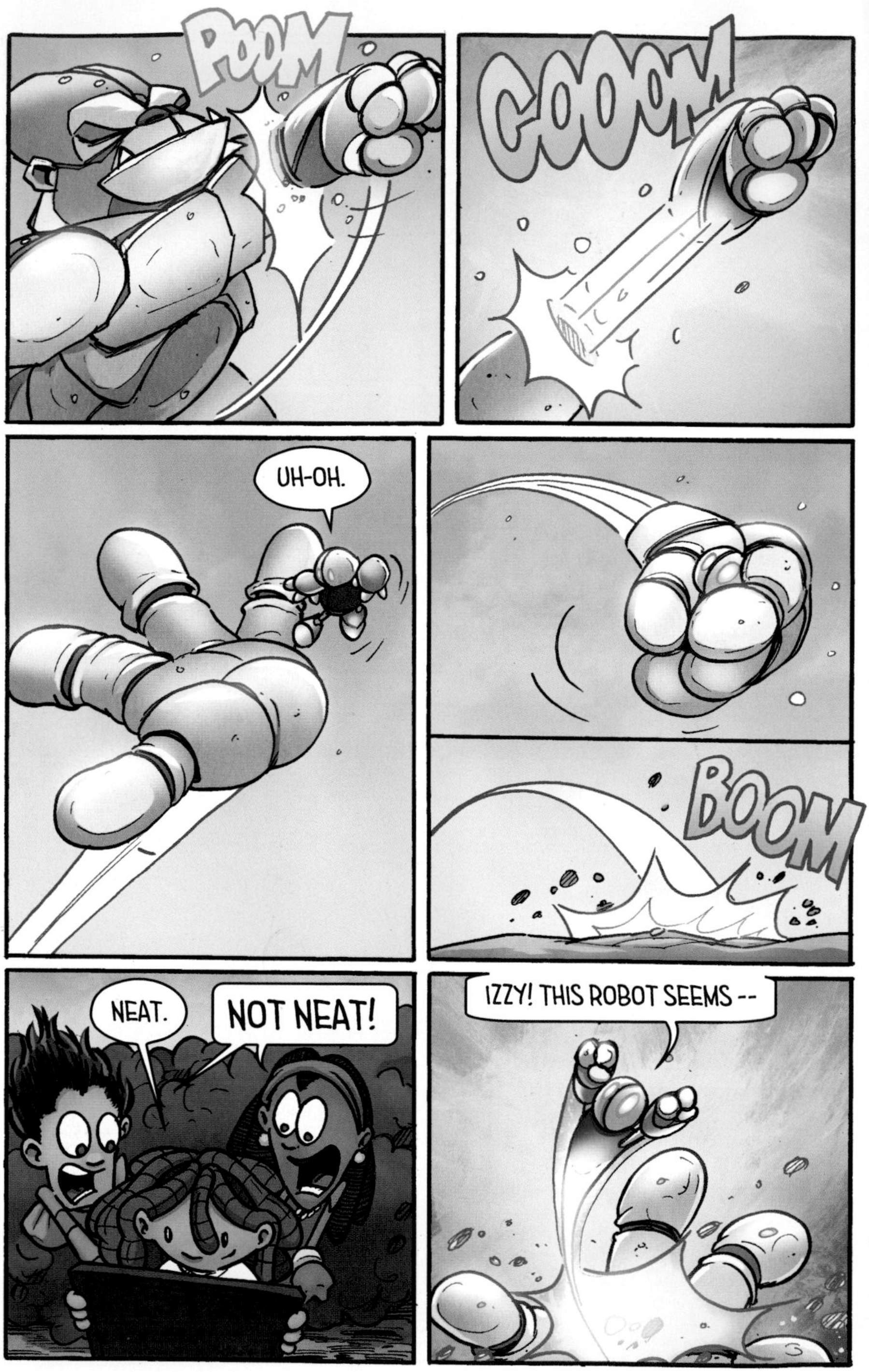
POOM
GOOOM
UH-OH.
BOOM
NEAT.
NOT NEAT!
IZZY! THIS ROBOT SEEMS --

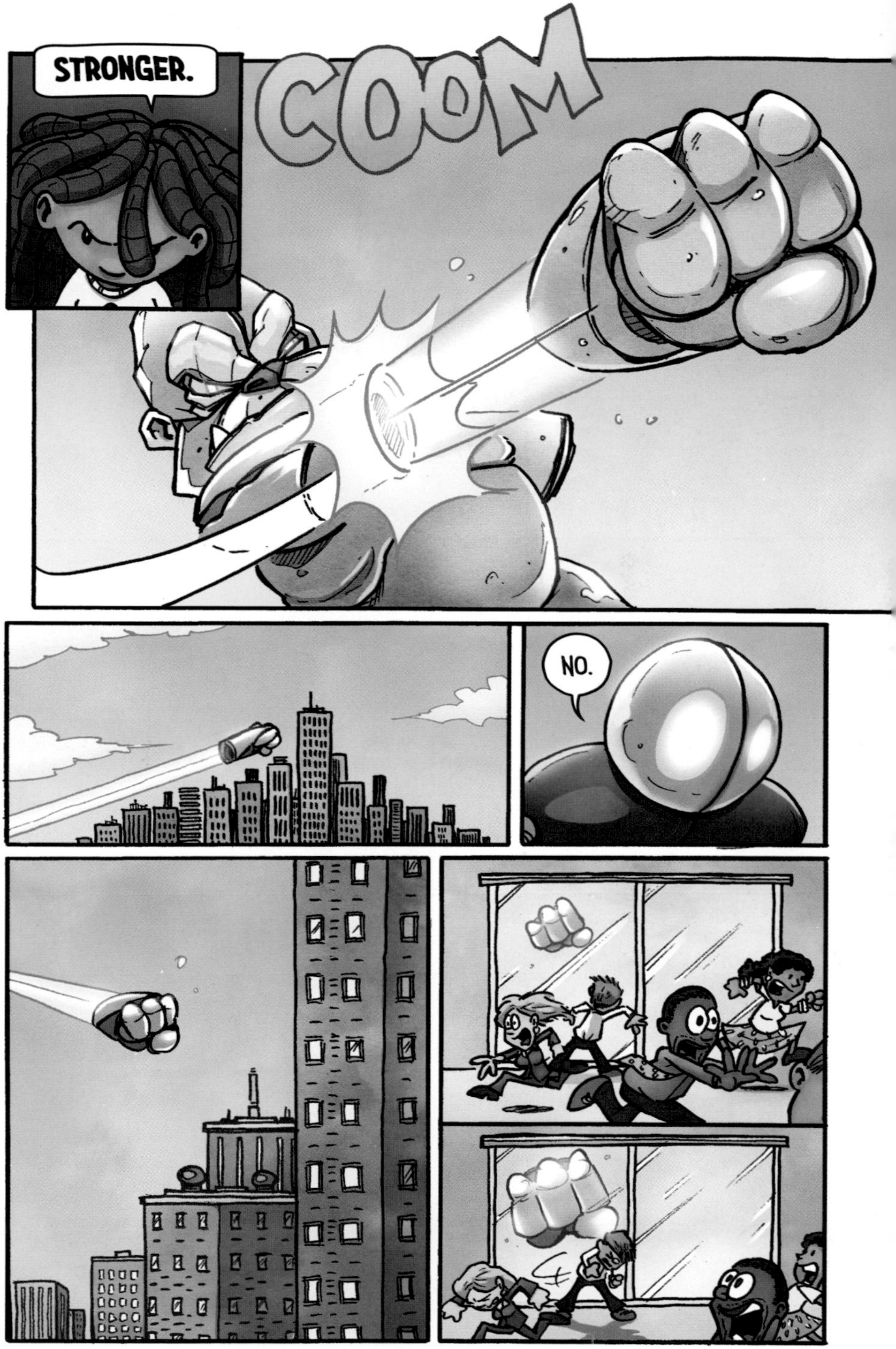
STRONGER.
COOM
NO.

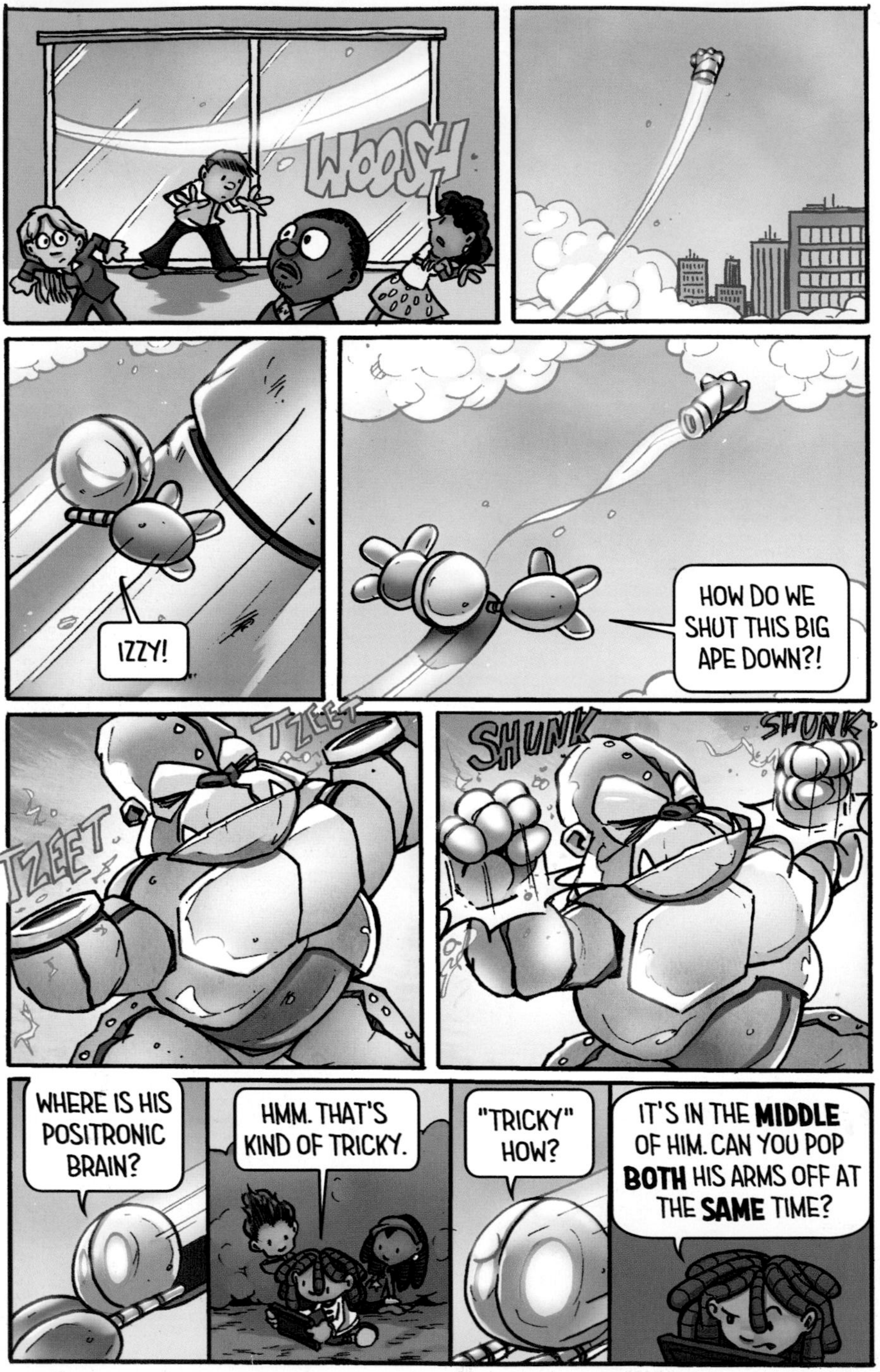
WOOSH
IZZY!
HOW DO WE SHUT THIS BIG APE DOWN?!
TZEET
TZEET
SHUNK
SHUNK
WHERE IS HIS POSITRONIC BRAIN?
HMM. THAT'S KIND OF TRICKY.
"TRICKY" HOW?
IT'S IN THE **MIDDLE** OF HIM. CAN YOU POP **BOTH** HIS ARMS OFF AT THE **SAME** TIME?

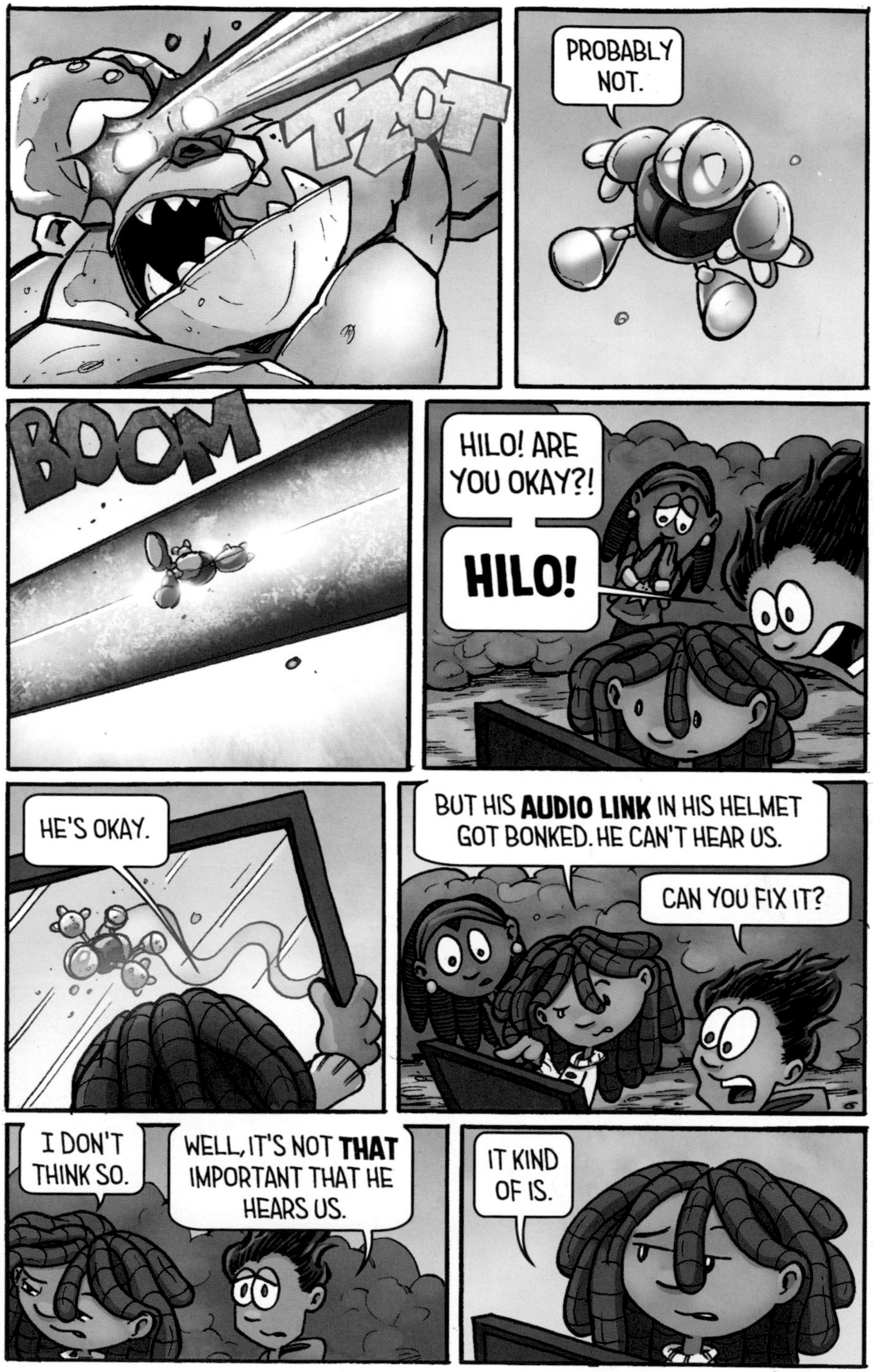
TZZOT
PROBABLY NOT.
BOOM
HILO! ARE YOU OKAY?!
HILO!
HE'S OKAY.
BUT HIS **AUDIO LINK** IN HIS HELMET GOT BONKED. HE CAN'T HEAR US.
CAN YOU FIX IT?
I DON'T THINK SO.
WELL, IT'S NOT **THAT** IMPORTANT THAT HE HEARS US.
IT KIND OF IS.

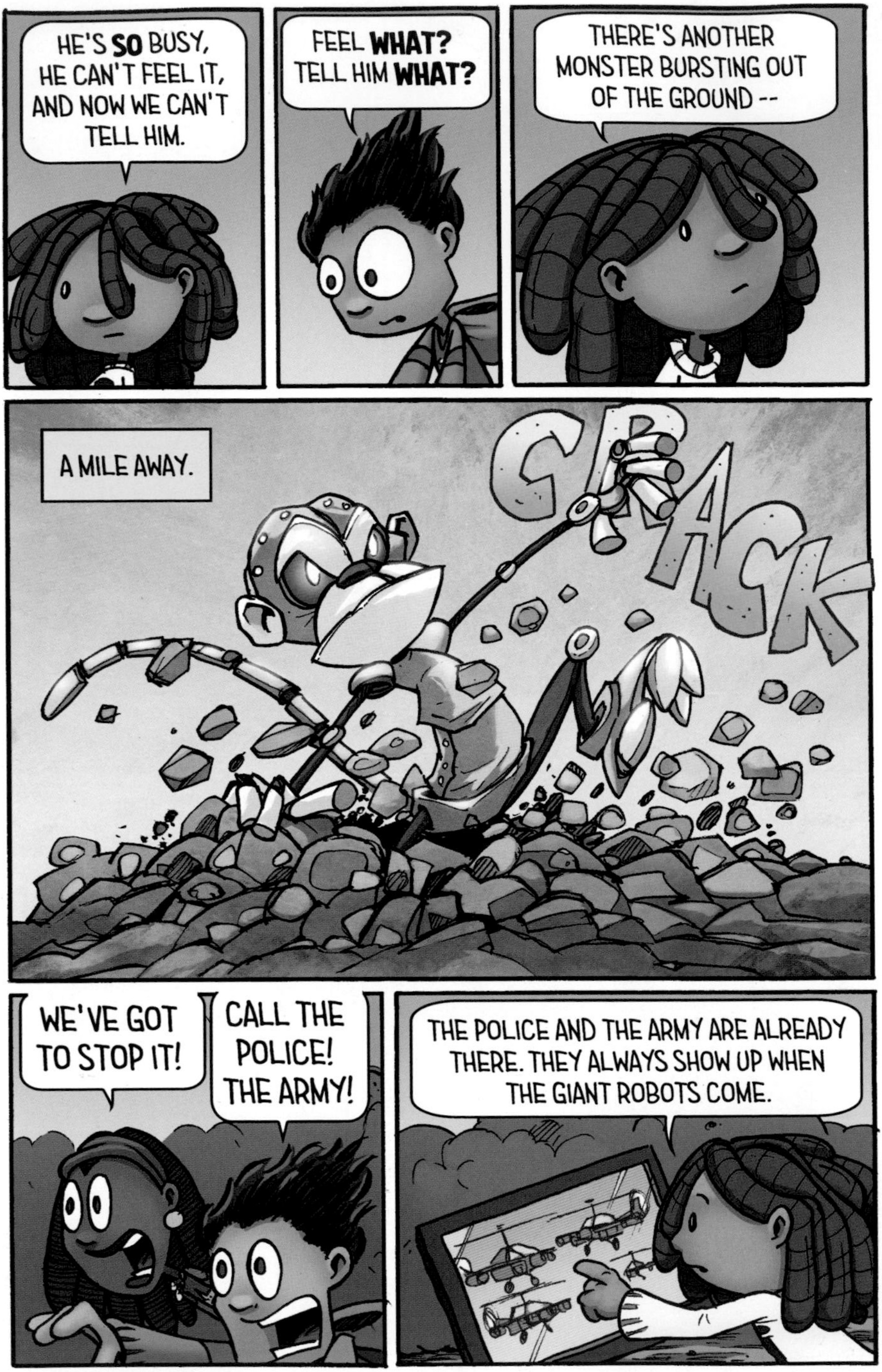
HE'S **SO** BUSY, HE CAN'T FEEL IT, AND NOW WE CAN'T TELL HIM.
FEEL **WHAT?** TELL HIM **WHAT?**
THERE'S ANOTHER MONSTER BURSTING OUT OF THE GROUND --
A MILE AWAY.
CRACK
WE'VE GOT TO STOP IT!
CALL THE POLICE! THE ARMY!
THE POLICE AND THE ARMY ARE ALREADY THERE. THEY ALWAYS SHOW UP WHEN THE GIANT ROBOTS COME.

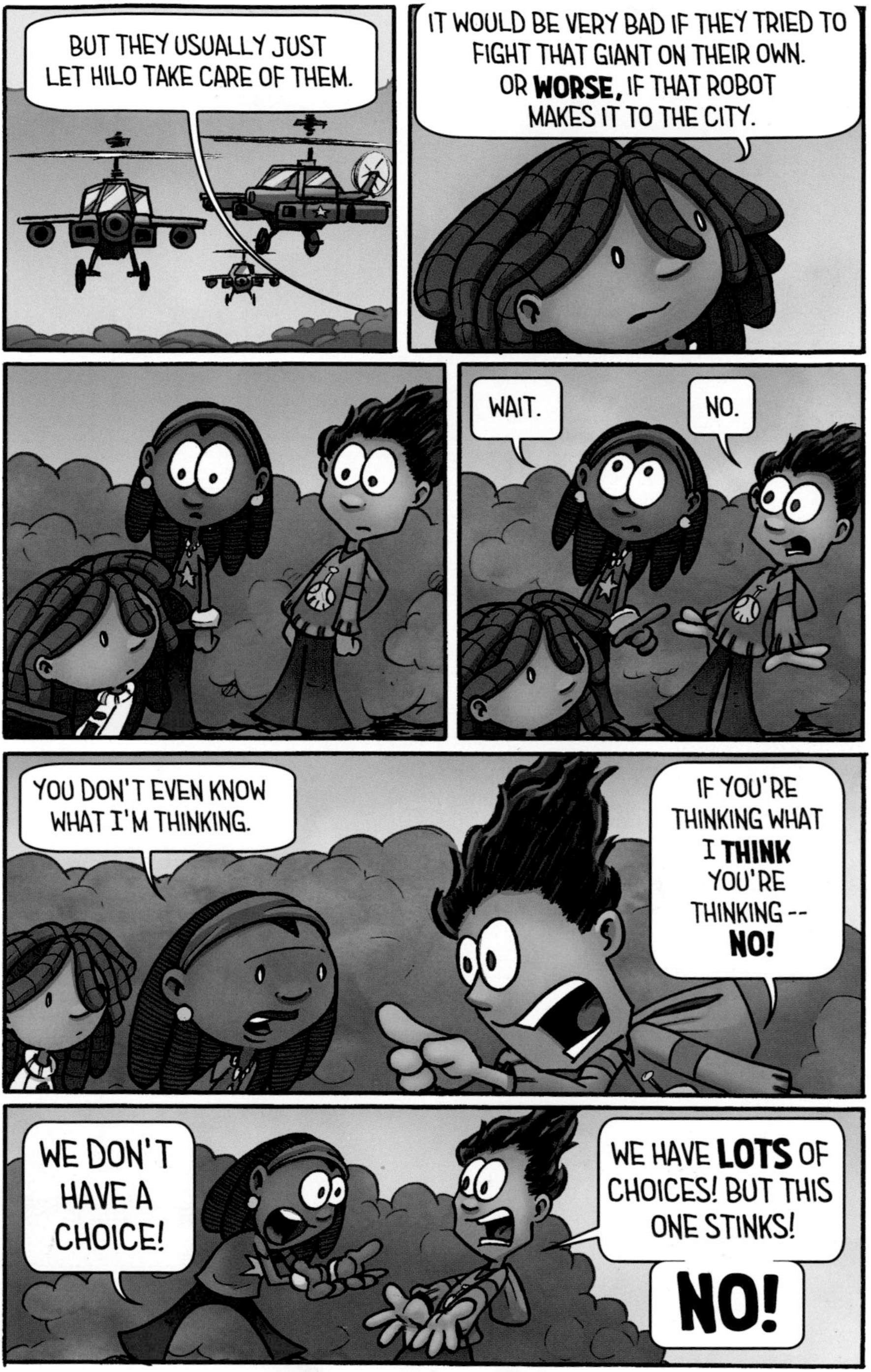
BUT THEY USUALLY JUST LET HILO TAKE CARE OF THEM.
IT WOULD BE VERY BAD IF THEY TRIED TO FIGHT THAT GIANT ON THEIR OWN. OR **WORSE,** IF THAT ROBOT MAKES IT TO THE CITY.
WAIT.
NO.
YOU DON'T EVEN KNOW WHAT I'M THINKING.
IF YOU'RE THINKING WHAT I **THINK** YOU'RE THINKING -- **NO!**
WE DON'T HAVE A CHOICE!
WE HAVE **LOTS** OF CHOICES! BUT THIS ONE STINKS!
NO!

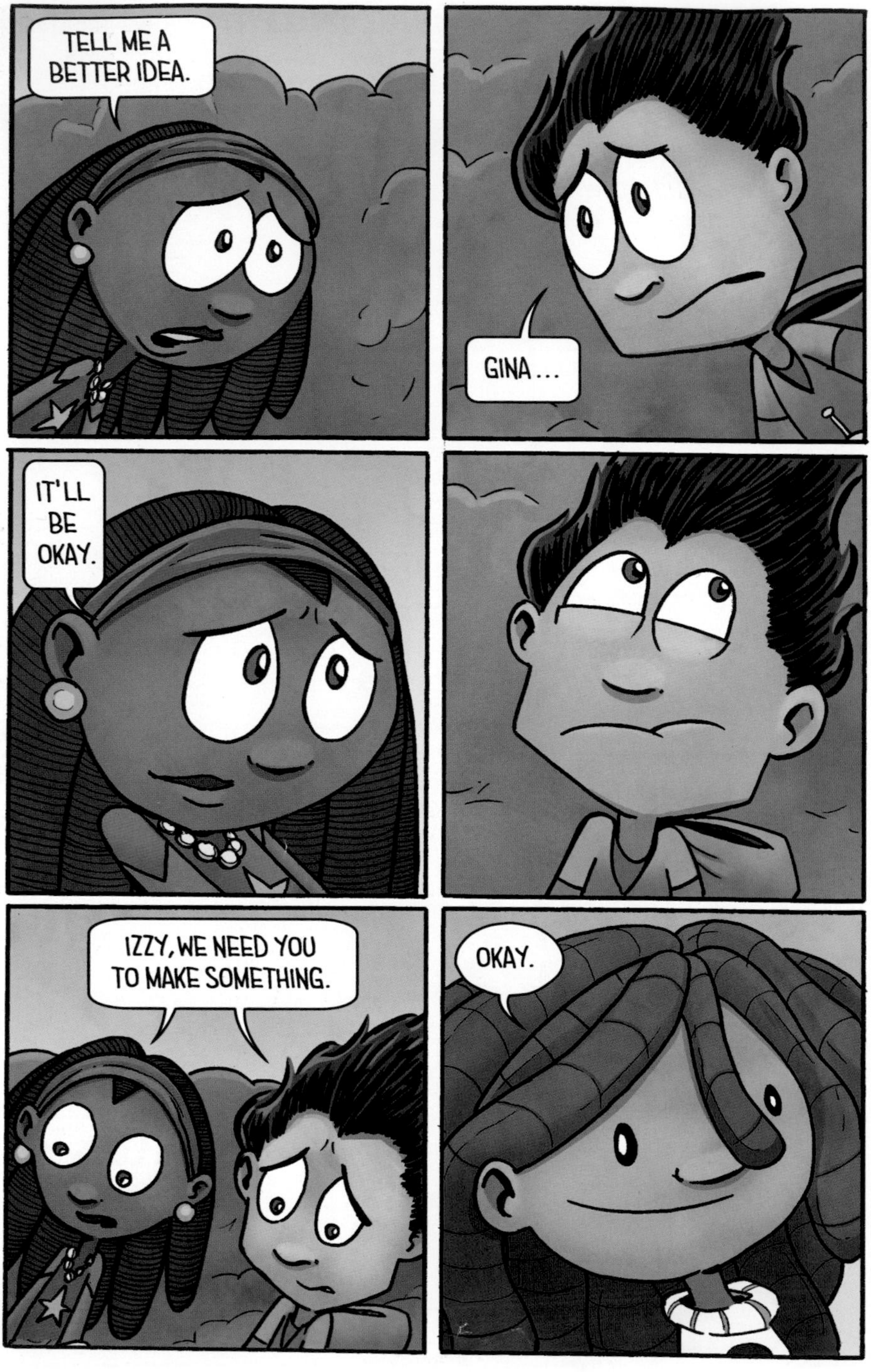
TELL ME A BETTER IDEA.
GINA . . .
IT'LL BE OKAY.
IZZY, WE NEED YOU TO MAKE SOMETHING.
OKAY.

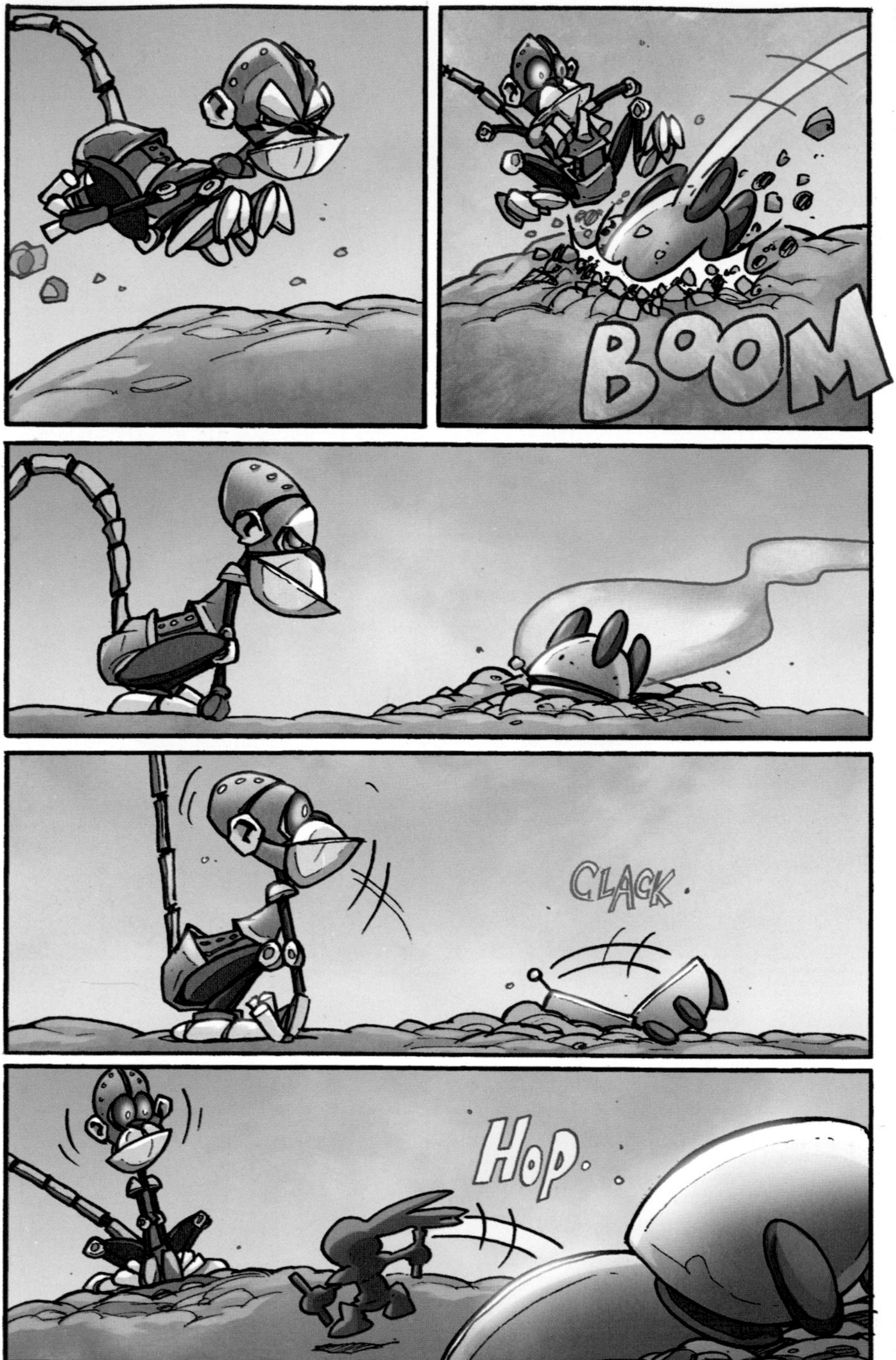
BOOM
CLACK
HOP

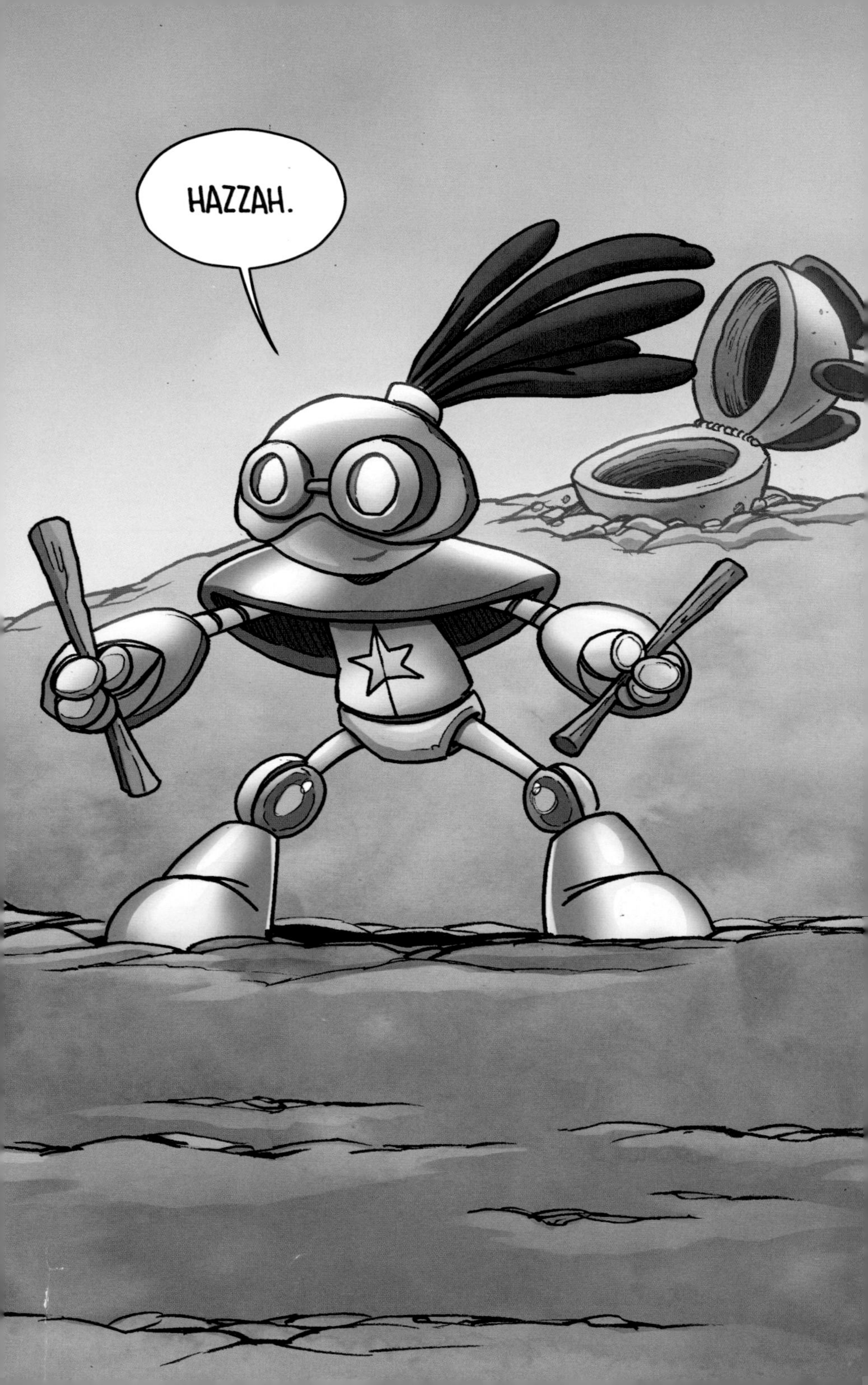
HAZZAH.

5

HAZZAH

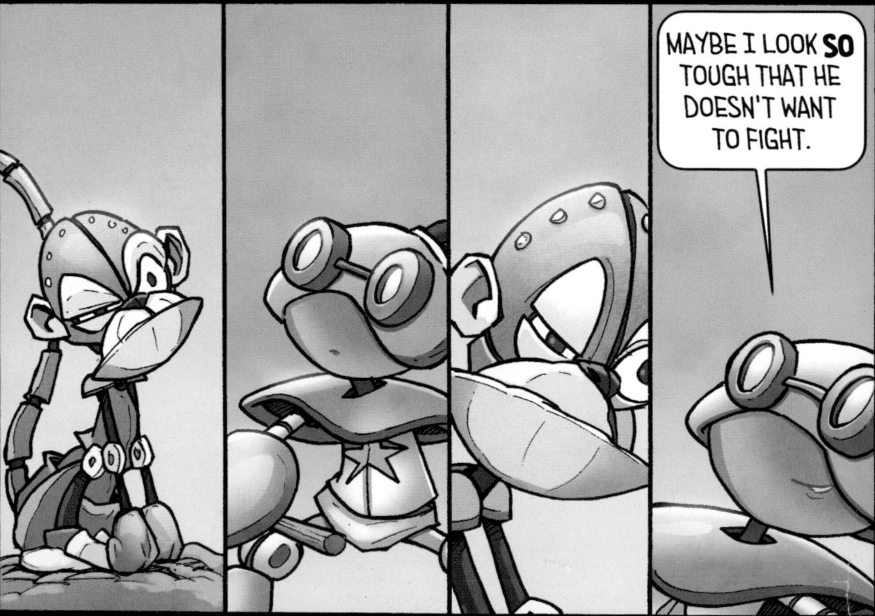
MAYBE I LOOK **SO** TOUGH THAT HE DOESN'T WANT TO FIGHT.

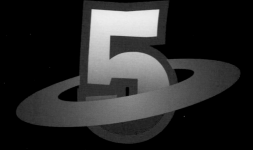

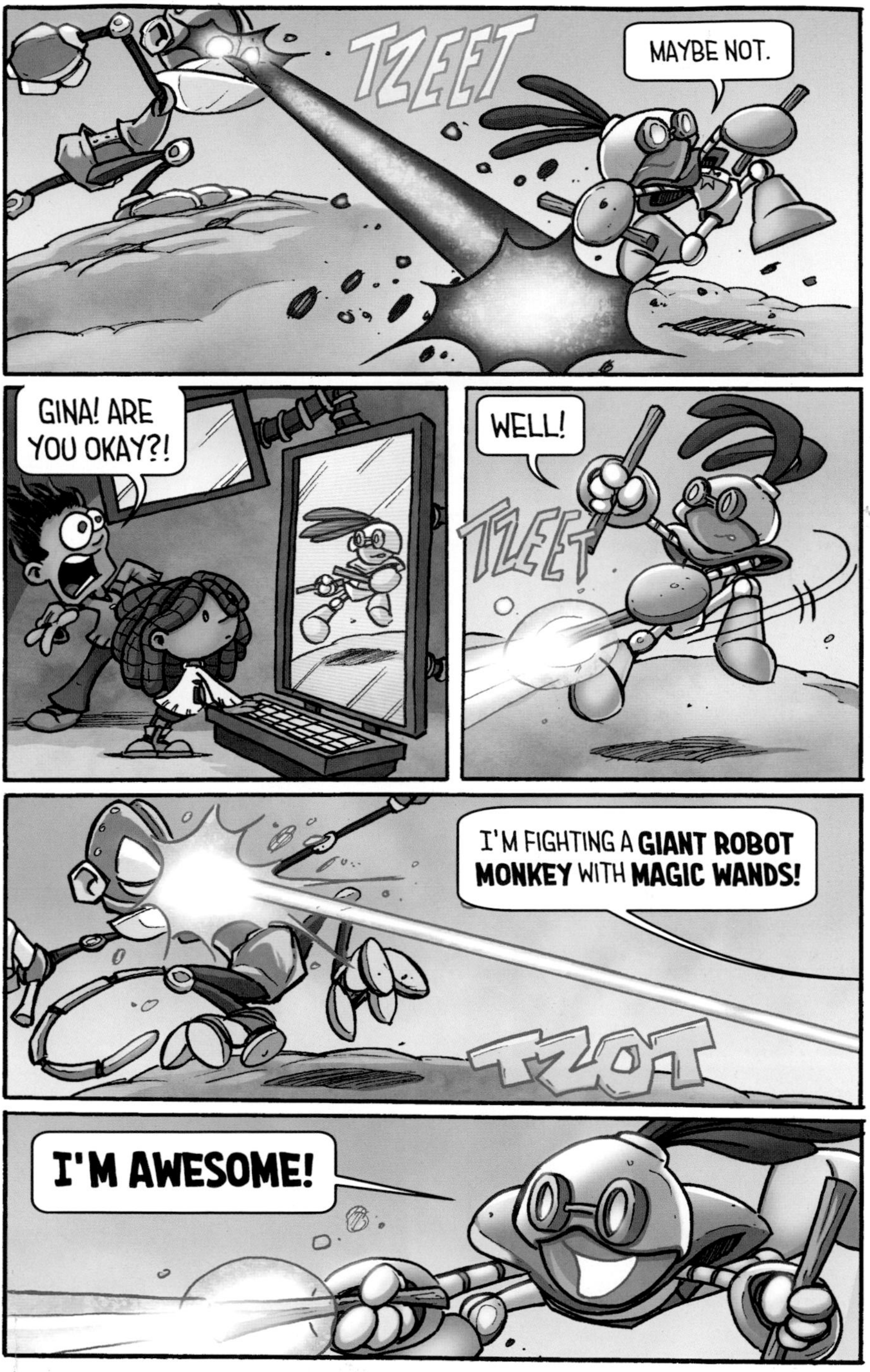
TZEET
MAYBE NOT.
GINA! ARE YOU OKAY?!
WELL!
TZEET
I'M FIGHTING A **GIANT ROBOT MONKEY** WITH **MAGIC WANDS!**
TZOT
I'M AWESOME!

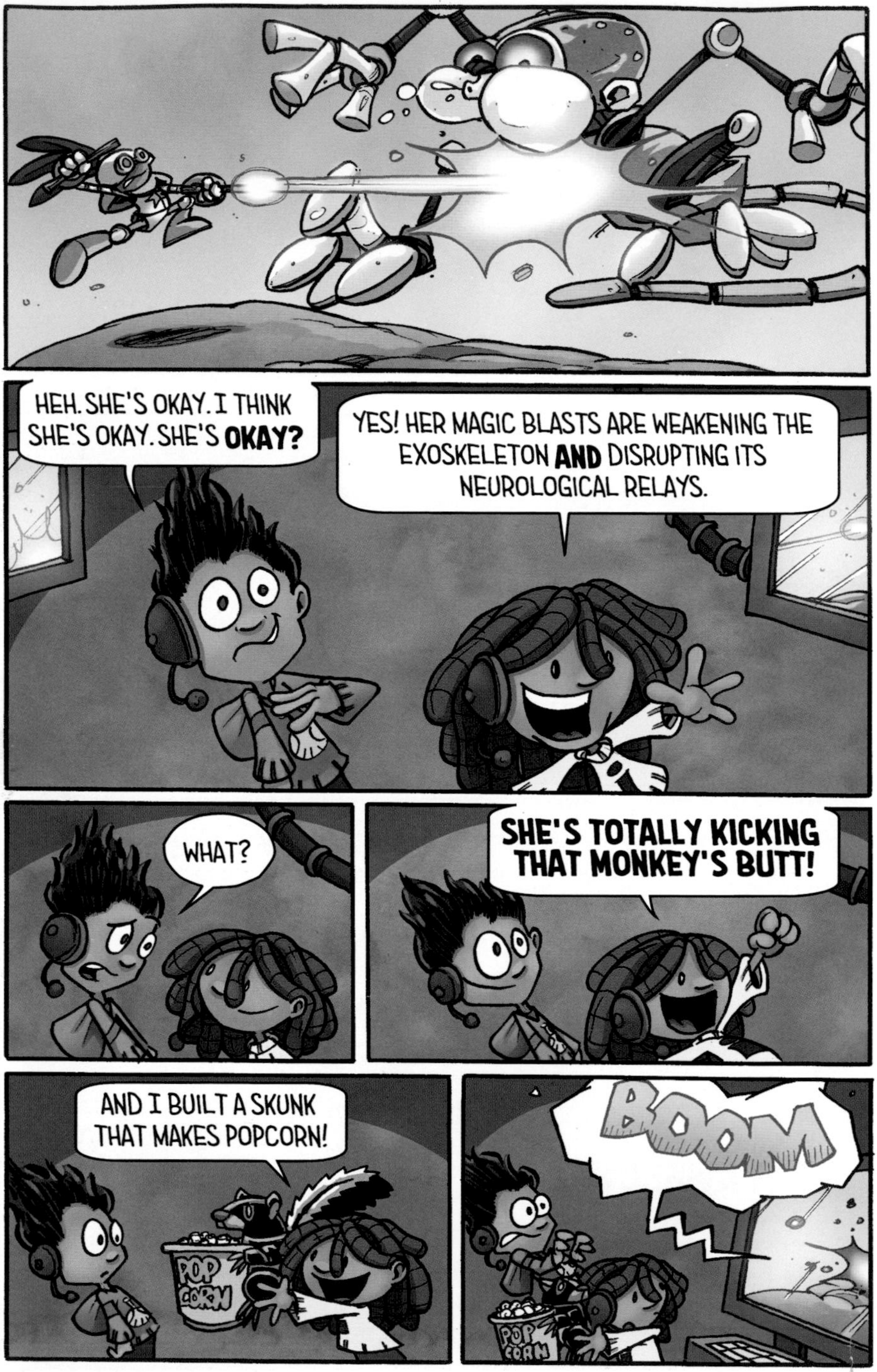
HEH. SHE'S OKAY. I THINK SHE'S OKAY. SHE'S **OKAY?**
YES! HER MAGIC BLASTS ARE WEAKENING THE EXOSKELETON **AND** DISRUPTING ITS NEUROLOGICAL RELAYS.
WHAT?
SHE'S TOTALLY KICKING THAT MONKEY'S BUTT!
AND I BUILT A SKUNK THAT MAKES POPCORN!
POP CORN
BOOM

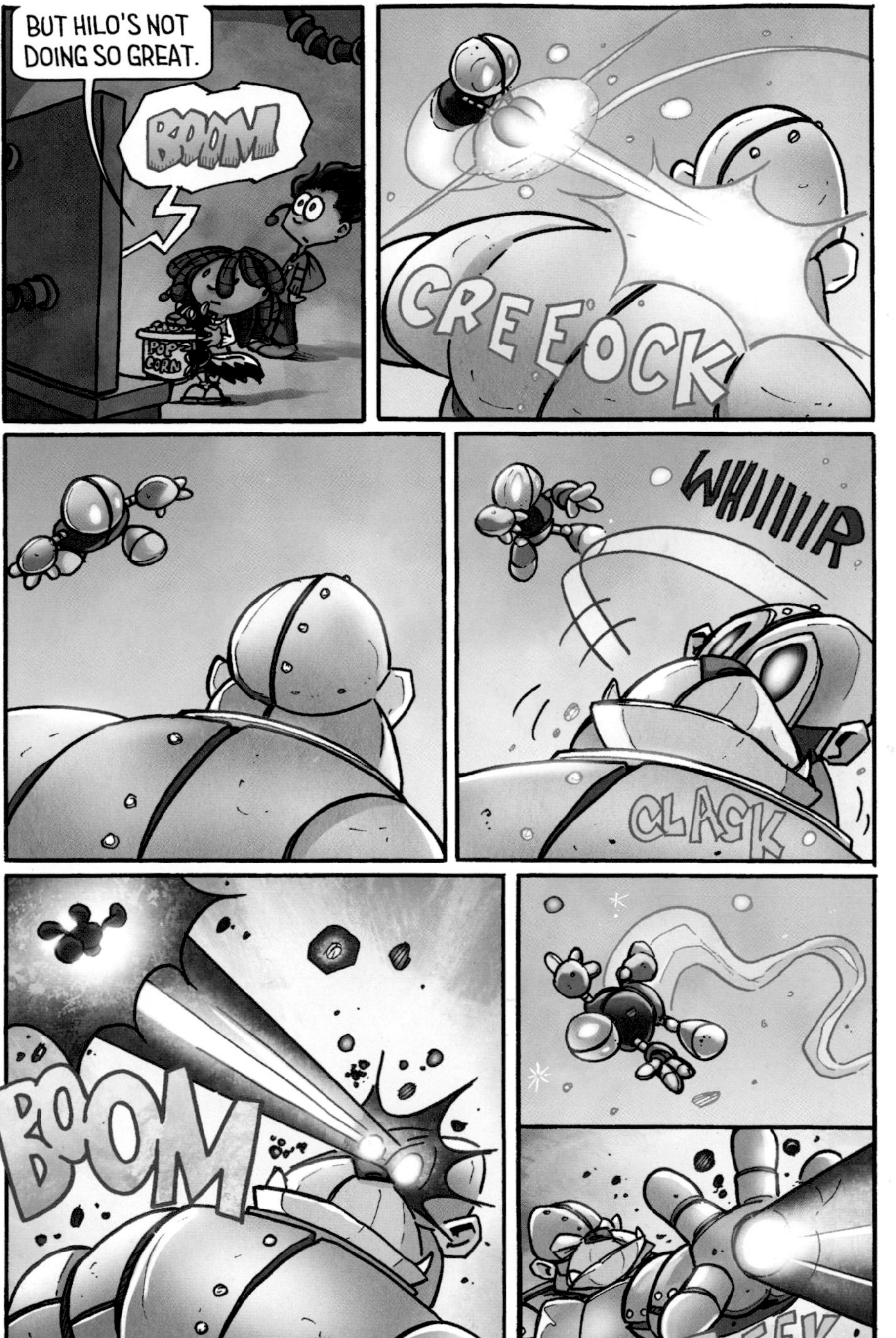

BUT HILO'S NOT DOING SO GREAT.
BOOM
POP CORN
CREEOCK
WHIIIIR
CLACK
BOOM
TZEEK

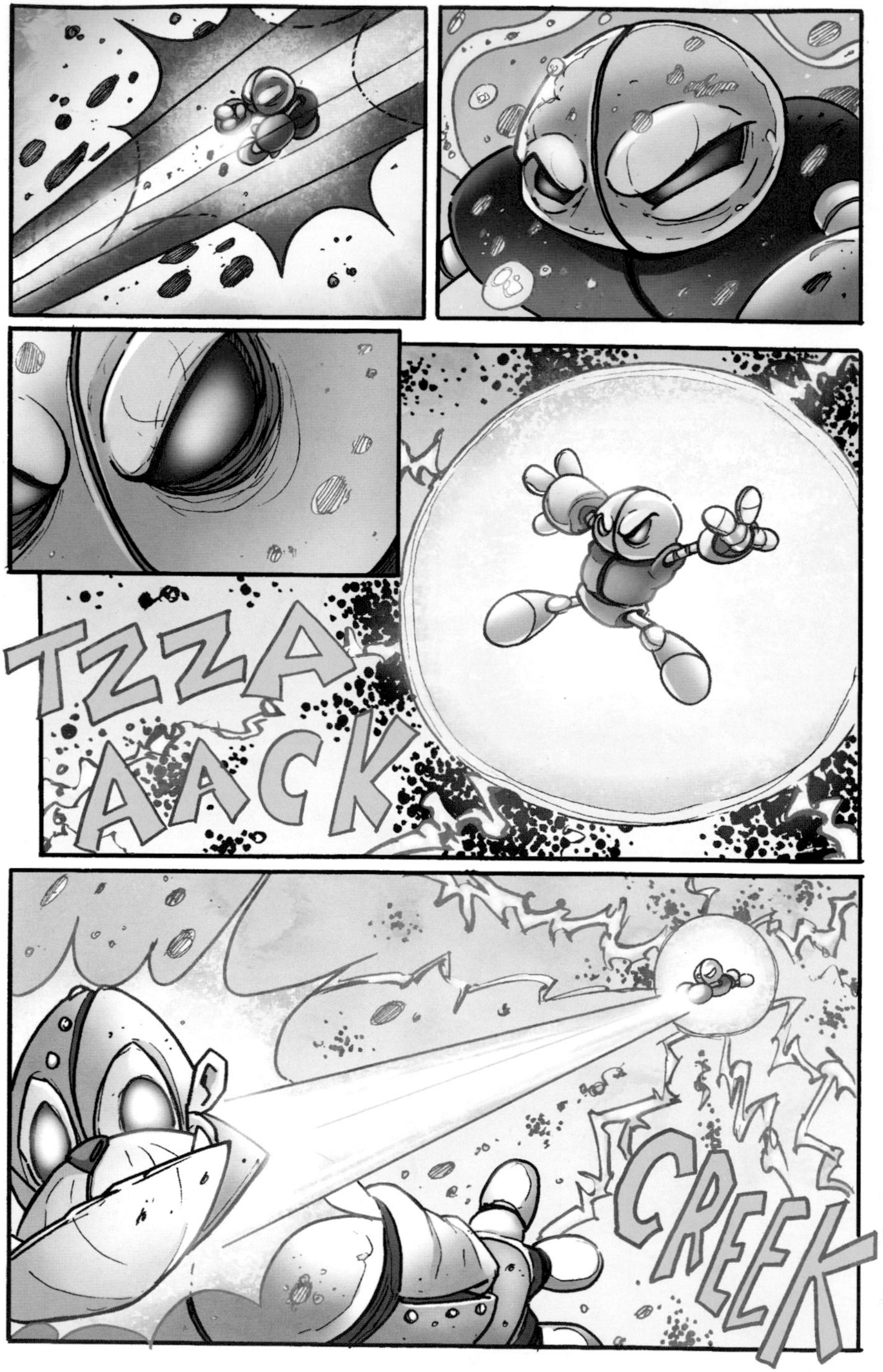
TZZA
AACK
CREEK

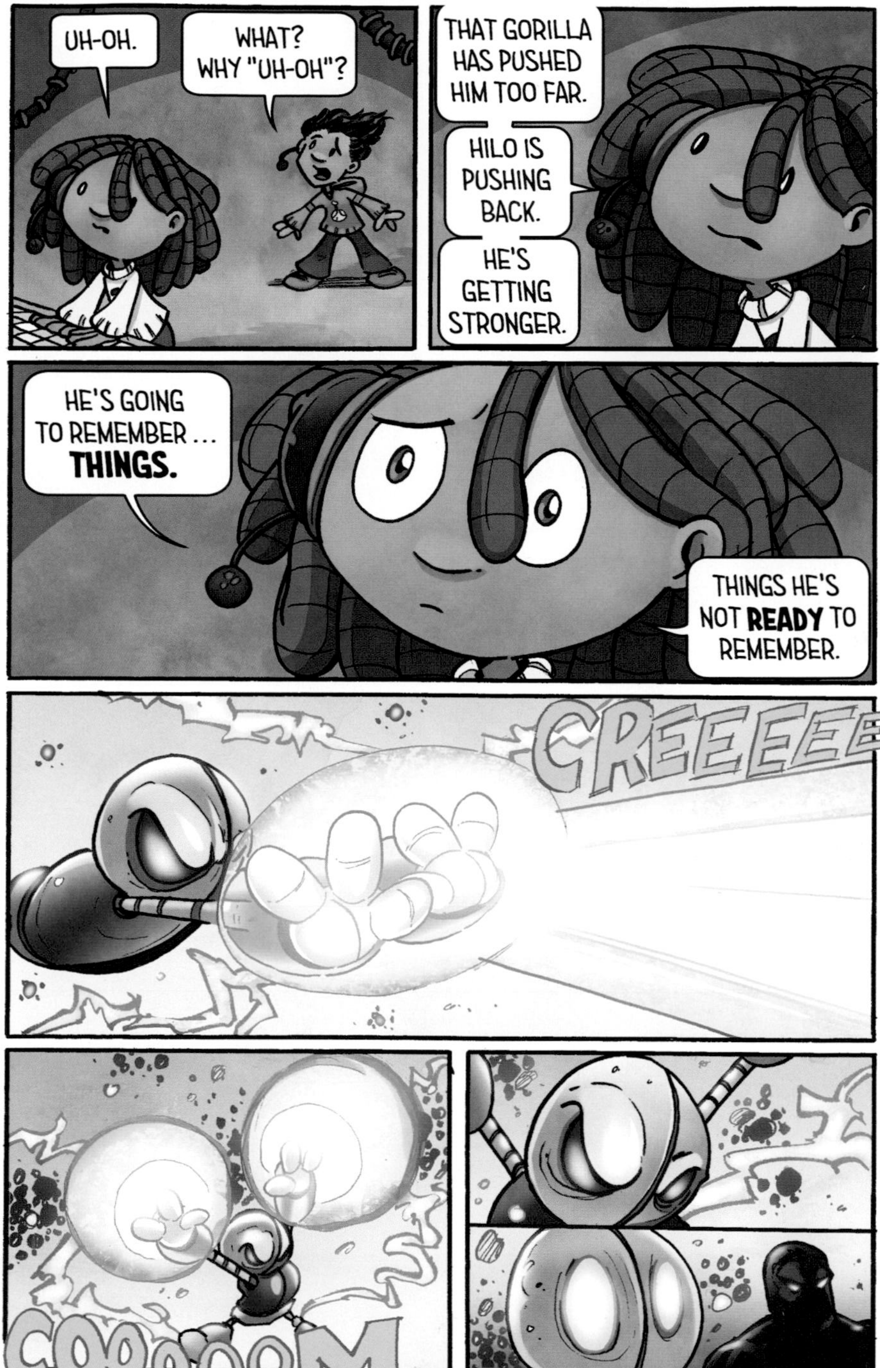
UH-OH.
WHAT? WHY "UH-OH"?
THAT GORILLA HAS PUSHED HIM TOO FAR.
HILO IS PUSHING BACK.
HE'S GETTING STRONGER.
HE'S GOING TO REMEMBER ... **THINGS.**
THINGS HE'S NOT **READY** TO REMEMBER.
CREEEEE
COOOOOM

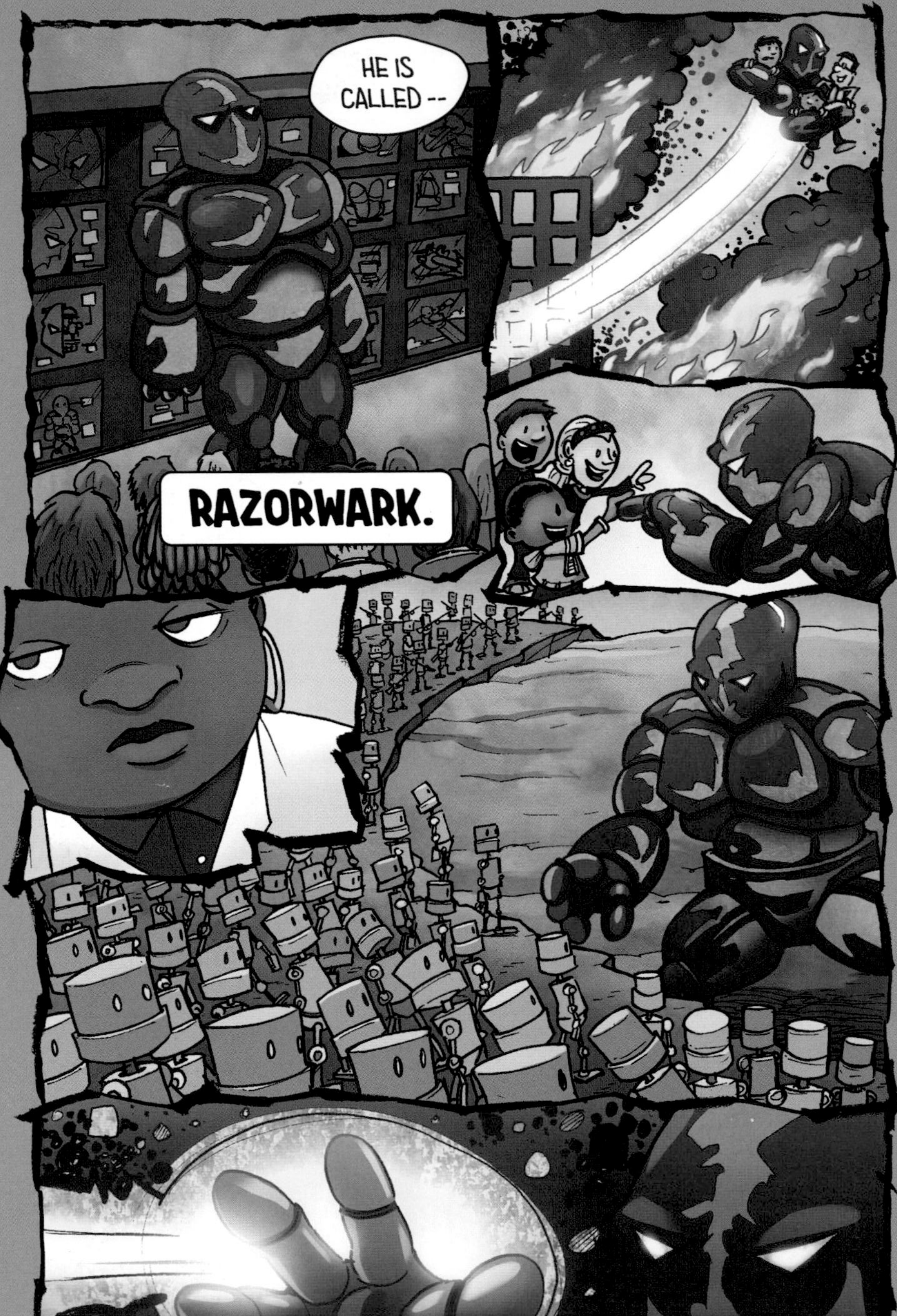
HE IS CALLED --
RAZORWARK.

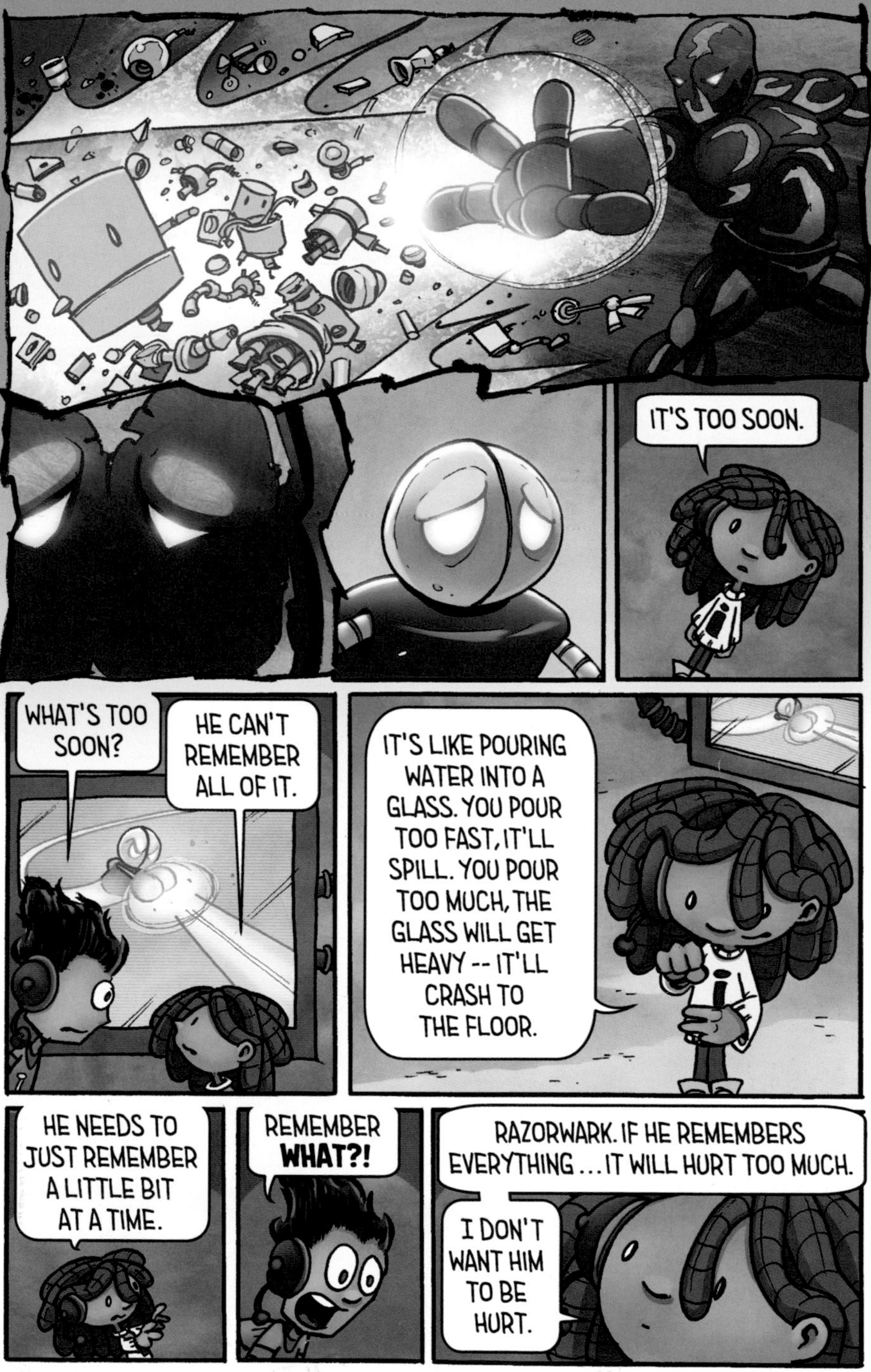
IT'S TOO SOON.
WHAT'S TOO SOON?
HE CAN'T REMEMBER ALL OF IT.
IT'S LIKE POURING WATER INTO A GLASS. YOU POUR TOO FAST, IT'LL SPILL. YOU POUR TOO MUCH, THE GLASS WILL GET HEAVY -- IT'LL CRASH TO THE FLOOR.
HE NEEDS TO JUST REMEMBER A LITTLE BIT AT A TIME.
REMEMBER **WHAT?!**
RAZORWARK. IF HE REMEMBERS EVERYTHING ... IT WILL HURT TOO MUCH.
I DON'T WANT HIM TO BE HURT.

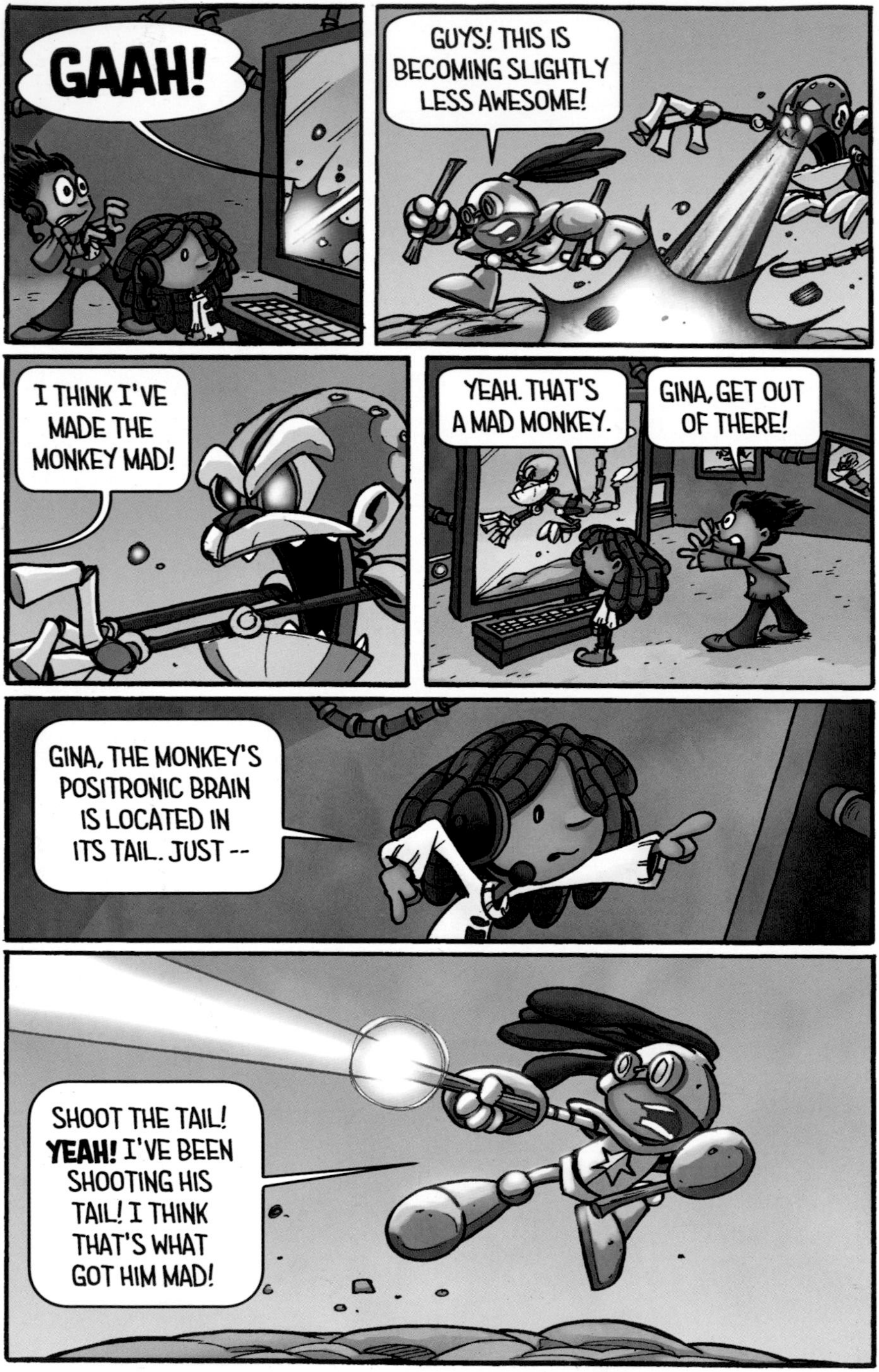
GAAH!
GUYS! THIS IS BECOMING SLIGHTLY LESS AWESOME!
I THINK I'VE MADE THE MONKEY MAD!
YEAH. THAT'S A MAD MONKEY.
GINA, GET OUT OF THERE!
GINA, THE MONKEY'S POSITRONIC BRAIN IS LOCATED IN ITS TAIL. JUST --
SHOOT THE TAIL! **YEAH!** I'VE BEEN SHOOTING HIS TAIL! I THINK THAT'S WHAT GOT HIM MAD!

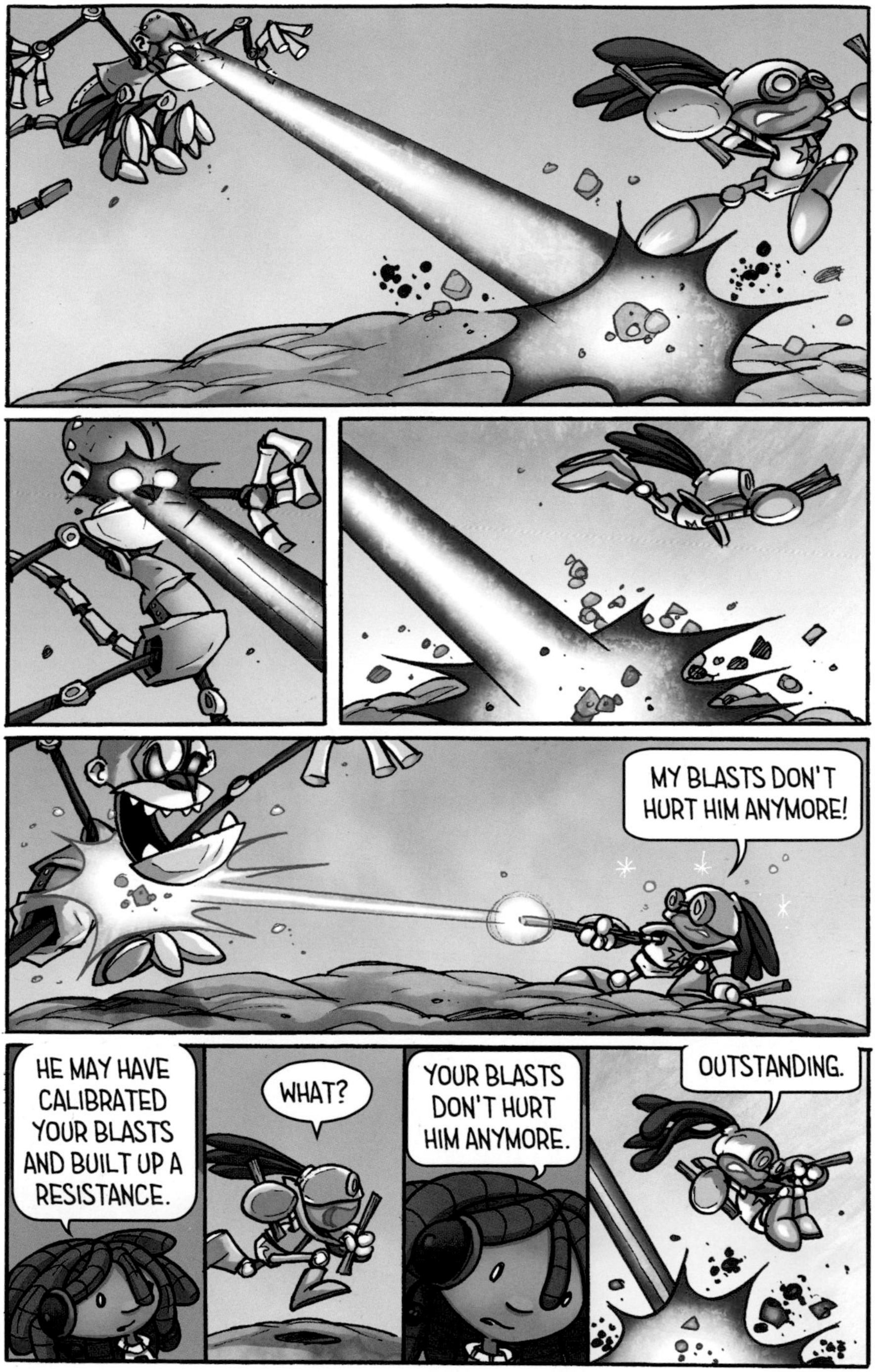
MY BLASTS DON'T HURT HIM ANYMORE!
HE MAY HAVE CALIBRATED YOUR BLASTS AND BUILT UP A RESISTANCE.
WHAT?
YOUR BLASTS DON'T HURT HIM ANYMORE.
OUTSTANDING.

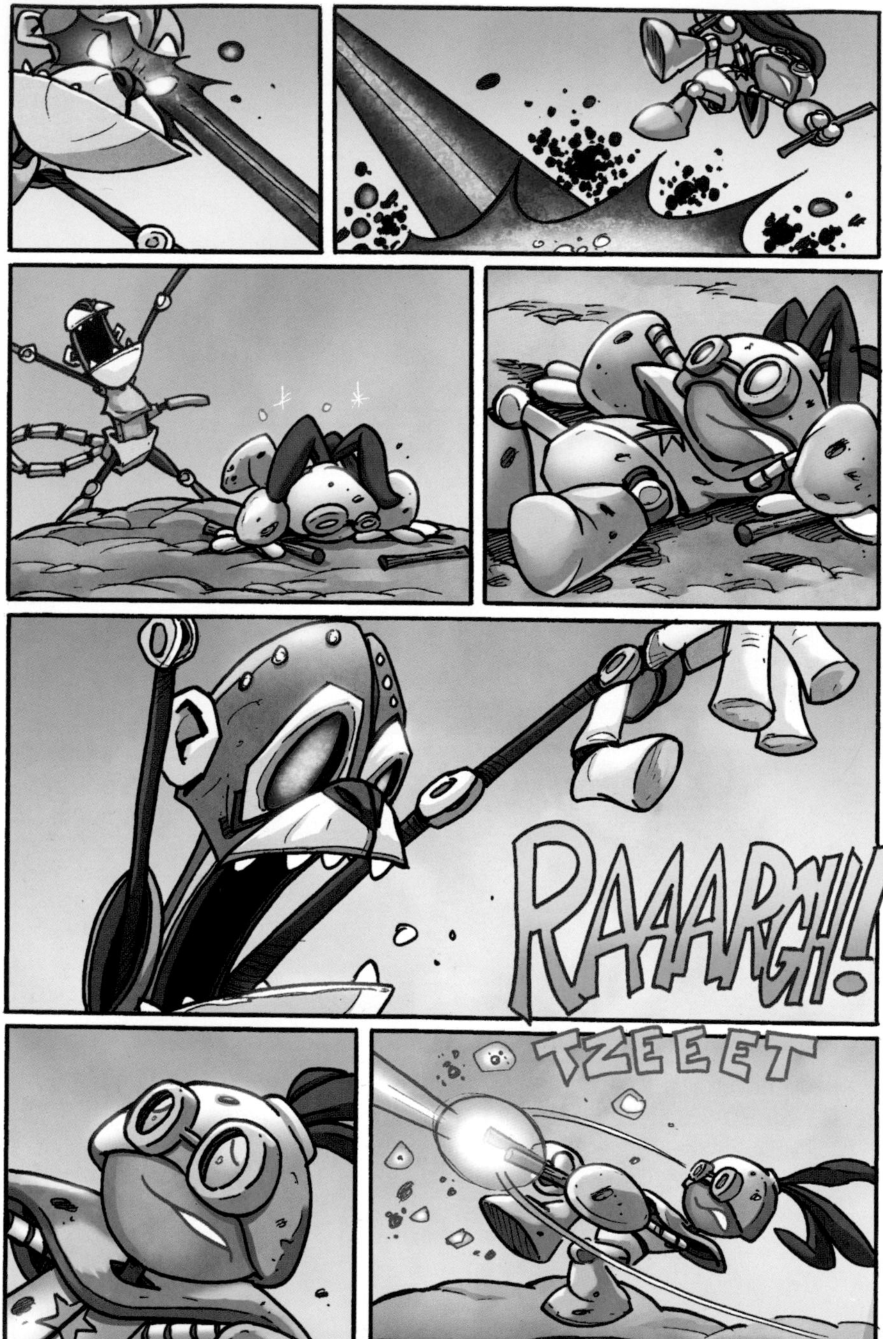
RAAARGH!!
TZEEET

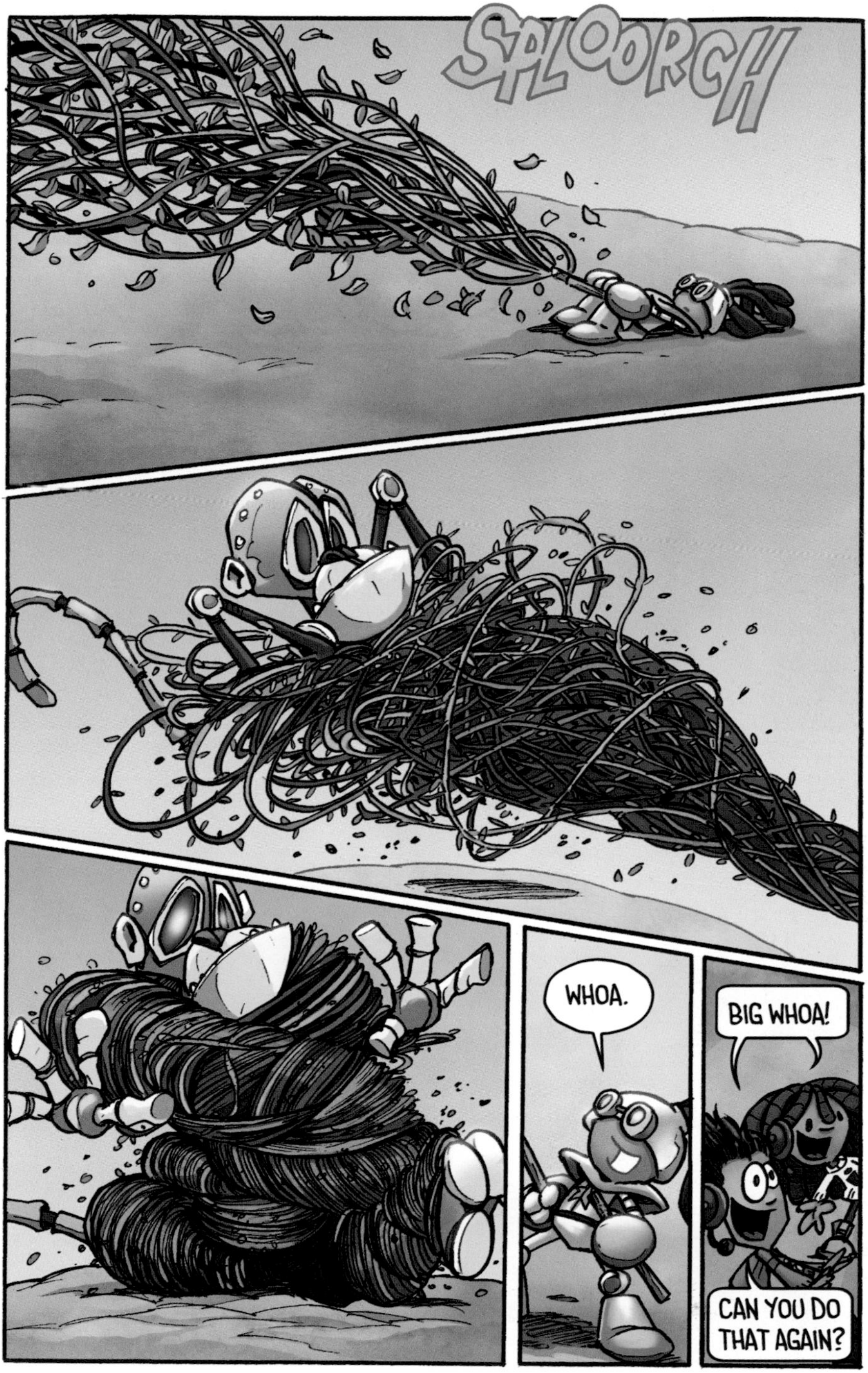
SPLOORCH
WHOA.
BIG WHOA!
CAN YOU DO THAT AGAIN?

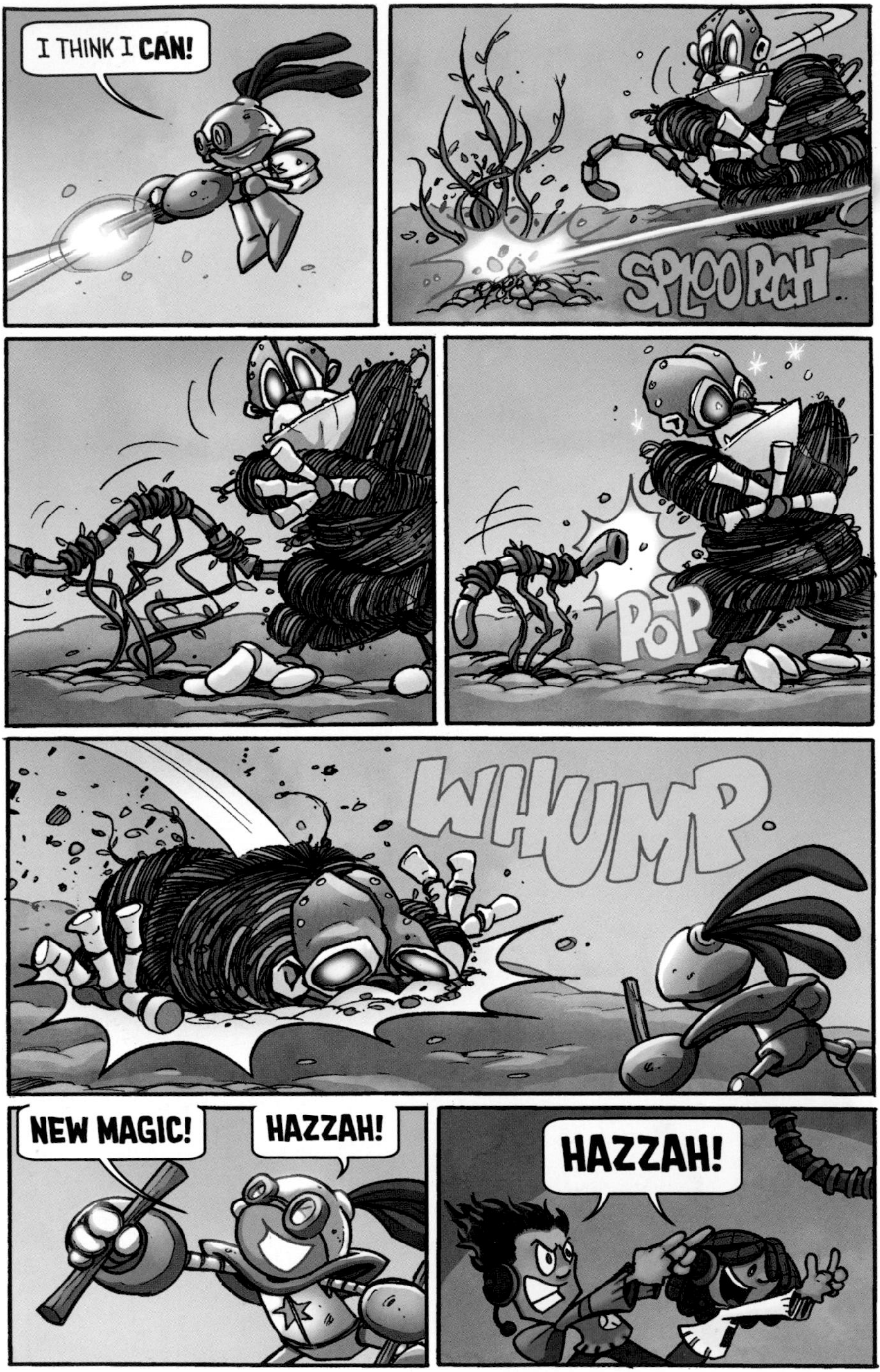
I THINK I CAN!
SPLOORCH
POP
WHUMP
NEW MAGIC!
HAZZAH!
HAZZAH!

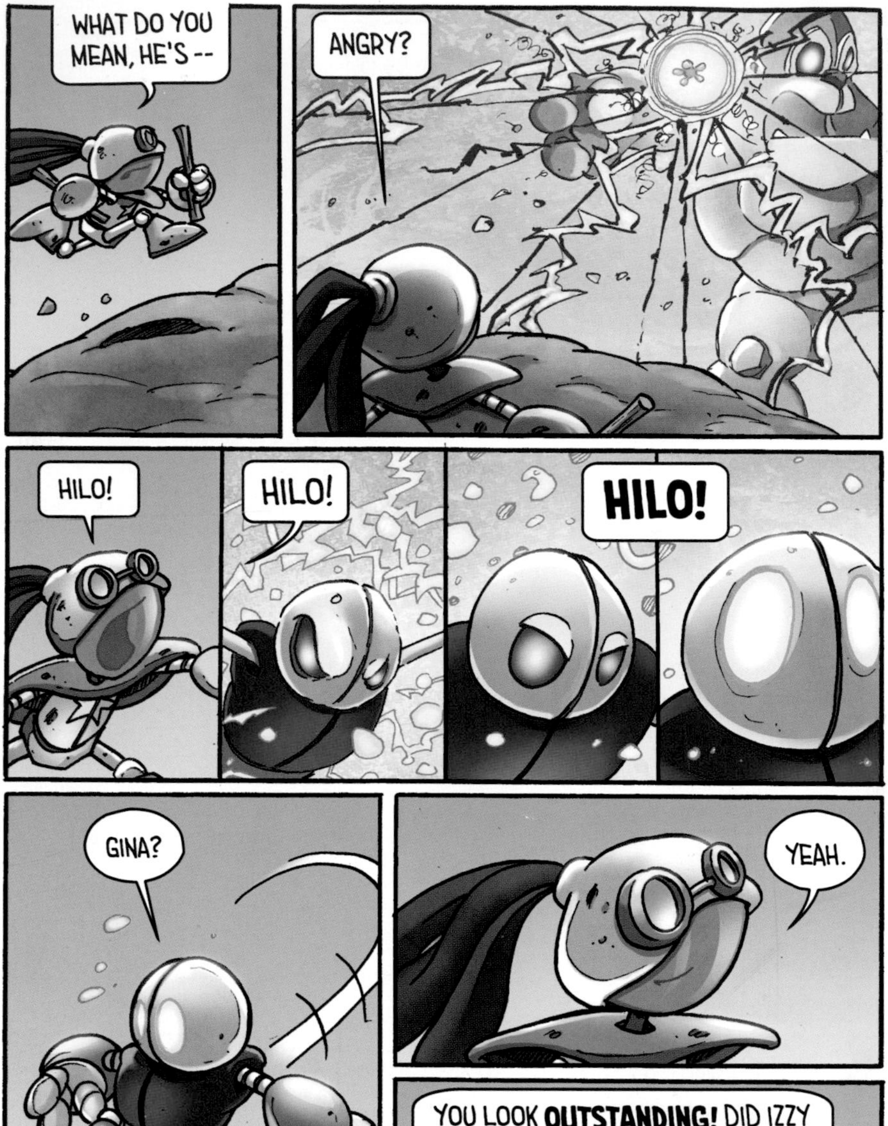
WHAT DO YOU MEAN, HE'S --
ANGRY?
HILO!
HILO!
HILO!
GINA?
YEAH.
YOU LOOK **OUTSTANDING!** DID IZZY MAKE THAT FOR YOU? YOUR **HELMET** IS WICKED NUTS!

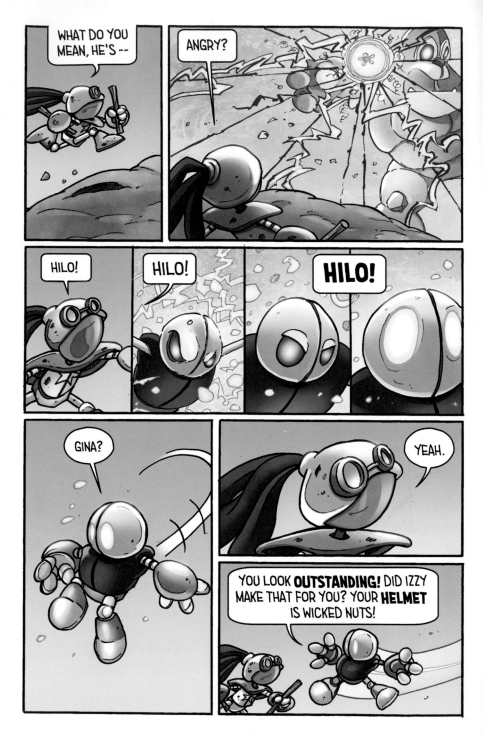

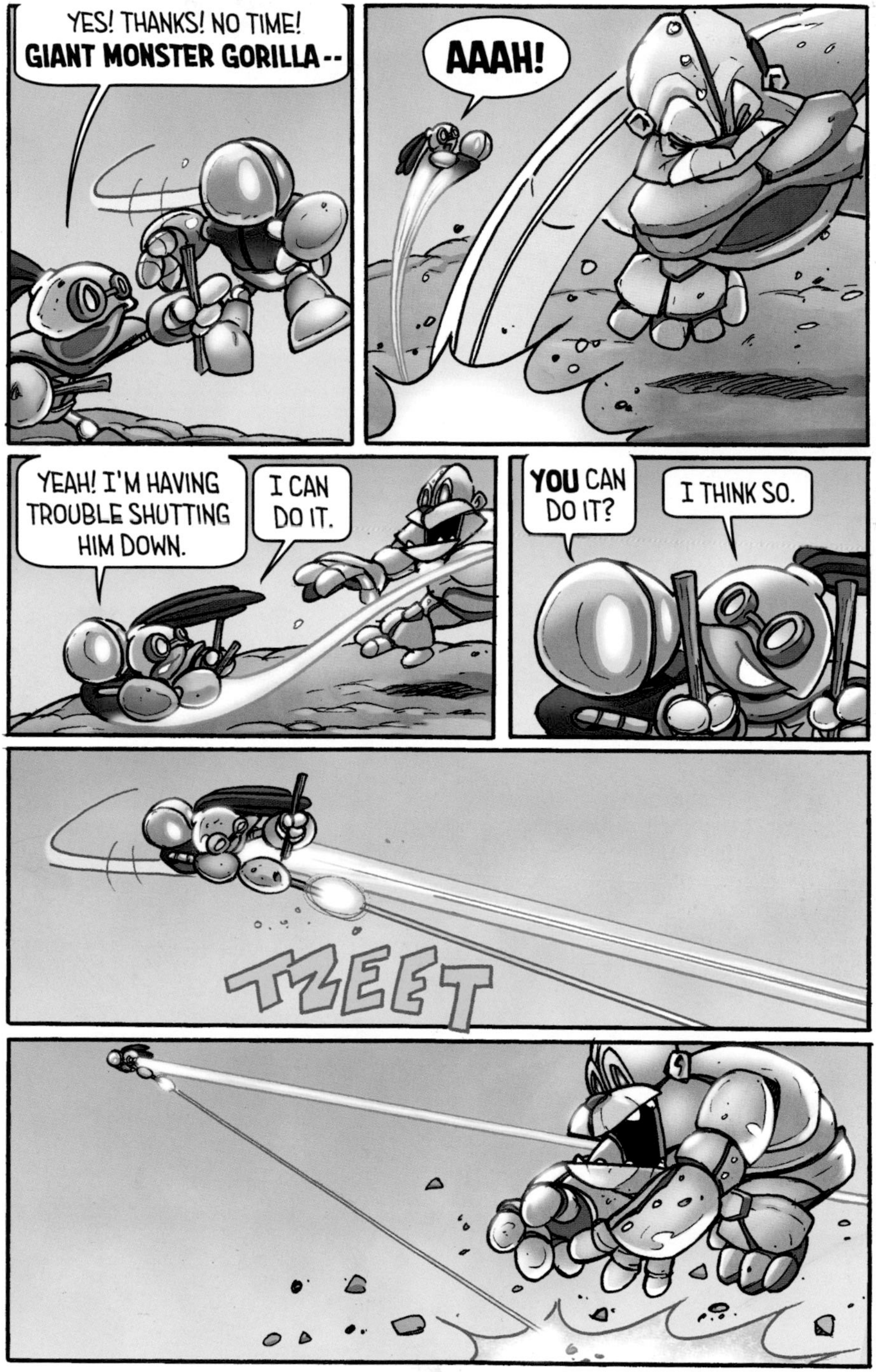
YES! THANKS! NO TIME!
GIANT MONSTER GORILLA --
AAAH!
YEAH! I'M HAVING TROUBLE SHUTTING HIM DOWN.
I CAN DO IT.
YOU CAN DO IT?
I THINK SO.
TZEET

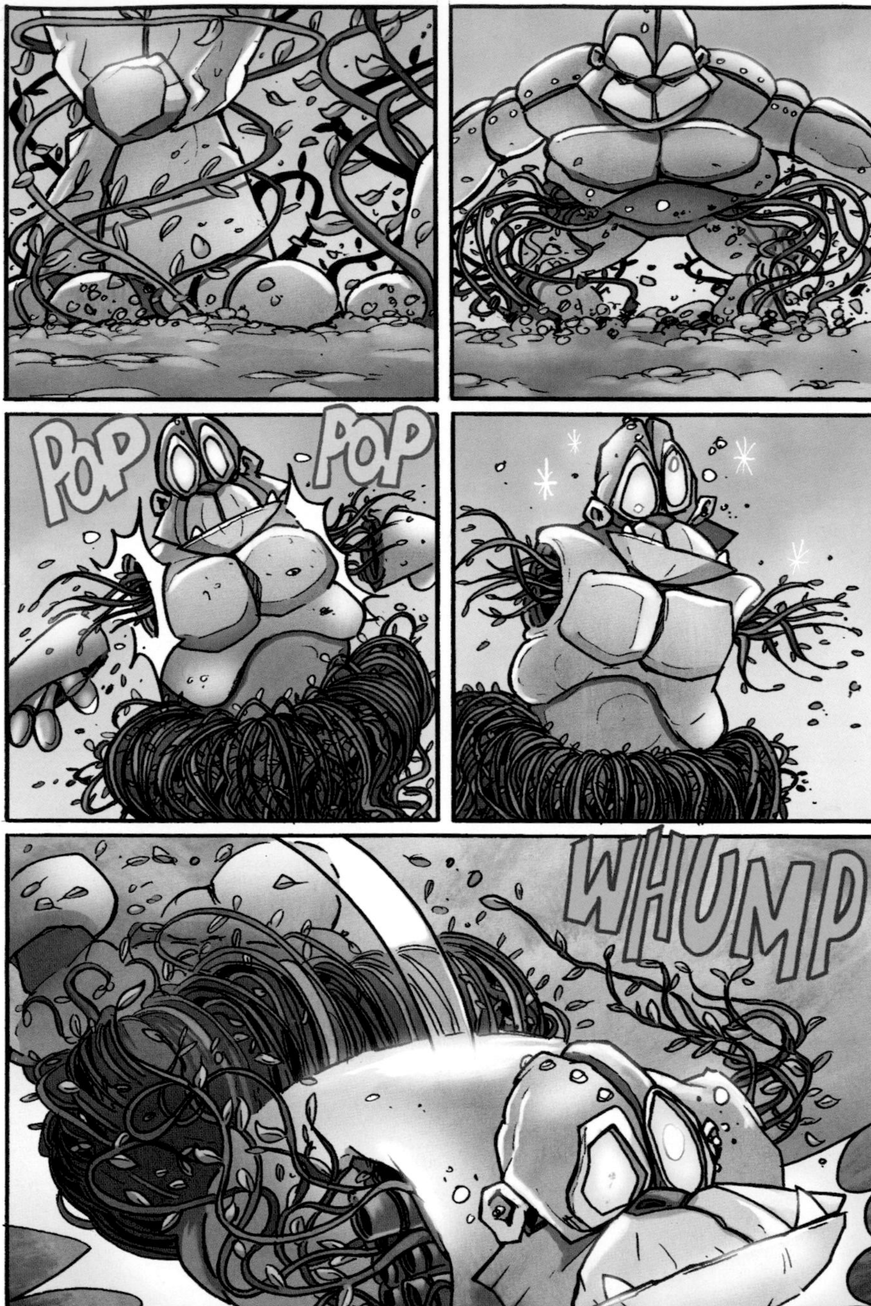
POP
POP
WHUMP

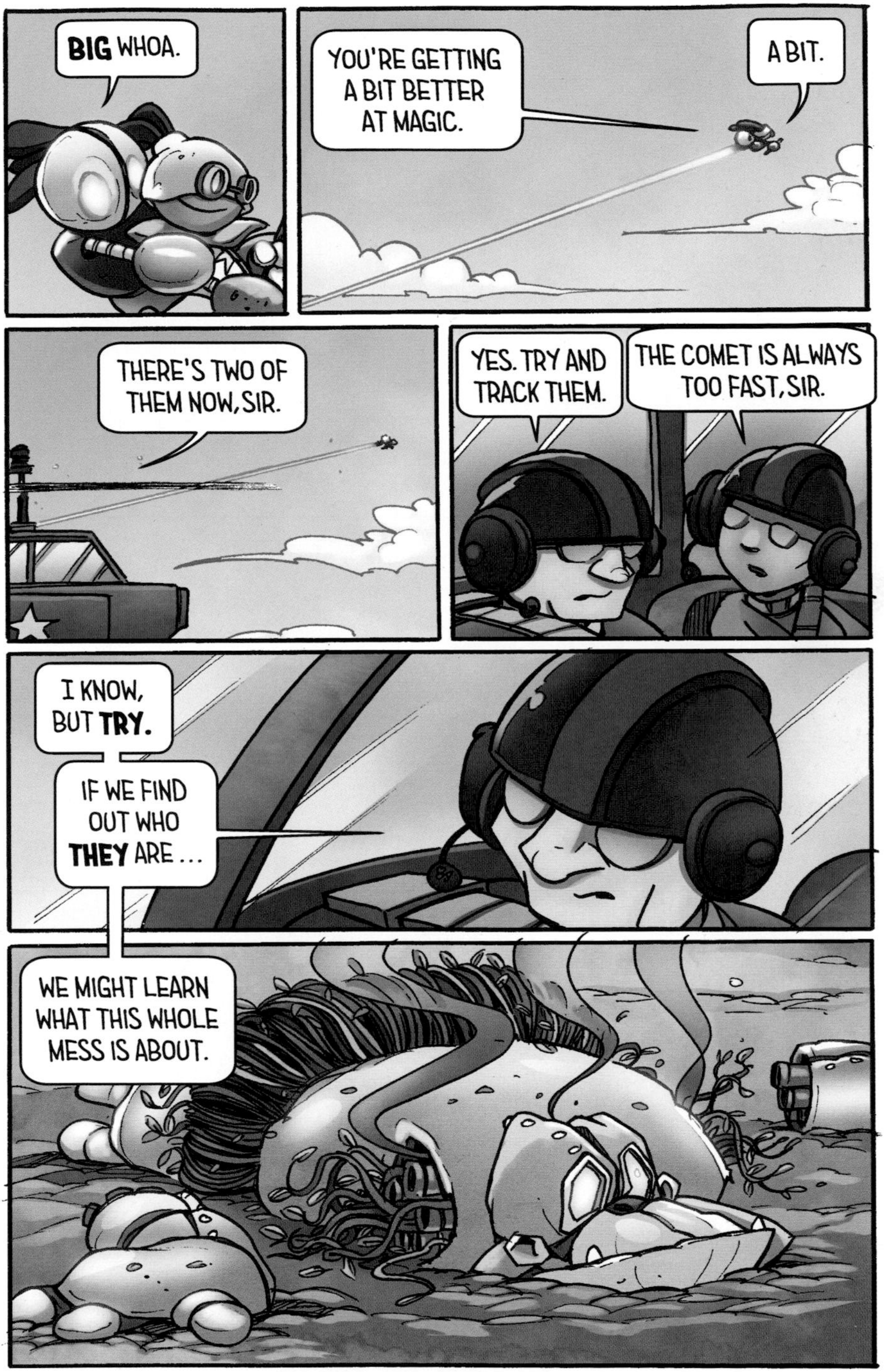
BIG WHOA.
YOU'RE GETTING A BIT BETTER AT MAGIC.
A BIT.
THERE'S TWO OF THEM NOW, SIR.
YES. TRY AND TRACK THEM.
THE COMET IS ALWAYS TOO FAST, SIR.
I KNOW, BUT TRY.
IF WE FIND OUT WHO THEY ARE ...
WE MIGHT LEARN WHAT THIS WHOLE MESS IS ABOUT.

CHAPTER 6

WE CAN BE HEROES

A GIANT METAL GORILLA AND A **HUGE** ROBOT MONKEY --
MARCHED ON THE CITY -- DISASTER SURELY JUST MOMENTS AWAY.
THIS TIME **THE COMET** CAME TO THE RESCUE WITH A **NEW** SUPERHERO BY HIS SIDE.

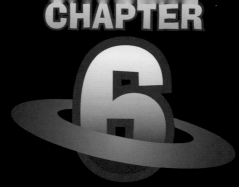

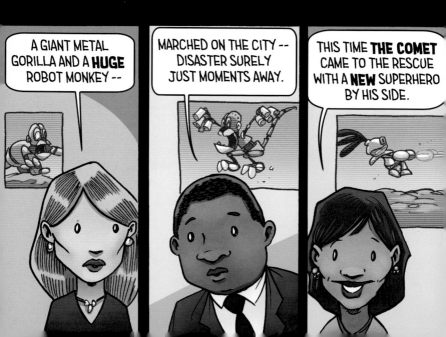

101

105

106

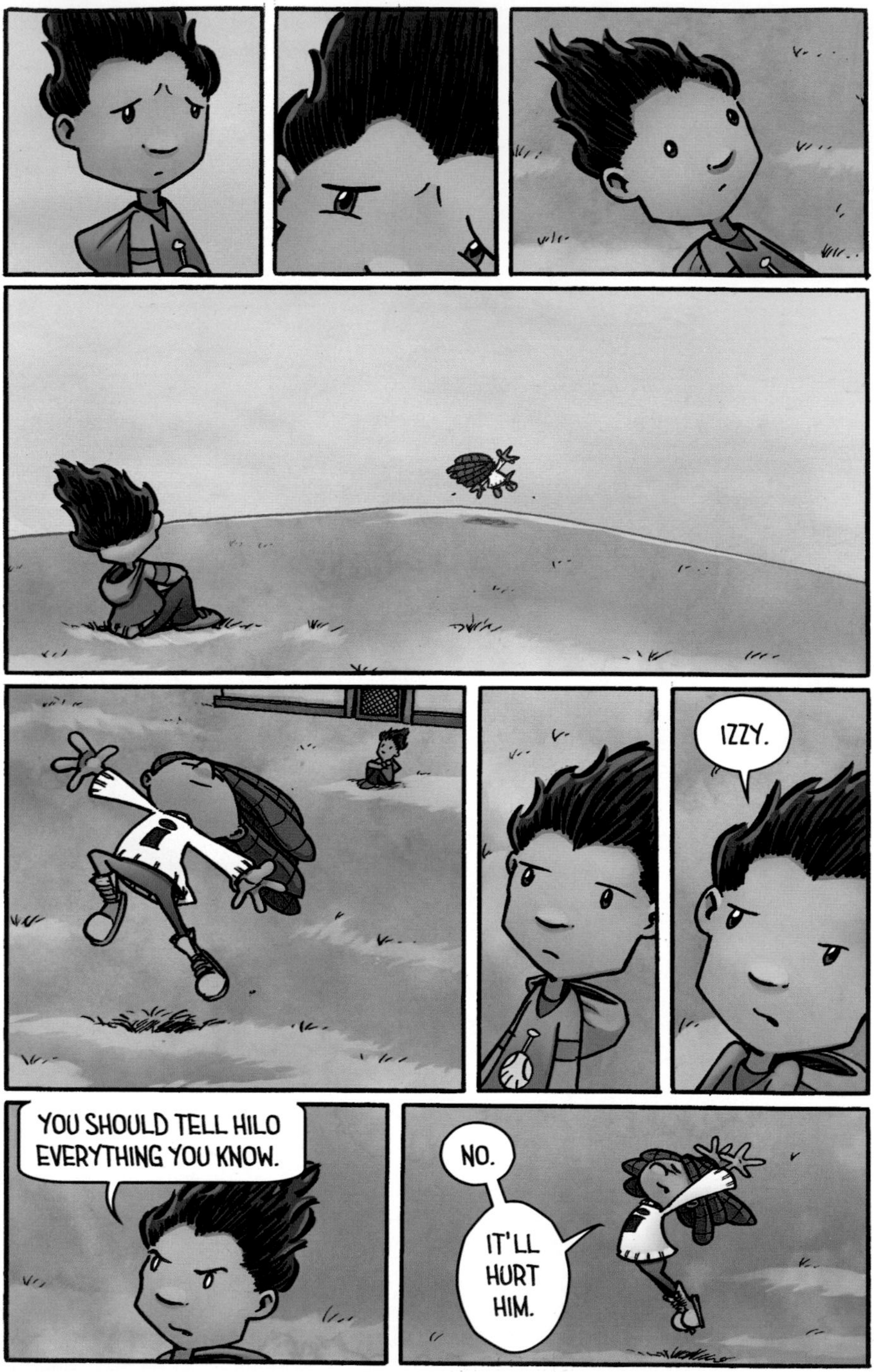
IZZY.
YOU SHOULD TELL HILO EVERYTHING YOU KNOW.
NO.
IT'LL HURT HIM.

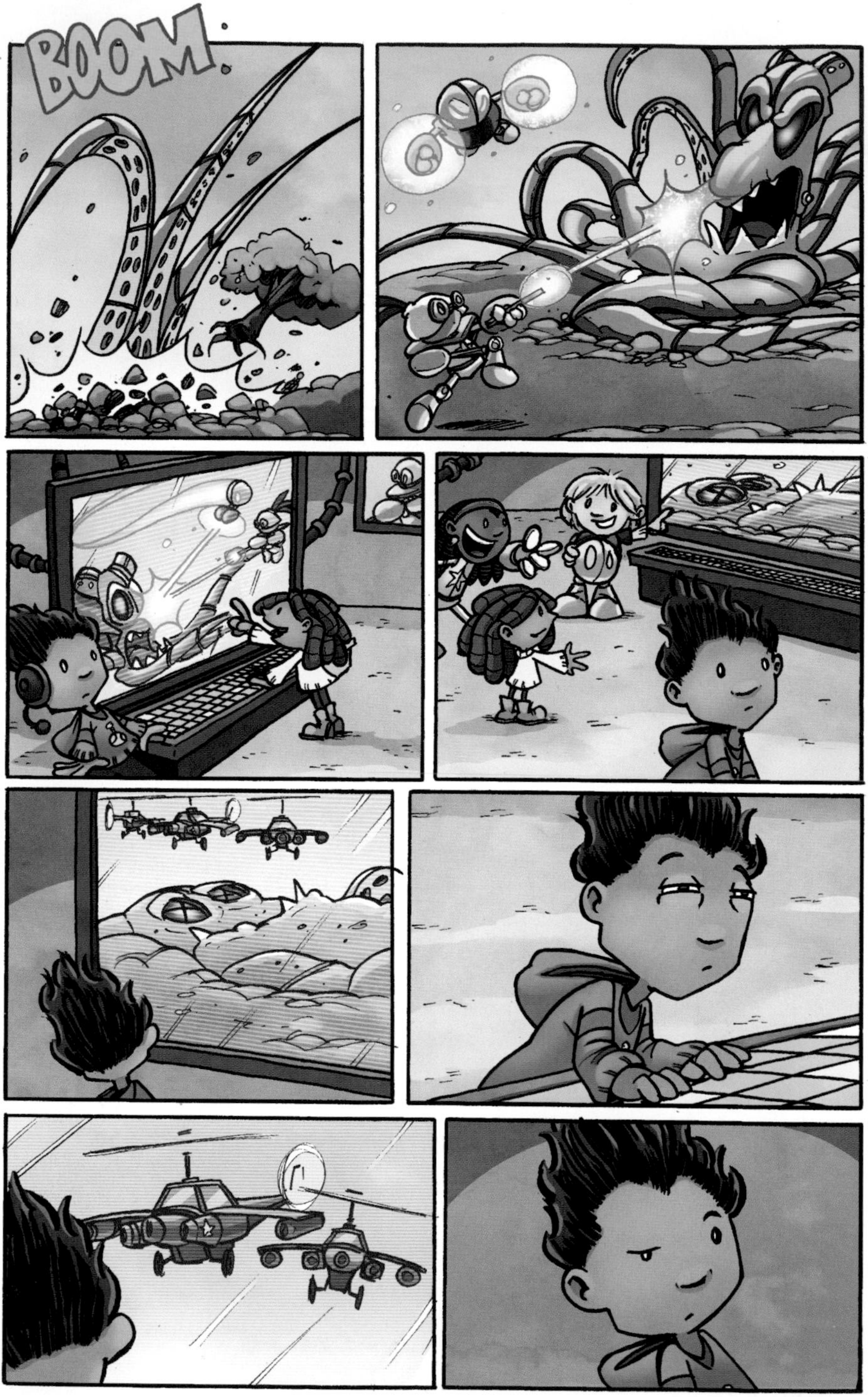
BOOM!

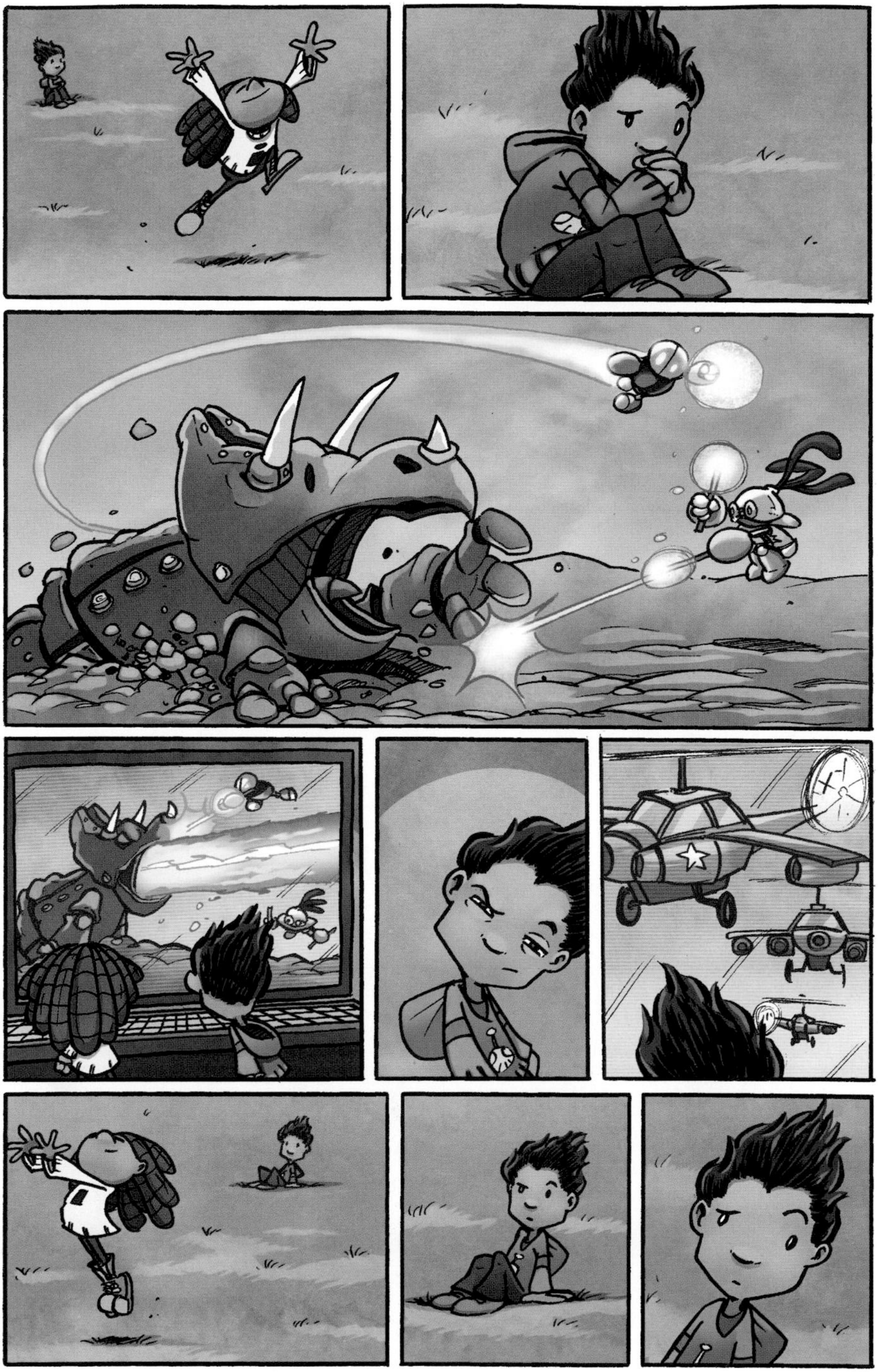

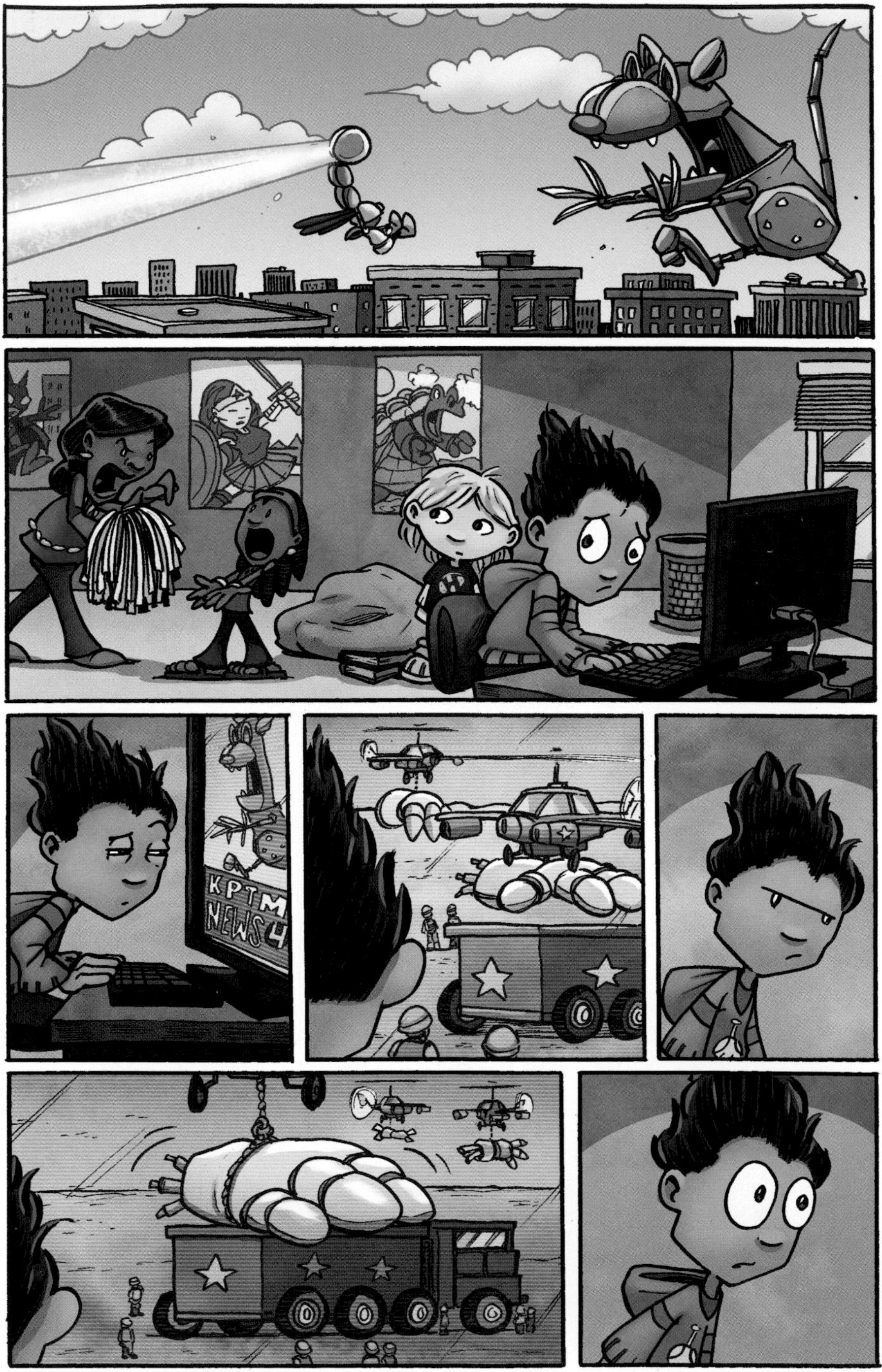
KPTM
NEWS 4

120

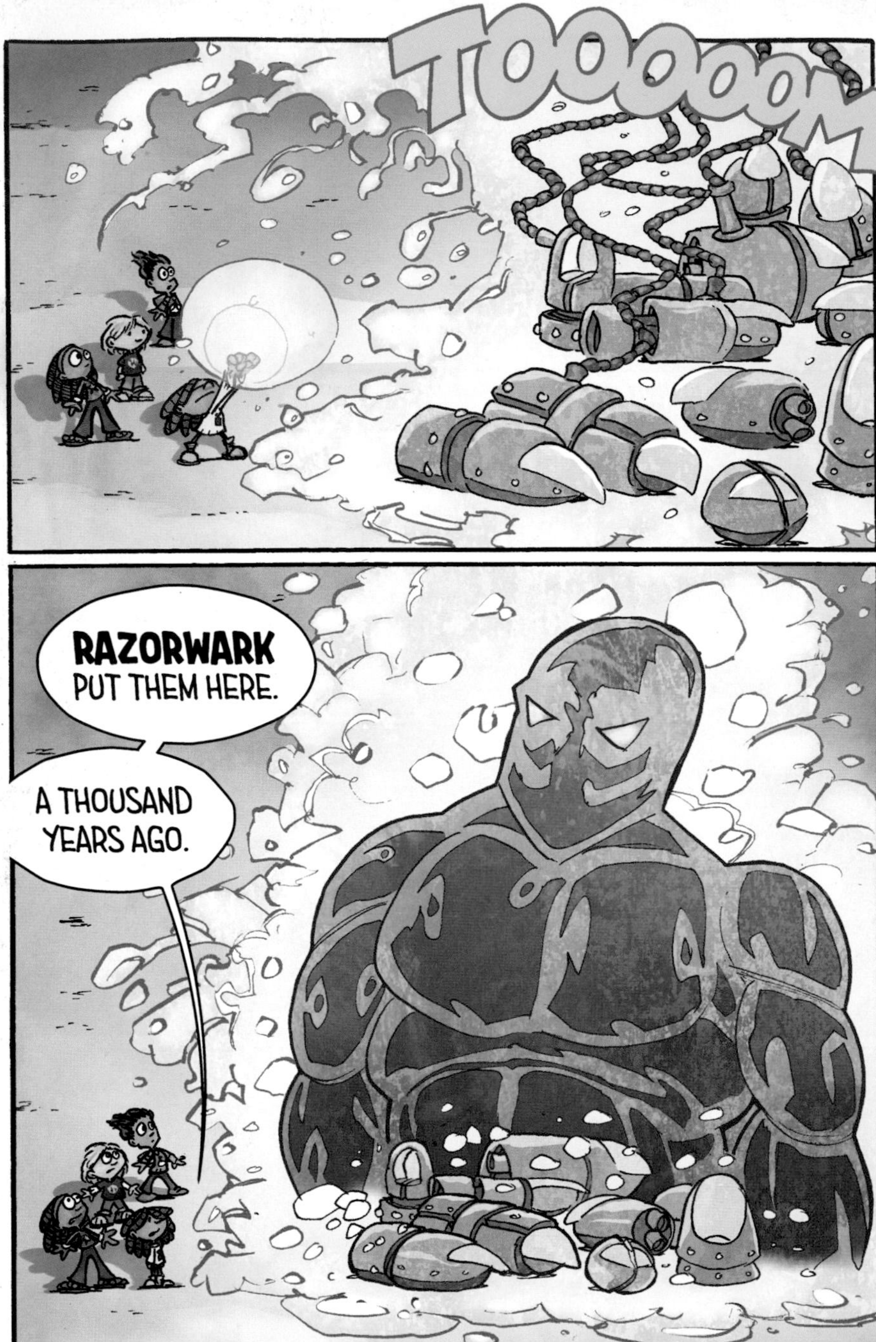
TOOOOOM
RAZORWARK PUT THEM HERE.
A THOUSAND YEARS AGO.

CHAPTER 7

SECTOR E

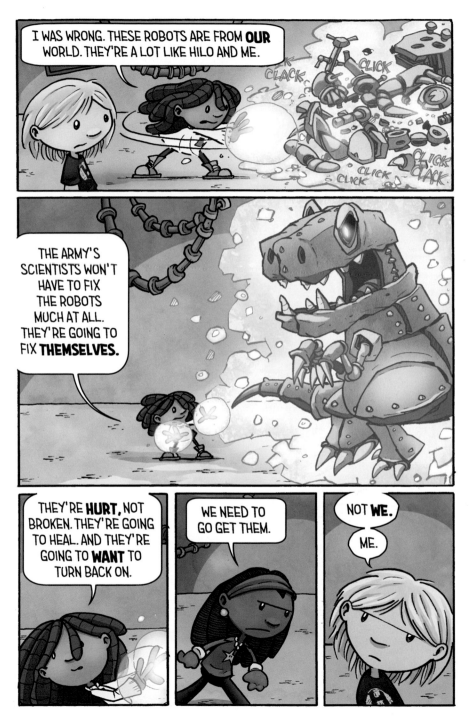

127

130

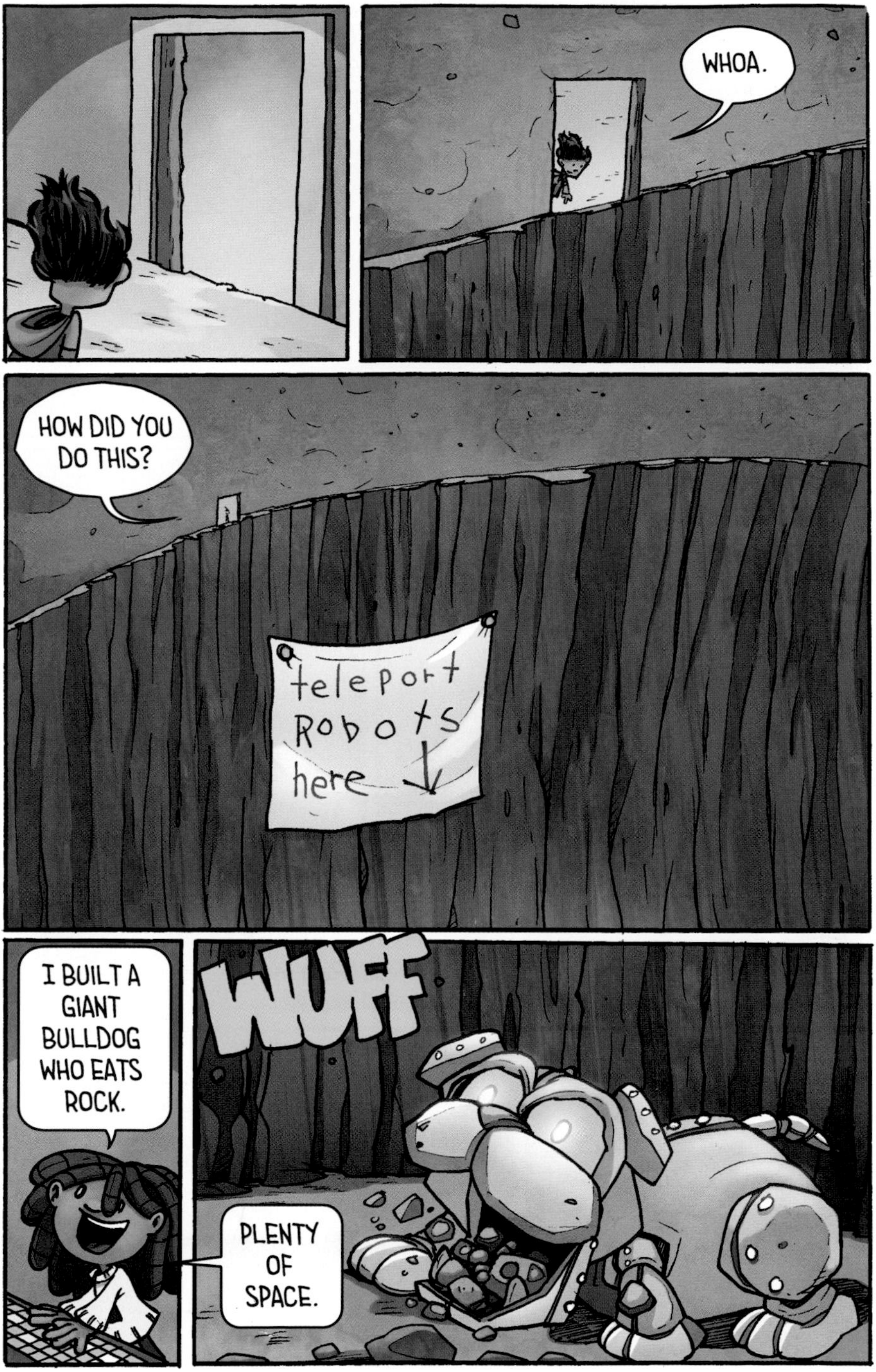
WHOA.
HOW DID YOU DO THIS?
teleport Robots here
I BUILT A GIANT BULLDOG WHO EATS ROCK.
WUFF
PLENTY OF SPACE.

139

CHAPTER 8

BANANAS

E
BOOM

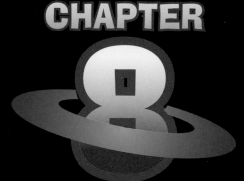

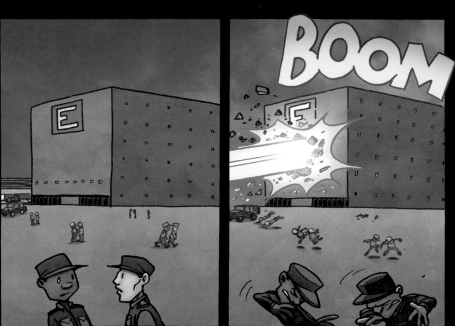

145

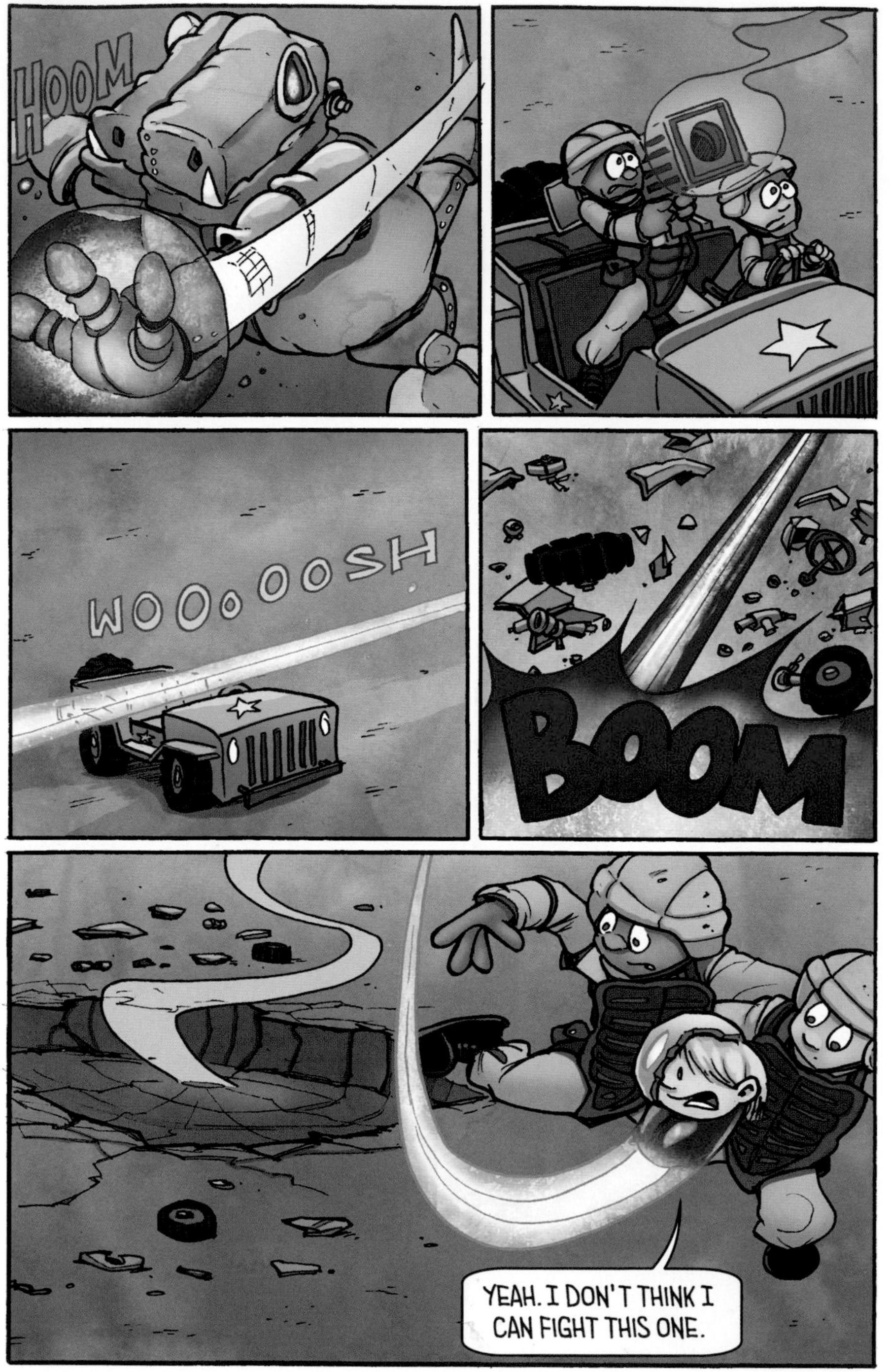

HOOM
WOO.OOSH
BOOM
YEAH. I DON'T THINK I CAN FIGHT THIS ONE.

147

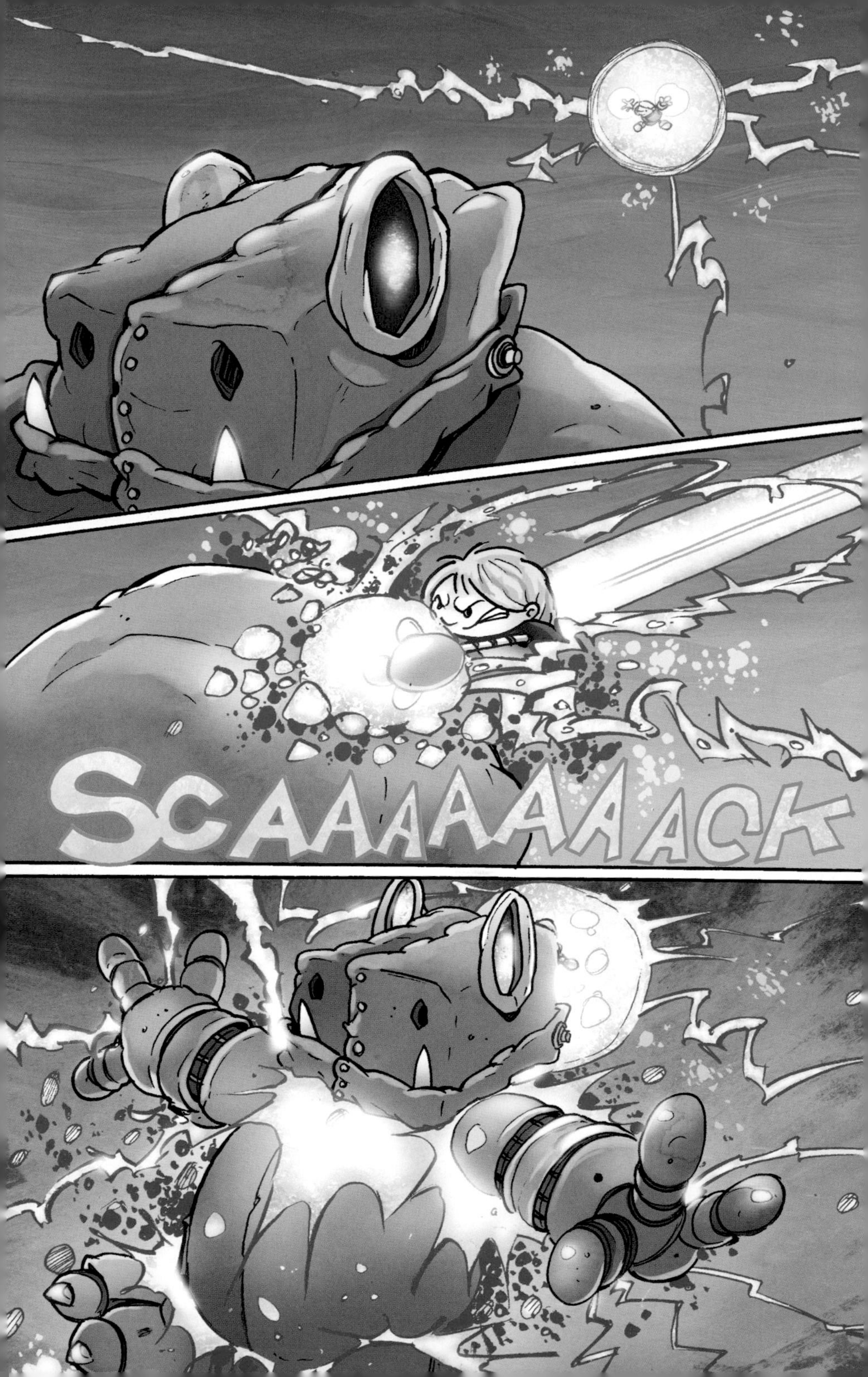
SCAAAAAACK

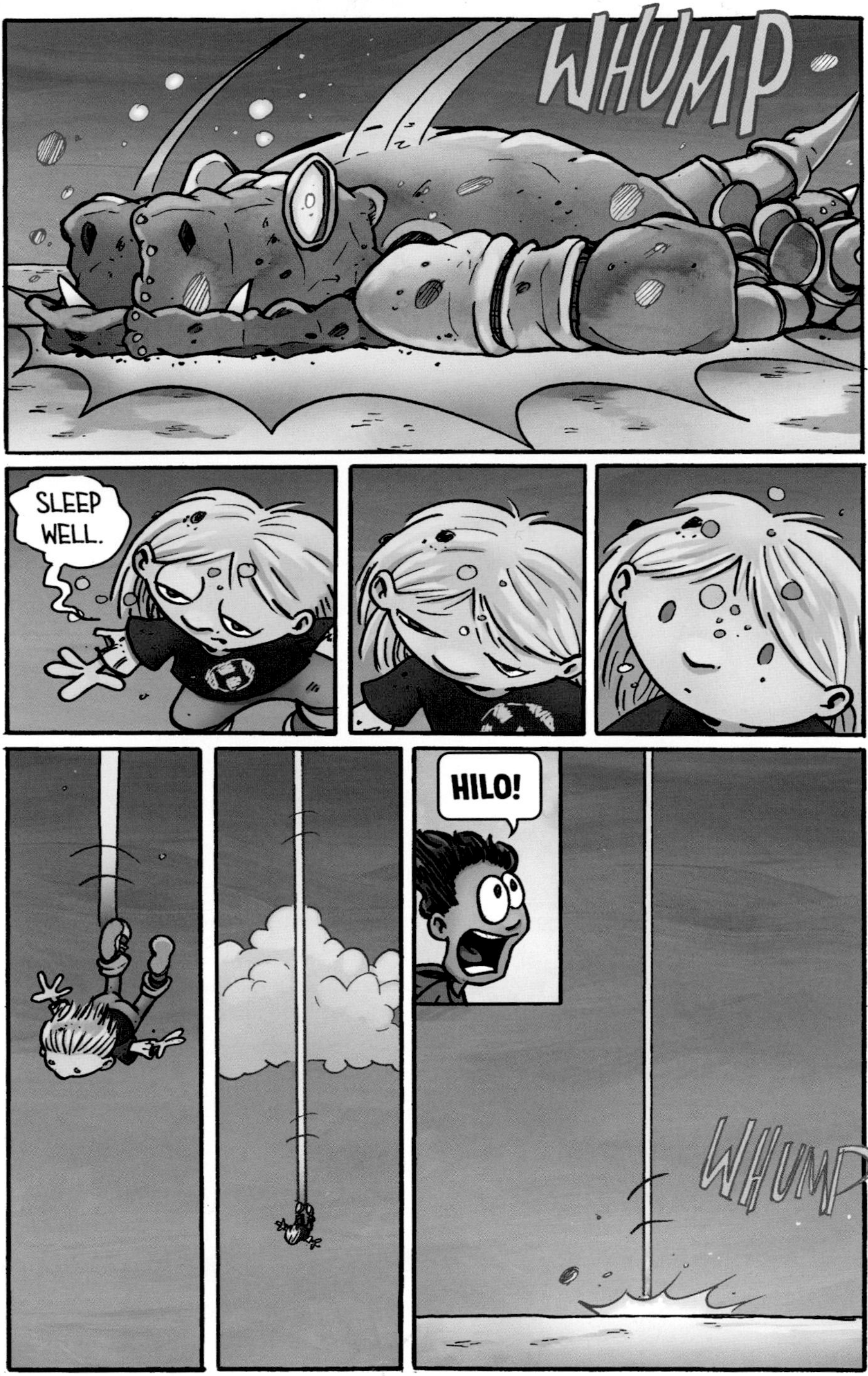
WHUMP
SLEEP WELL.
HILO!
WHUMP

152

153

154

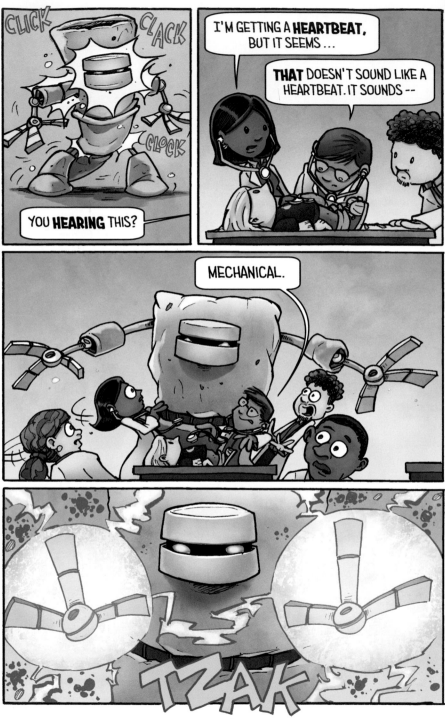

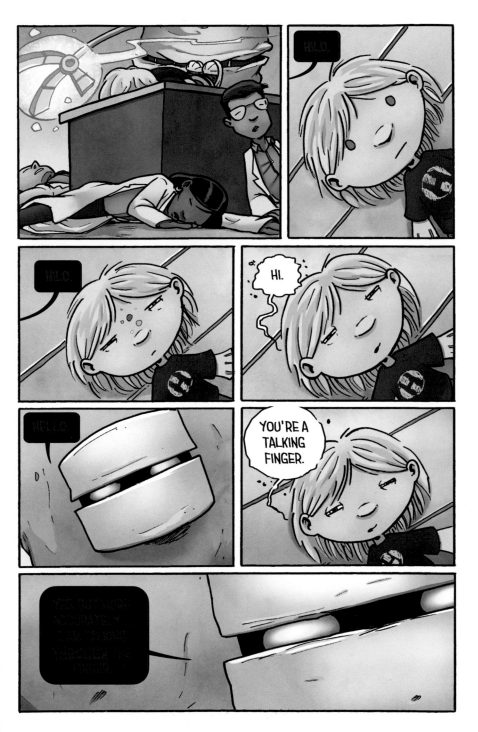

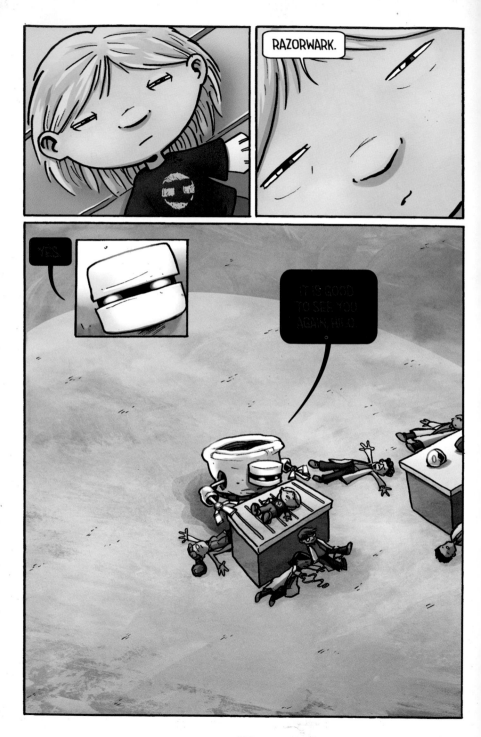

CHAPTER 9

LIKE YOU. LIKE ME.

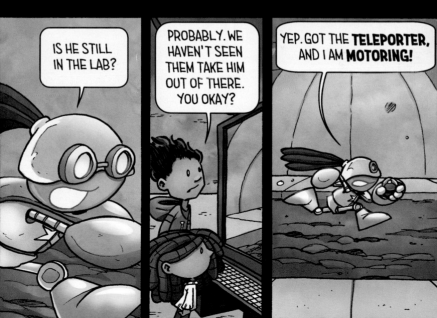

160

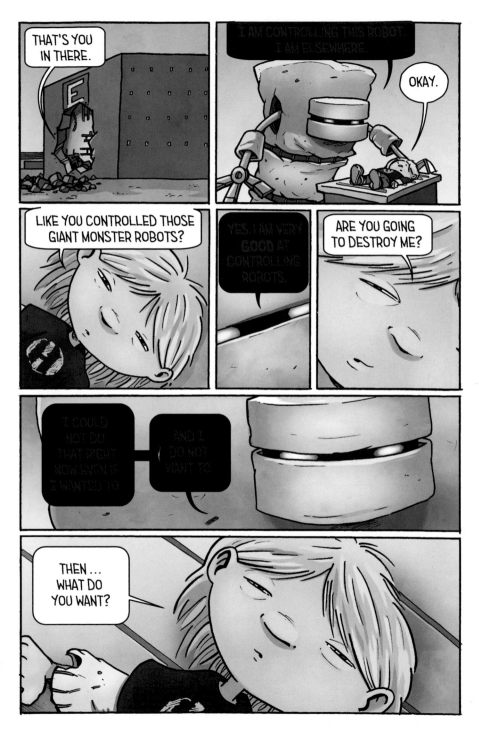

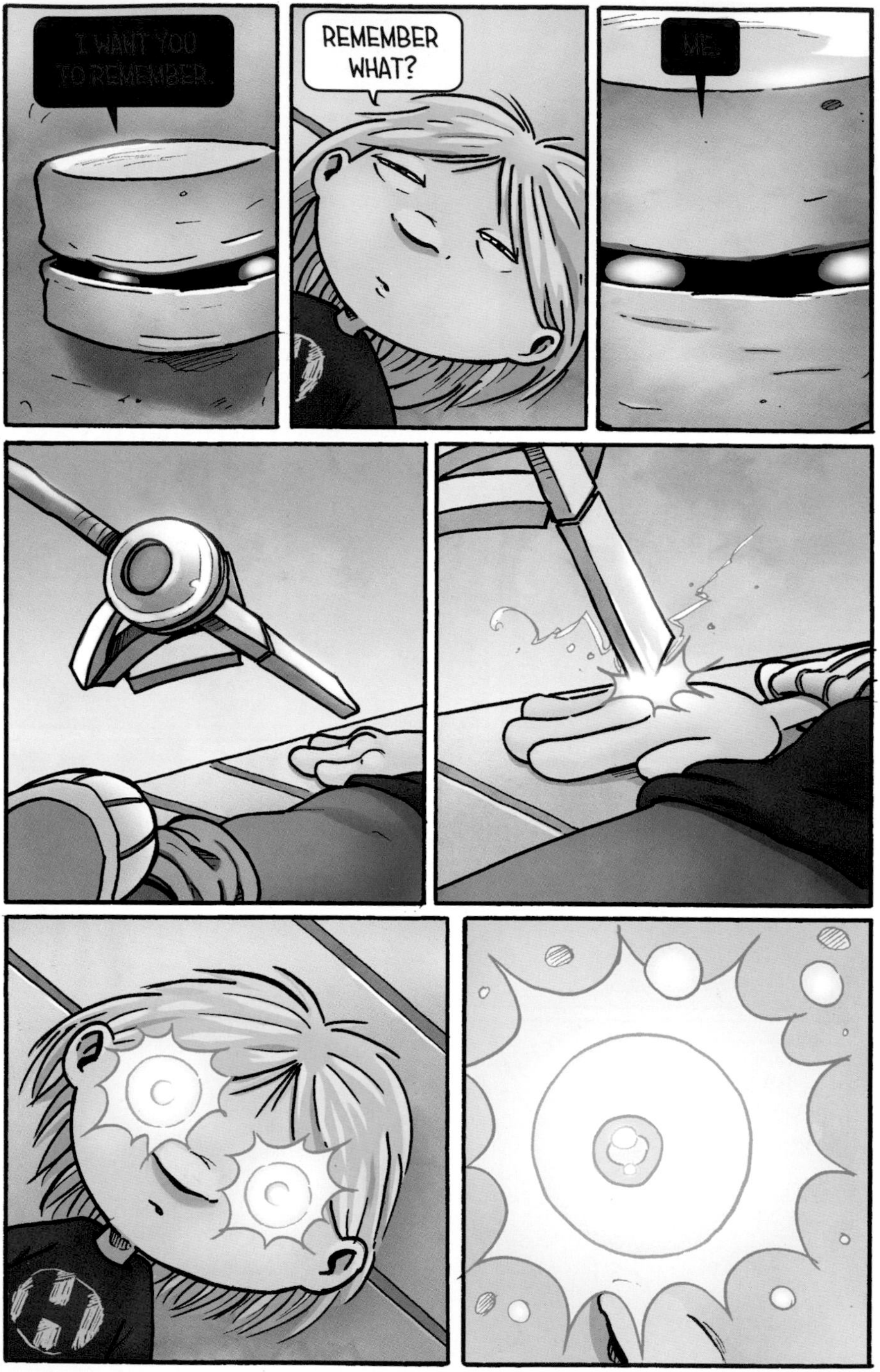
I WANT YOU TO REMEMBER.
REMEMBER WHAT?
ME.

163

164

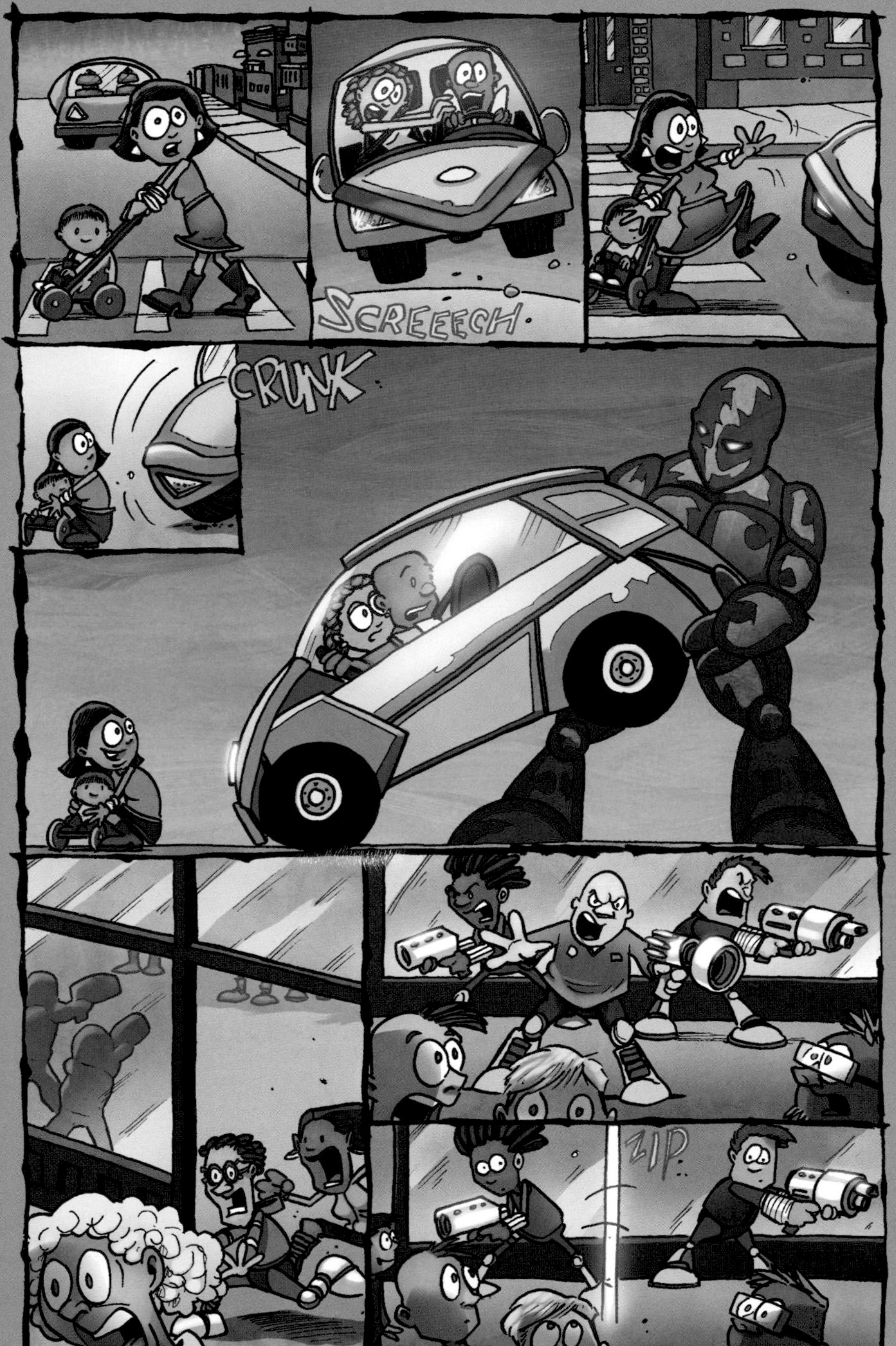
SCREEECH
CRUNK
ZIP

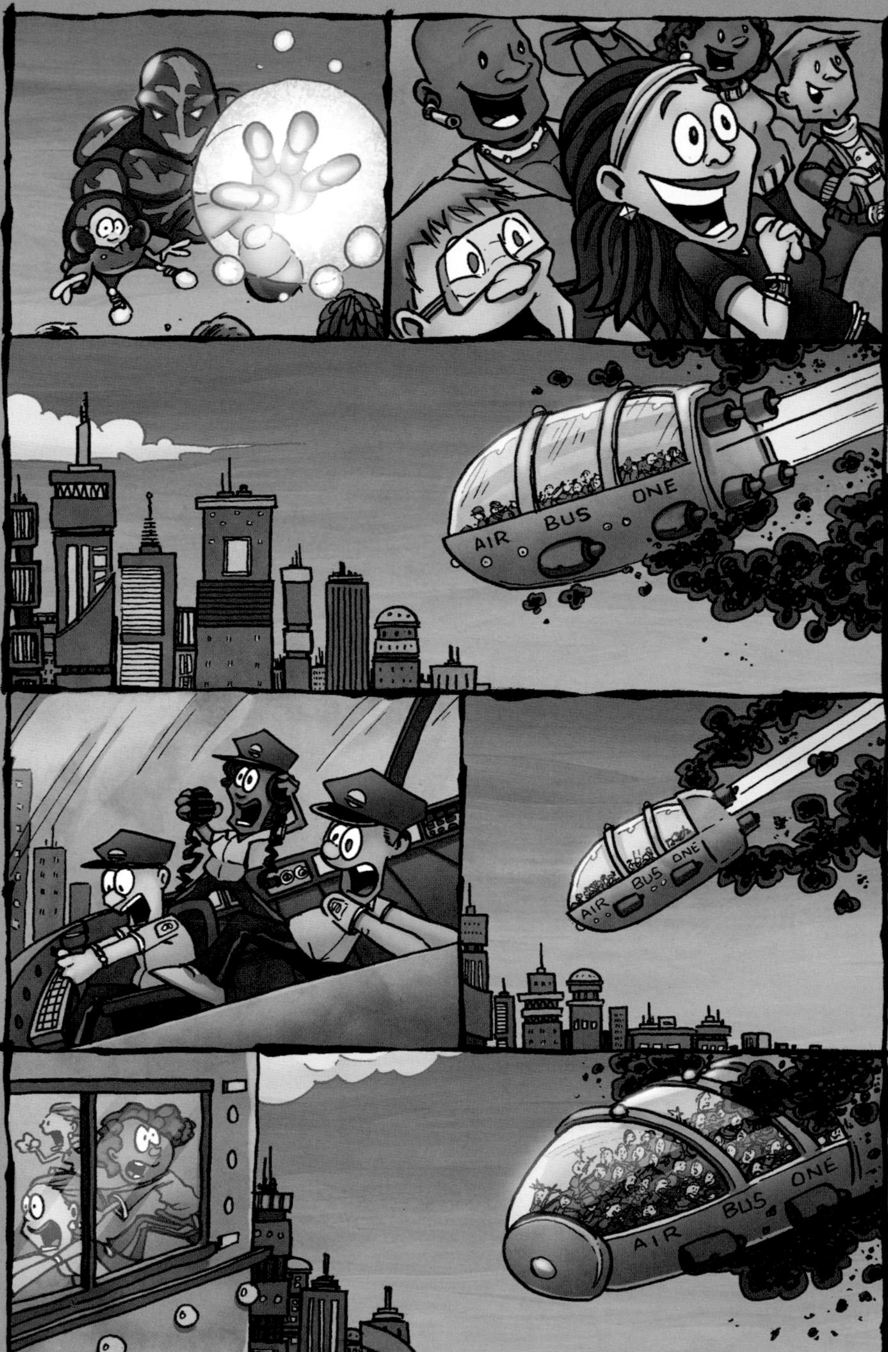
AIR BUS ONE
AIR BUS ONE
AIR BUS ONE

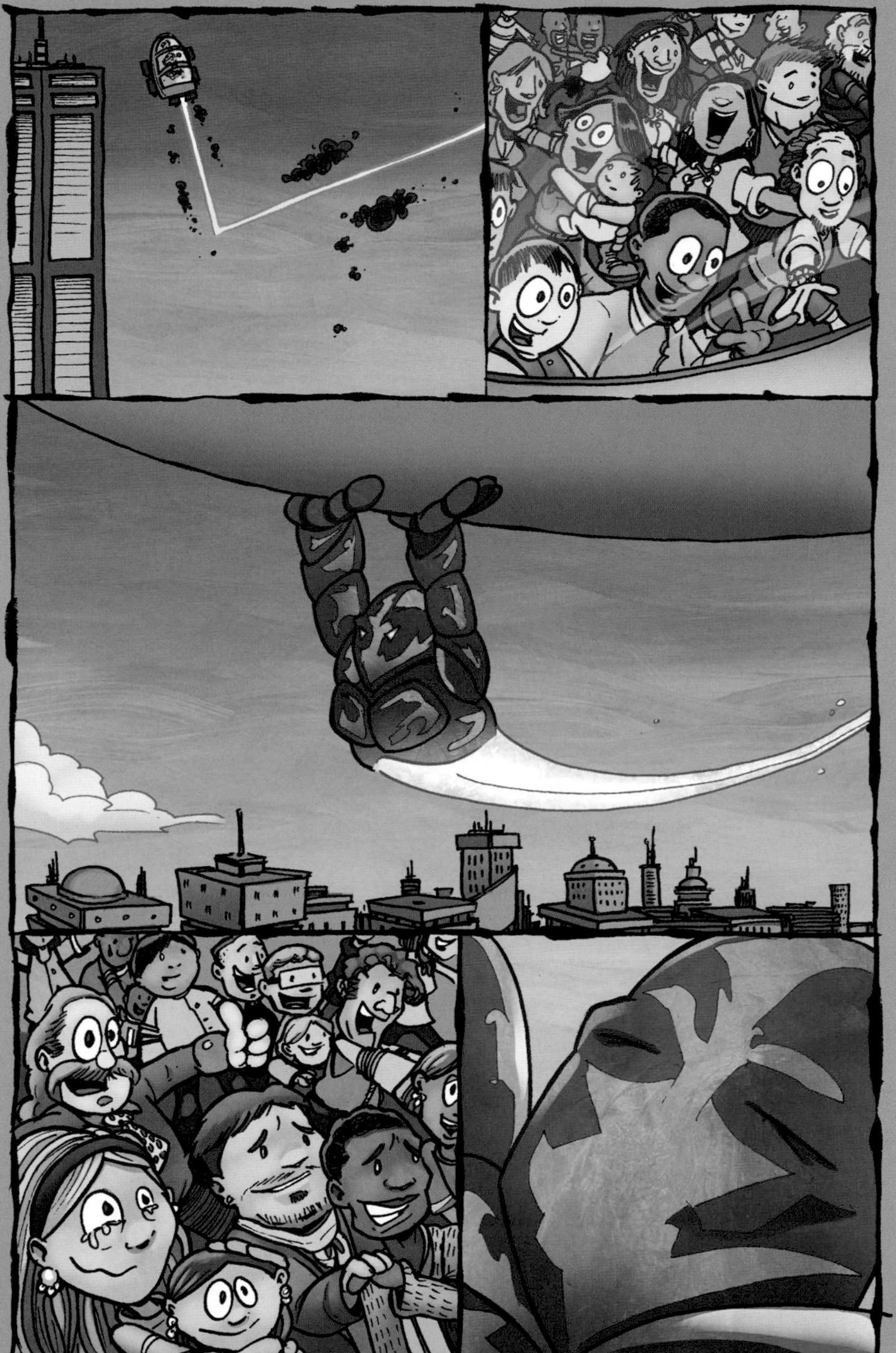

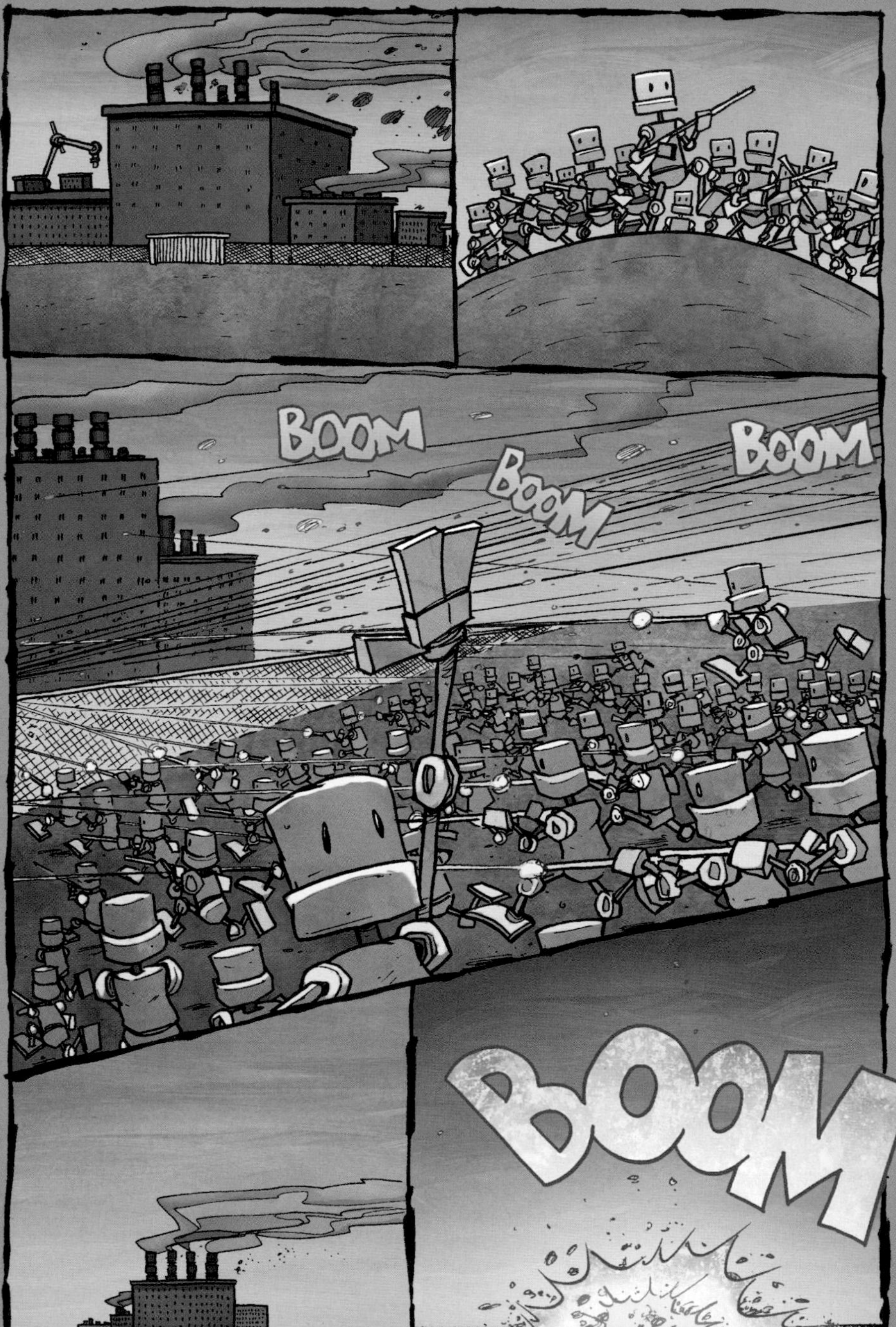
BOOM
BOOM
BOOM
BOOM

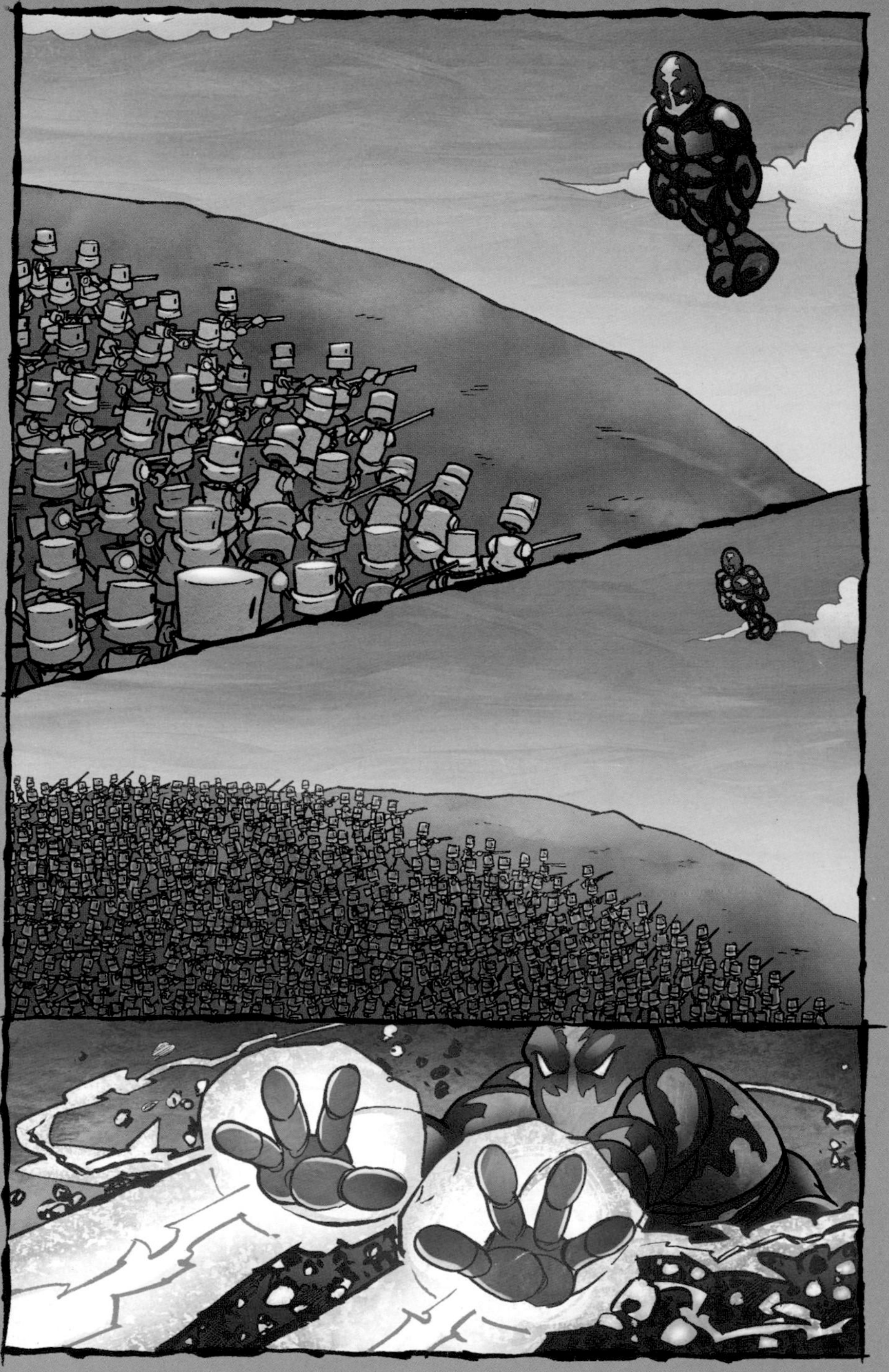

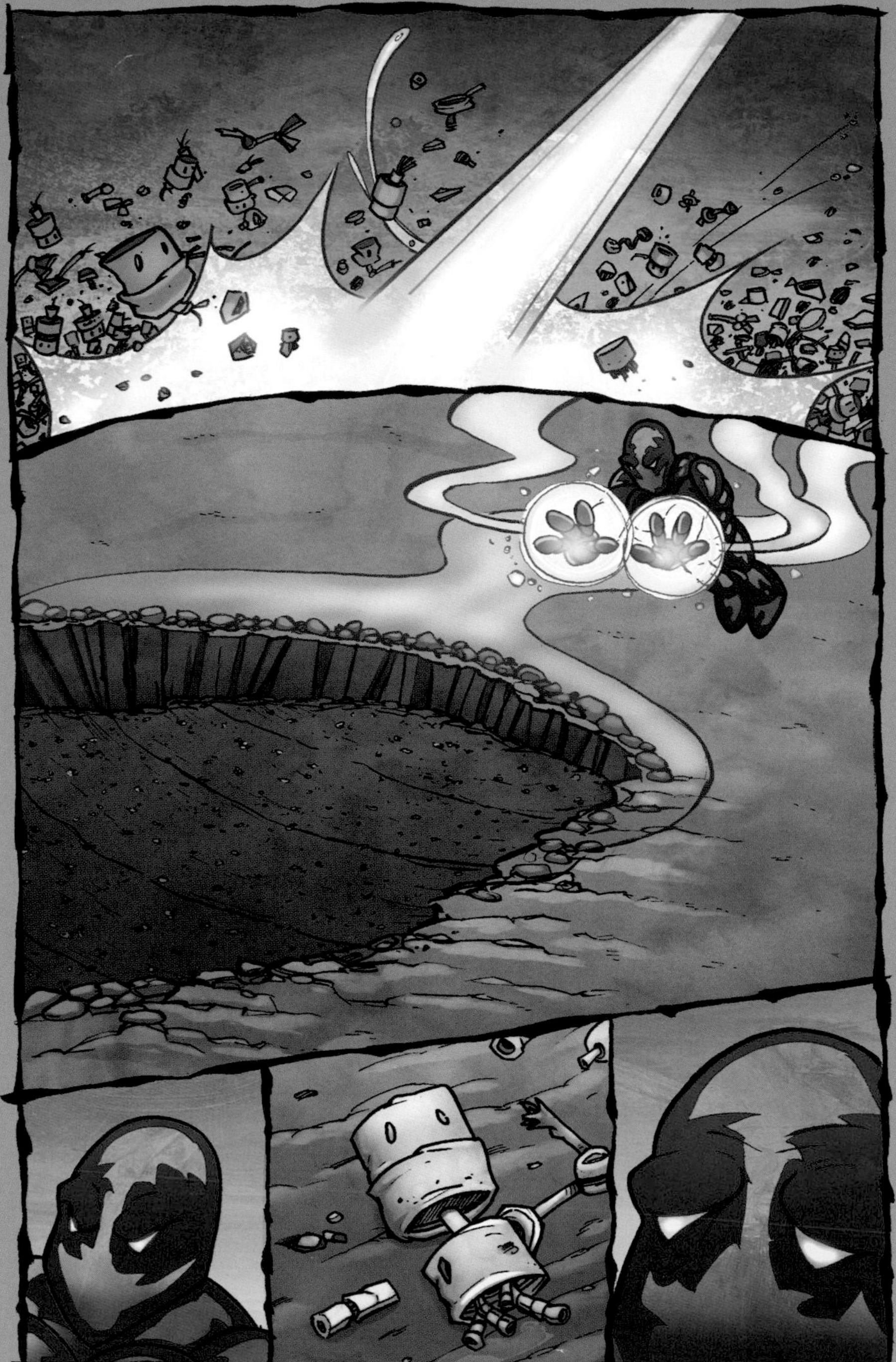

173

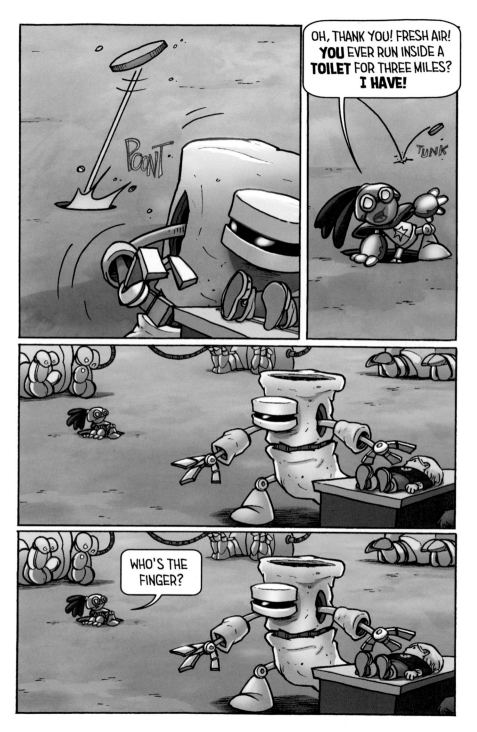

CHAPTER 10

THE LAST DANCE

177

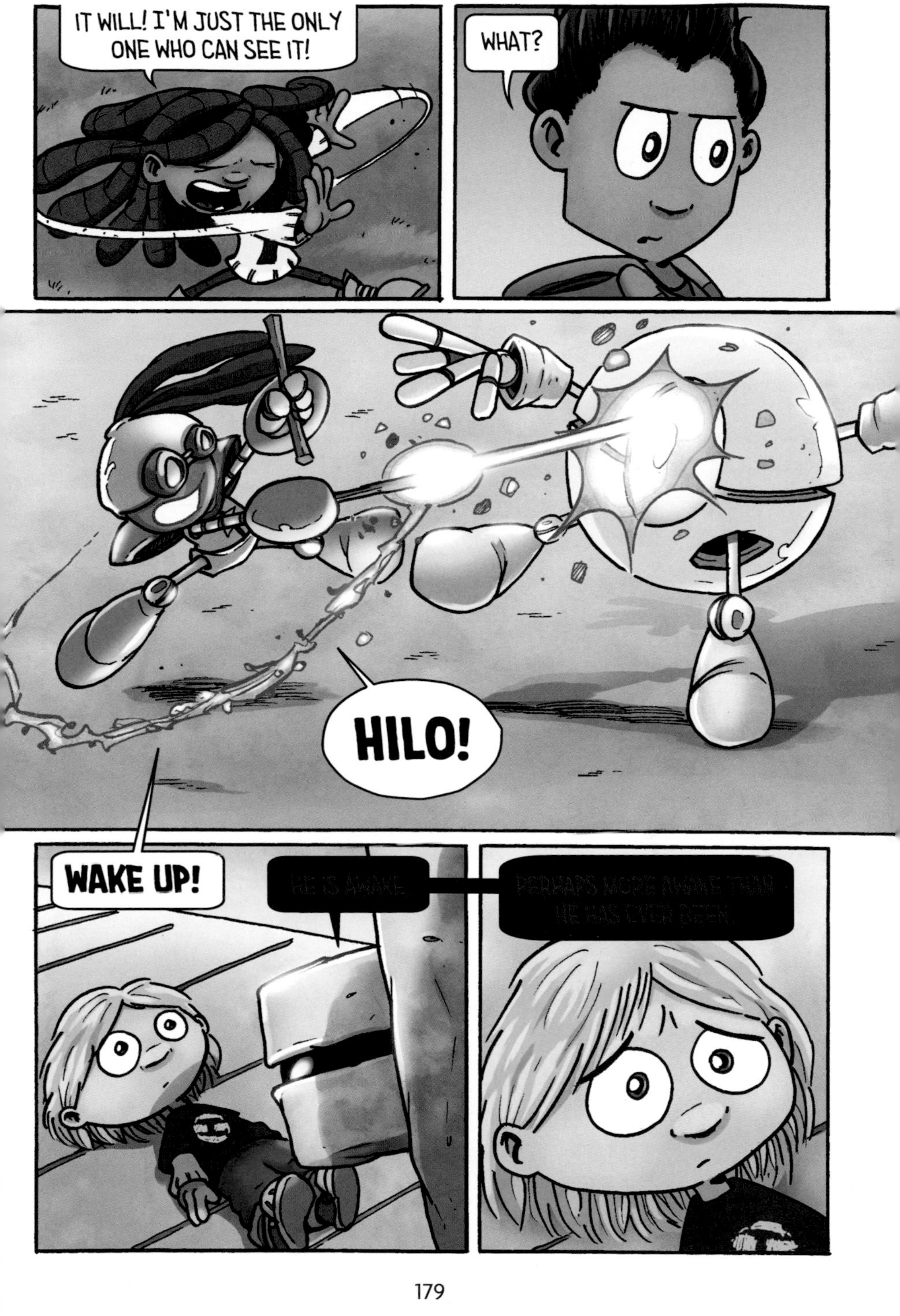
IT WILL! I'M JUST THE ONLY ONE WHO CAN SEE IT!
WHAT?
HILO!
WAKE UP!
HE IS AWAKE.
PERHAPS MORE AWAKE THAN HE HAS EVER BEEN.

181

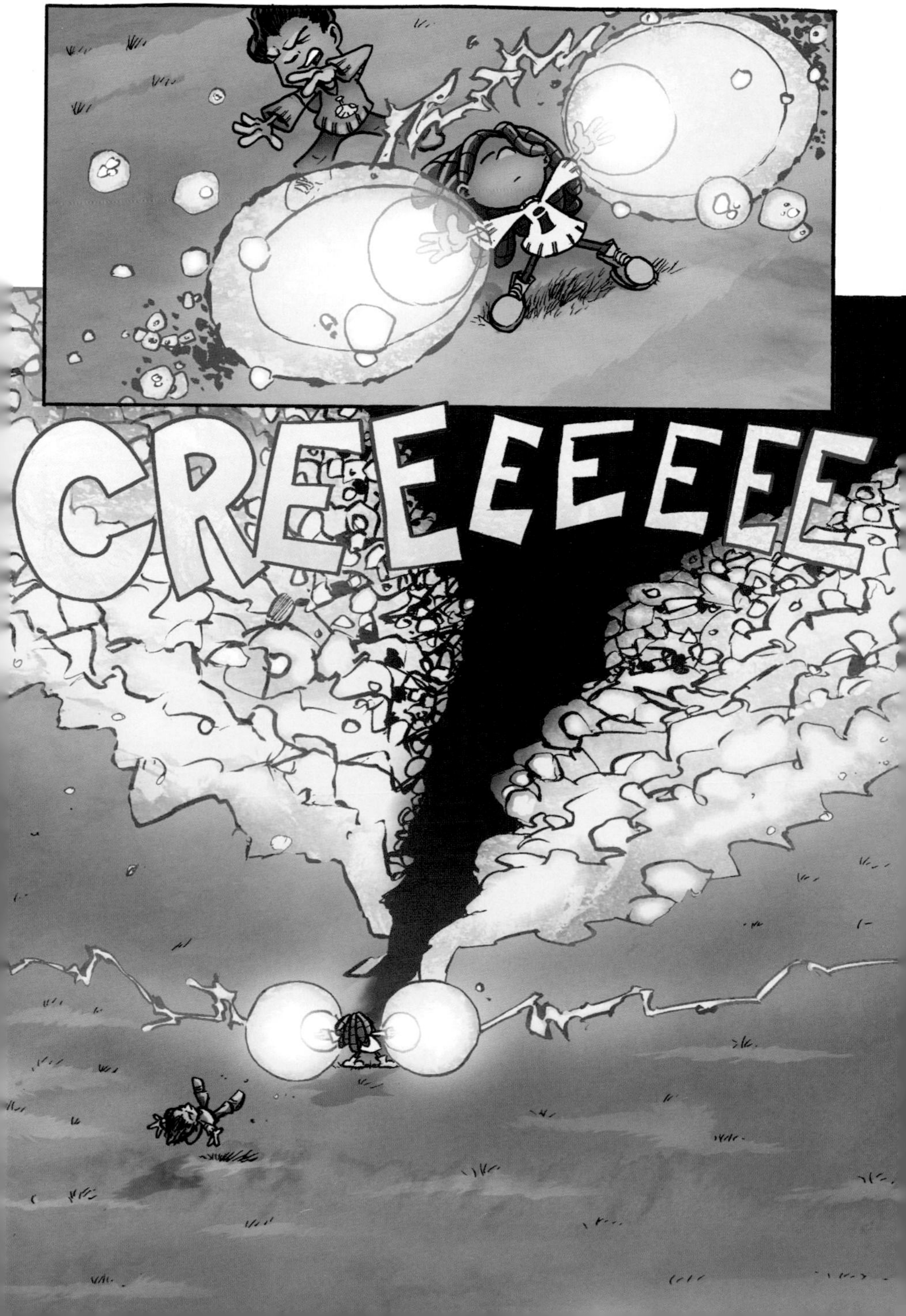
CREEEEEE

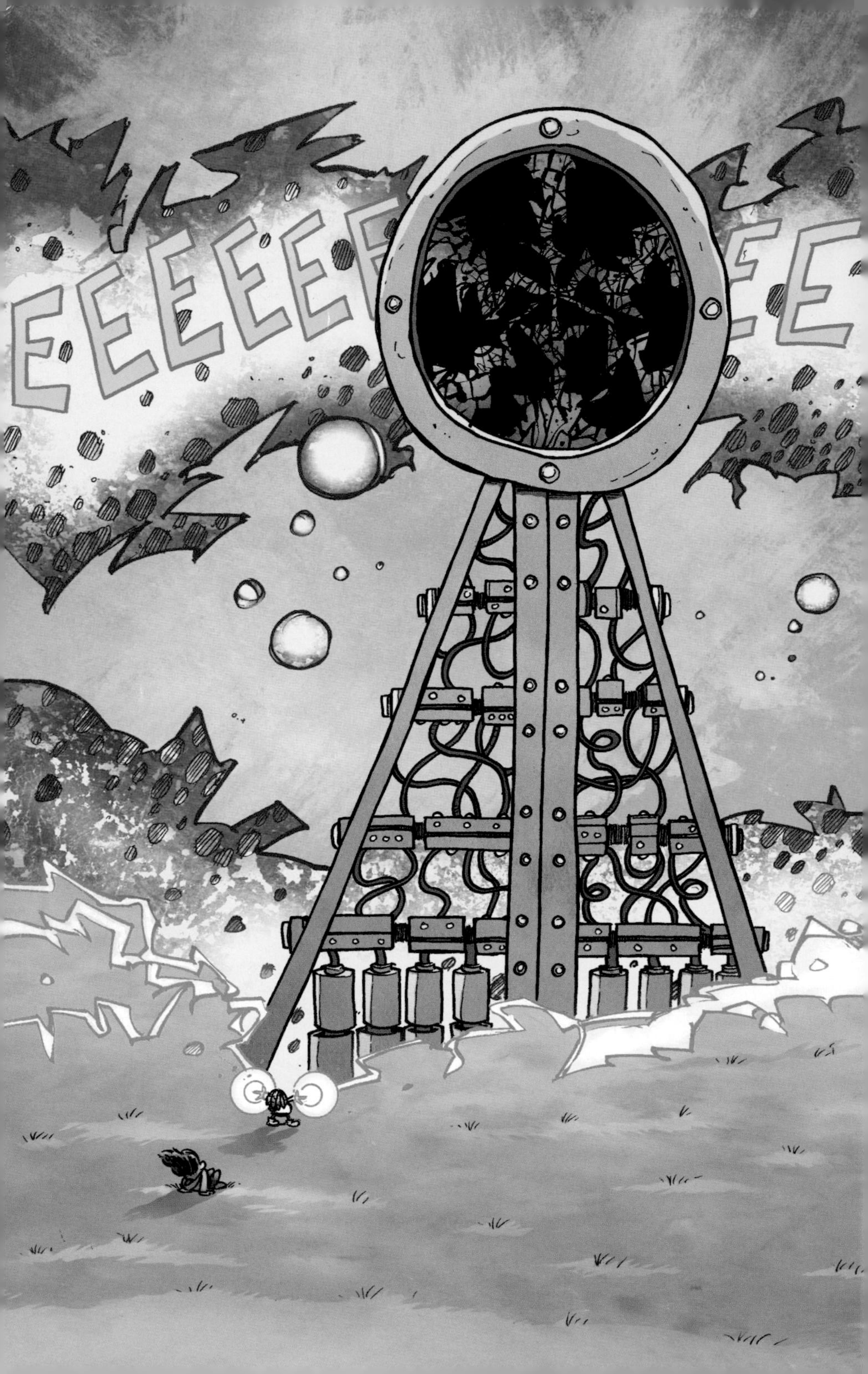
EEEEEE
EE

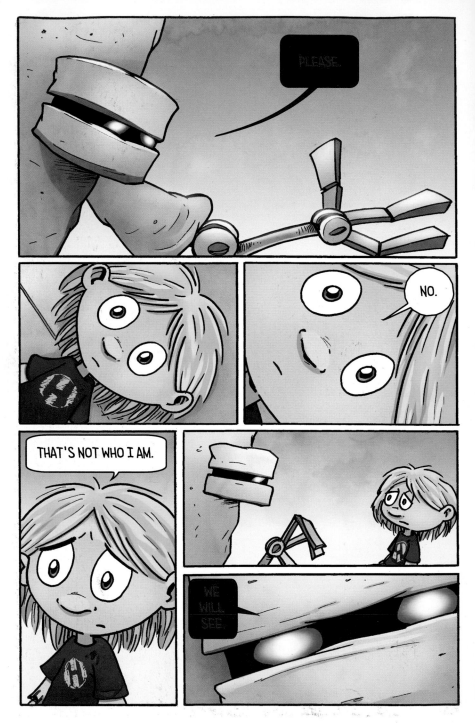

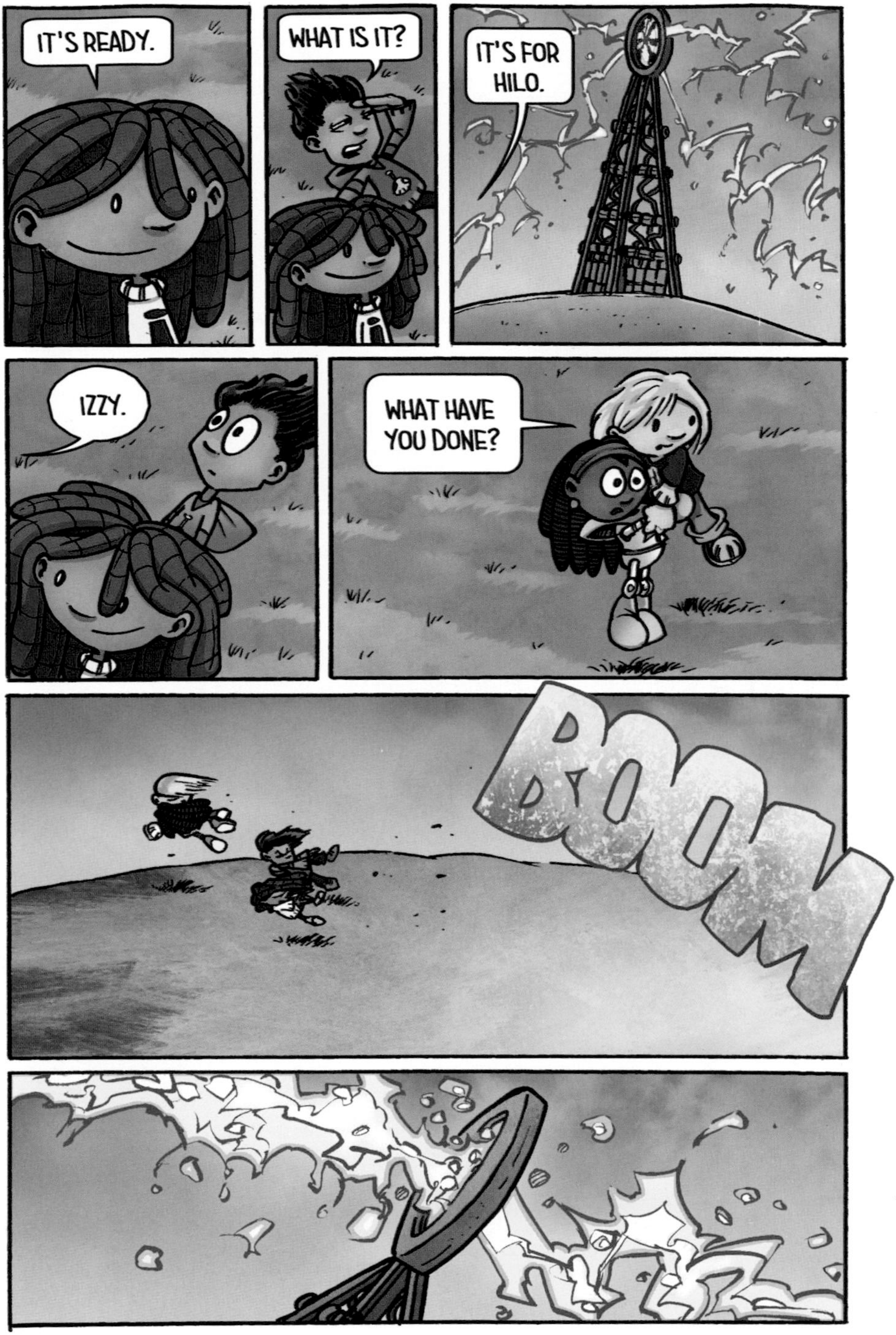
IT'S READY.
WHAT IS IT?
IT'S FOR HILO.
IZZY.
WHAT HAVE YOU DONE?
BOOM

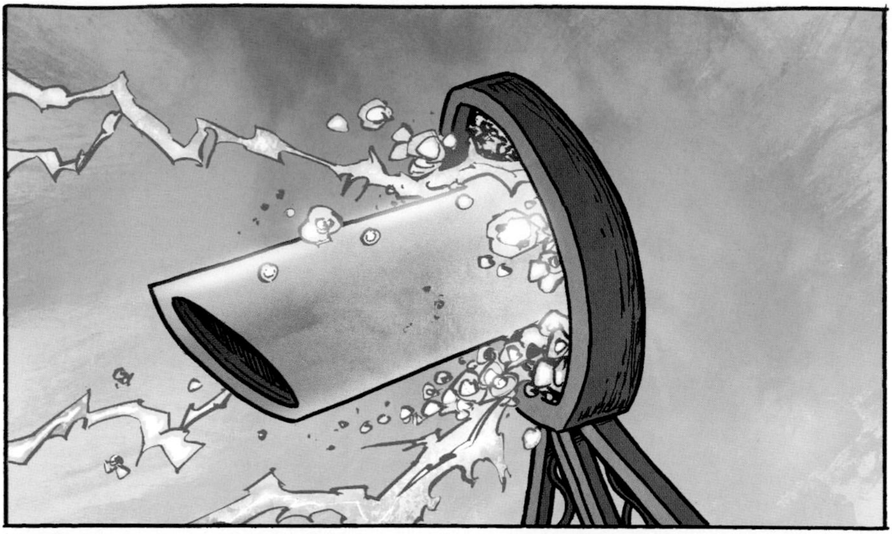
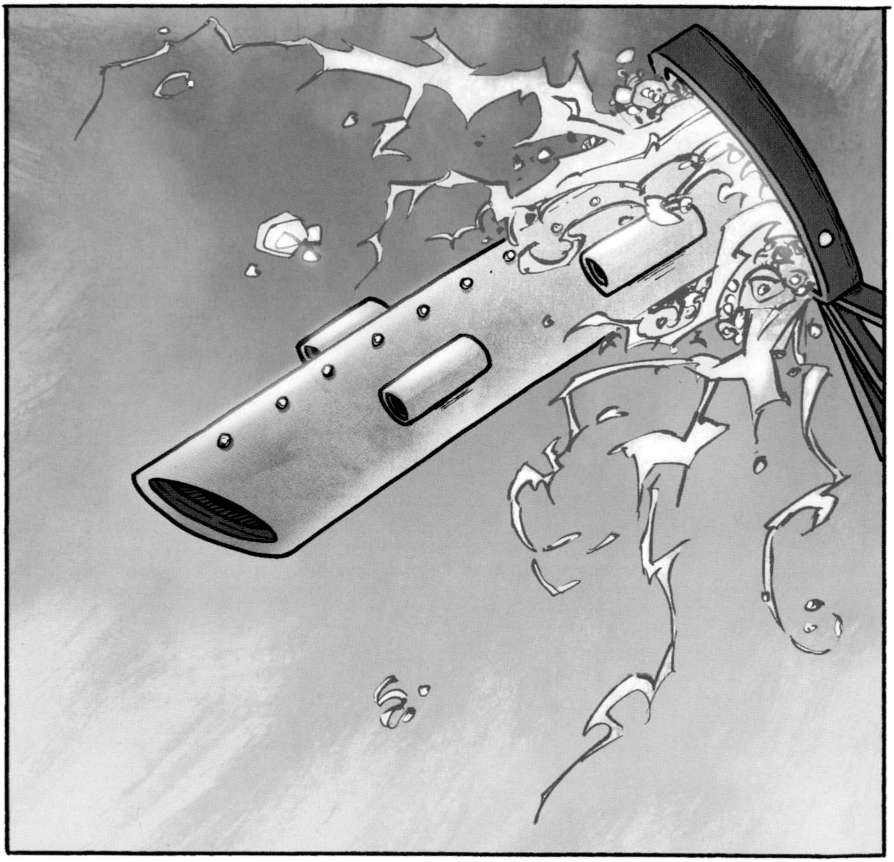

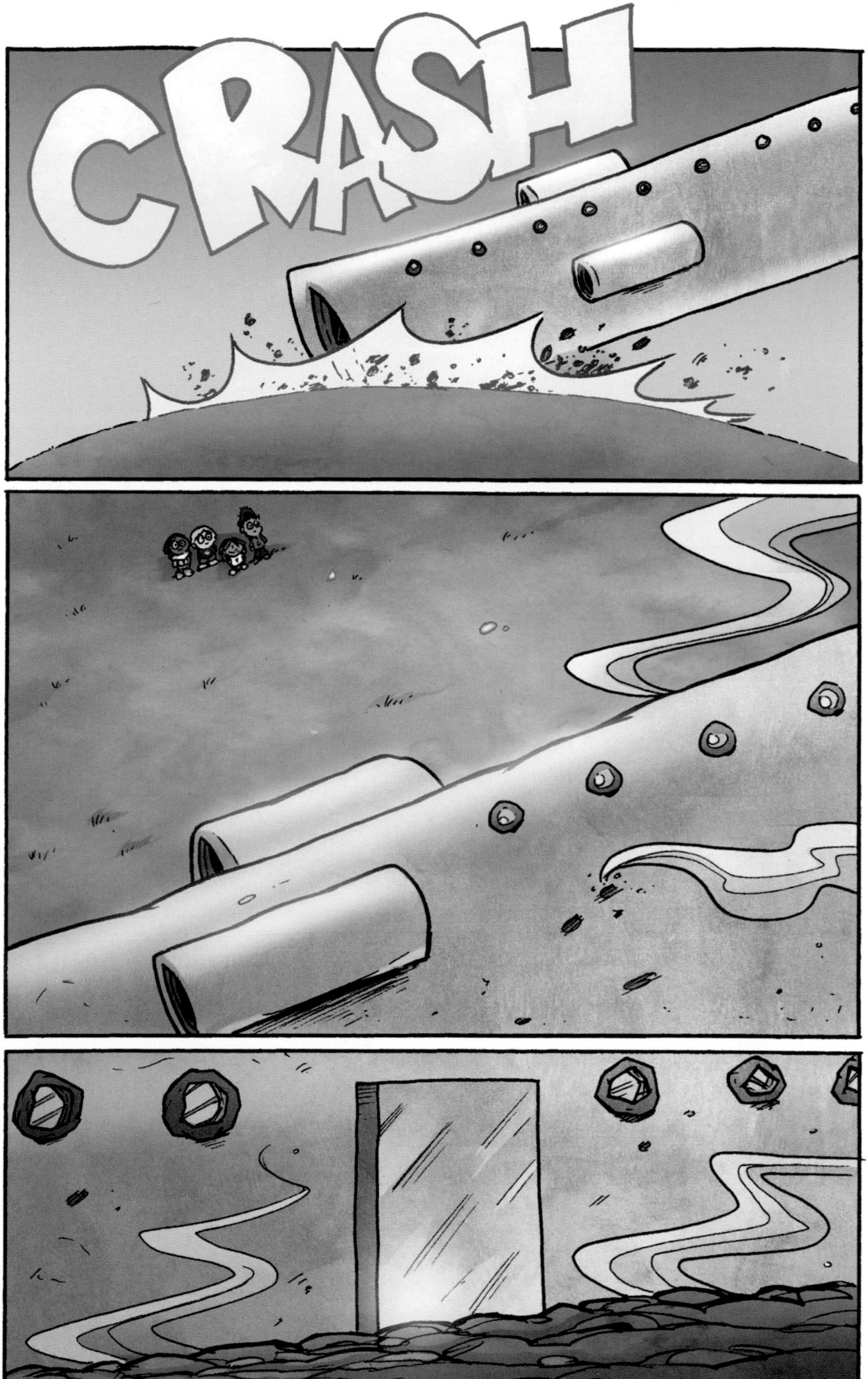
CRASH

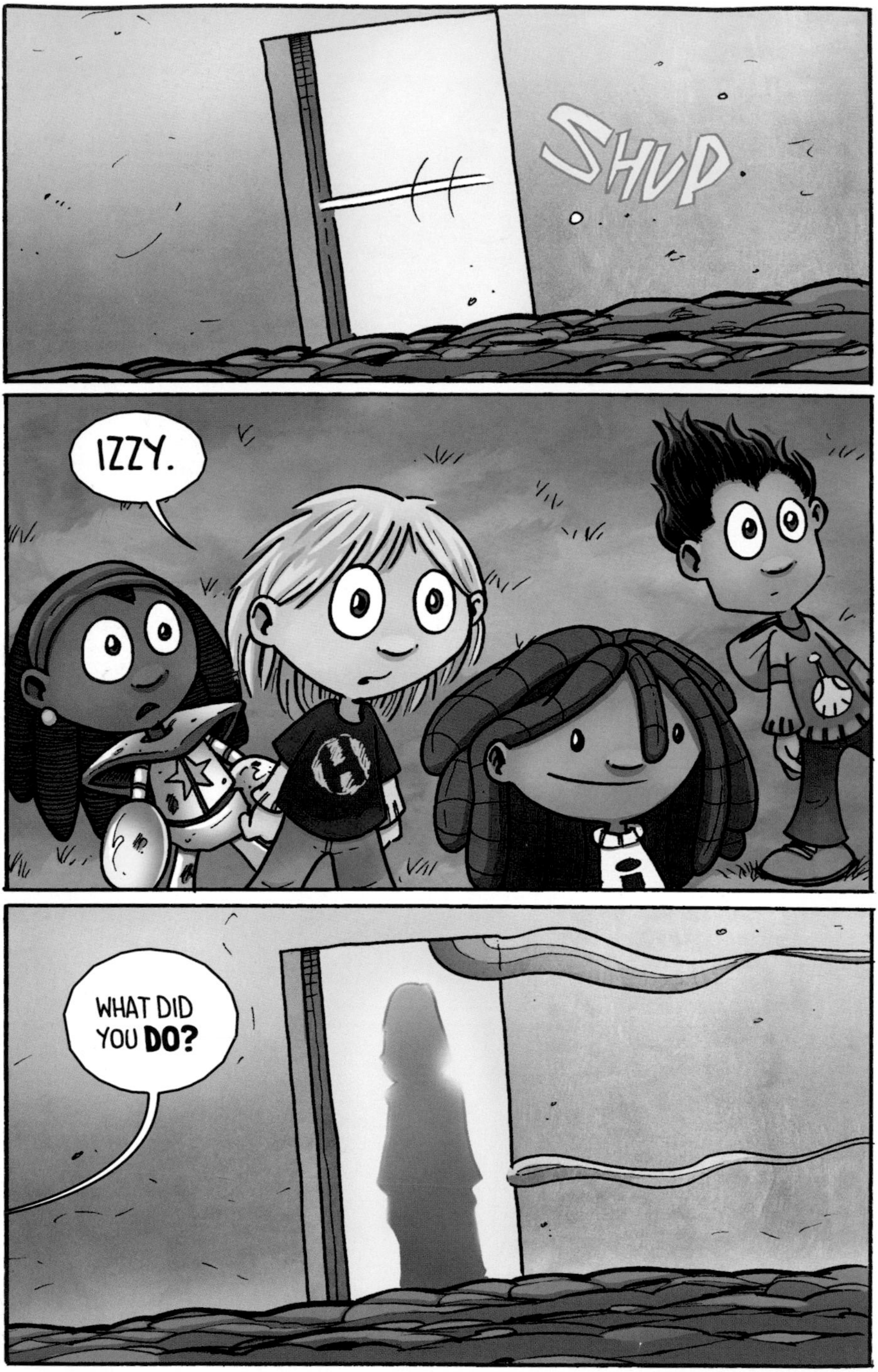
SHUP
IZZY.
WHAT DID YOU DO?

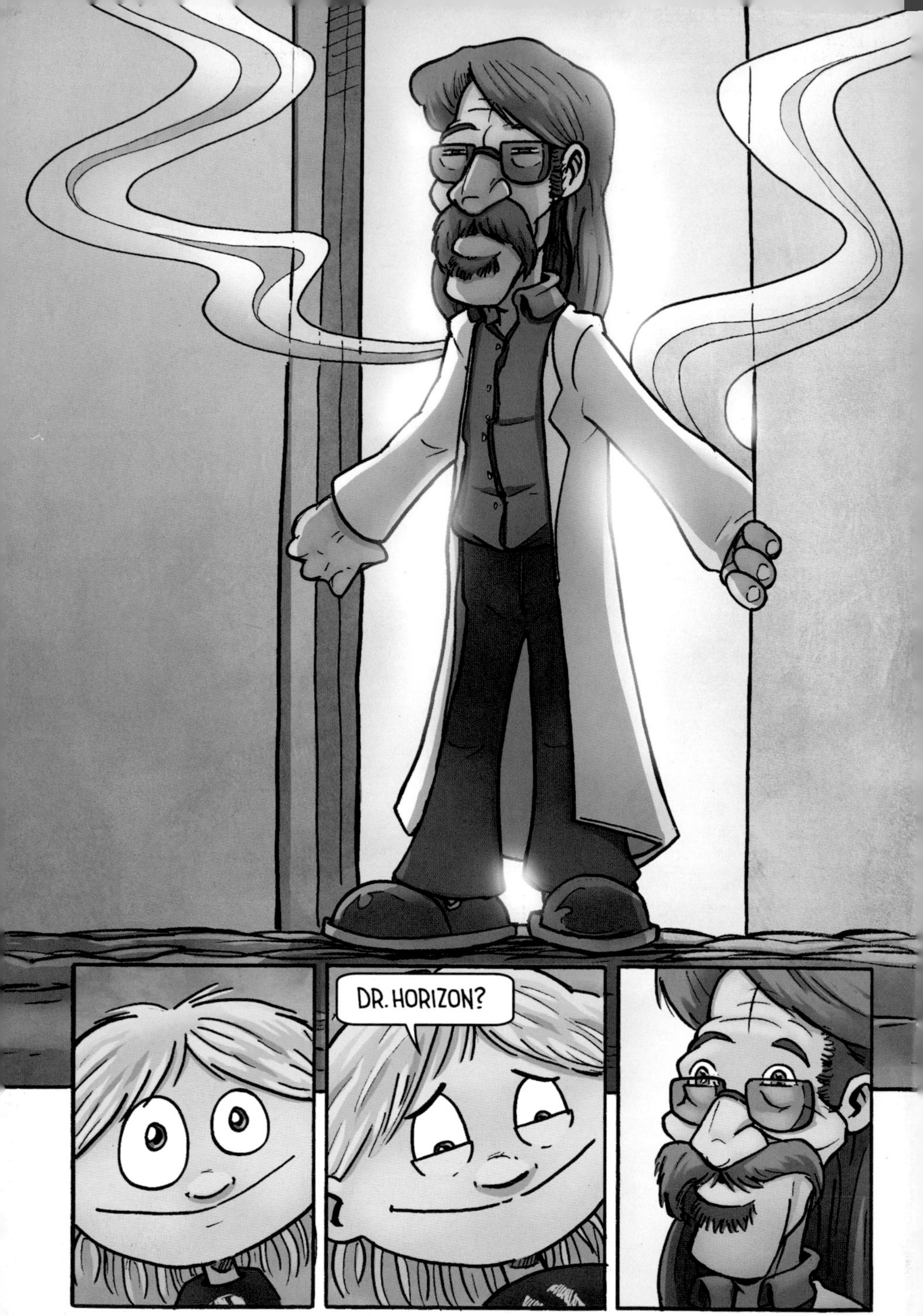
DR. HORIZON?

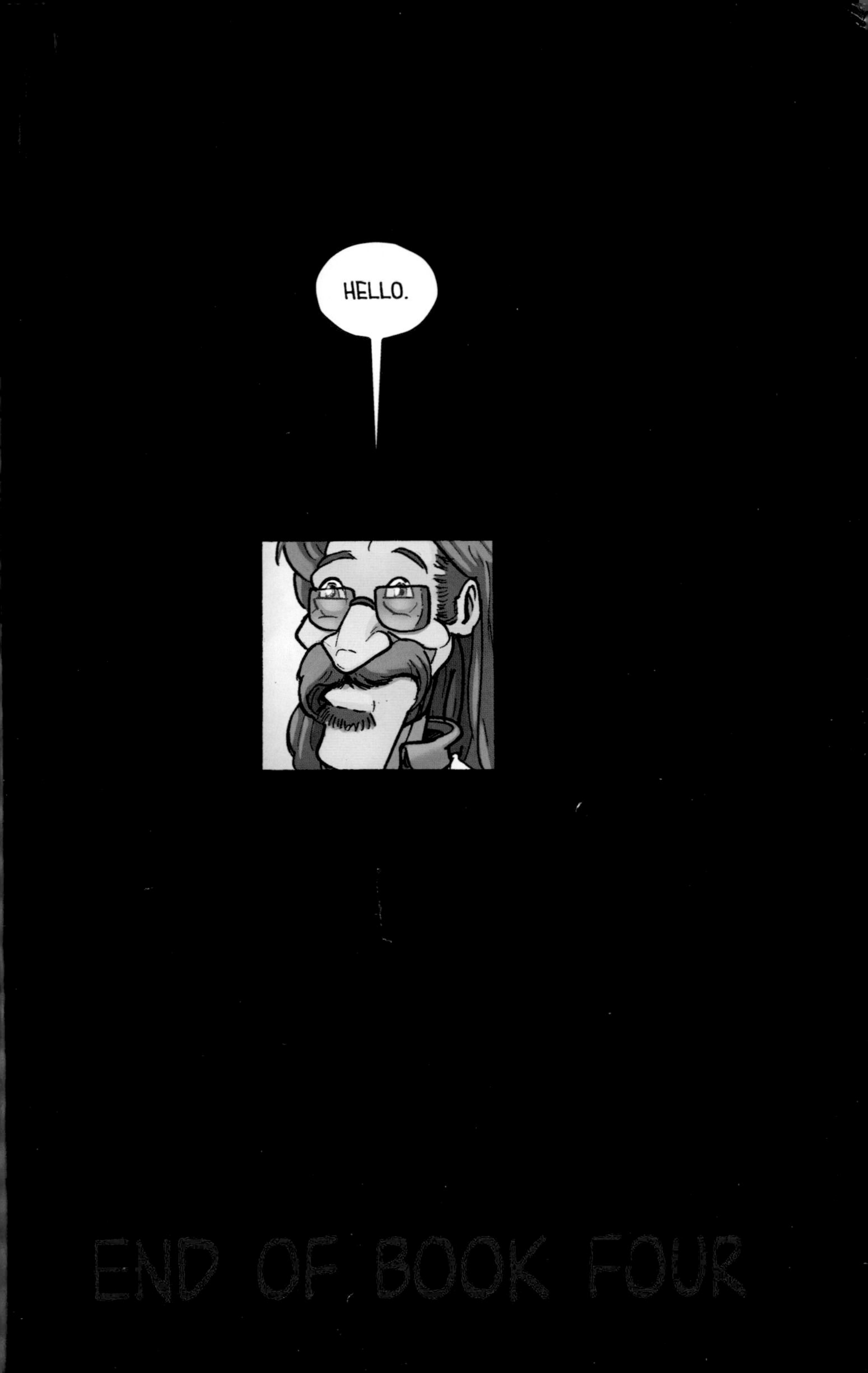
HELLO.
END OF BOOK FOUR

FIND OUT WHAT HAPPENS NEXT IN

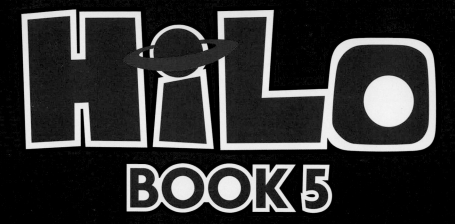

BOOK 5

COMING TO A PLANET NEAR YOU IN 2019!

SAVING THE WORLD HAS NEVER BEEN SO FUN!

WANTED

**FELONY CARTOONING. DRAWS CHARACTERS WITH FOUR FINGERS.
DEPICTS TALKING CATS. EXCESSIVE BURP JOKES.**

JUDD WINICK is the creator of the award-winning, **New York Times** bestselling Hilo series. Judd grew up on Long Island with a healthy diet of doodling, **X-Men** comics, the newspaper strip **Bloom County**, and **Looney Tunes**. Today, he lives in San Francisco with his wife, Pam Ling; their two kids; their cat, Chaka; and far too many action figures and vinyl toys for a normal adult. Judd created the Cartoon Network series **Juniper Lee**; has written issues of superhero comics, including Batman, Green Lantern, and Green Arrow; and was a cast member of MTV's **The Real World: San Francisco**. Judd is also the author of the highly acclaimed graphic novel **Pedro and Me**, about his **Real World** roommate and friend, AIDS activist Pedro Zamora. Visit Judd and Hilo online at juddspillowfort.com or find him on Twitter at @JuddWinick.

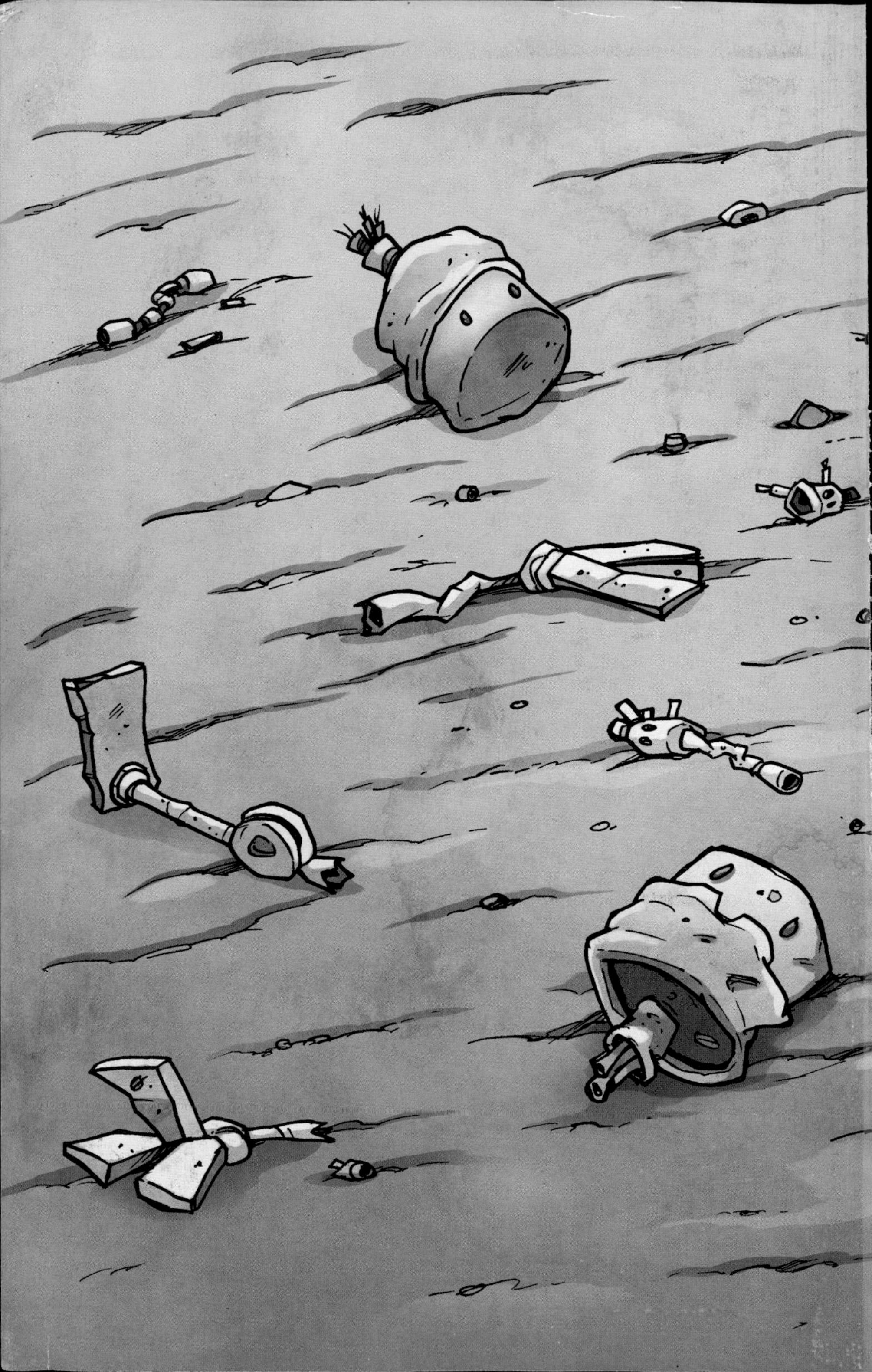